Kenneth Gregory is a Bel
outskirts of the city with h
writing since 2006, and in
Centre to participate in
Polaris Whisper is his first novel.

THE POLARIS WHISPER

KENNETH GREGORY

BLACKSTAFF PRESS

ACKNOWLEDGEMENTS

Christine O'Hare – Mark Gregory – Tina Gregory
Without you there is no Polaris World.

Linda Gregory, Helen Wright, Stuart Quate, Blackstaff Press,
Bernard Meehan, Pauline O'Hare, Tim Bates, Donal McKeown,
Jim Fitzpatrick – your artistry and humanity are an inspiration –
Paul Turner, and to all my family and friends, too many to mention.

Jackie Gregory, for believing in a dreamer.

First published in 2013 by Blackstaff Press
4D Weavers Court
Linfield Road
Belfast BT12 5GH

With the assistance of
The Arts Council of Northern Ireland

Typeset by CJWT Solutions, St Helens, England

Printed and bound by CPI Group UK (Ltd), Croydon CR0 4YY

A CIP catalogue for this book is available from the British Library

ISBN 978 0 85640 912 7

www.blackstaffpress.com

Dedicated with all of my heart
to my wife
Jackie
and my family,
Michelle, Danielle, Fiona,
Cara & Conn

PROLOGUE

LEAP OF FAITH

'They're here because of me.'

The abbot's palm pressed against his chest. 'All the more reason for you not to face them. They must not find you.'

'But ...'

Abbot Étgal interrupted – his voice, like his manner, serene and soothing. 'The Lord has chosen a different path for you.' He whispered a short blessing, signing the cross as he did so. 'Now go,' he said, turning to join his brethren in the chapel.

Every instinct in him rebelled against the abbot's words. He was not one to run from a fight – yet he had to obey.

The sounds of angry feet and clinking weaponry grew louder. The Norsemen were close. Their noisy ascent had alerted the monks to the raid long before their silhouettes had broken free of the mist that clung to the base of the island. The intruders were making steady progress up the steep rocky steps to the cluster of huts on the top of the island monastery of Sceilig. At points along the route, the steps clung precariously to the side of the rock face. The Norsemen had to be careful – one slip would have sent them crashing to their death.

Unfortunately, their quarry's delay proved costly – the Norsemen caught a glimpse of him as he scaled the outer wall.

With the dawn offering little light, the fugitive had to be vigilant as he ran between the lichen-covered rocks, down the steep incline to the cliff top. He could not afford to trip on any of the stones that protruded from the barren soil. In his haste, he stumbled into the burrow of a nesting puffin. The frightened bird took flight, scaring him witless, the commotion creating a ripple of piebald plumages, as puffin after puffin took to the air.

Behind, the raiders had cleared the monastery wall. Although tired, having climbed hundreds of steps to the summit, the sighting of their quarry gave them fresh impetus. They jeered and catcalled as their target fell, their Nordic language waking memories of his past. They were here to either kill him or bring him home.

A shiver ran down his spine as the sound of monks chanting filled the air. He admired their faith. An almost-forgotten story came to his mind. He had heard the first-hand account of a young monk who, in hiding, had endured the agony of hearing Norsemen butchering his friends. Determined that history would not repeat itself, he resolved to get off the island.

To the east, barely visible in the bad light, lay Gannet Island. The monks kept currachs there. If he could swim there, he had a chance of hiding out until nightfall. Then, he could use the cover of darkness to row to the southwest coast of Erin, and safety. Reaching the cliff edge, he stared down into a massive precipice. Below, the jagged rocks of the cove raised themselves out of a carpet of fog. It was impossible to judge where the rock ended and water began. He knew that it would take a mammoth leap to reach the ocean. Glancing back, he was not surprised to see that Iarl, his oldest foe, had outpaced the rest of the group and was closing rapidly. Taking off his woollen tunic, he skipped on to a protruding ledge and stood motionless, deep in concentration, forgetting momentarily the danger behind him.

Closing one eye, the tall Norseman took aim, his action contorting the scar that ran from under his left eye along the side of his nose and down his cheek.

Although the water sounded calm, the desperate man knew better. He listened as the waves slapped – it was vital to hit the water as the tide ebbed otherwise the incoming waves would smash him against the rocks. If, when he jumped, he managed to land clear, his troubles would only be beginning. He imagined spears and arrows raining down as he fought the swell. Even if he cleared the cove, it was not as if his pursuers would simply abandon their chase.

With a yell, Iarl launched his spear.

The hunted man remained focused on the water as he timed the gap between waves.

The spear's course was true.

Rocking backward and forward, the man leapt.

The spear pierced him, high in his back.

Momentum carried him into the ocean.

CHAPTER I

IN THE YEAR 830 AD

The sun broke through a rent in the clouds. Its warmth on Vidar's nape contrasted with the cold blustering wind against his face, mirroring his mixed emotions. He was happy to be under sail but despondent to be leaving. Sucking in the briny air, he held it deep; it tasted refreshing. His thoughts drifted until a seagull caught his attention. He watched it climb, hover, and then dive. The black tip of its grey wing skimmed the surface of the water, as if teasing the waves. Vidar envied its carefree abandon. He continued to follow the bird's flight until he lost it amongst its flock.

Vidar focused on Morton, the captain, who was busy steering the ship out of port. Tall, broad, and heavyset, Morton had a beard, speckled with grey, that hid much of his face. He wore knee-length boots and a grey tunic over breeches held up by a worn tan belt. Although he was a gruff man, with a temper hotter than a forge fire, he was respected and liked by his crew.

'How long has it been?' Morton shouted, hurrying from the side-rudder.

'Over seven years,' Vidar replied, running his hand through his unbraided hair. Ignoring Vidar's outstretched hand Morton hugged him. 'It's great to see you, lad.'

Vidar was elated. He was finally standing in front of the man who held the answers to many of the questions that had haunted him throughout his self-imposed exile.

Following their captain's lead, the crew broke from rowing and surrounded Vidar.

'It's great to have you on board again,' said Rune, the captain's first mate, patting Vidar on the back.

Someone threw him a bucket. The sight of it stirred unpleasant memories. All too soon, he would be standing knee-deep, baling water from the hull.

'Stop crowding him, back to work,' ordered Morton. 'We have a ship to sail.'

Vidar, standing at the helm, watched as they settled into their places at the front and the rear of the ship.

Torre set the pace: 'One-two, pull. One-two, pull.'

Responding, the rowers took two paces forward before pulling back on the oars with their callused hands. Their synchronised strokes rolled off the rowlocks. The oars scythed through the green glass water.

A few moments passed. Vidar shuffled uneasily from one foot to the other. The longing to learn of his son's welfare ate at him. 'What of Niclaus? Tell me of my son, is he well?'

Morton's face broke into a wide smile. 'He is fit and healthy, and grows strong. He's from good stock. He's popular and pleasant, a son any father would be proud of. In fact, he reminds me of you when I first took you sailing all those years ago. You remember that journey, don't you?'

Vidar nodded, breathing a sigh of relief; his son was alive and well, and he was soon to meet him. It seemed just a moment ago that he stood on Erin's shoreline watching Gilder, his dearest friend, sail off with his newborn son. Since that day Vidar had been consumed by guilt that he had not been there for Niclaus' childhood. But he took solace from the knowledge that Niclaus was safe with Gilder, who was raising him with his own son Orrin.

'She's better than the last one,' Morton said of his boat, quickly changing the subject as one of his crew neared. He was clearly proud of his new, freshly caulked knarr. 'She's deep and wide, sturdier than any dragonboat. She's able to sail the most treacherous of seas.'

Vidar eyed the vessel – but for a few minor adjustments, it appeared an exact replica of the previous one.

'She might look the same but come here and see,' Morton said, bending down and pulling back the wax covering to reveal the deep hull. 'Reinforced, double the number of crossbeams, and held in place by forged metal ends. It's the same with the support ribbing – it's extra strong,' he said, pointing to the thick strips that ran from the gunnel to the single-piece oak-keel. 'The *Ice Maiden*, she's the strongest boat ever made. She'll take you wherever you want to go.'

'We'll need her where we're going,' agreed Vidar, now impressed by the strengthened ship.

Walking to the stern, he stood and watched as Erin slowly disappeared from sight, swallowed up by the great sea. There were many whom he would miss – the villagers of Newgrange and Magority, not to mention the monks of Ceanannus Mór. And there was Fiona. He would feel further from her now.

Behind him, Torre released the final tie, unfurling the sail. Instantly stretching in the bellowing wind, it pulled the boat further into open water.

'I love to see wind in the sail,' said Morton, as he rejoined Vidar.

'You don't like harbours, do you?' said Vidar.

'I hate the offing. It's the one place you'll be guaranteed that trouble will find you. Come here,' he said, ushering Vidar to a quiet spot on the boat. 'I'm sure there is much you want to know.'

Only after Morton had told Vidar all he knew of Niclaus and his life in the fjord, did they begin to discuss the upcoming trek.

'Cado has sent me to discover a place in the frozen north,' Vidar explained.

'It's hard to believe …' Morton said, as he rubbed his beard.

'What is?'

'That Cado paid me to take you on this journey nearly thirty years ago.'

Vidar looked at Morton, incredulously. 'What? He paid for this trip before I was born?'

'Yes, even now, after all I have heard and seen, I still find it hard to believe. All those years ago, Cado negotiated a price for this and many more trips; gave me dates, places to be, things to bring. Like these,' he said, handing Vidar new boots and clothing.

Vidar eyed his scuffed and salt-stained boots, his faded tunic, and frayed cloak with its broken amber brooch. He imagined how those who had once admired and feared him would have reacted if they saw him now.

Morton sighed. 'I thought Cado was mad. I thought I was taking payment from a fool. Paid me full in advance. The little man played me well, got off lightly.'

'You mean to tell me he got one over on you?'

'He did that. Not for a moment did I believe that I would have had to fulfil my side of the bargain. If I had, I'd have charged him tenfold. For all that, he made me wealthy.'

'How many more sailings has he organised for me?'

'Afraid I can't tell you. Part of the deal, you see. He gave me an extra ten per cent if I promised not to divulge any details.'

'He won't know,' said Vidar.

Morton eyes widened, 'Even you don't believe that now, do you?'

Vidar shook his head.

'Right, lad, training begins now,' said Morton, loading a heavy bag on to Vidar's back. 'You'll have to carry this on your own for weeks. Get used to it.'

Vidar stood motionless.

'Go on, lad, climb the mast.'

Knowing by the set of Morton's jaw that it would be pointless to argue, Vidar reluctantly began. The straps of the bag cut into his shoulders and its weight sat uncomfortably in the small of his back.

'Quicker, lad, a girl could do better,' said Morton.

As each day passed and Morton put him through the same exercise, Vidar's confidence grew, as did his speed. By the end of the week, Vidar's technique had improved to such a level that Morton's insults ceased.

They were a few days from Folda when the weather turned, a strong easterly wind bringing ice-cold rain. Vidar was relieved, believing he would have a day off from climbing.

'Come on you, get up there,' barked Morton.

'You can't be serious?'

'I'll tell you what serious is. I've seen it on the island. A fine day'll turn quicker than a blink. Next thing, you'll be on the side of the mountain with a blizzard blowing. It'll be freeze or climb. Go on, get moving.'

Vidar grimaced. Trying to climb in cutting wind and driving rain was bad enough, but on a rolling ship it was downright reckless. He stretched out his hand, wrapped his fingers around the wood, and hauled himself on to the first beam. Having clawed his way to near the top, Vidar reached for the masthead. As he did so, the boat pitched. The sudden jerk sent him tumbling, crashing into the beam below. His stomach took the full impact. Winded, he continued to slip. In danger of falling from the second beam, he somehow managed to cling on by the fingers of one hand.

'Quick, help Vidar,' shouted Anders, the youngest crewmate.

Jorun, being closest, rushed forward.

'Leave him be,' yelled Morton.

Vidar tried to grip the beam with his free arm. He missed and missed again.

'He needs help,' implored Rune.

Morton ignored him.

The entire crew watched, aghast.

Hanging as a dead weight, Vidar's hand cramped. 'I can't hold on.'

'No one can help you where you are going,' retorted Morton, as the others looked on helplessly.

Gradually Vidar lost the feeling in his fingers but still he held tight.

Jorun instinctively took a step toward Vidar. The boat listed, forcing Jorun to grab the block and tackle to keep from falling.

'I said, leave him be,' roared the captain.

Vidar cursed the captain as his hand slipped and his body crashed on to the deck. He was fortunate to land on the hull cover – it softened the impact.

'Keep away from him,' warned Morton, as he stood between his crew and the fallen man.

Vidar looked like an upturned beetle floundering on the deck.

'No one will be there to help you on the island,' said Morton. 'You'd be dead already.'

Spurred on by anger, Vidar righted himself and stood shakily before the captain.

'Don't just stand there, get climbing.'

Once again, Vidar pulled his battered body up the rigging.

*

Although the sea was choppy, the cloud overhead had broken; the day held potential as Morton walked to Vidar. 'How are you, lad?'

Vidar, still seething, ignored the question.

'It's a harsh world out there.'

Again, he ignored the captain; the humiliation of the previous day was still too fresh. Vidar replayed the incident in his mind. Why had Morton let him fall? He could have been seriously injured or worse, killed. Vidar bent to pick up his satchel. 'Why didn't you let them help me?' he asked, struggling to keep his anger in check.

'I was making a point.'

'What point?'

'If you persist with this venture alone, the slightest mishap – one fall, a broken bone, or a twisted ankle – could be fatal. And think of snow bears. You need to take someone with you.'

'So you nearly kill me to prove how dangerous the island will be. That makes sense,' spat Vidar.

The boat sailed off a large wave, dropping rapidly. The swell was strong. Vidar felt his stomach rise but Morton carried on talking seemingly oblivious to the rocking boat, moving freely as though attached to the deck by invisible strings.

Morton tried to reason with Vidar as he had throughout the voyage. 'Won't you reconsider? If not me, let Rune or Torre accompany you. It'll be safer. I can always hire an extra man at Folda, it wouldn't be a problem.'

Vidar shook his head. 'Don't you understand?'

'Understand what?'

'You're not the only one who has made promises,' he said, grabbing the gunnel to counterbalance the lurching of the boat.

'To Cado, no less.' Morton finally understood.

'Yes, I too have made an oath to him.'

'I'm sorry,' said Morton, his voice calmer. 'I thought you were being pig-headed. It seems that this little man has the ability to get us all to do his bidding.'

The apology helped soften Vidar's mood.

'Come on, you've done enough climbing,' said Morton, guiding Vidar to a covered section at the back of the boat.

They spent the rest of the journey planning Vidar's first expedition.

'After we stop off at Folda and get fresh supplies, I will take you further north. Then it's up to you, you'll be on your own.'

'I know. I'm prepared. I know the way.'

Morton laughed, a little sarcastically. 'I don't think anything could prepare you. Remember, once out of the fjord, you'll have a vertical climb. Many of the mountains will be snow-covered.'

Vidar nodded. 'I've to find the lee side for pitching my tent. And I'm not to risk climbing if I have any doubts about the weather. And …'

'Remember what I taught you. It'll get easier on the other side. But easier doesn't mean safer. You'll be skiing over frozen snow and ice. Many a good skier has perished skiing over a ravine, so be attentive.'

Vidar did not know which frightened him more, falling off a mountain or plunging down a ravine. Neither held much chance of survival.

'From there, if you make it that far …'

'Thanks for the confidence,' muttered Vidar, taking the comment in the light-hearted manner it was meant.

'It's straightforward, keep heading north.'

Morton had supplied the names and locations of a few fur trappers and fishermen who braved the winter; men who would appreciate Vidar's company and the labour he would supply in return for his board.

'Listen,' said Morton, seriousness etched on his face. 'View this trek as a beginning; the first of many such journeys. For now, the challenge is survival, nothing more.'

Absorbing Morton's advice, Vidar was racked with doubt. The more he thought about it, the more daunting the task became. What if he was not up to the challenge, what if the weather conspired against him or what if he had an accident or a fall?

An easterly wind prevailed as the mainland came into view. The coastline became more picturesque the further north the *Ice Maiden* sailed. Passing numerous islands, they approached Folda late that evening. In the twilight, the village looked as Vidar remembered. Little had changed. A stream, fed by a cascading waterfall, flowed through fertile fields dotted with log cabins. Beyond the village, a backdrop of snowy peaks stretched into the distance.

Nearing port, Morton took Vidar aside. 'My men are exhausted. And seeing as we are in Folda, I was thinking we could extend this stop by a day or two. What do you think?'

'Thank you,' replied a delighted Vidar, not fooled by Morton's flimsy excuse. It was a generous offer. Aware of the boat's tight schedule, Vidar knew that the crew were looking forward to a longer break later in the month. Morton was stretching the stopover solely for Vidar's benefit, giving him longer with his son.

CHAPTER 2

IN THE YEAR 830 AD

Niclaus struggled to keep up with his father as they made their way to the smokehouse. Beside them, their little workhorse Trovil thrashed through the spongy ground, pulling the cod-laden cart. One of Niclaus' loose-fitting boots squelched and sank. He wriggled his toes into the boot before pulling it free, picking a firmer spot for his next step.

'Come on, hurry up,' called Gilder, not bothering to disguise his foul mood. His good nature had been lost to a deep frown and a sharp tongue.

Niclaus was worried; he had never seen his father so agitated. The previous evening he had heard his parents talking long into the night. Unable to make out the mumbled conversation through the dividing wall, he heard enough to recognise anxiety in their voices. He was sure he had heard his mother crying.

Overhead, low-lying cloud obscured the top of the fjord, the steep granite ice scars that marked the boundary of Niclaus' homeland. He was aware of a bigger world beyond the mountains – to the south, the land of Odin and, to the north, the snow-covered glaciers. He had grown up listening to his father's stories.

They fuelled his imagination and invaded his dreams in the form of mystical lands and monsters.

'Come on back there,' shouted Gilder to Niclaus' twin brother Orrin, who pulled a second, smaller cart. Orrin had spent the day working alongside Jarl, the best fisherman in the fjord. Niclaus believed he did so in the hope of improving his own technique.

Though the boys were very different, their bond of brotherhood and loyalty was unshakeable. Niclaus was lean and wiry while Orrin, broad and angular, was a miniature version of their father. Niclaus had an abundance of natural talent whereas Orrin took time to master a new skill. What Orrin lacked in ability he made up for in application and determination. Turning to look back, Niclaus could see the distant Lofoten Islands, their jagged peaks hidden by cloud. With an agreeable tide and a favourable wind, he estimated it would take a full morning to row out to them. He shuddered at the thought that one day he would undertake the same crossing as part of the Trial of Endurance.

'Niclaus, we need to talk,' said Gilder, breaking his son's reverie.

'Yes?' answered Niclaus, biting nervously on his lower lip. He shivered as he walked, whether from fear or cold, he was not sure.

'After last night ... well, it's nearly too late,' said Gilder, as much to himself as to Niclaus.

Niclaus' heart raced. What had happened? 'Is mother sick?'

Gilder's face softened. 'No, your mother's fine. It's you we are concerned about.'

Niclaus was confused.

'Niclaus, your mother and I have been talking about your future.'

Gilder paused, unsure of what to say next. 'I know you hope to follow in my footsteps and become leader of the village but we think that your life may hold different challenges.'

His words hit Niclaus like a cold slap. His only dream was to succeed his father.

Gilder tried to reassure him. 'I have no doubt that you would make the finest of all leaders, it's just we believe that this is not the path that has been set for you.'

'I don't understand. Do you not want me to enter the Trial?' Niclaus asked, afraid that his father's preference lay with his brother.

'No, not at all. We, your mother and I, are convinced that leading the village is not what you were born to do. We believe something greater awaits you.'

'Do you know what it is?' asked Niclaus, curiosity adding to his fear and confusion.

'We will see, time will tell,' said Gilder, with a smile.

Niclaus had many more questions to ask but they had arrived at the smokehouse and Gunnar stood at its door. Whatever it was, it would have to wait.

'Run along,' said Gilder, lifting the first creel. 'You've done more than your share.'

Free of any chores, Niclaus rounded the side of the smokehouse to wait for his friends by the main stream that ran through the heart of the village. He sat watching the gushing water as it churned and brown froth gathered around a few stubborn boulders. Normally,

Niclaus found the spot relaxing but his father's words weighed on his mind.

'Wait until you hear this,' cried Orrin, excitedly, as he came to join Niclaus. 'There's a new man in the village. He arrived on Morton's boat late last night. Just now I heard father and Gunnar …' Orrin stopped, interrupted by angry voices emanating from inside the smokehouse. Its door flew open and Gunnar stormed out, muttering incoherently as he went. His voice rising, he turned and shouted back. 'I don't care what you say, he's not welcome.'

'I say he is,' retorted Gilder.

'For all we know he could be one of Odin's men. We should have nothing to do with him.'

'He stays,' shouted Gilder, adamantly.

Gunnar swore. Gilder responded in kind.

Niclaus tried to make sense of the unfolding events. Was his father's mood related to this stranger's arrival? Until today, he had always opposed any outsider's attempt to join their village.

Ludin, tall and broad for his age, was wandering to the smokehouse to meet his friends when he caught the end of the commotion. 'I saw him earlier,' he said.

'Who?' Niclaus asked.

'The stranger, I saw him earlier.'

'What was he like?' asked Orrin.

'See for yourself, here he comes now,' replied Ludin.

Niclaus sized up the newcomer. Slightly taller than Gilder, his tunic, cloak and boots gave him an air of importance. His dirty-fair hair was tightly braided and his beard closely cropped.

'He's not welcome,' shouted Gunnar, in the direction of Vidar and the boys before hobbling homeward.

'Do you think he's talking about me?' asked Vidar, giving the boys a mischievous grin while shrugging his shoulders.

'Don't worry about Gunnar. He's like the wind, he'll calm,' said Orrin.

'You could be right,' said Vidar. 'I think it might be better if I leave it until later before I make his acquaintance.'

'A good idea,' agreed Orrin.

'I'm Vidar.' He offered his hand.

'Orrin.'

'It's an honour to meet a son of Gilder.'

'Hello again,' said Vidar to Ludin, before turning to face his son. 'And you must be Niclaus.'

CHAPTER 3

IN THE YEAR 801 AD

The sound of clattering spoons echoed around the refectory as Tomás offered his own silent grace. The previous day had been one of fasting and he was ravenous.

'Well, is it true?' whispered Damian, as he shovelled in a mouthful of oats.

Tomás, mesmerised by a tendril of smoke as it drifted high into the rafters, was not listening.

'Tomás.'

His concentration broken, Tomás glanced to the top table where Abbot Father sat. Talking was not permitted during mealtimes.

'Yes?' he whispered, trying not to draw attention to himself.

'Is it true?' repeated Damian.

'Is what true?'

'Is Bresal dead?'

'Yes,' replied Tomás. 'I'm sorry – you were close weren't you?'

'Yes, I was very fond of him. As a novice, he was my first abbot. It was he who convinced me to leave Iona, that God needed me here.'

'Well he was wise, for you are indeed a fine scribe. I shall pray for him.'

'Thank you,' said Damian. 'And is Connachtach to be the new abbot of Iona?'

'Yes, but not a word. It's not official yet.'

'When does he leave?'

'Tomorrow. Mind you, with his health, he'll probably not last …'

'That one, he'll outlive us all,' interposed Damian, with a hint of spite towards his superior. 'And what about you, with Connachtach gone, have you been named as his successor?'

'Yes, but shush – it still has to be announced.'

'Congratulations, you deserve it.'

'Thank you,' replied Tomás, still trying to keep his voice down.

'Head Scribe, would you believe it? And at your age? I thought only old wrinkly men ever earned such positions. You must be delighted.'

'I am,' replied Tomás, as he lifted a slice of still-warm bread from the trencher.

Having finished breakfast, Tomás and Damian walked back towards the scriptorium. Droplets of dew flicked off their sandals as they crossed a section of open grass. From there they walked under the cloisters in the cold shadow of the church. Above, a clear sky, stretching as far as the eye could see, held the promise of a hot and sunny day. Tomás hated the notion of being stuck indoors in fine weather. Housed above the chapel, the scriptorium had little ventilation and quickly overheated. Yet as soon as he lifted his quill, he lost himself to his work. Tomás believed he was fortunate to serve God in Ceanannus Mór.

'I hear the new head scribe is a real tyrant,' teased Damian, as they walked.

'Worse than that, I hear he's looking for replacements for the old ones – doesn't think much of their talent,' countered Tomás.

'He should think himself lucky,' said Damian. 'But with Connachtach gone, we'll need another scribe.'

'Father Abbot's intention is to bring in someone experienced, probably from Bangor Abbey in the north.'

Rounding the corner of the church, Tomás noticed the familiar figure immediately. 'Stay back. He hasn't seen you,' he whispered, his outstretched hand preventing Damian from moving into view. 'With a bit of luck we might catch him.'

'What makes today any different?' replied Damian. 'Every time we try to catch him, he just vanishes like a wisp of smoke.'

Tomás kept his eyes on the stranger who sat on the grassy mound by the edge of the nearby forest – a perfect vantage point for seeing over the monastery's high outer wall. To Tomás, Ceanannus Mór was merely a small settlement made up of workshops and wattle and daub houses. Yet it was clearly of great interest to the little man and Tomás was determined to find out why. Like many of the brothers, he feared that the dwarf was intent on stealing their Holy Bible, the most lavish Bible ever written. Its jewel-encrusted cover alone was priceless.

'The corner of the wall has blocked his view. I'm sure he hasn't seen you. Quick, go over the wall at the back, circle round and he'll not get away.'

With the surrounding land used for grazing, Damian would be instantly visible when he cleared the outer wall. His best hope lay in catching the stranger off-guard. Once before, he and Tomás had tried staking out the little man's route, preparing to ambush him as he cleared the trees but, on that day, as if guided by a sixth sense, the dwarf failed to show.

Damian hesitated.

'Come on,' Tomás urged, sensing his reluctance. 'Aren't we forever warned to be vigilant and reminded of what happened at Iona – our brothers massacred for the very same treasure we now protect.'

'Yes,' agreed an agitated Damian. 'But they were attacked by Norsemen, not by a single dwarf.'

'How many died in 795?'

Damian did not answer.

'Isn't our Bible dedicated to the same martyrs, their names inscribed on the inside cover? Can't you recite every last name? We pray for them often enough.'

Damian nodded, acknowledging Tomás' point.

'Haven't we all promised to protect the Bible since Connachtach brought it here for safekeeping?'

'Yes, Tomás, you are right,' conceded Damian.

'Go on then, get after him.'

Even if he believed it a pointless exercise, they still had to try. It was becoming embarrassing, two fit men unable to catch a dwarf.

Tomás was intrigued. There seemed to be something familiar about the interloper who stood no more than an ell in height. Tomás and Damian, as well as many of their brothers, had been trying to apprehend the little man for over a month. The dwarf, who Tomás suspected could easily have been mistaken for a youth, had managed to evade all their best efforts. Tomás was convinced he came from Newgrange, a village situated close to a bow in the Boyne River, a good half-day's walk away. Newgrange was the subject of much debate between the monks, their discussions dominated by one peculiar fact – its entire population were dwarfs. The monastery's forefathers had branded the villagers as heretics. The village was shrouded in secrecy, and tales of witchcraft and magic abounded. The tales had grown in intensity to such an extent that the sight of a dwarf now frightened many people.

Out of sight, Damian inched around the circular wall. Removing his heavy habit, he stood in his once-white leggings. He bent down and tightened his sandals before breaking into a run.

Tomás pulled the belt of his robe tight, letting the three knots in the cord drop to his side before he edged discreetly towards the open gate. He intended to sprint to the wood further to the right, cutting off the stranger's escape. He made a sign of the cross as he passed the small graveyard. To its side stood a large sculptured crux dedicated to the memory of Patricius and Colm Cille. He reached the entrance in time to see Damian dashing down the sun-baked path in the direction of the little man. Tomás doubted if the half-naked runner had given any thought as to what he might do if he ever caught up with the visitor. He chuckled at the unfrocked monk's ungainly run, his skinny legs resembling a strutting chicken. Being taller, fitter, and quicker, Tomás believed he would have been more likely to catch him.

Damian had covered three-quarters of the distance and still the little man had not moved. He appeared unaware of Damian advancing.

'You can do it,' Tomás whispered, breaking into a run himself.

Glancing over his shoulder, before entering the wood, he could see that the dwarf was running. If Damian could keep chasing him in the same direction, they stood a chance. Tomás crouched behind a thick oak tree. Hearing footsteps, he peeped around the trunk. The dwarf was still heading his way. Sunlight, breaking through the canopy of trees, lit up the forest floor. The dwarf was clearly visible. He was still heading Tomás' way. Waiting until the last possible moment, Tomás sprang out to catch the unsuspecting stranger. Only he was not there.

Tomás stood still, astonished.

'Did you get him?' Damian shouted as he came into view.

'No.'

'I was right behind him, he was running this way. You must have seen him?'

There were no hiding places, the floor of the forest was bare but for ivy and a few hearty shrubs.

Tomás heard a soft voice but he couldn't make out the words. 'What did you say?' he asked.

'I didn't speak. It must be that damned dwarf. He must be close.'

Tomás and Damian searched for the little man without any success. Close to giving up, Tomás heard another whisper. He looked about, again seeing no one.

Something brushed his hand. Startled, he let out a yell.

'What's wrong?'

'Someone touched me.'

'It's your imagination.'

Again, Tomás heard the voice. 'Didn't you hear it?' he asked Damian.

'Hear what?'

The two monks stood still, hoping the dwarf's movement would lead them to him.

'Why do you chase me?' called the voice, breaking the eerie silence of the forest.

Tomás swivelled around but still saw no one.

'What?' Damian asked.

'There it is again.'

'Stop it, Tomás,' said Damian, clearly unsettled by his friend's behaviour.

Tomás wiped sweat from his forehead. He was sure he had heard someone. He grabbed Damian's arm. 'Let's get out of here,' he said, as they broke into a run.

Almost out of the forest, Tomás looked back. The little man stood directly in his line of vision, some fifty paces or so away. Again, he heard the whisper. 'We have much to discuss.'

The dwarf was too far away; his voice should not have carried.

Frightened, Tomás did not stop running until he was well out of the wood.

'That's it. I'm finished chasing after him. I'll not do it, not even if Pope Leo III commands me,' said Damian, trying to catch his breath.

'Neither will I.'

Tomás smiled half-heartedly, revealing a slightly chipped front tooth.

'What happened in there?'

'I think my imagination got the better of me. I frightened myself,' said Tomás, trying to convince himself as well as Damian.

Retrieving Damian's habit, they walked back towards the monastery in silence.

*

As they walked, Tomás recalled the previous summer when he and Damian had travelled to Newgrange. Damian had unintentionally instigated the outing. Perched at the top of the high round tower of Ceanannus Mór, the two friends could see the raised mound that they believed was the home of the mysterious little folk. Jokingly, Damian had dared his friend to go to the village and convert them. Tomás took up the challenge and much to the annoyance of Damian, who had instantly regretted his suggestion, sought out Abbot Monicurr.

'I've robbed the king,' declared Monicurr, as Tomás entered his study.

Monicurr looked extremely pleased as he sat counting a mound of coins. 'And Áed mac Néill has promised us another hundred calves.'

Tomás understood. Áed mac Néill, King of Tara, High King of Erin, had visited earlier that morning to deposit his yearly stipend. All the kingdoms of the island donated to the monastery's upkeep. The extent of their generosity, laid out on the abbot's table, surprised Tomás. Realising that the abbot was in a good mood, he wasted little time in making his request.

'… and if Damian and I go to the village, there's a chance we can convert them.'

Monicurr sat at his carrel. As Tomás looked at him, he thought again that his nickname was most apt. With his white hair, narrow eyes and beaky nose, he did indeed look like a White Owl. Tomás prayed for a favourable response to his request. The abbot twisted his cross, a familiar but unconscious action that indicated that he was deep in thought. Tomás waited patiently, watching as the gold cross reflected rays of light across the room.

Eventually, Monicurr answered. 'It's an excellent idea.'

'So we can go?'

'No.'

'But you said it was an …'

'I'm sorry, Tomás, I can't spare either of you. Your work on the Holy Book is too important.'

'But what about the villagers?'

'You're right, the Lord's word must be spread.' Monicurr's brow creased as he contemplated who to send. 'Perhaps it would be more fitting if I went myself. It is not that far, I could be there and back in a day.'

'Father, if we make up the time we spend away, will you consider letting us go? I can think of nothing more rewarding than spreading the Gospel.'

Monicurr relented. 'If you and Damian do extra work and

make the time up before you go, you have my blessing to follow this calling.'

'We will. Thank you, Father.'

*

Tomás and Damian travelled eastwards, following the winding river of the Blackwater until it merged with the Boyne. From there they tracked the larger river's meandering path through the wooded countryside, knowing it led to the village.

'I hope this is worth all those extra hours spent slaving in the scriptorium,' complained Damian. Of late, Tomás had noticed an abruptness to his manner. At times he was snappy and sharp, and easily riled. This wasn't the first time he had voiced his dissatisfaction at spending his days at work in the scriptorium.

'It won't be too long until we find out.'

As they walked, Tomás sensed Damian's anxiety. Having lived most of his life close to shore, Damian was unfamiliar with the forest that covered the land. Emerging from the shadow of a group of alder trees, they startled a red deer. From Damian's reaction, Tomás reckoned he had been more frightened than the animal. Free of the forest, they were soon sweating under the hot sun.

'These satchels are too heavy,' moaned Damian, complaining of the leather-bound gospels that they carried.

'Nearly there. Only one last hill.'

'Praise the Lord,' said Damian, as they cleared the top.

Ahead, run-down houses surrounded a great earth mound.

'Seems very quiet,' noted Tomás.

They were both surprised to find that the unusual village had clearly been deserted for quite a while. The stone buildings were moss-covered and the roofs of the outbuildings had collapsed inward. Tomás pondered what had made the inhabitants leave.

'It seems to be more of a monument,' said Damian.

'Some sort of holy site,' agreed Tomás. 'Best not to hang about.'

'Yes, you're right.' Looking to the southeast, Damian spotted smoke rising in the air.

'That way,' he pointed.

As they drew closer, they were awestruck by the sight of a second mound.

It was huge and circular, walled by glittering quartz, and surrounded by massive, evenly spaced boulders, each one decorated with artwork. To Tomás, the builders of the monument had positioned the rocks with precision, but he could not work out why. Perhaps the stories of heresy were true.

Damian stopped at a slightly raised bank that circled the monument. 'Tomás I don't want to go on. There's something about that place.'

'Nonsense, come on, we've come this far. It's only down there.' Tomás pointed to the village below.

'I'm going no further. If you want to go on I will wait here for you.'

CHAPTER 4

IN THE YEAR 830 AD

Vidar stood before his son. He was pleased to see that the boy looked strong and fit. Niclaus had his mother's blue eyes and his grandmother's raven hair. Fiona would have been proud. Vidar composed himself. He had dreamt of this moment, hoping that Niclaus would instinctively recognise him as his father. Now, he realised how unrealistic his thinking had been.

'Is it true? Are you planning to live in the village?' Ludin asked, brazenly.

'Yes, although I will be away a lot of the time.'

'Where do you go?' asked Niclaus.

'Sailing with Morton. Way up north to where the ice bear rules.'

'What takes you up there?' asked Ludin.

Vidar drew the boys close. 'Can you keep a secret?'

The boys all nodded emphatically.

'It's a special place.'

'What makes it special?' Orrin asked.

'It's where …'

The creaking of the smokehouse door interrupted Vidar mid-sentence.

Gilder stepped out.

Vidar could only imagine how Gilder must be feeling, seeing Niclaus with him. Yes, he was sure it was difficult – but no harder than seeing your own son raised by another man.

'Did you sleep well?' Gilder enquired.

'Like a lord,' answered Vidar.

Gilder laughed, enjoying the private joke.

Vidar and the crew had spent the night in the main barn. It was draughty but more comfortable than the boat.

'Boys, do you mind if I take Vidar with me?'

The boys were crestfallen, dying to know more about Vidar's adventures.

'I'm not sailing for a day or two. Perhaps we'll catch up later?' said Vidar.

'Come on, we have much to discuss,' said Gilder, as he led Vidar away.

*

During the lay days, Vidar spent as much time as possible with his son. He was finding it difficult to motivate himself for the trek ahead. He would gladly give it up for a life in the fjord with Niclaus at his side, if only that were possible. Due to Cado's intervention, Niclaus was alive and his future safety depended on Vidar following Cado's instructions. He would go to the frozen island and search for the Vestibule. He knew not the importance of the place, only that Cado needed him to find it. He suspected it was important in Cado's battle with Bram. The very thought of Bram, the man who destroyed his family, stirred Vidar's anger. There was no one he despised more. Vidar had sworn vengeance and he always kept his word.

Cado warned of dark times, he spoke of Bram's power and the influence that he yielded. Bram would kill Niclaus unless Vidar killed Bram first. Vidar was resolute; he would keep his son from Bram's clutches and then, when the time was right, he would exact his revenge.

*

With Vidar due to sail on the evening tide, he and Gilder took an early morning stroll. He could feel Gilder watching him as they walked. He sensed the unasked questions in his eyes, hearing them without a word being said. 'Yes, there is a mountain of grief still locked in my heart,' he said, in response. 'But I am a lot more content now.'

His words caught Gilder by surprise. 'I didn't know you could read minds.'

They walked out of the village, in comfortable silence, along the water's edge as the sun rose behind them.

Gilder spoke. 'Do you remember the first time we sailed out of Folda?' His words started an avalanche of youthful memories, of sailing on Morton's boat and of secret summers spent in Erin.

'How are we going to tell Niclaus?' asked Gilder, finally.

'I don't know. I don't even know if it's the right time.'

'There'll never be a right time. This indecision is too much for Selina. Each day she waits anxiously to learn if we have told him.

It's killing her. She is terrified that he will be so hurt that he'll turn his back on her and me.'

'I know it's difficult for you both,' said Vidar, concealing his own anguish. They could not begin to imagine the hurt that came with seeing Gilder with his son or the pain that he felt at not being able to tell Niclaus. Vidar locked away his heartache, turning his thoughts to Selina and the torment she was suffering. Her initial delight at seeing him had curdled. He could hardly blame her.

'But I'm thinking of Niclaus,' he said. 'I'm not prepared to break it to him yet.'

'But he has a right to know,' replied Gilder.

'It not fair on Selina or you but it's best for Niclaus. I can't tell him I'm his father and then leave. He wouldn't forgive any of us.'

'But when will we? We can't put it off forever,' said Gilder.

'We'll know when. Although perhaps it might be better if we do not tell him at all,' he said, despondently, agonising at the thought of leaving his son for a second time.

Gilder patted Vidar on the shoulder, 'Somehow, we'll sort it out.'

Later, with the *Ice Maiden* ready to sail, Vidar was preparing to board.

'Come on,' instructed Morton from the deck. 'Sooner we sail, the sooner you'll be back.'

Gilder and Selina, having walked to the shore, joined Vidar.

'Gilder has told you then?'

Selina nodded; the last few days had left her pale and drawn, her eyes red from crying. She cried again – with relief that they did not have to tell Niclaus for a while longer – as she hugged him. 'Be safe and return to us.'

Vidar appreciated her words, especially as his return would cause her more heartache.

*

The *Ice Maiden* sailed north before heading into the massive fjord of Ofot. Morton walked to the front of the boat, to where Vidar stood. 'I didn't remember it being so long,' he said, referring to the length of the inlet.

Ahead, the fjord's steep sides rolled away to reveal a picturesque landscape of snowy forests. To the north, wintry mountains rose up towards the heavens. Morton claimed that beyond lay some of the harshest lands known to man.

'I wish I was going that way,' said Vidar, pointing towards the gentle land to the east.

'There's no challenge that way,' laughed Morton. 'That'll take you to Lake Torne.'

'What makes a man want to stay in the north?' asked Vidar.

'Some of them have no choice; they have been exiled. They hope to be forgotten. Others prefer to live in isolation, avoiding contact with most people. I'm probably one of the few men they deal with. The more successful ones, they live in small communities. There is a fortune to be made if you know what you are doing. Fish, seals, whales; the seas are teeming with them. The northern hunters, who live in the area where you are going, they also hunt the ice bear. You would not believe how much people will pay for their pelts. They trade me oil, fish, meat and skins. In return, I bring them the essentials that are hard to come by where they live.'

Vidar recalled two ice bear pelts that adorned the walls of Hakon's banqueting hall. He wondered if Hakon had paid a large sum for them, or if he had claimed them as booty.

'If the hunter gets really lucky he might catch himself a bear cub. If he did, well he could name his price for it. And if he's unlucky …' Morton laughed, 'he ends up as bear food.'

'What's so funny about that?'

'With no hunter to trade, I get to collect all his furs and pelts for free.'

'Well, I plan to be waiting for you when you return.'

It was mid-afternoon when Morton gave orders to drop anchor. 'I'll row Vidar ashore myself,' he said. 'We'll use the currach.'

'This isn't the same boat you stole from Brother Tomás back at the monastery?' said Vidar.

Morton gave him a conspiratorial grin. 'If my memory serves me well it was you who rowed it from shore.'

Vidar laughed. 'You told me Brother Tomás gave it to you as a present.'

'He did, lad. He just didn't know it at the time.'

They put to shore and Morton ran a final check of Vidar's provisions. 'Have you got everything?'

'You know I have, you've been over it a thousand times.'

Vidar stamped the ground. Unlike Folda, it remained frozen under foot.

'I'll be fine,' he said, mainly to reassure Morton. 'If I can't last here, how will I manage on the island? I really need to do this.'

35

Morton hesitated.

'Go on, get going.'

With that, Morton stepped into his currach.

'See you early next summer,' Morton called back, as he rowed to the *Ice Maiden*.

Vidar took heart from the knowledge that Morton planned to return – Cado had obviously paid for at least one more sailing.

Although apprehensive, nervous of the challenges ahead, Vidar mostly felt a sense of relief. At last, his journey was beginning. He planned to spend the next few days close to where he landed, acclimatising before venturing further north. He had half a day's sunlight and much to do. His first priority was to make camp. All too soon he would begin his trek for real. He would navigate a way through the forest and traverse the mountains. From there, he would travel to the northern point of land. There, Morton explained, he would find the hunters. While these men lived by the shore, in ice-free conditions, they often ventured further north. They would give Vidar an insight into life on the ice. Their knowledge and experience would be invaluable.

Morton had explained that the *Ice Maiden* sailed to the camp many times throughout the year. He would have plenty of opportunity to see how Vidar was faring. All being well, they agreed that Vidar should stay with the hunters until the beginning of the following summer, when Morton would return to take him to Svalbard, where his quest would really begin.

CHAPTER 5

IN THE YEAR 801 AD

'This is a stupid idea,' protested Damian, as they walked in the rain.

'Look, he's been sitting in the very same place every afternoon for weeks now. Of course he'll be here,' said Tomás.

'Well, who ever heard of leaving food for someone who, in all probability, is plotting to rob you? We should be chasing him away not welcoming him.'

Since the incident in the woods, Damian seemed more disagreeable by the day, especially with regard to the stranger. He was clearly discontent with life in the monastery, and had even mentioned leaving Holy Orders. Tomás, by contrast, was convinced that he and the dwarf had made a connection and, as a result, his desire to meet him had grown. He recalled the whispering in the forest, 'We have much to discuss.' But how were they to discuss anything if the dwarf ran off when Tomás approached?

Rather than chasing after him, Tomás had decided to try to gain the dwarf's trust.

'If he was plotting to steal from us, wouldn't he have done it already?' said Tomás, aware that the best moment for a robbery had passed – a few days earlier, he had waved goodbye to Brothers Colm and Eoghan as they departed on one of their regular trips to Iona. They carried a heavy load; enough coinage to last a year. It was a well-known secret that Monicurr had been financing the upkeep of Iona since his inauguration.

'Besides, if he was going to rob us, he wouldn't be so brazen, would he?'

'A waste of good food, if you ask me.'

Tomás sighed. 'Listen, Damian, I have a feeling about this one. There's something about him.'

'If he's not up to something then why is he skulking around, answer me that?'

'I don't know. Maybe he's frightened of us.'

'Do you really think so?' replied Damian. 'No, he'll bring nothing but trouble. Remember, I warned you.'

'Come on, let's get back,' Tomás said, setting down a calfskin of water, an apple and a slab of bread.

'What sort of idiot would sit out here on a day like this unless he was up to no good?' grumbled Damian.

*

'Benedícat vos omnípotens Deus. Pater, et Fílius et Spíritus sanctus,' sang the celebrant.

'Amen,' responded the congregation.

The blessing received, the chapel resounded to the harmonious chanting of the final psalm.

' … misericordia Excelsi non decipietur.'

The hairs on the back of Tomás' neck rose as the voices

increased in volume and tempo.

As the service ended, the chapel filled with the sound of murmuring voices and shuffling feet. Filing out, Tomás and Damian followed the throng to the refectory.

'He's not there,' said Damian.

'That's strange,' agreed Tomás. 'He's always here by now.'

'Perhaps he's had his fill of our food,' muttered Damian.

A familiar routine had developed over the last number of weeks – Tomás leaving food out for the dwarf, who came and ate, sat a while and then retreated into the forest.

Throughout the day, Tomás checked to see if he had arrived, but the offering remained untouched.

During vespers, he prayed for the stranger whose name he did not know, asking God to keep a watchful eye over him. There was no sign of him the next day either. The next days followed the same routine. Tomás would check to see if he returned and then, disappointed, he would meet up with Damian before walking to the scriptorium.

The smell of Cal's latest batch of mixed dyes filled the room. Tomás loved the strong scent of the iron-gall ink. Stewing crushed oak apples and sulphate of iron in gum and water produced not only a brown dye but also the sweetest of aromas.

The elderly monk returned to his work, busy pricking miniature indentations into the vellum, a technique that the monks had developed to rule the sheets of the Holy Bible, ensuring that the writing was straight. 'I've cut you new ones,' he said, pointing towards a pile of quills. Cal was responsible for much of the preparation in the workshop and, of late, had not only been carrying out his own work but Connachtach's as well – checking the manuscripts to make sure that no drawing, illustration, or passage was ever duplicated, as was deemed imperative by Abbot Monicurr. 'The Lord does not accept imitations, and neither should we when we praise his work,' the abbot repeatedly asserted. 'When people look upon these pages they must believe that angels descended from heaven and wrote the book themselves.'

Cal also had the ability to rectify errors and smudges so skilfully that the untrained eye could not see them. 'Now, where's yesterday's work?' he asked, keen to begin his inspection.

Tomás reached across his desk, lifting the single page. He checked it, ensuring that there were no smudges, before handing it over.

'Do you have anything?' Cal asked Damian.

'I'm still working on this,' said Damian, pointing to his latest illustration.

Tomás watched nervously as Cal's hands lifted his previous day's labour. Holding it close to his eye, he scrutinised the page as if he were examining a priceless jewel.

Tomás breathed a sigh of relief as his page passed its inspection.

'What's wrong with you?' asked Damian, noticing his friend's sullen face.

Tomás attempted a smile. 'Nothing.'

'Why the frown, then?'

'Oh, I was thinking of the dwarf – it has been some time since he came here.'

'That's good, if you ask me.'

Tomás, not wanting to get into a discussion, buried his head in his work, his mood reflected in his choice of ink. He usually steered away from the dull brown he was now using, preferring brilliant purples and reds or the intense carbon black. There was no disputing the fact that Tomás was the most skilled of the copiers. Damian often made barbed comments, complaining that Tomás was Connachtach's favourite. The abbot had encouraged Tomás' flamboyancy, which was in stark contrast to his own timid and sober hand. Tomás was exuberant with his quill; his scribing flowed in unconstrained style. As a novice, he had tried very hard to emulate the sedate style of his mentor but he could not restrain his flair, often finding himself unintentionally finishing the lower limbs of letters with ornamental flourishes.

Having completed another chapter, Tomás turned to the next page in the Bible. As he did so, Abbot Monicurr entered the workshop, accompanied by a gust of wind that blew a few more pages of the book over. Monicurr stood in his usual spot and gazed admiringly at the Holy Book. Tomás recalled an earlier incident that he could still see vividly in his head. Abbot Monicurr had stood at the very same spot arguing with Connachtach over the accuracy of the contents of the missal he was now copying. Monicurr was adamant: the scripture in Connachtach's missal was not right. 'It should be *gaudium* not *gladium*. "*I came not only to send peace but joy*" not "*I came not only to send peace, but a sword.*"' Connachtach's bullishness swayed the argument, and the text of Bible they were scribing, rightly or wrongly, became the unabridged text of St Jerome. Connachtach had left the book as a parting gift.

Tomás lifted his quill and began copying what he thought was the correct page. 'Good afternoon, Father,' he said.

'Good day,' Monicurr responded. 'How are you getting on?'

'We're doing well,' answered Tomás, twisting his neck to ease its stiffness. He reached for a virgin sheet of vellum.

Monicurr's visits had become much more frequent since Connachtach's departure, the atmosphere in the workshop being much more relaxed.

'Tomorrow, Cinaed is going for supplies. Are there any materials you need?' Monicurr asked, directing the question to Cal, who was now rinsing out a few brushes made of marten pine fur.

Cal rubbed his hands dry on the front of his cassock. Shufflling a few pages, he found and passed on his list. He turned to Tomas. 'Is there anything you need?'

'I don't think so,' replied Tomás.

Damian said nothing, too engrossed in painting his picture of the Virgin Mary and child. He had been working on the piece for several weeks. Madonna and Child sat, centred on the sheet, surrounded by an arabesque border. On each corner, an angel gazed adoringly upon the pair. Damian was using a compass to draw symmetrical semicircles between the angels, which he would fill in with a design. The picture was exquisite, the colour and detail surpassing any illustration he had ever created.

Tomás, feeling the draught of the open door as Monicurr left, placed a hand on the Bible to keep his place. His attention broken, he began to work, not realising that he was duplicating a previously copied text from St Luke's gospel describing Jesus' meeting with Simon.

His thoughts returned to the dwarf. Given another chance, Tomás would not hesitate; he would walk straight up to the little man. If there was to be a next time ...

CHAPTER 6

IN THE YEAR 830 AD

Aching muscles, along with scuffed knuckles and a gash to his forearm were the physical rewards of a successful climb. Vidar felt exhilarated, his confidence was high – he had conquered the mountain.

Making his descent, the strong breeze blew spitting rain into his face. Above, patches of blue sky broke up the swirling white and grey clouds. The weather would hold, he told himself as he skied over thick snow. He was relieved; snowstorms were commonplace even in summer. Tempted by unending daylight, Vidar ignored good sense and, over the next few days, pushed himself too hard. Resting little, he set an unsustainable pace. The rain came, carried on an icy wind. Keeping dry should have been Vidar's priority. A minor cough soon turned into a heavy cold and still he refused to heed the advice he had been given prior to his departure. By the fourth day, he was exhausted. Vidar struggled to put up his tent before collapsing inside it. He remembered little of the next days, drifting in and out of sleep, waking either drenched in sweat or shivering uncontrollably. His good fortune had been that, having reached the low lands, he had cleared the deep snow. In his tent, where he was dry and sheltered, the temperatures outside were not threatening. After the fever broke, Vidar took a few extra days rest, making sure he had regained his strength. His lesson learned, he restarted his trek. The sun shone, the gentler wind danced through the lazy grasses, as he trekked across a land dotted with glistening lakes. The terrain gradually changed, becoming boulder-strewn as he got closer to the coast.

Three-and-a-half weeks after setting out, Vidar walked down to the stony shore. Across the bay, lay the flat-topped island that Morton claimed housed a small settlement. The foreshore was uninhabited. The only way to get to the island was to swim, and it looked roughly a thousand strides, perhaps as much as a full vika, away. The distance did not disturb Vidar as much as the unknown currents of the stretch.

The breeze was strong, making the day feel colder than it was. He combed the shoreline for anything that would float. Disappointingly, there was nothing.

He packed only the clothes he was wearing into his sack. With the tide on the ebb, he found the narrowest crossing point. The initial coldness of the water passed as he acclimatised. The current was with him for most of way, and he only had to swim against it as he neared the island. Once ashore, he dressed and was soon walking northward.

Long before Vidar found the settlement, his nostrils filled with a foul smell. Eventually, below lolloping hills, the settlement came into view. It was a disappointing sight. Around ten wooden shacks and barns lay in a semi-circle facing the sea. Beyond the last cabin on the eastern side, birds hovered and dived, scavenging off a huge mound of decaying carcasses. Next to the rotting mass was a series of woodpiles. The smell grew more pungent as he neared. Close to the wood, large pots simmered on open fires, the source of the obnoxious aroma.

By the water, a group of men was busy unloading a cargo of seals.

A figure appeared from a shed next to the woodpiles. He was tall and bearded, with a messy head of dark hair. He carried a mountain of blubber over his shoulder. With a shrug, he slopped it into one of the pots. His shoulder and the right side of his shirt were wet, stained with blood.

'Hello, I'm Vidar.'

The man looked at the hand as if offended. 'What do you want?' he asked.

'Captain Morton told me I'd find a place to stay here.'

'He did, did he?'

Over the man's shoulder, Vidar could see men approaching with a cart filled with seal carcasses.

'Who's this?' the nearest man called, seeing Vidar. 'Fleinn, aren't you going to introduce us?'

Fleinn grunted inaudibly.

The newcomer introduced himself. 'I'm Knutsen,' he said, proffering his hand.

'Vidar.'

Knutsen was around the same age and had a similar build to Vidar, perhaps a little broader. His hair was fair and his beard bushy. Vidar liked him immediately.

'Well, you are most welcome. This is Þórarna.'

'Call me Þó,' said the elderly man.

Knutsen put a friendly arm around the newcomer. 'Now, Vidar, how long do you plan for us to share your company?'

'I was hoping to stay until the summer.'

'Any objections?' Knutsen directed his question to Fleinn.

'As long as he brings no trouble and does his share.'

'Come on, time to earn your keep. There's flensing to be done,' Knutsen said, leading Vidar towards the biggest shed in the settlement.

Vidar worked tirelessly, slicing strips of blubber before throwing them into the large pots where they were reduced to oil.

The summer months were busy. Vidar learned to hunt seals, whales and walruses. Using their boats to drive them to shore, they harpooned them and stripped their blubber in the bloody shallows. He fished, using numerous methods. When not hunting, there was plenty of work to keep Vidar occupied. He made oil, the barrels to hold it, and transported the filled barrels to the trading ships – that and a hundred more tasks. The work was hard and at times dangerous but the experience would prove invaluable when he undertook his own treks. Knutsen took Vidar under his wing and taught him all he could, and even Fleinn mellowed.

In early autumn, not long before the sun was gone for the winter, Knutsen led seven of the men on an expedition. They left the eldest men to look after the camp.

'So, how do we catch the ice bear?' Vidar asked.

'At this time of year, he is hungry. The ice is soon to form and then he will have his pick of the seals, but we have a few days when we can set a trap for him. We cut a blowhole in the ice and leave a dead seal next to it. The seal's scent is overpowering. When the bear comes in to feed, we harpoon and spear him. As big as a walrus but more ferocious, he'll put up a hell of a fight. If we're lucky, we'll find us a mother. If we do, we'll track her cubs.'

The sea was choppy for the entire sailing. Vidar was relieved when they finally reached the ice field. They sailed along its rim, watching for signs of the ice bear. A few times, they found paw prints but Yngvar, the most experienced among them, thought the tracks were old.

Yngvar studied the latest prints. Standing up, he pointed his index finger to the sky and twirled it. The signal meant that the trail was fresh. The hunt was on.

The men loaded a dead seal, spears and eight large harpoons on to a sleigh. Working in pairs, they took turns to pull it over the ice.

Yngvar stopped to examine animal droppings. 'It's fresh. He's close. He's probably already picked up our scent.'

Vidar felt a knot of excitement tighten in his stomach.

Knutsen studied the landscape. They were standing on open ice but there were plenty of ridges where they could lie in wait.

'Here is perfect. When the ice bear goes for the bait, we will close in from four different angles,' said Knutsen.

Gríss began cutting the ice.

Knutsen unloaded two harpoons.

'Létta and Múli, behind that mound,' he said, handing the weapons over and directing the two men to their positions.

Fleinn and Baggi manhandled the dead seal on to the ice next to the blowhole. Small and stocky, Baggi was acknowledged as the best hunter of the group – his accuracy with a bow and arrow was unrivalled.

Baggi sliced into the seal's blubber before pulling out its stomach and guts.

Fleinn looked at the spilt blood and guts on his partner's gloves and coat. 'I hope he doesn't smell the scent on you,' he said, grabbing a set of harpoons.

Yngvar and Gríss took their place as Vidar handed out long spears.

The hunting party remained well back.

'Keep your eyes open,' Yngvar warned. 'He won't be long.'

Kneeling behind a ledge, Knutsen gave Vidar some final advice. 'Remember, our weapons are tied for a reason. Once the bear starts eating we run in together. Whoever's closest harpoons it. Aim high on his front legs or shoulders. No matter what, make sure you do not miss and that the harpoon attaches. If I launch before you, then drive your weapon into the ice, bury it deep enough to hold the beast. We don't want a wounded bear running amok.'

Vidar's anticipation grew. He had grown up on tales of the ice bear's formidability but he was still to see one.

Létta whistled, signalling the predator's approach.

Then Vidar saw it. It was much bigger and more muscular than he had imagined. Its mouth and paws were huge. To his surprise, it moved without making a sound.

'You'll have to be quick if we want to beat Baggi. First to land a harpoon claims the kill,' whispered Knutsen.

A glaucous gull, spotting the seal's carcass, landed to feed.

The ice bear moved past Létta and Múli, some thirty paces to their left.

Vidar watched, mesmerised, as the animal stopped and dropped to a sitting position. It was taking in its surroundings. Its furry coat appeared yellowish against the white terrain.

Hunching, the predator moved stealthily toward the bait and pounced. Powerful hind legs propelled the ice bear forward. Landing with feline agility, it sprang again, landing on its prey, its jaws instantly ripping the animal apart.

Vidar was up and running a moment after Knutsen.

Simultaneously, a commotion kicked off to Vidar's right.

'Help,' shouted Baggi.

Vidar caught sight of Baggi running, trying to escape a second ice bear. Pouncing, it crushed him to the ice. The helpless hunter writhed and screeched in agony as the beast bit and ripped at him and then shook him wildly from side to side. Blood splattered in all directions. Fleinn was nowhere in sight.

Baggi's horrific screams ceased.

Múli had been quickest of all. With harpoon in hand, he was closer to the original bear. Létta was a few steps behind him. The bear, alert to the ambush, had turned to face Múli. To attack head-on would have been suicidal. Múli's priority changed from attack to defence. The ice bear howled as it pounded the ice. Dropping his harpoon, Múli pointed his longest spear toward it. Létta did likewise. Both men tried to back away from the beast.

With the first bear concentrating on Múli and Létta, Vidar, Knutsen, Yngvar and Gríss rushed to Baggi.

Vidar and Knutsen reached him first. They were too late. The animal raised itself on to two legs. It had Baggi's crushed head in its mouth; his mauled body dangled limply. The sight was sickening.

Without thought of consequence, Vidar rushed at the bear.

Dropping on to its massive paws, the bloodied monster tossed Baggi aside.

Behind, the original bear retreated, taking the seal with it.

Vidar launched his harpoon and rolled sideways, trying desperately to stay clear of the bear's reach. Unfortunately he was not quick enough, and the ice bear clawed him, tearing his side, his buttocks and the back of his thigh.

But his aim had been true. The harpoon buried itself between the bear's neck and shoulder.

Knutsen, following behind, had little choice – to drive his harpoon into the ice would have meant Vidar's death. Instead, he ran straight at the bear and drove his harpoon through its thick neck and into its chest.

Vidar could only watch as Yngvar and Gríss followed up, driving their weapons into the midriff of the animal.

Wounded, its rage spent, the ice bear collapsed.

Knutsen and Yngvar immediately turned their attention to Vidar. 'They're a lot better than I thought they would be,' said Yngvar, as he bandaged the wounds. 'You'll be sore but you'll live.'

Fleinn, who had been knocked unconscious when the bear charged at him and Baggi, was back on his feet.

'Thank you, lad,' he said to Vidar. 'It was a brave thing you did. The bear could well have attacked me next.'

Vidar studied his party. Although they were a hardened bunch,

Baggi's death had shaken them all. Knutsen organised a burial of sorts. He said a few words over Baggi's body before they dropped him into the blowhole.

Yngvar and Gríss hacked and cut, skinning and boning the ice bear. Knutsen helped Vidar on to the sleigh while the rest packed up.

Vidar recovered well from his injuries and the mild winter came and went. The returning sun was a welcome sight. Morton was soon to return.

CHAPTER 7

IN THE YEAR 801 AD

Hunching his shoulders against the strong breeze, Tomás walked along the side of the church. The building was roughly a hundred paces in length by forty in width. Its walls were the same thickness as the monastery's outer perimeter. It had a steep roof with narrowing eaves. Monicurr's scriptorium was above its chancel, which was divided into three workshops. Tomás and Damian had renamed it White Owl's Cages.

'Well, I'll be …,' exclaimed Tomás, as the silhouette broke from the tree line.

The dwarf was back.

Tomás rushed toward the stranger, determined not to let this opportunity pass. Afraid that he might scare him again, he stopped, still a little way off. 'I promise I won't chase you. Anyway, you're too quick for me.' He sat down. 'I am glad to see you are back. I trust you are well?'

'I am fine. Unfortunately I cannot say the same of the weather,' replied the man, eyeing the swirl of black clouds.

'What brings you here?'

'I'm here to meet a friend.'

He introduced himself. 'I am Brother …'

'Tomás,' finished the dwarf, who, up-close, seemed more round. Dressed in a brown tunic, the little man wore a woollen hat that covered his head and most of his ears. 'I heard your name mentioned by one of your brothers. My name is Cado,' he said, offering Tomás his hand. Tomás was surprised at the firmness of the handshake from someone so small. Having waited an age to make Cado's acquaintance, Tomás felt a mixture of trepidation and excitement.

'Why did you run when we first came to meet you?'

'I did not run from you. Rather I ran from Damian.'

'Why would you run from Damian?'

'The heart is perverse above all things, and unsearchable, who can know it?' said Cado.

Tomás was more than intrigued – how was Cado able to quote the Bible and what made him believe that Damian was wicked?

'You must be mistaken. Damian is a God-fearing man.'

'Do you doubt that a disciple of the Lord can be led astray?'

'Not Damian.'

Cado's perception of his friend's character irked Tomás. Yes, Damian could be moody and at times resentful of religious life but Tomás was sure that he had a good heart. Tomás' much-anticipated meeting with Cado was not going the way he had hoped. The conversation dried, the lull making Tomás uncomfortable.

Tomás remained resolute; he would discover the dwarf's intentions.

'And what is it that we have to talk about?' Tomás asked, referring to the encounter in the forest.

Cado cleared his throat. 'We, the people of my village, have decided to broaden our horizons, and to do so we must meet and talk with those who walk as tall as you.'

'What, have you never met a person like me before?'

'Of course I have. Only you, you have been chosen to learn of our ways.'

'Chosen? Me?'

'Yes.'

'Why me?'

'Indeed, I asked the same question. In time, all will become clear. That is, if you want to learn of Newgrange.'

'I would be honoured,' Tomás said, believing he had made a small breakthrough in his mission to convert Cado and his village.

Cado, having said what needed to be said, changed the subject. 'The weather is turning and I have a long walk ahead of me. I shall return tomorrow and we can talk more.'

'I would like nothing better,' replied Tomás, feeling the nascence of a friendship. 'Perhaps you will allow me to accompany you on part of your journey home?'

As they walked, Tomás told Cado of his previous visit to Newgrange.

'And what happened?' asked Cado.

'We – that is Damian and I – we got as far as your monuments.'

'Did the monolith impress you?' asked Cado, deftly steering the conversation.

'Very much, but I worry as to the use of such a building.'

'And why would that be?'

'Rumour has it that you do not follow the true Lord, that you are heretics.'

'Fear not Tomás. Our ways may seem strange but we have a common belief.'

His words, as reassuring as his tone, put Tomás at ease. His plan to convert the people of Newgrange was progressing. Tomás was fascinated as Cado explained the great effort required to build the monolith. He wanted to learn of its purpose but believed it better not to pry. Cado would reveal more in due course. They talked freely.

'Until today, it has always been our custom to avoid people like you,' explained Cado.

'Are you not the least bit curious about us?'

'No,' he replied, matter-of-factly.

'Well, I am pleased to have met you, Cado.'

'And I you.'

'This should do,' said Cado. 'You have already escorted me over half the way back. You should make for home.'

With a quick goodbye, they separated as the first few drops of rain fell. Tomás pulled the cowl of his habit over his head, as the drizzle grew heavier. Walking home, Tomás thought hard about the mysterious little man. He wondered why he had been chosen to learn of the ways of Newgrange and how Cado could have been so mistaken about Damian. Not only was he devoutly religious, he was also Tomás' best friend and confidant. By the time he arrived back in the monastery, his habit was sodden. Unsurprisingly, White Owl was waiting for him. Tomás would have to tread carefully or he would suffer the abbot's wrath. To leave the monastery without first obtaining permission was unheard of.

'Father, I was on my way to find you. I have some wonderful news.'

White Owl's jaw was taut, a sure sign of his annoyance. Tomás' news needed to be good.

'I met the dwarf, the one who has been loitering around the grounds.'

'And he is reason enough to forsake your duties to the Lord?'

'Oh, no, Father, I have not forsaken my duties. If you ask Brother Cal, he will vouch for me. I have been working extra every day since the summer. My promise of observance to both you, Father, and to God, shall always come first. I would not have left the monastery this afternoon if you yourself had not given me your permission to spread the word of God.'

Tomás' words softened White Owl's mood. 'I did not realise you had been working so hard,' he said. He looked pleased.

'He wants to meet me again.' Tomás paused, 'Tomorrow. If you only allow me some time with him, I believe I can convert him to the Lord's path. It would only be for a short while in the afternoon. And I'll make sure that I keep keep ahead of my duties.'

'Very well, you may meet with him. So long as it does not interfere with your work,' agreed Monicurr, reluctantly.

'Thank you, Father,' said Tomás.

'And Tomás,' added Monicurr, as an afterthought. 'I will have Cal keep an eye on your work and if he sees it dropping in quality I will have to re-visit my decision.'

*

With Monicurr's blessing, Tomás started meeting the dwarf regularly and any doubts as to Cado's motivation soon dissipated. Days stretched to weeks, and weeks into months as their friendship flourished. Tomás used the time to preach of Jesus and the church and, determined to spread the word of the Lord, he pressed for an invitation to Newgrange. He learned all he could of Cado and his village and their traditions, whilst, at the same time, he spoke of his role as a scribe, of the Bible he was working on, and of the privileged position that he held within the monastery.

'You never told me you were inscribing such an impressive Bible,' said Cado.

Tomás' hopes rose. 'Have you read the Lord's book?'

'I have read many books,' answered Cado.

Although Tomás was anxious to convert Cado and his village to Christianity – White Owl would not allow their meetings to continue indefinitely without evidence of progress – he knew the wisdom in patience. He did not press the matter.

'It is Abbot Monicurr's intention to tell the story of the life of the Lord Jesus Christ in the most exquisite book ever made,' he explained.

'Will you show me this wondrous book?'

Tomás, now entirely relaxed with Cado, believed his request to be nothing more than natural curiosity. 'Unfortunately that is impossible. No one, except those working on the book, is allowed inside the workshop for any reason.'

'What's the point of having such a book, if you hide it away?'

'It's very valuable,' said Tomás, suddenly uncomfortable with the conversation.

'I'm sorry. I shouldn't have asked.'

Cado had a valid point – what was the sense in having such a book if he could not use it to convert a pagan? Tomás wanted to show Cado the Bible he was working on, believing his refusal must have seemed like an affront. Moreover, if he did not let Cado see the book, what chance would he have of learning more about Cado, his village, and the mysterious monument?

*

'I won't be here tomorrow,' said Cado.

The day was bitterly cold and the hard frost refused to lift.

'Is anything wrong?'

'No, not at all. Tomorrow is a night of great festivity in my village.'

Tomás checked the date in his head, comparing it to his religious calendar. It was insignificant. 'What festival is it?'

'The longest night. The beginning of the strengthening sun. God's greatest gift to the world,' explained Cado.

'God's greatest gift was his only son, Jesus,' responded Tomás, to whom the mention of a pagan festival was offensive. 'Does your celebration take place in your monument?' he asked, trying to learn more.

'It does.'

'Your monument fascinates me. You built it so perfectly. Is there a reason for its precise shape?'

'There is indeed.'

Tomás waited for an explanation, which did not come.

'Well, aren't you going to tell me?'

'No.' Cado's grin was enough to let Tomás know that he was not going to find out.

Cado elaborated. 'I'm sorry, Tomás. Only the Head Elder can tell you of our secrets.'

Tomás believed he understood. They both would have shared everything had it not been for the constraints placed on them by others.

*

Tomás leant over his vellum, working on his latest illustration of Melchisedek. He paused, deliberating over whether the character's trousers should be the same colour as his undergarment. His quill hovered before dipping into the blue dye, made from the leaves of the woad plant.

White Owl, who stood at his shoulder admiring his artistry, permitted himself a smile. 'Tomás, I have just been talking to Cal. He says that, even allowing for your meetings with the little man, these last few months have yielded some of your most productive work. He has been greatly impressed.'

Tomás was elated. It was rare to receive such praise. He tried to suppress a smile of his own, knowing that Monicurr loathed pride. It was one thing to receive praise, and it was another to gloat about it.

'Thank you, Father,' he replied, solemnly.

'So, you are telling me that this little man, what's his name again?'

'Cado, Father.'

'… that he is well versed in the Bible.'

'Yes, Father, he quoted scripture to me. And it was Vetus Testamentum. Lucam. "O God, be merciful to me a sinner."'

White Owl's face lit up. 'This is wonderful news. Perhaps I should offer him some sort of encouragement.'

'He mentioned he was partial to mead.'

'Indeed, a worthy reward for a believer in Christ. Have Cinaed bring you a cask from the cellar, one of the smaller ones. You may take a little longer this afternoon.'

*

That afternoon, the conversation returned to the topic of Tomás' work.

'Your Bible sounds fascinating,' Cado said. 'I long for the day that you will be able to show it to me.'

Tomás believed Cado meant no harm, but sensing a test of friendship and feeling less inhibited because of the mead, he offered to show Cado the manuscript. Deep down, he had always known that the moment would arrive.

'Not today, my good friend. Maybe tomorrow.'

On reflection, Tomás was relieved that his friend declined his hasty offer.

The following morning, Tomás left early for the terce service. Knowing that he should not have offered to show Cado the Bible, he was intent on saying a few prayers of contrition. After exchanging a few pleasantries with Eamonn, he left his fellow brother busy spading an overgrowth of brambles by the side door of the refectory. As he crossed to the church, Tomás spotted Cado standing close to the monastery's entrance, gesturing for Tomás to come to him. Before today, Cado had usually arrived around midday.

Tomás' stomach churned as he hurried through the open gate. He was certain that something was amiss. The abbot would punish him if he were late for the service so he would have to make his meeting short.

'What's wrong?' he asked.

Cado looked at him sternly. 'Can you keep your word?'

'Not very well, it appears. Only yesterday, I was offering to break my oath to the abbot by showing you the manuscript.'

'Yes, indeed you did, and I was disappointed.'

Cado's comment stung.

'I, I …' Words failed Tomás.

Tomás had always believed that his would have been the role of teacher in their friendship. Now, standing before Cado, he accepted he was, once again, the novitiate, and it stirred memories of the uncertainties he had encountered settling into religious life.

'Tomás, have you given any consideration to the fact that I might have befriended you to steal your manuscript?'

Damian's warnings rang in Tomás' head, 'This one'll bring nothing but trouble.' Tomás digested the question. 'Cado, I should not have offered to show you the Bible but if by showing it to you I can bring you closer to the Lord, then my actions were …' he paused unsure of what to say.

The dwarf's expression became even more serious. 'Tomás, I think it is time.'

'Time for what?'

'These are grave times and my village is in great danger. Will you help me?'

Tomas saw an opportunity. 'If I agree, will you allow me to teach you and your people of Jesus and Christianity?'

'Yes.'

'Then, I am happy to assist in any way I can. Now, how is Newgrange in danger and what can I do?'

'Tomás, what I am about to share with you will change your life. I will be burdening you with a great duty. You will be the first tall walker to be trusted. Even I am afraid to anticipate the outcome. It may cause you great pain. Are you sure?'

'I am a servant of the Lord. If by helping you, I can bring your people closer to Him then I am more than happy to do what I can.'

'To begin with, I must be totally honest with you. I have no interest in stealing the manuscript. If I had, I could have taken it when I read it.'

'But you could not possibly have read it,' protested Tomás.

Cado gave Tomás a look that he was getting used to.

'Your work is truly exquisite. Without doubt, you are the most talented scribe.'

Tomás was astonished. There was no way Cado could possibly have got into the workshop. Tomás possessed the only key to the scriptorium and he did not let it out of his sight.

'Believe me, Tomás – I have read your book. In fact, I have found a mistake that both you and Cal have failed to spot. Cal attached the page with the error to your Bible only last week.'

'You tease me.'

'No, Tomás, I do not, for I now need you to understand the power that I possess, and the importance of the task that I am asking you to complete. Go and look for yourself, but be careful when you handle the book.'

'I'll be early tomorrow, so that we can begin our work. Now, go before you are late for your service.'

Hurrying back to the chapel, Tomás took his seat as the choir broke into song.

Tomás was desperate to examine the bible but the service seemed to go on forever. Finally free, he rushed up the spiral staircase to the workshop. Opening the book, he scoured the most recent pages for the mistake. He read the text again and again and then systematically checked every single word and every single letter. Cado was wrong. Slamming the book shut in frustration, he cut his finger on the edge of a page. Preoccupied by finding the so-called mistake, he did not remember Cado's warning.

*

Tomás rose early after an unsettled night's sleep. Why had Cado made such an accusation and why had he lied? He turned over the questions in his mind as he walked to the scriptorium. Whatever the reason, he was going to demand answers when he met Cado later in the day.

'Good morning,' called Cado from the open gate.

Surprised to see Cado so early, Tomás crossed the path to meet him. 'There's no mistake,' he called.

'If you say so, it must be true. How's your finger?'

Tomás looked down at the paper cut. Cado's words came to

mind. How could he have known? The thought frightened him a little. 'Why do you torment me these days?'

'I do not mean to,' replied Cado. 'But you definitely have duplicated the text about Mary Magdalene washing Jesus' feet. Cal has missed it and added the parchment.'

How could Cado have known that he had been working on that section unless he had seen the manuscript? It made sense – it was a mistake that was only obvious if you knew what to look for.

'Come on, there is much to discuss,' said Cado.

'No, I have work to do and I want to see the error for myself.'

'You can see it later,' said Cado, forcefully, 'I need you to begin writing a manuscript for me.'

Surprised, Tomás followed Cado to the grass bank where they sat.

'I do not have time to start another ...'

'This will not be an intricate book – it's a private one.'

'What sort of book?'

'It will be the history of my people, detailing the building of our monument, uncovering the reasons why we built it and the amazing journey we have taken.'

'But surely someone from your village could write it?'

'Tomás, you have been chosen. It has been decided that you shall be the first tall walker to learn of our history and our many secrets. This is your destiny.'

CHAPTER 8

IN THE YEAR 831 AD

The *Ice Maiden*, as scheduled, had returned early in summer and whisked Vidar from Knutsen and Fleinn's camp to Svalbard, the island where he was to find the Vestibule. The summer's heat, aided by a warm current, pushed back the ice-cap boundaries, freeing Svalbard from its isolation. The reprieve, although short-lived, offered an opportunity for Vidar to explore its shores.

'Look, dolphins,' cried Anders.

Vidar leaned over the gunnel to get a better view. He watched, amazed by the speed and grace of the mammals as one jumped high out of the water to his left.

'A good omen. The gods of the sea send them to watch over us,' explained Anders.

The white-nosed dolphins looked majestic as they escorted the boat, their arrival coinciding with an increase in turbulence in the water.

'It'll be choppy for a bit. We're crossing a riptide,' warned Anders.

The archipelago was teeming with wildlife. Nesting kittiwakes, easily recognisable with their black-tipped wings and distinctive white plumage, were dotted all over the high cliffs. Below, an assortment of seals, fighting for basking rights, dotted the shore, as a few Arctic foxes scavenged, feeding on hatchlings dislodged from the ledges above. Eider ducks and barnacle geese swam on the shallow waters and a pod of killer whales patrolled the shoreline, eating any seal foolish enough to venture into the sea.

'Out there,' called Walrus.

While his words were indistinct behind his drooping whiskers, his meaning was clear. He pointed to what at first looked like stillness in the water – closer inspection confirmed that he had spotted the first ice slab.

The appearance of ice heralded long shifts for the crew, as they watched for jagged pieces above and below the waterline. Working with long timber poles, the crew cleared a path through the ever-increasing jigsaw, pushing frozen debris out of their way or sailing around larger pieces. The ice thickened on either side, leaving a channel of clear water. They sailed until it narrowed, when the way ahead became an impassable field of churned sludge.

'That's as far as even the *Ice Maiden* can risk,' said Morton. 'We'll put you ashore here.'

'Thank you,' said Vidar, gratefully.

'We were lucky that the south of the island was ice-free. Got you a lot further up the coast than I expected. I'll come back for you the same way, as far as is possible. Mind you, I can't promise that the conditions will be as favourable.'

'I'll wait where the ice ends,' said Vidar.

'Remember, it's a big island and there's no guarantee you'll find what you're looking for. Whatever it is,' Morton said.

Vidar suspected he was still annoyed that he had not taken him into his confidence.

'You know I can't tell you. I promised Cado not to speak of it.'

'I know, lad. Anyway, consider this a learning experience – you'll be slow and unconditioned. I'm sure we'll be back here a number of times before you find what you seek.'

'A number of times …' The words registered with Vidar.

'Keep to the schedule,' warned Morton. 'The summer will be shorter than you think.'

Morton had devised a timetable that included rest days, and a safety net of extra days to compensate for any adverse weather or mishaps.

'The rest days have been included for a reason,' said Morton, sternly. 'Remember how you did not heed my advice last time. You learned the hard way.'

Vidar began smearing seal fat over his body, a technique the northern hunters had taught him – the fat acted as an insulator.

'That stinks,' complained Rune, as he and the rest of the crew moved upwind of the scent.

Vidar found himself retching at the smell. 'It stops me sweating,' he explained.

'Think I'd rather sweat,' said Rune.

'Not out there, you wouldn't. Sweat freezes and burns into the flesh, and hurts worse than you can imagine – especially on the insides of your legs.'

Vidar put on woollen socks, inside out. The wool allowed the skin to breathe and soaked up perspiration. Next, he put on another pair with the fur to the outside, creating a pocket of warm air, followed by leggings of deerskin, under breeches made of young sealskin. Over this, he put his sealskin boots. He had shaved the sealskin himself and stitched it with seal sinew that expanded when wet. On top, he wore two woollen fleeces – one wool against skin, and the other with wool outside – before he slipped on a hooded coat filled with eiderdown. He had stitched wolverine fur to the hood, as it was water resistant and did not freeze. Finally, he put on mittens and a furred face cover.

'You look like a bear,' laughed Torre.

'I feel like one.'

The clothes looked less comfortable than they really were. Like his utensils and equipment, they had been scrutinised in minute detail, it being vital that they not only protected him from the harsh conditions but also that they allowed him freedom of movement.

'Why so much wood?' asked Torre, seeing the large pile he had packed on to the sleigh.

'The island has none. I'll need it for cooking and keeping warm.'

'We shan't be stopping,' said Morton. 'We'll be sailing straight away.'

The men groaned. Rune rolled his eyes. Morton caught his expression. 'Only a foolish sailor rests in perilous waters.'

'Would it kill us to rest up for the night?' asked Rune, when he and Morton were out of earshot of the others.

'I don't like these waters,' whispered Morton. 'It's so quiet that even the animals stay away.'

'It's colder here,' replied Rune, trying to explain their absence.

'I have a bad feeling.'

Vidar found Morton's words unsettling; Morton rarely worried.

'I've heard tales of the sea freezing over in a night, trapping ships, crushing them to splinters. I don't want to take any risks.'

Rune accepted the decision. Vidar doubted he would have argued even if he had disagreed.

'The sooner we get Vidar ashore, the sooner we can be away,' Rune said to the men.

The crew gathered to wish Vidar good luck.

'Hurry back,' said Anders.

'Godspeed,' said Torre.

'And keep safe,' added Arne.

Vidar gripped the locket around his neck before kissing it for luck.

'What's that?' asked Arne.

'Oh, this old thing,' said Vidar, raising it to have a look at it. 'I've become quite attached to it – it's my lucky charm. Brother Tomás gave it to me. He claims it saved his life once and wanted me to have it. He says it might do the same for me some day.'

With goodbyes and good wishes exchanged, and the *Ice Maiden* sailing into the distance, Vidar checked over his sleigh for the umpteenth time, running his hands along the ivory runners and leather covering. He had spent an age stitching it – making it waterproof and buoyant.

Vidar walked to where the grass met the shore. A few paces further ahead lay the summer snow line, the end of the thaw. He eyed the divided land: the south was in bloom while the north was a vast lifeless tundra. Vidar stood, motionless, a solitary figure in the pristine Arctic. He remained transfixed until the glare from the snow broke his stare, forcing him to shield his eyes with cupped hands. He would need to put his visor on. Its eye-slits helped to protect his eyes from the glare that reflected off the snow.

The land embraced him with a beauty and purity he believed he would never experience again. Exhilarated, he stepped off the grass, crunching on to the ice for the first time. The noise shattered the silence and, with it, Vidar's illusion. This was not just a picturesque place, he reminded himself – it was the most hostile place he would ever face.

'Get a move on,' he said aloud.

The sleigh moved smoothly over the polished surface. As he walked, he replayed past conversations with Cado in his head, trying to remember if he'd said anything about where to start looking.

'You are to find a Vestibule in the ice on a frozen island,' Cado had told him.

'You want me to search an entire island to find a cave? How will I know if it's the right cave?' he had asked sceptically.

'It's not like any place you have ever seen. Its entrance is lit up by a spectrum of reflected sunlight.'

'Give it to me in language I understand,' Vidar had said.

'The sunlight reflects off the ice of the Vestibule, creating a rainbow in the ice. It's a remarkable sight.'

At last, Vidar understood. 'So, I'm to find a cave with a rainbow at its entrance.'

'No, not a cave. A Vestibule, in the mountains, that leads to a massive underground valley. The escaping heat from the earth's core melted the frozen water of a great lake from the ground up and the Vestibule acts almost like a chimney. The temperature above remains so low that the ice failed to melt, meaning that there is a land above ground but below frozen waters. A roof of ice replaces the sky. The sun penetrates the frozen water, bringing light to the hidden land. It is a truly remarkable sight,' Cado paused, 'and I need you to find it.'

CHAPTER 9

IN THE YEAR 835 AD

'Aslak, will you fetch some water for me?' asked his mother.

Aslak grabbed the bucket and started for the stream. Tall and gangly for his age, he was the eldest of five siblings. He had shaggy blond hair, protruding front teeth and the reputation of being unlucky. Over the years, Aslak had gathered up an impressive list of injuries: broken bones, sprains, concussions, black eyes and insect bites, not to mention numerous cuts and bruises. Even swimming in the fjord proved dangerous. Taking a dip on a summer's day, he felt a sudden movement in his half-length trousers. Something was wriggling. His friends Niclaus, Orrin, and Ludin watched in horror as Aslak splashed wildly in the water. Swimming to shore, Aslak struggled for what seemed an eternity before he wrestled a snake the length of his forearm from his trousers. He lifted it by the tail and instinctively it lashed out, biting his hand. Aslak screamed in agony as he dropped the snake, which slithered back to the water.

Sobbing uncontrollably, Aslak started shaking and then passed out. After a few minutes he came round – the snake had been harmless. He had merely fainted. It took him ages to live down the embarrassment, and his friends teased him mercilessly for having a snake in his trousers.

It was already twilight as Aslak hurried to the stream. Reaching the steep bank, he jumped down without looking and landed on an unsuspecting Henik, sending him sprawling into the stream. Aslak knew instantly that he was in trouble.

'I'm sor ... sorry,' he stuttered.

Henik, born of a reindeer herder and a young village girl, tended to travel with his father, Berit, and the nomads of the north. He was older than Aslak and big for his age – muscular and pugnacious.

Henik rose, his eyes flashing with anger, his nostrils flaring. 'You'll be sorry when I'm finished,' he thundered.

Aslak tried to run but Henik twisted both his arms behind his back. Henik did not need an excuse to make life difficult for the younger boys.

He shoved Aslak head first into the water. Aslak tried desperately to resist. His lungs were close to exploding when Henik finally yanked his head up. Aslak tried to gasp air but instead gulped a mouthful of water. Henik was enjoying himself now. 'This'll teach you to jump on me,' he said, plunging Aslak's head into the freezing water once more.

*

Having heard the commotion, Niclaus rushed to the stream to help Aslak. 'Leave him alone,' he yelled.

Henik, laughing wildly, released Aslak and faced Niclaus.

'Why, what are you going to do to stop me?'

Niclaus, without thought of the consequences, threw a quick, straight punch that caught Henik full on the nose, and sent him crashing to the ground. But he was soon on his feet and, lifting a thick branch, he hit Niclaus with it. Niclaus tried to block the blow but he was too slow. Its force almost knocked him out and he was unable to defend himself as Henik rained blow after blow. Niclaus tried to stay on his feet, tried to bring his arms up to defend himself but Henik switched attack, dropping the branch and going for Niclaus' kidneys and stomach. Niclaus' guard dropped. Henik threw a series of powerful jabs into his unprotected face. One crashed into Niclaus' mouth, splitting his bottom lip. A vicious uppercut followed, clattering teeth. The force of it caused Niclaus to bite heavily on his tongue. Pulling him down by the hair, Henik brought up his knee, delivering a knockout hit to the temple. Niclaus' limp body fell to the ground, chased by a stampede of kicks that completed the beating. Satisfied, Henik ran off, leaving Aslak sprawled by the water's edge, and Niclaus lying motionless by his side.

Aslak, trying to rouse his friend, splashed a handful of water over Niclaus' face. Slowly, Niclaus came round, groggy and in a lot of pain.

'Come on, Niclaus, we need to get you home.'

Niclaus took a moment to test his aches and pains, assessing how much damage he had suffered. He licked at the coagulated blood on his fat lip and fingered his bloodied nose. His chest hurt when he breathed. Niclaus got to his feet but nausea overcame him.

'I'll get your father.'

'No, don't. I'll be fine, just give me a moment.'

Niclaus forced himself to stand. 'Aslak, we shan't tell anyone,' he said through gritted teeth, the pain in his chest almost unbearable.

'What'll you tell Gilder?'

'Don't worry, I'll think of something. Just pretend you came to the water and found me lying here.'

Niclaus winced; he clutched his arm around his chest in a feeble effort to ease the pain. With Aslak's help, he climbed the bank before stumbling home. His family had just sat down to their evening meal when Aslak helped him through the door.

Gilder rushed to help. 'What happened?'

Niclaus did not attempt an answer.

'I was getting water,' stammered Aslak. 'I found him lying by the stream.'

'Gilder, not now. Go and bring me a basin of water,' ordered Selina, taking charge. 'Good night, Aslak. Thank you for bringing Niclaus home.'

'But ...' Gilder went to argue.

'Later,' said Selina, her tone forbidding argument. 'You can find out later. First we tend to Niclaus.'

Niclaus lay on the large rug in front of the fire as Selina washed dried blood off his face. She removed her son's clothes with a mother's tenderness, checking every abrasion and laceration. Next, she washed Niclaus' battered face and applied moist dressings. 'You'll feel worse in the morning.'

'I hope not,' said Niclaus, taking comfort from his mother's attention.

Gilder had waited for Selina to finish before he prodded his son for information. 'Tell me, Niclaus – what happened?'

'I can't remember. The last thing I recall is standing by the stream, the rest, I just don't know.'

'Niclaus, tell me,' demanded Gilder.

Niclaus looked his father in the eyes, holding his stare. 'I can't remember.'

'I'll find out,' said Gilder, as he marched towards the door.

'I'm coming too,' said Orrin.

'Gilder, wait,' called Selina. 'Don't go, not tonight. It will keep to morning. Sleep on it, please.'

Reluctantly, Gilder agreed. 'I'll get to the bottom of this; I'll find out who did it, though,' he declared.

It was Selina's turn to agree. There was no doubt. Gilder would find out what happened. 'Just not tonight,' she said.

CHAPTER 10

IN THE YEAR 835 AD

The next morning, Orrin, impatient to discover what had had happened, jumped out of his bed, landing noisily on the wooden floor. A groan confirmed that he had succeeded in waking Niclaus.

'Well? Who did it?'

Niclaus, not in the mood for questions, rolled over to face the wall, wincing with pain.

'Come on, Niclaus. Tell me. Who did this to you?'

'Not now,' Niclaus moaned, feeling as though somebody was trying to scrape out the inside of his head with a spoon. He was sure he looked a mess. His left eye was swollen and completely closed. He had a fat lip, which stung, a bruised left cheek and every breath of air irritated a freshly chipped tooth. He was also finding it uncomfortable to breathe through his swollen nose, bunged as it was with dried blood. Niclaus licked his forefinger and put it up his left nostril, bringing air to the passageway. He repeated the exercise with the right one.

Selina bustled into the boys' bedroom, a worried frown on her face. The cramped room had barely enough space for two beds, a chest, and a roughly made table. Upon the table rested an extinguished, half-burnt candle, the draught from under the door having blown the flame off centre, melting the wax unevenly down one side.

'Come on, Orrin, out and get your breakfast. Leave Niclaus alone, he needs his rest,' she said.

Niclaus knew that Orrin would hear about the fight from Aslak.

A daylight check revealed the full extent of the injuries.

'Well, are you not going to tell your mother what happened?' she asked, as she rubbed a healing lotion into the deeper cuts and abrasions. 'Who did this to you?'

'All I remember is going to the stream for a drink. The rest … well, the rest I can't recall.'

Gilder came in. 'How are you?'

'I've had better days.'

'Well, what happened?' Gilder's mood was more relaxed than the previous night.

'He says he doesn't remember,' Selina answered.

'Well, it looks like you made a fight of it,' said Gilder, pointing to his swollen right hand. 'I'd like to see the face that that connected with.'

Over the next days, Niclaus stuck to the same story. He remembered nothing of the incident. His parents could get no further information from him. Orrin, as Niclaus suspected, had discovered what had happened from Aslak. Henik, for his part, had left the village the morning after the fight.

*

As it was a warm day, Niclaus, Orrin, Aslak and Ludin met at the water's edge. Their talk once again returned to the attack on Niclaus and Aslak.

'Let it rest, you got off lightly,' said Orrin.

'Yeah,' agreed Aslak.

'He nearly killed you. Have you forgotten that?' protested Niclaus.

Aslak voiced his desire to let the matter drop. The incident had shaken him. 'Forget it,' he pleaded.

'Forget this?' said Niclaus pointing to the fading purple bruises on his face. 'No way. Henik will pay for this. I will have my revenge.'

*

Henik only stayed in Folda when the herds were close. Even then, he stayed mostly with his father, only returning to his mother's home to sleep. Niclaus watched him for a couple of nights. He walked the same path every evening, allowing Niclaus to scout the route and select an ideal spot to execute an attack. It was a straightforward plan, a surprise ambush on Henik as he took the quickest way home, through a grove of small trees.

Niclaus waited until the evening. He collected a webbing of fishnet that was hanging to dry by the shore. He spread it evenly over the ground in the grove, keeping some slack in his hand. As he had hoped, the semi-darkness worked to his advantage. Henik was oblivious to both the net and to the waiting Niclaus. As soon as Henik stood on the net, Niclaus sprang from his hiding place, charged and threw the remaining net over the startled Henik, who, twisting and wriggling, was soon sprawled on the ground.

The more he fought, the more he entangled himself. Niclaus did not waste a moment, rapidly lacing kicks into Henik's midriff. Snared perfectly, Henik was powerless to defend himself. Revenge felt good.

'Not so big now,' shouted Niclaus, as he landed a punch. Blood spurted from Henik's mouth. Before he could scream, another blow drowned out his cry. Another followed another.

'That's for Aslak,' he said, smashing another fist into Henik's jaw.

Grabbing Henik's head, he banged it off the ground.

Henik was whimpering, pleading for mercy, still writhing trying to free himself.

Niclaus knelt on his chest. 'Stop struggling or I'll make it worse for you.'

With no option, Henik did as commanded. Niclaus threw a few more punches to his stomach and ribs.

Determined that this would be an end to their fight, Niclaus warned Henik. 'Now you listen, and listen well. This ends now. Do you understand?'

'Yes,' moaned Henik.

Niclaus took his knee off Henik's chest and stood. He was satisfied. Now they were even.

*

After a restless night's sleep imagining Henik still ensnared, Niclaus had risen early and hurried to the grove. He was relieved to find Henik gone. He gathered up the netting – he planned to replace it before anyone noticed it was gone.

'Where are you going with that?' asked Gilder, spotting Niclaus by the shore. 'I thought I heard someone leaving the house early.'

Niclaus cursed his luck.

'We were using it for a game last night.'

'Catch a big fish on land, maybe? You think you can keep secrets, do you? You think your dispute has not been the talk of the village?'

'I wanted to sort it out myself.'

'And you think I would have interfered? You should know me better than that. I would not fight another man's battle.'

It felt good that his father had called him a man. 'You told me yourself. I have to stand up for myself.'

'I know, son. But if you continue with this there will be repercussions and I'll not be in a position to help you.'

Gilder reached for the twisted netting and began helping Niclaus unravel it. They worked in silence.

'A man is born with honour,' Gilder finally said. 'He can choose to wear it with pride or he can give it away freely. It is your choice, but remember: once your honour is lost you'll wear its memory like a stain. Guard it well.'

His father's words picked at Niclaus' conscience as an ache to a tooth.

CHAPTER II

IN THE YEAR 800 AD

Hakon's powerful arm brought the sharp blade down, cutting deeper into the right side of the wooden training block. He pulled back the sword, swung it over his head, and smashed it into the trunk from the opposite side. Hot from his exertion, he paused to remove his leather jerkin and fleece undergarment. His strong torso glistened with droplets of perspiration. He wiped sweat from his forehead with his leathered wristbands. The freshness of the air tickled his exposed flesh, sending a shiver up his spine. He readjusted one of the three bronze amulets he wore on his sword arm. The last ring – the loose one, a dragon's head of twisted copper – had been a gift from his father, Siegford, in recognition of Hakon's bravery.

Siegford had unwittingly disturbed a wild boar on a hunt. It was close to goring him when Hakon launched his weapon. Siegford swore he heard the spear swish past his ear before it landed deep between the animal's eyes. He often teased Hakon after the incident, claiming that the boar was a mere gilt, but that was not what he had said at the time. Hakon remembered his words clearly: the beast had been fierce – few men could have killed it with a single spear. Siegford had taken off his prized amulet and given it to his son. It was the proudest moment of Hakon's life. Holgarth, the farrier, had offered to adjust it but Hakon had refused, claiming he would grow to fit it. The fact that the amulet was still loose on his arm was a source of embarrassment.

Stay calm, he told himself as he sat outside the great wooden hall. The announcement was imminent. Siegford, the Great Lord, was close to death. He had been ill for some time and – having come to terms with the fact that he was going to lose his father – the prospect of succeeding him excited Hakon. With age came weakness. If Siegford had not taken ill, younger, more virile men would have challenged his authority. There would have been infighting and unrest. Many powerful settlements had been lost during such disputes.

His father, as with everything, had planned meticulously for this eventuality, so much so that he had instructed his son on where he was to be when the time arrived. For all of his twenty-three years Hakon had lived under his father's strict regime and now everything was going to change. The mantle of responsibility was going to fall upon Hakon's shoulders.

Hakon was, like his father, an imposing figure: tall, broad, and majestically Nordic. His blond braided hair, piercing blue eyes, strong square jaw, and chiselled features made him pleasing to the eye of many of the women he encountered. Yet for all his charm, the threat of danger was never far away.

The dying man's final breath prompted a chorus of wails from the women in attendance. The high-pitched screeches marked the beginning of the mourning period. The women exited the banqueting hall, making their way up the slight incline to Hakon.

Each woman half-bowed, affirming him as their new master. Simultaneously, the men of the village, who had waited by the shore, began banging their shields in honour of their new lord.

Hakon watched as Oto, his closest friend, began calling out instructions. Oto was revelling in his new position. His chest was puffed out and his shoulders arched to give the impression of being taller than he really was. Hakon often teased Oto that his temper was born out of the anger he carried from being small.

Hakon gave his first orders. 'Men, let us pay tribute to my father. We shall celebrate his memory. After we have honoured him, we shall place him on the *Hammer* and send him on his journey to Valhalla,' he said, pointing to his father's dragonboat, which was anchored by the shore.

Aware of the greatness of the title bestowed upon him, Hakon was anxious not to disappoint. He clenched the charm around his neck, a silver hammer of Thor, a gift from his father in recognition of his transition to manhood. Then Envik, his father's most loyal follower, left the main body of men. Tension rose as the massive, bearded soldier strode slowly and deliberately forward. If he challenged Hakon, they would duel to the death, the conqueror becoming lord. Siegford had taken power the very same way.

Expecting to face some challenge, Hakon had taken a high position with the sun on his back.

The two warriors stood like rutting stags, preparing to do battle for mating rights.

Envik drew his massive sword from its sheath.

Hakon took a step back, raising his own sword in readiness for the fight.

Envik strode on until he was just short of striking distance. He dropped to his knee. 'I swear my allegiance to Lord Hakon. I will serve you as faithfully as I did the Great Siegford. My sword is yours,' he said, handing over the blade, hilt first.

A further chorus of cheers erupted and the banging of shields resumed.

'Hakon, Hakon,' they called, wildly.

Hakon was delighted. With his father's most trusted soldier swearing allegiance, the older men in camp would now fall into line. Now his only other concern was Barid.

Hakon placed a hand on Envik's shoulder. 'Do not kneel in front of me. Rather stand at my side as my counsel. In recognition of the esteem in which my father held you, I think it fitting that you act as the flame-bearer for his dragonboat.'

Pride swelled in the older man's face. Such was the prestige of sending Siegford to the next world that the young lord had won his allegiance.

Hakon continued. 'Now we honour the dead. Let us give my father a send off worthy of the great Odin himself.'

Then there was a stirring from the back of the group. Someone was pushing through the lines of men.

'So Envik is not man enough to face you,' said Barid, 'but you shall not lead my village while I still hold breath.'

Barid looked supremely confident as he stood before Hakon.

Face to face, the men sized each other up.

It was as his father had predicted. Hakon would have to kill Barid. 'If that is so, then you may join my father on his voyage to the afterlife,' replied Hakon.

CHAPTER 12

IN THE YEAR 835 AD

Vidar's annual summer treks to Svalbard continued without success. Although he was yet to find the Vestibule, he took comfort in the fact that, with each trip, the search area grew smaller. Back in Folda, over the years, he had gained the acceptance and trust of the villagers, through his hard work and good nature. Of late, even old Gunnar had made a point of inviting him to his house so he could listen to Vidar talk about the exploits of his youth. Gunnar said that in all his years he had never heard a better storyteller.

Returning from his latest trek, Vidar had been shocked to learn that Magnus, one of the villagers, had fallen into a deep ravine, his body lost. He left behind a wife, Elwin, and four young daughters. As it was customary for the village to take care of widows and their families, and given that Vidar was one of the very few unmarried men of the village, he started to help the family without discussion.

Initially, it was a very difficult time. The family was struggling with grief and here he was – a stranger – around them all the time. Wisely, Vidar kept out of the way as much as possible. Although he had no intention of trying to take Magnus' place, he could not help becoming attached to all of them. The younger girls, Dylla and Helga, took to Vidar much quicker than the older ones. Soon they were hugging and kissing him and pleading with him to play with them. At night, they demanded that he tell them bedtime stories. The older girls took longer to thaw: Fenja, the eldest, snubbed him at every opportunity, and Eve, the second daughter, was polite, but always withdrawn.

And Elwin was like Eve. Vidar found it uncomfortable to be around her for she was very beautiful and stirred feelings he had long forgotten. He fought hard to suppress them. Elwin remained ignorant of the memories she evoked. Innocent looks or smiles, the way her lips curled, the way she brushed past him and a hundred other little things: they all reminded Vidar of Fiona and of what he had lost in Erin. Once, he had entered the house to find Elwin, with her back to him, singing gently, *'Hand entwined hand. Warm, soft, and tender as summer's sun.'* Unsure of the words, she hummed the tune, unaware of the song's significance. Vidar had named it 'Fiona's Song', it being the first one he had ever heard her sing

For all the difficulties, Vidar's place in the family gradually became established and permanent, and the children became used to seeing him emerge from the barn after a night's sleep.

One day Elwin, stirring oats, noticed him from the window. She walked to the door. 'It's freezing out there,' she said, as she tugged on the thick shawl around her shoulders, the first of the winter nights having arrived.

'It's not the worst, try sleeping in the ice further north. It's so cold that even the ice bears wear coats,' he said, trying to be funny.

Elwin smiled, perhaps appreciative of his effort. She looked up at Vidar who stood a good head taller than she did.

'I won't have you getting sick on my behalf. No, I think you should come into the heat at night.'

Vidar nodded, she was right. It was getting too cold to sleep in the barn. He understood that Elwin's invitation was only into her home and not into her room.

*

Gilder walked to the stable to find Niclaus. Summer would soon be here and Morton would come to spirit Vidar away, only this time Vidar had responsibilities. He needed someone to take his place looking after Elwin and the girls.

Gilder watched as Niclaus groomed Trovil, fascinated as always by the boy's way with the little horse.

Gilder coughed to make his presence known. 'He's a fine worker,' he said.

'There's no better in the village,' agreed Niclaus.

Gilder hesitantly brought up the thorny topic that he really came to speak about. 'Niclaus, Vidar has asked me for a favour.'

Niclaus stopped brushing. 'What sort of favour?'

'As you know, he will soon leave the fjord for a few months.'

Niclaus looked at his father. 'How does this concern me?'

'With Vidar soon to depart, he needs someone to carry out his duties. He has asked that you take on the responsibility of helping Elwin and her daughters. It's a big responsibility.'

'I would love to but I can't. I need to prepare for the Trial.'

'Niclaus,' Gilder said sternly, 'I would be grateful for your help.'

Trovil whinnied as Niclaus took out his anger by brushing him too roughly. 'I can't do it. I'd have no time for my training.'

'Niclaus,' said Gilder. 'This is not for discussion; this is how it will be.'

'I won't, I can't do it. Let Vidar find someone else. Ask Orrin or one of the others.'

'Orrin has already agreed to carry out your duties and his own.'

'Why can't Orrin deputise for Vidar?'

'We both thought that the work would suit you better.'

In temper, Niclaus threw down his brush and walked out. The raised voices made Trovil restive. Gilder spoke reassuringly and patted his neck gently. Lifting the brush, he resumed grooming. Gilder could find no way out of his predicament; he could see Niclaus' point. When he had finished, he went looking for Vidar, and found him working at the front of his cabin. He was punching leather, mending a worn strap, while Elwin stood nearby, distaff in hand, threading and spinning flax on her loom.

Vidar stood up to greet Gilder as Elwin excused herself to the kitchen.

'I think it would have been easier for you if Morton had not brought you on that first trip all those years ago,' said Vidar, seeing the expression on Gilder's face.

'Rubbish,' replied Gilder. 'If I had not taken that trip, neither Selina nor Orrin would be alive and God knows what would have become of Niclaus. Without you, I would have nothing. It's just … it's a difficult situation. I understand why you want Niclaus to look after Elwin and the girls, but it's hard for him to understand why he should. I don't like having secrets from him.'

'I know it's difficult. I shall go to him,' replied Vidar, as he put a hand on Gilder's shoulder. 'I'll see if I can persuade him.'

*

Niclaus had taken himself to the waterside. He was going to get out of this. There was no way he was going to take over Vidar's responsibilities. Why should he? His father should know better. Why would he agree to such a request when he had his training to complete? To Niclaus, it seemed that Vidar and his father were working to some sort of secret agenda, always talking privately. Vidar's influence was growing increasingly evident.

Vidar found Niclaus and sat beside him. 'Niclaus, I need you to listen. It's very important.'

His tone was calming. He had a way of putting Niclaus at ease.

'Certain things, of which you know nothing, are unfolding. Soon it will all become clearer. You know Gilder; he only does what's best for you. Trust him. Please. And I promise you, if you undertake my duties I will repay my debt to you.'

'How do you intend to do that?'

'What if I train you for the Trial myself?'

'What would you know?'

'I may surprise you,' said Vidar. 'I'll make you a deal. You undertake my duties when I'm away and when I'm here I will train you better than anyone else could.'

Niclaus looked at Vidar doubtfully.

'If my training isn't good enough, you can cancel the deal.

What do you say?'

Niclaus started to argue, and then thought again. He would do as his father asked.

'Niclaus, do you give me your word that you will carry out my duties when I am away?'

Reluctantly Niclaus agreed. 'Yes, I give you my word. I shall do as you ask.'

'Be sure now, Niclaus. A man lives by his word. Once given, it cannot be taken back. Are you sure?'

'Yes, I'm sure. You have my word. I will not let you down.'

'And I promise you, I shall prepare you better than you could ever imagine.' Vidar reached a hand to his boy and pulled him to his feet.

That same evening Vidar sought out Orrin to thank him for agreeing to undertake Niclaus' duties. In return, he agreed to train Orrin for the Trial too.

CHAPTER 13

IN THE YEAR 836 AD

Orrin shook his brother. 'Wake up, Niclaus. Come on.'

Niclaus, trying to ignore him, pulled his woollen blanket tighter to his body.

Orrin, undeterred, snatched the blanket.

'Are you mad?' Niclaus protested. 'It's still dark outside. What's got into you?'

'Come on, our training starts today.'

Accepting that he was not going to get any peace, Niclaus rolled over and sat on the edge of his bed. 'What training are you talking about?'

'Some fool made a deal with Vidar yesterday, something about training for the Trial of Endurance.'

'I suppose he's training you as well?'

'Well, the way he sees it, it would be wrong to leave me out. Especially as I have to do your work while you are helping Vidar. That is, unless you object?'

Niclaus stretched. 'What does my opinion matter?' he said, as he dressed. Both boys crept to the main room and were soon on their way to meet Vidar.

*

Vidar stood at the water's edge, watching the boys hurrying to join him. The dark clouds overhead were threatening and the wind was chilly. 'Morning, boys. So the deal is, I train you to be the finest competitors in the Trial of Endurance and in return Niclaus will deputise for me when I am away and Orrin will carry out all the chores at home.'

'What takes you away from here?' asked Niclaus.

'That is of no concern of yours,' said Vidar. 'Do we have a deal?'

The two boys, soon turning fourteen, looked at each other. Niclaus shrugged his shoulders as Orrin nodded consent.

'This is not the first time I have helped train someone for this type of race, so I have more experience than you might think. My methods may seem unusual but they work. When does this Trial take place?'

'Not for another few years but we have lots to learn,' said Niclaus.

Vidar pretended to be unfamiliar with the tasks ahead. 'And refresh my memory as to the details of the Trial.'

'It begins with a kayak from the island of Lofoten to the side of the fjord,' explained Orrin. 'Next we have to climb the fjord to the summit, then ski over the glacier top, before sleighing over the frozen land to the finish.'

'It sounds tough,' said Vidar.

'It is. Three full days,' answered Orrin.

'Where do you sleep?'

'There are checkpoints at various sections of the Trial. We get to sleep after we climb the fjord and the next night after we complete our ski.'

'And what is the prize?'

'The winner becomes Ugter, leader in waiting. He'll learn from Gilder how to lead the village.'

'Ah, yes, back in Erin we call the leader a tanist,' said Vidar. 'Right, boys, I'll teach you everything you will need to win. By the time I've finished with you, there'll be no match for the pair of you. Whichever one of you has the bigger heart and greater desire will triumph.'

He took them to the water's edge.

'Clothes off,' he ordered.

Bemused, the two boys did as were instructed.

'Jump in.'

The fjord's steep sides meant a drop into deep water. The boys hesitated.

'Now,' roared Vidar.

The boys plunged into the ice-cold water.

'I think I lost something when I hit the water,' shouted Orrin.

Niclaus laughed, swallowing a mouthful of water.

They both shivered.

'Swim to the far side and back, quick as you can,' ordered Vidar.

'What if we get into trouble?' asked Orrin.

'Then you better hope that your brother rescues you.'

'I'll watch out for you,' promised Niclaus.

With a headwind, a strong undercurrent and quite a way to

the far side, it was a tough swim. The boys were only accustomed to swimming in the summer and, even then, they rarely swam any distance.

Orrin matched Niclaus stroke for stroke. It took a great effort, as Niclaus was the stronger swimmer.

Vidar bawled instructions to the boys as they reached the far shore but they could not quite make out what he was saying. However, they got the gist of his meaning: they were to swim back without a rest.

'Out, quickly, come on,' ordered Vidar, as the boys reached the shore.

Niclaus stood doubled over, hands on his side, breathing deeply, while Orrin collapsed on the bank.

'Come on, boys. You aren't telling me you're tired, are you?'

They both nodded, unable to speak.

'Well, you've only started, in again.'

Vidar smiled to himself; the exercise reminded him of sailing with Morton on the *Ice Maiden*.

'You can't be …' protested Niclaus.

'Now.'

The boys swam the fjord for a second and a third time before Vidar called an end to their session.

'Same time tomorrow,' he said.

Vidar allowed himself a smile as he marched home. The two boys had impressed him. Both had survived their first day.

'I can't feel my legs or my feet,' muttered Orrin.

'I'm staying in bed tomorrow,' moaned Niclaus, his teeth chattering. 'I think he tried to kill us.'

Joining their friends, they relayed the details of their training to Ludin and Aslak.

Orrin complained of his aching limbs, 'I think it'll take a month for my arms to recover.'

The next morning, Niclaus and Orrin arrived promptly but looking less enthusiastic.

Vidar smiled as he gave out new instructions. 'Today, boys, we learn a different discipline.'

Niclaus and Orrin were relieved.

'Today, I want you to stand perfectly still.'

Having explained the exercise, Vidar walked off. 'I will check on you after I eat,' he called, not once looking back.

Gilder, aware of the new regime, ventured out to enjoy the spectacle, meeting Vidar on his way. 'It brings back some painful memories,' he said, with a grin to his old instructor.

'I fear they would rather die than lose to one or other. They are better than you ever were, you know?'

'Never,' grunted an indignant Gilder.

CHAPTER 14

IN THE YEAR 800 AD

'I knew it would be you,' said Hakon, as he locked his gaze on Barid, the first dissenter in camp.

Barid took off his cloak and threw it to the ground. 'How could I not challenge you? We both know you are not my equal.'

Slightly stocky in stature with short arms, Barid was renowned for his great strength and, despite his size, for his nimbleness and agility. The man posed a serious threat.

'I am no longer the young boy you toyed with,' warned Hakon.

Barid, a few years older, had grown to manhood safe in the knowledge that he was the superior warrior. However now they were both men, Barid's extra years counted for nothing.

Hakon began taunting his nemesis. 'Did you know my father had me spar with you deliberately? I know it is hard to believe but he knew we would fight. He made me study everything about you. I know all your strengths and weaknesses better than you know them yourself.'

The challenger tried to ignore the provocation as he advanced but Hakon continued. 'Do you know that you over thrust with your right arm? If I sidestep, your body is exposed.'

Barid flushed with anger as Hakon continued. 'And do you know that when you strike with your weaker arm you compensate by balancing too much on your front leg? Barid, you are no match for me. There is no shame in accepting me as lord. Do not make me kill you.'

Hakon's words were having their intended effect; he could see doubt in his opponent's eyes.

Barid closed. Holding the short-handled axe of Thor in his left hand, he unsheathed his dagger with his free hand. Hakon dropped his sword and armed himself with his dagger and axe.

Both circled as the men and women of the camp clambered around, trying to get the best view. Barid was first to attack, rushing at Hakon, feigning with his dagger while swinging at the head with his axe. Instinctively, Hakon dodged the blow. Barid followed up, lunging with his dagger, forcing Hakon to jump backwards. Circling and prodding, both struck and parried with limited success. All the while, Hakon was moving around, trying to take the higher ground and keep the sun to his back. Again, Barid tried a quick thrust. Hakon read the attack as easily as he had predicted. Overstretching, Barid left himself unbalanced and exposed. Seizing the chance, Hakon sidestepped the thrust and brought his axe down, slicing deeply into Barid's wrist. Involuntarily the wounded hand released its weapon. Hakon switched attack; dropping to his knee, he buried his dagger in Barid's foot, pinning it to the dark soil. Hakon raised his axe once more, with the intention of finishing off his rival.

Bera, watching from the sidelines, had been horrified when

she saw her brother Barid throw down his challenge. Impulsively, she pushed her way through the throng and, armed with a knife, rushed to protect him. Without thought of the consequences, she pressed the knife to Hakon's throat.

Hakon turned to stare in disbelief at Bera. A dark-haired beauty, she had a face and body to enchant Odin himself.

Behind them, Barid struggled to free his pinned foot.

'It appears you have my attention.' Hakon said, eyeing the silver key that hung on a chain around her neck, a sign that she was not betrothed. In his eyes, that key was more of a challenge than the enemy he had just faced. As leader, he could take her as his own – in theory at least. He was confident that he could disarm her easily enough but, given that she was prepared to risk her own life to stand against him, he doubted that she would ever succumb to him freely. It would be impossible to tame Bera unless she consented. She was much too free-spirited.

'How do you propose to settle this awkward situation we find ourselves in?' he asked.

'Spare my brother.'

'I cannot. By Odin, he has challenged me. He shall go to Valhalla with honour.'

'By Odin, you must spare him.'

Looking puzzled, Hakon asked what she meant.

'Odin's laws demand that you must protect your family,' she explained.

'He is no kin of mine.'

'He shall be if you spare him. Do not banish him – treat him as your brother.'

'And why should I do so?'

'For I could not love a man who killed my brother but I could love one, a great lord, who spared his life.'

Hakon looked into her hazel eyes, 'I will take no woman who satisfies me to save her brother.'

'You misjudge me. I would never dishonour my lord any more than I would my brother. He would more surely prefer to die than submit to such an arrangement. If this is to be agreed, it will be of my own will. I believe I will not disappoint you,' she whispered as she lowered the blade. Hakon walked to the water's edge to think, leaving Bera to attend to her injured brother.

'I will not allow this,' said Barid, 'I would rather die a thousand deaths than let you unite with him.'

'Listen,' she whispered. 'You have tried to slay the wild dog and have been bitten. You are fortunate to be alive.'

'I cannot let you do this.'

Bera had the final say. 'I have made my decision. You shall respect him as your lord and your brother.'

With the excitement over, the men set about preparing the festivities, leaving Hakon to his thoughts. Considering Bera's proposal, he conceded that he would spare Barid and allow him to remain in the village, but only if he declared an oath of allegiance.

His mind wandered before settling on the White Cross Followers. Under Siegford, they had plundered many parts of the Western Isles, but not nearly enough. He would set this to right. He detested them. Their plague was spreading like a wild fire. Now, as lord, he would extinguish it. They would feel the might of Odin and Thor. Hakon had lost count of the raids he had carried out, the names of Lindisfarne and Jarrow, two of the numerous monasteries that sprung to mind. Free of his father's shackles, he would raise a flotilla to terrorise the White Cross Followers.

In the distance, he heard Envik giving out instructions, 'Who will accompany our great chieftain on his journey?' he called.

He chose a widow, and her two daughters. Hakon saw the wisdom in Envik's selection – there would be no dispute over his choice. It might have been a different matter if he had picked attractive women or those with strong family connections.

The revelry started immediately and continued for the full duration of the mourning period. The villagers drank copious amounts of wine, mead and ale. One of the older men drank himself to death. He was still clutching his drinking cup as they carried his body onto Siegford's dragonboat.

On the tenth day of mourning, Hakon ordered Envik to commence the final ritual, allowing Siegford passage to Valhalla.

'Prepare Lord Siegford,' he instructed.

The body was dressed in full fighting regalia.

'Most trusted, carry Lord Siegford to his boat.'

Hakon led a group of men as they carried the body on board and placed it on soft cushions next to a pyre. The dismembered remains of Siegford's favourite dog rested at its master's feet. Envik lifted Siegford's sword, placing it in Siegford's hand.

A procession of women brought wine, fruit, herbs, bread, and meat on to the ship. The three women chosen to accompany Siegford were next to board. They resignedly passed personal belongings to friends and family. They were strapped to the base of the mast.

The ritual now almost complete, a group boarded and proceeded to cover the sacrificial women and Siegford's body in a hastily erected tent of fine cloth. The act was a symbolic gesture to keep Siegford comfortable on his journey to Valhalla and also an attempt to obscure the next stage of the ceremony. The men standing by the shore began banging their shields as three assassins made their way on to the boat. The noise drowned out the last gasps of the women as their throats were cut.

Finally, Envik ignited the kindling placed beneath Siegford. Other men threw their own torches on to the boat. A strong breeze fanned the fire as the boat drifted. The crowd watched in silence as the *Hammer* floated out to the sea, blazing in the dusk sky.

CHAPTER 15

IN THE YEAR 836 AD

The path was a quagmire. Daylight, which was minimal at that time of year, was soon to depart, and the bitter wind that had spat rain for the last few days had finally eased. A cold cloudless night lay ahead.

Orrin struggled to find a dry patch where he could put his foot. 'He won't train us this late in the afternoon.'

'I'm sure he'll find something,' replied Niclaus.

Vidar stood waiting. 'Come on, you two, into the barn.'

Inside, they were surprised to find that Vidar had locked the animals into the stalls, leaving a large space in the centre where he had positioned two stripped tree trunks, both buried deep enough into the ground to stand freely.

Vidar knelt down and began unrolling a large cloth. Metal inside the cloth clinked, immediately arousing the boys' interest.

The cloth fell away to reveal two swords.

'Can I hold one?' asked Orrin, excitedly.

'You can, indeed.'

Orrin lifted the blade and slashed the air. Both he and Niclaus had played with their father's sword but it was lightweight by comparison.

Niclaus lifted the second sword and swung it widely.

'This'll be fun,' said Orrin.

Vidar gave Orrin a look that let him know that the training would be anything but fun. The swords were cumbersome and of poor quality. However, they were perfect for what he had planned.

Getting started, Vidar taught the boys basic blocks and safety techniques.

'Remember, more people hurt themselves by accident than are ever wounded in a fight,' he warned.

It did not take long for the weight of the weapons to exhaust the boys.

Vidar corrected Niclaus' stance. 'Are you struggling?'

'No,' he lied.

'What about you?'

'They're a lot heavier than they look,' Orrin replied.

'Continue practising,' ordered Vidar, as he left the barn.

'My arms are killing me,' confessed Niclaus.

'So are mine. I can hardly lift this sword, never mind swing it.'

Both continued striking the large trunks but more slowly and with less vigour.

Vidar returned with two shields, and showed the boys how to hold them.

'Right, Orrin, strike at Niclaus. Niclaus, parry with your shield.'

The power of the sword sent Niclaus sprawling to the ground.

'Your go, Niclaus.'

Determined to equal Orrin's strike, Niclaus swung with all his might. Orrin yelled as he fell to one knee.

'Very good, Orrin. You managed to transfer much of the force to the ground,' said Vidar.

Orrin beamed with delight, it was not very often Vidar offered praise.

'Now, take it in turns. The loser's the one who can't get back on their feet or the one whose shield splinters.'

Vidar stood back and watched.

It soon became apparent that the exercise was draining Niclaus more than Orrin. Bracing himself before impact meant that Niclaus absorbed the force. He fell with every blow, but sheer willpower got him back on his feet.

The two continued their duel.

'Yield before I kill you,' taunted Orrin.

'Never,' replied Niclaus, as another strike sent him sprawling.

Surprisingly, his shield showed little sign of damage whilst Orrin's bordure had come off and its edges were splintering. Orrin winced with every counterblow but managed to keep upright. This meant that the impact was causing more damage to his shield.

Vidar watched, engrossed. A battle of wills was in full flow.

Again, Niclaus collapsed. He was breathing heavily. It was now a question of whether Niclaus would fail to get up before Orrin's shield split.

Niclaus swung again. Wood splintered. Another few strokes

and he would break Orrin's shield, of that Vidar was sure. It was becoming too dangerous to continue.

Standing between the pair, Vidar ended the duel. A relieved Niclaus crumpled to the floor.

'I had you,' claimed Orrin.

'Keep dreaming. Another swipe and I'd have taken your arm off.'

Orrin looked at his shield. Niclaus was probably right.

'If we ever have to fight, make sure you are by my side and not in front of me,' said Orrin.

Both brothers seemed satisfied with the outcome.

Niclaus was surprised to see thunder in Vidar's face.

'Have I taught you nothing?' he asked, angrily.

Niclaus and Orrin stood dumbstruck. As far as they were concerned, they had worked extremely hard. Neither spoke.

'Did I not teach you to think?'

Again, neither brother spoke.

'What did you hope to achieve by half killing each other?'

'We were learning to use swords,' said Niclaus, defiantly.

'Learning to use swords?' repeated Vidar, irately. 'I did not see anyone learning swordsmanship. From where I stood, all I saw was two idiots beating each other senseless. Haven't I told you, a thousand times before, to use your mind before your body? How did trying to kill each other improve your skill with a sword? I wanted one of you to see the stupidity of your actions. I wanted one of you to realise that it is sometimes better to lose than to suffer needlessly. Pride has no place here. Let the aches and pains that you have gained be a reminder to you.'

His lecture over Vidar again left the barn.

'Damn him,' swore Orrin. 'Yield, don't yield. Fight, don't fight. How are we supposed to know what he wants?'

'He'd have killed us if we had quit,' agreed Niclaus.

The barn door opened and Vidar marched back in.

'Rest time is over,' he said, as he collected the swords and began wrapping them in their cloth. Bent down, with his back to the boys, he allowed himself a smile. He believed the lesson learned. 'Come outside with me.'

The boys followed Vidar, and found him looking to the sky.

'It's freezing,' complained Orrin.

'There's an old Norse legend that claims that the vespertine stars are the old Gods who come to steal the heat of the land. That's why it's so cold. How many stars can you count?' Vidar asked, without dropping his gaze.

At first, Niclaus noticed only a handful, but as his eyes became accustomed to the night, more and more became visible.

'Too many,' said Orrin.

'Do you want to learn the ways of the stars?' asked Vidar. Aware of Newgrange and brought up on the stories of the stars by his father, Vidar had a lot to tell. 'Now, swear to me that what I am about to share with you will remain our secret.'

Both agreed – they could not wait to hear more.

'I used to live in the camp of a great Norse lord. His name was Hakon the Black.'

Orrin's eyes bulged. Hakon the Black was the most feared Norse lord.

'I am under threat of death from him.'

'Why?' Niclaus asked in astonishment.

'Like you, I now follow Christ. I renounced the Norse religion. The penalty for doing so is death. I just hope Hakon never finds me. Now, what do you think this is?' he asked, reaching into his pocket and taking out a crystal.

Both boys shook their heads.

'This is a sunstone. When the sun is out of sight, but has not yet set, the stone will change colour when pointed in its direction. Take it,' he said, as he handed it to Niclaus. 'Try it out, just after sunset or before sunrise, if you don't believe me. It also works on cloudy days. If you point it in the direction of the sun, it will glow.'

Niclaus rolled the crystal in his hand.

'It can be useful in storms and deep fog. It might come in handy during the Trial,' said Vidar.

'Do you have more than one crystal?' asked Orrin.

'Yes,' laughed Vidar. 'The crystals shall be my gift to you. I will give you both one before you begin your Trial. And did you know Hakon and his men can tell their way by the stars in the night?'

'Can't you tell us about Hakon?' asked Niclaus.

'Not now. I shall tell you all when the time is right.'

Niclaus could not hide his disappointment.

'You have my word,' promised Vidar. 'Back to the stars,' he said, as he pointed heavenward.

'Hakon tells a story that in the beginning there were only burning embers. Until, that is, the gods placed the embers above and below heaven and earth, creating the stars in the sky and the lights of heaven. If you know where to look, some stars never move. It's these ones we use to find our way.'

Vidar pointed out significant stars and constellations: the Chief Star, the Eyes of Thjazi, Frigga's Distaff, the Bloody Star and the Wain.

'Now there is one star that you must learn to find,' he said. 'It's the most important star in the sky. Find it and you will always know your way. It'll always lead you north.'

'What's it called?' asked Niclaus.

'Hakon calls it Lode Star; my friend, Cado, calls it Polaris. I prefer Polaris.

Orrin struggled with the pronunciation, calling it 'Po-lard-us.'

After a few attempts, he settled on giving it an easier name. 'I think I'll call it the North Star.'

'I don't mind what name you give it, as long as you know it and can find it. Come on, it's late and getting colder,' said Vidar, guiding the boys in the direction of home. 'When I'm finished with you, you'll know every star in the night sky.'

Over the next few months, Vidar taught Niclaus and Orrin how to fight. They learned how to thrust, feint, attack and retreat, and how to inflict wounds with the point and the edge of the sword. They learned tricks that disabled and disarmed, and to use all means at their disposal; a man's elbows, knees, feet, and head could be as useful as any weapon. Vidar also taught them self-defence techniques, how to fight barehanded, how to wrestle, and how to use spears, knives, and axes, much to Selina's displeasure.

'Why are you teaching us these techniques?' Niclaus had asked.

'There may come a time when you have to leave here. It is

better that you are prepared for every eventuality.'

Vidar's training was relentless. He knew exactly how far to push the boys. He made sure to keep them motivated. Some tasks were impossible to complete, the intention to test the boys' stamina and endurance. To Vidar, the most important part of the training was to teach the boys discipline and control. The brain was their greatest tool, so it was imperative that they used theirs.

He taught the pair to navigate using the stars, to calculate the time of day from the sun's position, to judge the depth of water by flotsam and seaweed, and to find their direction by following the different winds.

'A smart man can feel the breeze on his face and, by knowing the wind, can judge in which direction he is travelling,' he would say.

Vidar was a great storyteller, even better than Gilder. He spoke of strange lands and of unusual languages. Niclaus took to the languages that Vidar taught them. He enjoyed trying to use the strange dialects, whereas Orrin took no interest in them.

Unfortunately for Niclaus and Orrin, Vidar's treks did not offer a let-up in training. Vidar had the perfect deputy in Gilder. Determined that one of his sons would follow him as leader, he proved as tough a taskmaster.

CHAPTER 16

IN THE YEAR 837 AD

Deputising for Vidar, Niclaus was up early and, making too much noise, woke Orrin.

'I'll give you a hand if you want,' offered Orrin half-heartedly, instantly drifting back to sleep.

It was still dark as Niclaus crossed the ground to Vidar's barn.

As he walked, Niclaus contemplated going skating. Orrin and his friends planned to go to the frozen lake later in the day. It sounded fun. He had worked hard and deserved a break, he told himself. He decided that he would finish his wood-chopping a little early and catch up with them.

Niclaus started his work in semi darkness. Beginning his routine, he fed the animals and cleaned out the barn, finishing as the sun rose. He had earned the breakfast that was waiting for him in Elwin's house.

'It's me,' he called, before walking on in.

Elwin greeted Niclaus with a smile as she set down a plate of hot oatmeal biscuits. Lifting one, Niclaus blew on it as he juggled it from palm to palm, and then stuffed it into his mouth. It tasted delicious but stuck to the roof of his mouth, burning his palate.

He gulped down a cup of milk from the fireside ewer. Elwin gave a mock frown as Niclaus pocketed a few biscuits. He loved them.

'It's for a snack,' he said.

Elwin knew his ways and, as always, had made extra with him in mind.

'Are you coming?' he shouted into the back bedroom.

'Won't be long,' Eve replied, as she entered its doorway.

Eve had rosy cheeks, a tanned complexion and hazel eyes. A year younger than Niclaus, she had taken to helping in Vidar's absence. At first, Niclaus had declined her offer of assistance, believing he did not need the help of a girl, but he was soon grateful. She had proved herself a tenacious worker. He found her good company, funny and cheerful, and although he would have denied it to his friends, he enjoyed being around her.

'I'll get the sleigh. Catch me up,' he said, finishing his breakfast.

*

The red blanket lay strewn across a crystal white carpet, its splattered edges fanning out, staining the snow in a circle. Upon it rested a reindeer, its whirlpool eyes unflinching and strikingly beautiful.

Standing over the animal, frenzied and bloodied, the pack fed. They tore at the carcass, tearing off steaming flesh, bolting down the meat. They continued their feast until the lead wolf pricked his ears, raised his head and sniffed the air, catching traces of a scent. He could not be sure – his normally acute sense was dull, blotted by the spoils of his kill. He pawed at his stained nose and licked at the offending blood. Dissatisfied, he buried his nose in the snow, rubbing it clean. He howled as he caught the scent again. It was unusual and unsettling – he had to investigate its origin. The other snow wolves, responding to his call, growled, snarled and snapped as they huddled close in a council of war. A new hunt was underway.

*

As Niclaus chopped the wood, Eve worked too, collecting and loading the logs. Niclaus smiled as he watched her struggling with one particularly heavy basket, her step unsure on the snow. He should have known better but he could not resist offering a hand. 'Do you want me to lift it?'

'No.'

'Are you sure?'

'I'm fine,' she answered, curtly.

Her frown made him laugh and his laugh made her frown the more. He infuriated her and yet she rarely stayed cross for long. He liked her; liked her a lot.

Niclaus watched Eve out of the corner of his eye. She wore her hair tied back in a bun except for a golden tress that had fallen in a wave over her face. He had always thought of her as pretty but not in the way that he was thinking of her now. Not having enough strength to lift the dead weight cleanly, Eve brought her knee to prop the basket against the cart's side before she landed it with a final push. As she did so, her heavy cloak caught on the broken weave of the basket and lifted to reveal the outline of her maturing body. As Eve adjusted her cloak, she caught Niclaus staring.

He turned away, quickly. 'Come on, Eve, we've done enough today. Let's catch up with the others on the ice,' he said brusquely, trying to hide his embarrassment.

'So, that was why you took the reindeer.'

Niclaus laughed. 'Course it is. Trost would be too slow over the snow.'

'But I don't have anything to skate with.'

Niclaus smiled, holding up sanded-down animal bones, complete with leather ties.

'We don't have to go. We can always stay here, if you'd prefer.'

'No way,' said a delighted Eve. 'It's not every day I get the chance to teach you boys how to skate.'

*

Orrin pointed out the route, its length roughly a hundred paces. 'Over the frozen stream, down the slope, build up as much speed as you can, over the frozen waterfall and land on the lake below.'

'You're not serious,' said Aslak, 'That drop is twice my height.'

'You'll be fine.'

'You lot, maybe – but what about me?'

The rest of the boys laughed. Aslak did have a point; his record for mishaps was unsurpassed.

'What if it breaks?' Aslak asked.

'The ice is strong,' said Orrin. 'I wouldn't suggest it otherwise. If you are worried you can watch us first.'

'Come on, let's test it,' said Ludin.

Further to the right of where they planned to jump, Orrin and Ludin rolled two boulders over the ledge, the impact reverberating across the frozen lake.

'Looks strong enough to me,' said Ludin, inspecting the surface. Except for a few scratches, the ice remained sound.

'It's safe,' agreed Thorsfied, Gunnar's son.

The boys began tying their runners to their fur boots.

'Who wants to go first?' asked Orrin.

Thorsfied volunteered.

Although there were only a few years between Thorsfied and the others, he looked much younger than them. His father had been late to marry and his friends teased him, saying that he was old enough to be Gunnar's grandson. Thorsfied was brave, good-natured and renowned as a runner – Gunnar claimed he was quicker than a deer – but he was also foolhardy, and desperate to gain the acceptance of the older boys.

'Don't break your neck,' teased Orrin, as Thorsfied skated to the starting point.

The boys gathered by the ledge to watch.

They all accepted the risks: the ice could weaken and there was a possibility of falling through – it added to the excitement.

Thorsfied pushed off, following the course of the frozen stream, lined on both sides by pine trees. Gaining speed, he misjudged a slight bend in the course of the river, lost his balance and sailed off the ledge, landing on his backside with a thud.

The cackle of laughter grew as Thorsfied continued to slide across the ice. Finally he managed to get up and skate back. Using a few protruding rocks, he clambered back up to the ledge. 'I think I broke it when I landed,' he declared, as he rubbed his behind.

'Let me go next,' begged Magnus, son of Ragnall. He, too, was keen to gain acceptance from the others. He was the same age as Thorsfied, but slightly taller and broader. Although not as quick, Magnus' balance was better. Judging the turn well, he sailed off the ledge but failed to hold his landing. His left ankle buckled on impact, sending him sprawling across the ice.

'Good try,' shouted Orrin.

'You'll land it next time,' added Aslak.

*

They looked majestic as they raced over the snowy ground, six magnificent snow wolves cutting through the forest in single file. They moved swiftly, their every stride bringing death closer. Normally territorial, seldom venturing beyond their own boundaries, they did not hesitate as they passed the edge of their domain. Something powerful was drawing them, driving them beyond the realms of their previous existence.

*

'Do you want to see how it's done?' bragged Orrin.

'I hope you break your leg,' Ludin joked.

Orrin sailed off the ledge and landed perfectly. 'See, it's easy,' he gloated.

Aslak made a snowball. 'Let's pelt the show-off when he gets close.'

Orrin presented a perfect target.

'Now,' shouted Ludin.

Defenceless, Orrin took his pelting in good heart. 'I'll get you all back,' he warned, as he headed back to the others.

'Watch me land it,' said Ludin.

'You're too heavy – you'll crack the ice,' teased Aslak.

Making his way to the start, something caught Ludin's eye, a slight movement in the trees. No, he shrugged it off. It was just his imagination.

Again, he saw it. Only this time there was no doubt. The hairs stood on the back of his neck. Instinct took hold. Ludin knew what he had to do. The slight bend in the river meant that the other boys could not see what Ludin could see. They remained oblivious to the danger.

'Orrin, everyone, do you hear me?' he shouted.

Ludin tried to control his movements but it was not easy. All the boys were aware of the action they should take in the event of a wolf sighting. Ludin recalled what his father told him: wolves were nature's cleansers, who feasted on the weak and infirm, leaving the strongest to thrive. He had to behave in a confident manner, to use slow and deliberate movements, show no fear. If he could do this, he would send a signal to the wolf that he was both brave and strong, and prepared to face it. The wolf, so his father claimed, would look for a weaker kill. Well, that was the theory, not so easy in practice.

The panic in Ludin's voice instantly alerted Orrin. 'What is it?'

'You all need to head for …'

A great howl drowned out his words. Growls and whines answered. Ludin stood terrified. The howls were intimidating and disorientating. It was impossible to gauge how many wolves were out there – four, five or maybe even more. His best hope of escape lay in reaching the lake.

The lead animal broke from the cover of the tree line and stood sizing up Ludin.

The wolf was massive, at least twice the size of a big dog, perhaps as long as two-and-a-half ells from tip to tail, and with shoulders that would come waist high to a man. Ludin, now frozen with fear, felt drawn to the wolf's fulvous eyes. It stared back, not blinking, holding his gaze whilst baring its fangs.

Why was it waiting?

Inside, a voice screamed, 'Hurry – skate for the ice. You can make it.' Yet, as Ludin stood transfixed, the animal seemed uninterested. It seemed to be looking beyond him.

What was it doing? Why was it not attacking? Maybe the old tales were true. Perhaps if you did face a wolf down it would look for easier prey. He hoped it was so.

A second smaller animal broke from cover, followed by the pack.

Instantly, Ludin raced for the lake, not daring to look back. He could sense them closing. Clearing the final tree, he could see the ledge. If he could reach it, he had a chance. Just as he was about to jump, teeth sank into his right ankle. Ludin's momentum kept him sailing on. Both he and the wolf fell. The rest of the pack drew up before the ledge, not prepared to jump.

Landing free of the animal, Ludin regained his footing and made desperately for the centre of the ice, adrenalin masking any pain.

The wolf got up and leapt again, landing on Ludin, sinking its teeth into his shoulder. Ludin collapsed under the weight of the animal. Down, but not beaten, he pounded on the ice.

*

Orrin directed Aslak, Thorsfied and Magnus towards the centre of the frozen lake. 'Don't look back,' he ordered, as he ushered the boys away.

'We can't leave him,' pleaded Aslak.

Orrin pushed him. 'Keep moving.'

Magnus and Thorsfied, both clearly shaken, did as instructed. Aslak refused.

Orrin gripped him by his collar and shoved him forcibly. 'Don't make this harder, Aslak. It's bad enough.'

'We can't leave him.'

'We have to. We have to obey the Rule of Protection. We cannot risk all to save one.'

'Let's go back.'

'And do what? We have no weapons. What use would we be?'

Orrin lifted out his pocketknife and stared down at it. It looked pathetically inadequate.

'We have to try,' pleaded Magnus, spurred on by Aslak's defiance.

'No,' said Aslak, finally acceding to Orrin.

'What about Ludin?' Magnus pleaded.

Orrin jostled Magnus. 'He's on his own, now move.'

They moved on, leaving Ludin behind.

*

Nearing the lake, Niclaus and Eve heard Ludin's warning shout followed by the howls of wolves. Breaking from the forest path, they arrived at the frozen shoreline and caught sight of Ludin and the wolf as they fell off the waterfall above. To their right, the land rose sharply, obscuring their view of most of the lake. They did not see Orrin and the boys.

Niclaus pulled his sleigh to a stop and gestured to the reindeer.

'Quick, Eve, hold Rugt's head tightly. Don't let him see what's going on.'

Eve gripped the reins.

'Help,' screamed Ludin.

Niclaus grabbed his axe and rushed toward the ice.

Hearing the reindeer bucking and realising that Eve was struggling, Niclaus turned back to help her.

'I'll let Rugt go if I have to,' she said. 'Ludin needs you.'

Niclaus rushed off. He was fewer than fifty paces from his friend but still too far away. He watched in horror as the wolf pounced on Ludin.

'Hang on,' he shouted, as he reached the shoreline.

The other wolves came into view. They had taken a slightly longer route that avoided the drop. Niclaus stood on the ice halfway between Eve and Ludin. Standing at the shoreline, roughly twenty paces in front of Niclaus, the wolves were now equidistant from Eve and Ludin.

Niclaus' plan changed from helping Ludin to driving the new arrivals away. The wolves pulled up short of the ice. Niclaus deduced that they were afraid of it. The first slowly tested the surface. The others held back, snarling in anticipation.

Ludin was screaming, writhing in agony as the wolf tore at his shoulder and neck. Halfway between the sleigh and Ludin, Niclaus lifted his axe and drove it into the ice repeatedly, until it cracked with a noise like the loud snapping of a branch. Water hissed from the opening. Niclaus repeated the action. The first stroke sent the four wolves scurrying away, Niclaus hoped for good. The second swing was more effective, splitting the ice in all directions.

The ice below Ludin, already weakened, gave way. Both boy and wolf fell into the freezing water. Seizing the opportunity, Niclaus scuttled over the splintered surface. The wolf was yelping and slowly pulling itself from the water. Ludin, too weak to get himself out, was struggling to keep a grip.

Having covered the remaining ground, Niclaus swung his axe, burying it deep in the defenceless wolf's skull.

*

Orrin, Aslak, Magnus and Thorsfied had stopped running and were watching the unfolding events.

'Oh, no,' cried Thorsfied, as the four wolves came into view.

Magnus cursed.

'No,' Orrin screamed, seeing Niclaus raise his axe.

'He doesn't know we're here,' exclaimed Aslak.

Niclaus chopped at the ice. The impact reverberated across the length of the lake.

The group, far from shore, did not move as the ice creaked. Fortunately, it held.

'We have to get off,' shouted Thorsfied, looking to Orrin for leadership.

'It could give way at any moment,' agreed Orrin. 'Back towards Niclaus and Ludin.'

Hurriedly retracing their steps, the group cheered at the slaying of the wolf, alerting Niclaus to their presence.

Orrin stopped the boys. 'The ice in front will be weak. It's better if we split up, spread the weight. Aslak, take Magnus and go that way,' said Orrin, pointing to the far shore. 'Thorsfied, we'll go this way,' he said, leading him the shorter route. Unknown to Orrin, he was heading in the direction of Eve, who remained out of sight, obscured by the jutting shoreline.

'Thorsfied, I want you to get back to the village and summon help,' said Orrin, upon reaching the shore.

'The wolves … I'll be on my own.'

'We've walked from here to the village a hundred times and never seen a wolf. I'm telling you, this wolf came from the north. You'll be fine. And Ludin needs you – your speed could save his life.'

Thorsfied sprinted off, concern for his friend taking precedence over his own fears.

*

Niclaus grabbed hold of Ludin and began pulling him out of the bloodied water. As he did so, the ice below gave way and he, too, fell in. He managed to catch hold of an edge and pull himself out. A few tugs and Niclaus hauled Ludin out of the water too. He dragged his friend to shore, leaving a trail of blood. Ludin's injuries looked horrific – he was bleeding profusely from his mauled neck and shoulder and was shaking uncontrollably from both shock and cold, Niclaus assumed. He packed the wound with snow and ice, which turned pink in colour as it mixed with Ludin's blood. Next, he removed his coat and tucked it around Ludin.

*

The cracking of the ice had sent the rest of the wolves scampering off. Unfortunately, their retreat was momentary. Regrouping, they found a new attraction. Howls rose as they feasted their eyes on Eve and her reindeer. They closed. She was focused on the ice and on trying to restrain her frightened animal, and remained unaware of the danger. Rugt was becoming more agitated. The sight of more wolves breaking from cover was too much. She screamed. The wolves responded in kind.

The four wolves stood halfway between Niclaus and Eve, and his route across the ice was broken. He was of no use to her; he did not have a weapon, having lost his axe as he dragged Ludin ashore.

*

Orrin, who had remained unaware of Eve's presence until her scream, rushed to help. When he saw her, he knew her predicament was hopeless. Even if he got to her, what could he do? Further to his right, he could see Niclaus running towards her desperately.

Aslak and Magnus were too far away. They would have to pass Ludin before they could contemplate helping.

The reindeer pulled on its halter, breaking free of Eve's grip.

Laden with a heavy sleigh, escape was impossible. The first two predators downed and killed the reindeer, leaving Eve to face the remaining wolves.

They closed, snarling and snapping. Eve had nowhere to go.

'Run for the lake,' shouted Orrin, charging toward her. Eve needed a miracle, not one boy armed with a tiny knife. The nearest wolf crouched, ready to pounce.

*

Suddenly the white alpha wolf, which had not joined the fray, thrust itself in front of Eve, snapping sharply at the attacking pair. Both withdrew to feed on the reindeer carcass, leaving the small pickings to their master.

Orrin neared. Eve stood paralysed with fear. The beast slowly and deliberately circled. Still, it did not strike. Instead, it sniffed her, recognizing the same scent that had taken it far from its home, only it was not as strong as it should have been. Something was not right.

Knife in hand, Orrin rushed at the wolf. Sensing his approach, the beast turned and snapped at him. Its action was enough to force Orrin's retreat. The beast feigned another lunge, making Orrin jump back. The wolf repositioned itself to ensure a clear view. It howled at Orrin, warning him to stay back.

Then miraculously the wolf dropped to a sitting position.

'What should we do?' asked Orrin as Niclaus arrived.

*

Niclaus was amazed to find Eve alive and uninjured. He saw the wolf's ears prick up. Slowly it came towards him, losing interest in the others. Wasting no time, Orrin grabbed Eve's hand and pulled her away.

The wolf padded up to Niclaus, standing so close that he could feel its breath. Niclaus felt his body shake. He tried to reason with his panicking mind – the longer he could distract the wolf, the better chance Eve stood of getting away. His heart raced. He held his breath, not daring to exhale. Prepared for the worst, Niclaus was shocked when the animal sat at his feet.

Slowly Niclaus raised a trembling hand and stroked its head. It rolled its neck and pressed against his hand.

'What shall I do?' called Aslak, as he reached Ludin.

'Tend to Ludin; bandage him as best you can. And then pack more ice around his wounds, press it as hard as you can,' instructed Orrin.

Aslak then looked anxiously towards Niclaus.

'Don't worry about me,' said Niclaus. 'I think it's better if we don't antagonise my new friend. Besides, if this wolf wanted me for dinner, I'd be dead already. I think we'll have to wait this out.'

Orrin and Eve watched, astonished to see the wolf playing with Niclaus.

The rest of the pack kept their distance, feeding on the reindeer.

Niclaus knelt before the wolf, which pawed at him like a pet dog until it seemed to become restless. It gave a few howls, commanding his pack to leave. They disappeared into the woods.

Orrin and Eve rushed to hug Niclaus.

Niclaus grabbed Eve, squeezing her tightly, afraid to let her go. She was shaken but unharmed, and that was all that mattered. She had been his responsibility and he had neglected her; he should have made her safety his priority. It was no thanks to him that she was still alive.

He kissed her cheek in relief. 'I'm sorry, so sorry,' he said, repeatedly. 'Can you forgive me?'

'You have nothing to be sorry for. You saved Ludin.'

'How is he?' Niclaus shouted to the other boys; he had forgotten Ludin in the melee.

Aslak's face was ashen. 'I don't know. He looks bad. He's lost a lot of blood.'

CHAPTER 17

IN THE YEAR 802 AD

There was something troubling Cado. Tomás had been meeting his friend for over half a year and, in all that time, he had never seen him so agitated.

'What's wrong?'

Cado did not reply.

'Have I done something to offend you?'

'No, not at all.' With his friend not talking, Tomás sat on the grass bank and lifted his book. He began to read his most recent entry.

*

Cado's Initiation

The last rays of the amber sun signal the beginning of the ceremony and thankfully the bright moon offers a challenge to the darkness. This, the end of the shortest day, marks a turning in the yearly cycle. It is a time of rebirth, of new beginning, and so I take my place with my people as I prepare to enter the secret world of my forefathers. For I have been given the chance to join the Council of Elders.

Tomás recognised his own hand yet the words seemed unfamiliar. How could that be? Reading on, his memory cleared and he recalled the piece.

It is a time of great excitement as I watch my people march to the giant mound, our greatest creation. It has taken us hundreds of years of toil and sweat to complete the circular mound that stands as a beacon above Newgrange. It has been said that this sacred place is the very heart of our people. As I stand here, I believe it to be true.

The hushed anticipation is clear as our procession fans out to form a line of about fifty-by-twenty deep around the entrance to the mound. The crowd is dressed in identical hooded black robes. Embroidered on each are gold spirals, lozenges, arcs, and chevrons, stitched symbols of our secrets. The females in our gathering burst into a soul-piercing mantra as the centre of the congregation parts to allow my party through. We are the only ones dressed in white robes. It feels so strange to be the main focus of the group. I have knots in my stomach. The men in our assembly, following the women's lead, break into song, creating an antiphon that would grace the heavens.

I am struck by the contrast of the dark water-rolled granite stones that are interspaced in the white quartz wall, either side of the centred entrance of our mound. The moonlight reflects off the quartz giving it the appearance of dazzling light whereas the granite appears dark and almost threatening. I wonder if the wall has been built deliberately so, as some kind of warning. Does the darkness warn of evilness in the warmest of hearts? Somehow I know that I will face a challenge like never before.

I watch as two solemn flag bearers lead the procession; the first carries a black flag with a gold spiral motif; the second, a black chevron on a white background. Four pallbearers follow, carrying a dark ossuary encasing the cremated remains of those who have died during the last year.

Bram and I bring up the rear, our importance denoted by hoodless robes, the only ones in the whole assembly. We walk to the great-carved stone which lies lengthways, a few paces from the entrance. To the side of the entrance, a brazier filled with animal fat splutters plumes of stinging smoke into our eyes.

The pallbearers enter the chamber. Guided by a few flickering candles, they make their way up the gently rising passageway to the cross-shaped centre. The alcoves to the left and right house large stone basins, onto which they place the ashes. Their part in the proceedings over, they exit the chamber and join the waiting crowd.

I wait nervously for Bram to address our people. He is slightly taller than me. His hair is white and his crown bald. Confident and popular, many, including Bram himself, believe that he will be the next Head Elder, if we ever get round to voting. He is often vocal on the subject; no one deserved the title more. To him, his selection is long overdue. Yet, I cannot deny, I sense a sinister side to the leader-in-waiting. Behind his façade is a darkness, an evilness, a coldness that frightens me. Such is his popularity that I will not voice my concern. Who will believe me?

Bram raises his hand, signalling the end of the singing. He places a torch into the fire of fat. The icy wind fights, trying and failing to keep it from igniting.

'Take light from my torch,' Bram calls out. He pauses to emphasise the importance of his words. 'For out of death springs forth new life. Let our torches be the symbol of this new life.' Bram moves to stand in front of the gathering.

The light from his torch passes quickly from neighbour to neighbour, bringing illumination and a welcome heat to the ceremony.

Palls of smoke drift across the cold sky. The temperature is dropping and a hard frost will soon follow.

'Now, I call Cado to walk in the footsteps of the Elders.'

I look at those before me. They are my friends and family. They want me to succeed. Yet their faces, partially visible by the torchlight, take on the form of twisted and grotesque creatures. I look away, scanning the distant hills and the river Boyne. It is just possible to track the river's course by the mist that hangs above it.

Calm down. Selection in itself is an honour, I tell myself, as I again look at the crowd. I stare at one individual until his features become recognisable.

I, Cado, son of Boruc, step inside the chamber. I will face this challenge. I will meet my destiny.

'Godspeed on your journey,' a voice calls after me.

I pause. Ahead lies all that I dare to dream of, my future, all my hopes and ambitions. I will not fail. 'Remember,' I whisper, taking my first hesitant steps into the aisle, 'the centre of the universe only moves when I take a step.'

*

Tomás mind swirled. He could not recall any more of the book's contents. What devilment was taking place? Frightened, he flicked open the book and read another section.

*

As I take my seat, I read the inscription burnt into the wood before me. In the most elaborate calligraphy is the inscription,

Cado

Peace at Journey's End

Glancing at the last place setting, at the head of the table, I read the final task, however the name space is blank.

Father to Every Child

'What does this mean?' I ask.

Hannel, sitting opposite, explains, 'Everyone has had his name inscribed and underneath is written the challenge that lies ahead for him. Cado, it is for you alone to discover your task.'

Tomas breathed a sigh of relief as his memory cleared. He remembered all that he had written. Yes, he is still doing the Lord's bidding and Cado is very much his ally.

*

'Tomás,' Cado said, interrupting his friend's reading. 'I'm afraid I am going to have to ask you to stop writing the book.'

'Why?'

'It's just … what I ask is unfair on you. It is too heavy a burden.'

'Have I done something wrong?'

'No, no, that's not it, not at all. What I ask of you is too much.'

'Spreading God's word is not meant to be easy. I must continue..'

'No, Tomás. You will suffer great heartache. I cannot let you.'

'Why did you seek me out, if only then to deny me?'

'It was not I that found you; rather, it was the other way around.'

To Tomás, Cado was not making any sense. 'I want to finish what I've started.'

'We can't.'

'Can't or won't? If it is my decision, I ask that we continue.'

'It will be to your detriment if we do.'

'It is a chance I am willing to take.'

'Tomás, many will suffer; yourself included if we carry on this path,' warned Cado.

'Cado, how can the mere writing of a book do any harm?'

'It may turn hearts to stone, brother against brother.'

Seeing Cado's sullen face, Tomás tried to offer comfort. 'Take courage, and be strong. Fear not, and be not dismayed: because the Lord thy God is with thee in all things whatsoever thou shalt go to.'

He recalled learning the verse as a young boy, it was from the book Joshua.

'Because in much wisdom there is much indignation: and he that addeth knowledge, addeth also labour,' replied Cado. 'Ecclesiastes.'

Cado's ability to quote scripture surprised Tomás again, who reaffirmed his willingness to go on. 'This work is too important.

We have a responsibility to complete it, no matter how much it pains us. We must be prepared to suffer all the sorrow of this undertaking for it is God's will.'

'Oh, Tomás, you are right,' conceded Cado. 'However, there is more that I have not yet told you. There is a wickedness spreading through the hearts of many in my village.'

'What do you mean?'

'Let me explain. Long ago we, my people, created an Orb. We have been its guardians ever since. It has wonderful capabilities and continues to grow in size and strength. We are finding it increasingly difficult to keep its presence a secret. I fear I am losing control of it. In the wrong hands, it could wreak havoc and destruction. Times are changing. The future tells of a time when an outsider shall become leader of my people. Many fear this and are opposed to the idea. I believe that an ignoble leader will emerge. His heart is blackening as we speak. He wants the Orb for selfish reasons. Many, believing they are staying true to the old ways, will be fooled into following him. I will not carry enough support to overcome him.'

'What will you do?' asked Tomás, somewhat confused, but sensing Cado's fear.

'I have to locate a safe haven for the Orb, far away from Newgrange. When the time comes, those who remain loyal will help me transfer it to a new home.'

'But what has this to do with the book?'

'There will come a time when I will not be in a position to guide the future leader of Newgrange. This book will be needed then. All our fates rest on it.'

Cado proceeded to take out a leather pouch. 'Come closer, it's time for you to see.'

He poured a handful of coloured dust into his palm.

'What is it?' asked Tomás.

'It's the magic in the air, the most powerful force in our universe. A long time ago, a wise man, a little man –' he said, proud of his village's achievements – 'realised that the most important thing to us all was …'

'Air?' interrupted Tomás.

'No.'

'Water, it must be water?'

'Wait. Let me tell you. The most important thing is light. Without it, we would have no life. We know it is all around us and yet we cannot see it. Such a powerful force. Imter, our first elder, was sitting in a field when he noticed a rainbow. Try as he might, he could not reach it, so he retraced his steps and sat watching the weather as the sun strengthened and the rain cloud dispersed. He came to believe that each colour represented a part of the light. Over the next few years, Imter spent his days chasing rainbows. Each ray of light travels such a distance and at such speed, taking no time at all. He considered that perhaps the light was weightless, travelling in straight lines, never fluctuating. Furthermore, it transported vast amounts of energy – enough to illuminate the world. Imter believed that if he could harness the power of the light he could develop an amazing tool.

'If only we could split the light and dissect the colours,' said Cado, as he poured the coloured particles from hand to hand.

'Is this them?' asked Tomás.

'Yes, these are particles of captured light.'

'What's so special about them?'

'With these particles, it is possible to do many wonderful things.'

'Like what?'

'Under the right conditions, it can help me see both the future and the past.'

'I doubt it,' said Tomás, incredulously.

'Oh, Tomás, test me. Ask me a question, one only you know the answer to. Why not ask me which saint you pray to at night? Better still; why not ask me why it is you pray to St Thomas every night?'

'How …' Tomás stammered, struggling to find his words.

'This dust, in the right hands, can be used for many purposes. It is very powerful.'

Cado took a small knife from his belt. 'Watch this, my doubting friend.'

He ran the blade along his index finger; a trail of blood followed the knife's path. Next, he smudged a sprinkle of dust over the cut.

Tomás watched, wide-eyed, as Cado's finger healed before his eyes. There was no cut or trace of injury. 'What sort of sorcery is this?'

'Tomás, this is not magic, merely "wisdom beyond belief".'

'I've seen it with my own …'

'I would not lie to you. I need you to trust me.'

'If it's not heresy, it must be a miracle. Think of the good that it can be used for.'

Cado wore a stern frown. 'It can heal but in the wrong hands it can also destroy. Worryingly, for every good use, we have also found a counteraction. For every positive, there is a negative. It has the potential to cause great harm. We have already learnt that it can be used to manipulate people; it can make people forget one thing or believe another. Imagine how it could be used. Tomás, you are the first person outside of my village to be entrusted with the knowledge of this power. If this wisdom was ever to fall into the wrong hands it would be catastrophic for us all.'

The enormity of the responsibility was becoming apparent. 'I am honoured and will do all that I can to keep your wisdom safe, I promise.'

'Tomás, arduous times lie ahead. Many of your friends will leave your monastery never to return. Even the manuscript you write shall be lost.'

CHAPTER 18

IN THE YEAR 837 AD

Gilder drove the sleigh with Orrin by his side. In the back, Olaf held his unconscious son in his arms. Gunnar tried to stem the blood from Ludin's wounds.

Orrin looked to the sleigh behind. Lars, Aslak's father, sat next to Reseth, who was steering. Niclaus sat in the back between Magnus and Thorsfied, his arms wrapped around Eve.

'How is he?' Gilder asked Olaf.

'He's lost a lot of blood.' Olaf squeezed his son tightly to control his latest convulsion. 'He's shaking violently.'

Gilder looked back. 'It's a good sign,' he explained. 'His body's still fighting.'

Orrin wondered if his father was speaking the truth or if he had said it just to make Olaf feel better. He sneaked a glance at Ludin's wounds as Gunnar adjusted the makeshift bandage around his neck. Much of his skin was gone, ripped off. He could see where an exposed vein pumped crimson blood. It made him queasy.

'Who packed it with ice?' asked Gunnar.

'Niclaus and Aslak,' answered Orrin.

'You did well. It may have saved his life.'

*

The incident was quickly on everyone's lips. The next evening, the men convened a meeting in the hall, with all the boys who had been on the ice – except Ludin – in attendance. The only other notable absentee was Vidar, who was away on one of his annual trips.

The hall, used as a winter store for animals and feed, was the only place large enough to hold such a meeting. It smelled strongly of animals and damp. Niclaus and his friends had spent the day moving animals to other barns, carrying benches and seating inside, and placing fresh straw on the ground.

Flanked by Ragnall and Ealver, Gunnar sat at the head table. Torches of pitch brought light but little heat to the proceedings.

Gunnar stood. The fact that he was in charge was a surprise to many present.

'Are you sure he's up to this?' whispered Olaf.

'He insisted,' answered Gilder.

Gunnar was old and frail, and many had been relieved, and surprised, that he had survived the previous winter.

Gunnar gently rapped the table, hushing the gathering. They began with a prayer, giving thanks for the boys' safe return. Although the village had converted to Christianity years before, religious ceremonies were kept to a minimum. There being no priest, Gunnar assumed the role of religious leader.

Gunnar then started the meeting. 'We are here this evening to discuss the events of yesterday. It seems that the Rule of Protection may have been broken.'

'Rubbish,' countered a voice.

Gunnar gave a stern look. 'Yes, I agree that some of our rules may seem harsh but you all know why we have put them in place. No one has the right to endanger the wellbeing of the collective. Our first responsibility must be to ensure the safety of the village. I fear that individuals forgot this yesterday.'

'They're only boys,' someone shouted.

'If only that was the case. Unfortunately, they are all over thirteen. The law decrees them men. Given Niclaus and Orrin's involvement, Gilder cannot preside so I am to take his place. Ragnall and Ealver shall assist me. If laws have been broken, it shall be our responsibility to pass judgement.'

'And I could ask for no fairer men,' added Gilder.

Niclaus sat next to Orrin, his eyes fixed on his father. Gilder looked anxious. It was obvious – Niclaus was going to have to justify his actions on the ice.

Slowly the details of the day unravelled with each boy called to give his own account. In time, Gunnar called Orrin. He sat on a stool next to the main table, wringing his hands. Then he sat on them to keep them still. Then he wrung them again. Like the rest of his friends, this was the first time Orrin had attended such a meeting.

'So, Orrin, can you tell us what happened?' Gunnar asked. 'Just take your time.'

Orrin's apprehension was evident as he looked away from Gunnar and directed his answer to Ludin's father instead. 'Hearing the wolves, I knew we had to make for the centre of the ice. I didn't want to leave him.'

Olaf remained stony faced.

'How is he?' Orrin asked when he had finished giving his account.

Olaf was a powerful man whose scowl often frightened many of the boys. Yet it was clear that he had lost much of his menace. He looked drained, older even. His mop of hair and beard appeared greyer.

Olaf stood. 'Rula says the bleeding has stopped. She is sure he'll survive but how his wounds will heal, well, we'll have to wait and see.'

'I am sorry for Ludin's injuries but if I found myself in similar circumstances I would do the same again,' Orrin said. 'I had to protect the others.'

'Orrin, I would expect no less,' replied Olaf. 'You are wise beyond your years. If not for your actions, the wolves most certainly would have attacked you all. I thank God for your bravery.'

Olaf addressed his next comment to all in the room. 'As for Ludin, if he had understood the dangers he would not have led the pack towards the others. Of that I am certain.'

'Yes, what of Ludin? Did he fail to carry out his duty?' interrupted Gunnar.

Without hiding his annoyance, Orrin answered. 'Ludin acted as any of us would have. He tried to escape from a pack of wolves. In my eyes, he has done nothing wrong but, as to obeying rules, I find it unbelievable that you are questioning his part. Don't you think he's suffered enough? That wolf nearly ripped him to death. Aren't his injuries worse than any lash?'

'We get no pleasure from this,' said Gunnar. 'But the laws must be obeyed. The safety of our village depends on our rules. But it is clear to me that Ludin has suffered enough. Now, moving on to Niclaus, what of his actions?'

Orrin wriggled nervously on his chair. 'Without Niclaus' intervention, Ludin would be dead and perhaps more of us. There is no way of telling if the wolves would have attacked us. Niclaus should be commended not punished.'

Gunnar was becoming increasingly uncomfortable chairing the proceedings, which was hardly surprising given that his son had been one of the boys on the ice. It could easily have been Thorsfied standing in Niclaus' shoes.

Having mulled it over, Niclaus believed that, although he had saved Ludin, he had jeopardised an awful lot more. 'I wish to speak,' he said, walking to the centre of the room.

Gilder rose to stand by his son's side in a gesture of solidarity. His features remained in shadow making it difficult to judge his reaction to what was unfolding.

Niclaus felt small in the presence of his peers and elders. 'I … I …,' he stuttered. He stopped to compose himself. 'Yesterday, I set off with the aim of working hard,' he said, as confidently as he could. 'I hoped to finish early and go skating with my friends. I worked doubly hard. When I arrived, I heard and saw the wolf attacking Ludin. I'm truly sorry.' He bowed his head. 'I did not mean to put Eve in danger. It was wrong of me to leave her alone. My responsibility should have been to ensure her safety. I should not have left her.'

'I am grateful you did,' interposed Olaf.

'And it was complete madness to crack the ice. I put everyone at risk. I dread to think of the consequences if the ice had broken completely. By my actions, I endangered all that I should have protected and I am really sorry.'

The room fell silent. Gilder put his arm around his boy. 'I'm proud of you,' he whispered.

Gunnar rose from his chair and walked to the front of the main table. 'You have demonstrated more bravery than any man here. Moreover, it takes courage to stand before us and admit to your mistakes. You really are most remarkable.' Gunnar paused as the room echoed in agreement. 'However, I am duty bound. With a heavy heart, I find you guilty of breaking the Rule of Protection and as punishment, and in accordance with our rules, you must receive lashes. The minimum number permitted is four.'

The room erupted in disapproval.

Niclaus bit hard on his lower lip. He had never seen a lashing but he had heard that the leather sliced through flesh as easily as an oar through water.

There was a look of horror on his father's face as he ushered Niclaus out of the barn.

Behind, Niclaus could hear Olaf protesting at the decision. Niclaus did not look back.

*

'What can we do?' asked Orrin, as he joined his father and Niclaus in their cabin.

'I don't know. All that I know is that I cannot let this happen. I have seen first-hand the damage a lash can inflict and I will not stand by and watch Niclaus be whipped.'

Upon hearing the news, Selina remained silent. Niclaus suspected her silence was the loudest scream his father would ever hear. That night, no one slept well. Niclaus had half-expected to hear his parents muffled voices through the wall, arguing long into the night. He was surprised that his mother kept her tongue. Gilder had often claimed that she was the only woman who could speak her mind without uttering a word – Niclaus now understood exactly what his father meant.

Over breakfast, Orrin tried to console Niclaus. 'They'll have to stop it. Father won't let it happen, and Olaf: can you see him letting them whip you after you saved Ludin?'

Niclaus willed himself to keep a brave face. 'Look, Orrin, I am glad it happened as it did.'

Orrin stared at him as if he had lost his mind.

'If I had behaved as I should, I would have had to leave Ludin to the wolf and I would have lost a friend. For Ludin's sake, I am glad it happened as it did.'

'At least the threat of a flogging hasn't affected your appetite,' said Gilder, looking at Niclaus' empty plate.

Niclaus rose from the table. 'Come on, let's get this over with.'

Behind him, his mother started to cry. 'Don't think I am not coming with you. I am most proud of you,' she sobbed, finally breaking her silence.

Gilder looked disapproving, but the family walked together to the shore.

The day was dark and threatened a torrent, very much like Gilder's mood.

They walked through a knot of villagers towards the water's

edge. The main group had already congregated, both enthralled and disgusted at what was about to take place. Eve broke from the crowd

'I can't believe you are going to let them do this,' she said, belligerently.

Gilder ignored her and looked ahead.

Eve's temper was boiling. 'Niclaus acted so bravely, why won't you stop this?'

Gilder stopped walking and looked down at Eve.

Eve fumed. 'If Vidar was here he'd …'

'Stop it,' interrupted Niclaus. 'This is difficult enough. Please don't make it any harder.'

'She's right,' said Gilder. 'I will put an end to this madness.'

'No,' said Niclaus, urging his father onward. 'This is how it must be. What sort of leader would you be seen to be if you failed to punish your son? I did wrong.' He was adamant. 'Please, let me see this through.'

It seemed that the whole village had turned out. Even Henik was there to witness Niclaus' humiliation. Catching Niclaus' gaze, he sneered with pleasure.

Niclaus felt his legs quiver as he removed his tunic and positioned himself in front of the whipping block. He asked his father to tie the restraints as he steeled himself.

Reseth, with whip in hand, was already in position, he having the unenviable task of administering the lashes.

Although his father held Reseth in high esteem, Niclaus had always been afraid of him. With a splattered nose and dark eyes under a single brow, his scowl was enough to frighten many a man.

Niclaus shivered from a mixture of cold and fear.

Reseth hesitated.

'Get on with it,' interposed Gunnar.

Reluctantly, Reseth raised his hand to deliver the first lash.

'Wait,' shouted Olaf.

Removing his shirt, he strode forward and stood in front of Niclaus. 'Strike at the boy if you must, but make sure that it is my frame that takes the brunt. Do you understand?'

Reseth looked to Gunnar for guidance.

'No boy who saved my son shall ever be punished for it. Now do as I say,' demanded Olaf.

Gunnar consented.

Without hesitation Reseth delivered two vicious lashes, both landing on the left shoulder, running diagonally across Olaf's broad back.

Olaf winced.

Niclaus felt nauseous. His legs weakened. The next lashes would be more severe. The cord would slice through exposed tissue. Again, Reseth brought the whip over his shoulder.

'Wait,' called Gilder, as he stepped forward. 'I think these lashes have my name on them,'

'No,' argued Olaf.

'Olaf, let us not quarrel. I think you have done me enough of a service today.'

Olaf stepped aside as Gilder took his place in front of Niclaus. Reseth resumed.

Gilder gritted his teeth and tensed in anticipation.

Niclaus turned to see his father. Seeing the worried look on his son's face, Gilder forced a smile. He was thankful that Reseth was using the whip. No one had a better aim. His first lash landed close to his neckline. It was a deliberate stroke. Reseth was leaving plenty of room between the lashes to ensure he would not cut into an already opened wound. The whip cracked a last time. The lash stung viciously but, thankfully, landed on untouched skin.

*

'Are we satisfied?' asked Gilder to the crowd, after the final stroke.

No one spoke.

Gilder, Selina, and their sons walked back to their cabin.

Niclaus felt a mixture of guilt and relief. Guilt that Olaf and his father had taken the lashes meant for him and relief that he had survived his ordeal.

Inside the cabin, Gilder grimaced as Selina applied salves to his lacerations.

'How are you?' asked Niclaus.

'Never better,' smiled Gilder through gritted teeth. 'I am so proud of my two sons. I feared this punishment would split the village but instead I believe it has brought us closer.'

After the whipping, Niclaus returned to Vidar's duties with more vigour, trying to make amends for having left Eve alone.

*

Ludin's condition worsened. Infection set in and he developed a fever. Over the next days, his body flitted between burning with heat to shivering with cold. Ludin became so sickly that Gunnar was called to give him the last rites. Olaf and Rula watched over their son constantly. Eventually, exhausted, Rula had fallen asleep. Olaf carried her to bed before he once more took up his place on the stool next to Ludin's bed. 'Why God do you curse me so?' he asked aloud. 'Am I not a good man? What is it that I have done to offend you? Please, I beg you, spare my son.' He sighed. 'What do you care anyway? Have you ever helped me? No, not even when Gilder robbed me of my victory in the Trial all those years ago. The humiliation. And now are you going to take away my son and with it my only hope of regaining my honour? Please, not my boy.'

CHAPTER 19

IN THE YEAR 837 AD

Vidar imagined he was floating as he stepped off the currach into waist-high fog. He lost sight of the shore and his boat in just half a dozen steps. All was eerily quiet.

He readjusted the straps of the heavy woven sack before knocking on the door. Three loud bangs. The children inside, previously asleep on cushions in front of the dying log fire, screamed and jumped, giddy with excitement. He was home, at last.

Vidar laughed at their squeals.

'Are all the children asleep?' he called.

He kicked the side of the cabin, clearing snow from his boots before opening the creaking door and entering, dropping his large sack as he did so. Instantly, he was attacked by little Dylla, who only a moment before had been asleep on her sister's knee. 'He's back,' she cried, excitedly.

She, the youngest girl, only five, golden curled with wide eyes, rushed to Vidar. She flung her arms around his neck as he lifted and twirled her.

'Now, Dylla, let Vidar breathe,' said Elwin, giving him a warm smile.

It was evident that she had missed him.

Vidar set Dylla down and crossed to meet Elwin. They hugged and kissed, sending the girls into fits of giggles. It was clear their feelings had deepened, although they had not made the transition from companions to lovers. Breaking their embrace, Elwin gave a disapproving eye to his wet footprints.

'Sorry,' he said, as he went to the door and removed the offending boots and wet socks. He smiled as he caught sight of fleece socks hanging, warming by the fire, exactly as before. It seemed traditions were forming.

Dylla tugged at Helga's sleeve and whispered, 'Don't hug him – he's all wet and smelly.'

Helga laughed as she took her turn to embrace Vidar. Wrapped in his arms and facing Dylla, she held her nose, mockingly. 'You're right, he smells worse than horse pee,' she whispered.

Fenja and Eve, the older girls, huddled around Vidar amidst more hugs and kisses. It was great to see the girls so happy – they had suffered a lot over the last few years. Vidar did not want to replace Magnus; rather he hoped that one day all the girls would come to think of him as a second father.

Taking off his wet coat and settling in front of the fire, Vidar lifted the socks and put them on. Warming his hands, he gazed at the fire, watching the flames; he loved getting lost in their intensity. Helga waved a hand in front of his face to break his stare. Snapped back from his momentary lapse, his thoughts settled on his son. 'And how did Niclaus get on?' he asked. He had already confided to Elwin that he was Niclaus' father.

'He has kept the wood piled high, perhaps higher than you

would have yourself,' teased Elwin, with a woman's ease, gently steering the conversation away from further discussion of the boy. She had already warned the girls not to mention the incident with Eve on the ice. It would keep until morning.

Vidar began to ramble, deliberately testing both the children's resolve and Elwin's patience. All the time, the girls' eyes remained fixed on the sack by the door.

'That's enough, you've had your fun,' said Elwin.

'All right,' he agreed.

He went to the door and attempted to lift the sack, pretending it was too heavy. With Dylla's help and a wink, they dragged it to the fireside.

'Gather around, girls.'

Dylla could not contain her excitement. 'Me first, me first,' she screamed, jumping on to Vidar's lap.

'So you don't want a present?' teased Vidar.

'I do, I do,' she cried.

'And have you been well behaved?'

'I've been really, really good – ask Mummy.'

'Well, Mummy, has she?'

Elwin paused. Dylla frowned. Vidar supposed that there had been a tantrum or suchlike, nothing too drastic.

'Yes, Dylla's been good,' confirmed Elwin, finally.

All smiles again, Dylla stood at Vidar's side as his hand went into the bag.

'What would my little princess like? I thought long and hard before I settled on this,' he said, pulling out an exquisitely carved doll. She was beautiful, fully dressed, with arms and legs that could rotate full-circle, and hair made of dark mane and a painted face. The craftwork was intricate, perfect in detail right down to individual fingers.

'She's gorgeous,' exclaimed Dylla, rushing to show her mother.

'What will you call her?' asked Elwin.

'Why not call her Elwin after Mum?' suggested Helga.

Dylla laughed. 'Don't be silly, her name's Doll.'

The others all laughed too.

'Hold on a moment Dylla there's more than that.'

Vidar reached into the bag and brought out another doll; the only difference was that the second dress was red rather than green.

'What's her name going to be?' asked Helga.

'That's easy; her name is going to be Sister,' said Dylla, making everyone laugh again.

'What do you say?' Elwin asked.

Dylla immediately hugged Vidar, his thick greying bread tickling her nose, 'Thank you – they're the best presents ever.'

Vidar coughed, clearing his throat. 'Who's next?'

Helga beamed. She was nine years of age, and had hair braided into two long fair plaits, soft hazel eyes and a tanned complexion. She would break hearts in a few years, of that Vidar was certain. She reminded Vidar of Elwin.

The fire crackled, spitting an ember onto the woollen rug. Using tongs, Vidar threw it back into the fire. The singed wool gave off a pungent smell.

'So what could I find for my Helga?' he asked, pulling out a doll's house complete with miniature figurines. Helga's eyes lit up and she smiled, revealing a gap in her front teeth.

'It's perfect,' she squealed with delight.

Fenja, Elwin's eldest daughter, moved to sit next to Vidar.

Vidar shifted in his seat. 'On my trip, I heard a tale of a magical instrument that, when played by a girl, would enchant any man who heard it. I decided there and then that I had to have it for Fenja, given that she's close to marrying age.'

The girls sniggered. Elwin gave a scowl.

'Enough,' Fenja interrupted. 'Please, may I have my present?'

Vidar reached into the sack and pulled out a whistle made of tin. Her reaction impressed Vidar; she did her best not to show her disappointment. She blew it. 'I shall learn to make beautiful music to catch that handsome man.'

Vidar laughed. 'Don't you want the rest of your present?'

Fenja's face lit up. 'There's more?'

Vidar pulled out a pouch and gave it to her. Inside were a silver ring and a shiny necklace inlayed with coloured stones, the fire's reflection giving them a reddish glow. The ring was beautiful; it had a heart as its centrepiece encased between two silver hands. Trying it on, she was disappointed to find it much too large.

'It's called a lover's ring – you give it to the man who wins your heart,' he explained.

She loved it. From her expression, Vidar guessed she had someone in mind to wear the ring.

'That leaves Eve,' he paused. It was three days since the longest night. 'And this your birthday. What did I bring for you?'

Eve tried to sneak a peep. There was something large in the sack but Vidar was certain she would not begin to guess what it was.

'You are always the hardest to choose for,' he said as he lifted the present out. 'It's not full size; master it and I'll bring you a proper one.'

It was a wooden frame, standing about the height of an average person's hip, in the shape of half a heart, strung from top to bottom with strings of differing lengths and thickness.

Eve was a natural musician with a beautiful voice. Vidar loved hearing her sing.

'It is known as a harp. When played properly it makes the most beautiful music.'

Eve's face gave little away, Vidar was unsure whether she liked it or not.

'They tell me it is as easy to play as any stringed instrument.' Vidar kept talking. He was blabbering.

Eve was always so guarded. He wanted to break down her reserve but she was not making it easy for him. For a fleeting moment, Vidar wished he had changed presents, wished he had given Fenja's gift to Eve.

Eve gave Vidar a hug. 'Thank you, it is a lovely present.'

'Come on, girls, it's late. Off to bed with you,' said Elwin.

CHAPTER 20

IN THE YEAR 802 AD

'Never in the history of this monastery has anything like this ever happened. What have you to say for yourselves?' Abbot Monicurr asked, slamming his palm on his desk.

The slap on the table startled Prior Cinaed who stood at Monicurr's side.

Tomás sneaked a glance at Damian. He was not proud of himself. Damian had two black eyes and a split lip. There was no denying that Tomás had carried the fight – swollen knuckles were his only injury from the dispute.

'So, why is your brother so badly injured?'

'It's a private matter.'

This was the first time that Tomás had defied his abbot.

'There must be no secrets in the house of God,' said White Owl, angrily.

'On this matter I must keep the knowledge between myself and the Almighty,' replied Tomás, knowing his words would further enrage White Owl. He was resolute: he would not divulge the source of the dispute.

Tomás watched as White Owl, unused to disobedience,

struggled to control his rising temper. He exhaled forcibly, as he looked at Damian. 'So, how have you come to find yourself in this position?'

His tone was softer but still carried threat.

'I cannot answer.'

'Cannot or will not?'

'Both,' replied Damian, with conviction.

'Do you know what this is about?' White Owl asked Cinaed.

Tomás held his breath. If anyone were capable of unearthing the reasons behind the row, it would be Cinaed.

Cinaed shook his head. 'I am afraid I have heard no inkling.'

Tomás breathed a sigh of relief.

White Owl continued to question Tomás and Damian but both brothers chose not to answer. The chasm between them was too wide and the room remained deadly silent.

'What could be so bad that would result in you resorting to violence? Have no doubt; I will get to the bottom of this. I will not settle until this matter is resolved to my satisfaction.' He waited for a response.

It seemed that Damian had not uttered a single word since Brother Ciaran found him stumbling outside the chapel. Tomás' swollen hand was the only clue as to the fight.

Abbot Monicurr looked furious. Accepting there was nothing he could do to break their silence for now, he said, 'I ask you both to leave and to pray for guidance and forgiveness. I will deliberate long and hard before I decide how to proceed with this matter.'

The root of the discord was Tomás' secret work on Cado's manuscript. Before the dwarf's arrival, the two young monks had been inseparable. Unfortunately, Tomás' new undertaking left him little time, meaning that Damian felt suddenly excluded. Damian had enquired about the new friendship but Tomás had not been forthcoming.

'What's so important that you're spending all your time with this Cado fellow?' he had asked.

'You know that I am trying to convert him and his people.'

'I suspect there is more to it.'

'Yes, you are right. I'm working on something for him. When the time's right, I'll tell you all about it.'

The explanation, although not perfect, was enough for Damian to drop the matter for a while but soon he began to question Tomás again. 'And why can't I meet with this dwarf? Surely you can take me into your confidence?'

'He won't let me, made me promise.'

After the refusal, the two had worked in silence.

*

Believing something was amiss and with genuine concern for his good friend, Damian had set out to uncover why this stranger seemed to have such a hold over Tomás. Whatever it was, Tomás was leaving no clues. The answer came from the most unlikely source. Damian's painting of the Virgin and Child was close to completion. Using carved wooden stencils, he was adding interlacing designs – arches and loops – to the border. He sat back in his chair to admire his work. The full page was his finest piece of work.

Tomás stood up and stretched. 'I have to go and see White

Owl.'

Damian raised his head. 'What for?' he asked, annoyed that he was excluded.

'He's having a special lectern made to hold the book in the chapel. I have to give him the book's dimensions. I will not be long.'

Alone, Damian tried to lose himself in his work, but he was finding it more and more tedious. Taking less care than usual, he dipped his quill into the ink pot, and then positioned it over the vellum. A droplet splattered on to the picture. He grabbed at the blotting paper that was by his side. Rushing, trying to limit the damage, he knocked his cow-horn inkpot, spilling orpiment, the golden pigment, over his picture. His efforts to wipe up the spillage were in vain – the illustration was ruined. Months of painstaking work wasted. Damian lifted the sheet and, in a fit of rage, tore it. He sat still for a few moments, trying to regain his composure. Abbot Monicurr would be livid. He slid the offending vellum underneath a cupboard. It would give him time to consider what to do.

Having cleaned up the spill, he went to refill the empty inkpot from the jars stored in the adjoining room. Monicurr kept the ink in a cabinet in his study. Damian was sure the level of the brown dye, the most commonly used, should have been higher. Beginning with the copper green dye, he checked each bottle. The only one that looked low was the iron-gall brown. He would not usually have noticed, but he had filled the bottle just the day before.

Was Tomás writing something? What could it be?

He contemplated the answer all afternoon as he worked on a

new page. He decided to find out. As to his damaged illustration, if Tomás asked about it, he would tell him that he had made a slight mistake and that Cal was repairing it.

Over the next few days, Damian systematically searched the workshops for any hidden material, but found nothing. He also watched Tomás closely. The only time he could not monitor his fellow monk was for the short periods when Tomás went off with the dwarf.

Damian decided to break the inviolable rule of the monastery: he would search Tomás' room for clues. Tomás' excursions offered the perfect opportunity. Damian entered the sparsely furnished room. It would not take long. He surveyed the contents – a wooden bed, a rickety bedside table with a stone jug on top, a rail for Tomás' vestments and a kneeler for private worship. A poorly made wooden crucifix hung on the wall above the bed. Rummaging through the room, he found an empty ink bottle – confirming his suspicions – and a few scribbled jottings. Nothing of significance. He pulled a bundle of papers from under the bed. Damian flicked through the documents, discarding each one. They were mostly private thoughts and prayers. Having searched the last remaining hiding place, Damian concluded that Tomás had to be keeping whatever he was writing on his person. But Damian could not understand how Tomás could hide a book. Then he saw it. The answer was right in front of his eyes. Sitting neatly on his bed was Tomás' missal. That in itself was not out of the ordinary except that, of late, Tomás brought his satchel everywhere, not letting it out of his sight. If his missal was here, then what was he carrying around with him?

Tomás only needed his missal during services and having sat next to him, Damian knew Tomás had had it. Bringing in a second book would have been too conspicuous and besides, with everyone in the chapel, there was no risk of anyone ever finding it. Tomás must simply exchange his missal for the secret book before services, probably hiding it somewhere in his room. Then he retrieved it, leaving the missal as Damian found it now. That would explain why Tomás, of late, had made a point of going home after services.

To find the book, Damian would need to search the room during the joint services of Mass and Terce, before morning meal. He set about devising a plan to miss the service. It would be tricky as Monicurr expected even ill monks to attend so that they could offer up their suffering as penance.

Damian's anticipation continued to grow. For some reason he could not deny his unchristian feelings towards the dwarf. If he was honest, his hatred probably stemmed from jealousy over Tomás' and Cado's close friendship.

The night before his planned search, Damian said he was ill and scurried off to bed. Tomás checked in on him on his way to the early morning service, intending to help him to the chapel. As he reached the doorway, he heard retching. 'Is there anything I can do?' he enquired, as he entered.

Damian hoped he looked awful. Instinctively, Tomás covered his mouth with his hand.

'No, I'll be ready in a …' Damian retched again.

The odour was overpowering.

'Get into bed and I'll let White Owl know.'

Damian pretended to protest, 'I'll be fine.'

'No, into bed with you. You'd be better tucked up here rather than infecting everyone else. You'd kill half of them,' he said, in reference to the frail old monks.

'I'll check on you after Mass,' he called back from the doorway.

Having taken Brother Brendan's stomach-clearing remedy earlier, Damian had struggled to wait to vomit until the exact moment of Tomás' arrival.

The final peal from the bell tower over, Damian crossed the sun-hardened path to Tomás' hut and began his search. He checked the table, sifting through a stack of papers, a few sketches, and religious quotes. Once more there was nothing of note. Next, he searched the bed. He ran a hand over the straw-filled bedding. Nothing. Then he spotted something, wedged between the front leg of the bed and the wall. He had found it – a plain black leather book, the size of an ordinary missal.

Knowing he had plenty of time, the service being the longest of the day, he sat back on the bed and began to read.

CHAPTER 21

IN THE YEAR 837 AD

The weak sun failed to penetrate the hanging mist as Niclaus crossed the frosted snow to Elwin's house. He had slept badly. Vidar was due home any day and the prospect of facing him was daunting. Niclaus was afraid of how Vidar would react about what had happened; he had, after all, put Eve's life in danger and lost a reindeer.

Over the last few days and nights – when sleep would not come – Niclaus rehearsed how the conversation would go. He was certain of one thing; the waiting was always the worst part. He remembered the time that he and Orrin had taken their father's bow without permission. Unbeknownst to the boys, the bow's string was old and it snapped on Niclaus' first pull. They sneaked the weapon back, hoping that their actions would go undetected. Niclaus could still recall how his anxiety had steadily grown. It would have been better to blurt out his guilt and accept the punishment. How was he to know that his father would repair the bow without thought? How he wished he had just owned up.

His stomach sank as he caught sight of two sets of footprints near Elwin's house. One was probably Eve's, but the other, much larger set could only be Vidar's. He was home.

Niclaus walked nervously to the barn.

Made of rough timber, the barn was big enough to house two cows, two goats, four sheep, one horse and a few hens, and still leave space for a reindeer, if they had one. On seeing Niclaus, Vidar set down his wheelbarrow. Eve stood by his side, smiling, trying to soften Vidar.

'Run along, Eve. I need to talk to Niclaus.'

The barn was dark and damp, a few spaced tallow candles offering the only glimmer of light. The smell of animal urine was more potent than the steaming dung on the wheelbarrow.

'Elwin has told me all about the …'

'Vidar, let me explain.'

Vidar took a seat on the edge of the animals' trough. 'No, Niclaus, this was reckless; you went too far. How could you have been so foolish?'

'I, I'm sorry, I …'

'Eve could have been killed.'

'I know, I didn't mean to …'

Vidar was cross, Niclaus remorseful.

'How stupid could you be?'

'I didn't think … I would never do anything to harm Eve.'

Vidar checked himself. 'It's not all your fault,' he sighed. 'I placed too heavy a responsibility on shoulders so young. It is more my fault.'

The remarks hurt almost as much as if Vidar had struck him. Apart from this one incident, Niclaus had proved himself most competent. He was proud of his work. No shed had a bigger stockpile and all the animals were healthy, that is if you exclude Rugt. 'Perhaps you are right,' he said. 'It was a great responsibility you left me with. I have tried my utmost and, except for that one time, I believe I have served you well.'

Vidar agreed.

'And then,' continued Niclaus, 'I wonder what you would have done.'

'I would have thought of Eve first.'

'Really?' Niclaus pursed his lips, struggling to hold his tongue.

'Yes.'

'Your first instinct wouldn't have been to try and save Ludin?'

'No.'

Their voices were rising.

'I don't believe you. Maybe, if you're being honest, I think you would have …' He let his words hang.

Niclaus took Vidar's silence to be an acknowledgement that he was right. Vidar coughed. 'Niclaus, I understand why you acted as you did, and I am so grateful that you have taken such good care of Elwin and the girls. I know that I have asked a lot of you, and I am sure that you wish you had more time to spend with your friends.'

Niclaus laughed.

'What's so funny?'

'I thank God I was not with the others that day. Could you imagine if I had led all the boys to attack the wolves? I don't think I would have survived a bigger whipping.'

'What whipping?' Vidar asked.

Elwin, knowing how Vidar would react, had deliberately not

mentioned Niclaus' punishment.

'Are you trying to tell me they whipped you?'

'No, no,' Niclaus said, reassuring Vidar before he explained what had happened.

'What sort of village are we living in? It's not right.'

'It is village law,' defended Niclaus.

'Laws. Stupid laws made by stupid people.' Vidar offered out a large hand. 'Niclaus, I would ask no other to care for our family in my absence.'

They shook hands.

Niclaus noted the word *our* in Vidar's last remark. It felt good that Vidar considered him part of his family.

'And I felt it only fitting to bring you a gift, to say thank you for all your work.'

He produced a knife, shiny and new.

Vidar presented it blade first. 'It's a tool, not a weapon – always remember that.'

The finely crafted blade ran from a broad handle into a narrowing point, roughly the length of Niclaus' hand. He pressed his finger lightly against the blade to test it. It was razor-sharp. 'Thank you.'

'And with it comes a belt and sheath,' said Vidar, handing them over.

Trying it on, the thick black belt fitted Niclaus neatly and the knife slipped smoothly into its sheath.

'By the way, you still owe me for a reindeer,' said Vidar.

'I did you a favour.'

'And how do you reckon that?'

'Rugt was old and ate too much food. The way I see it, I saved you from having to eat him. Tough old meat, takes forever to chew.'

Vidar laughed. 'And tell me, how is Ludin?'

'Thankfully, he's on the mend but it'll take months before he's fully recovered.'

'So, tell me about this wolf. What happened?'

He listened attentively.

'Was he as big as Elwin had heard?' asked Vidar, when he had finished.

'Yes, he was a monster.'

'And yet he did not attack Eve. Why do you think that was?'

'I don't know. He must have had a full belly.'

'Let me tell you about wolves,' said Vidar, lifting his spade to resume mucking out. 'Wolves are nature's favourite animal. Tidiers of the forest: they kill the weak and cull the overpopulated.' He tossed the droppings into the wheelbarrow. 'They are the most trusted by Mother Nature. They maintain the right balance. It is said that they are the wisest of all animals and are blessed with knowledge of good and evil. Some say they were bestowed with an ancient magic that allows them to protect the good of heart.'

'That's old folklore,' countered Niclaus.

'Then why did the wild beast not devour you or Eve?'

'I honestly don't know.'

'Niclaus, I believe that it found something in you. That beast travelled a long way to meet you. I think he smelt your scent on Eve. That's why he prevented the pack from hurting her.'

'The wolf was there offering you his protection. I believe this was no more than an introduction. You will meet him again.'

Niclaus reflected on Vidar's words. Much of what he said rang true – he had felt a connection to the animal.

'Niclaus, given time, things will become a lot clearer. Your life will become a wonderful adventure. Even the voyages I undertake relate to you.'

Vidar was opening up, more than he ever had before.

'Can you tell me more? What is it that you are searching for in the frozen north?'

'I'm looking for a special place to hide a great treasure.'

'What treasure?' Niclaus asked, barely able to hide his excitement.

'I'm afraid I've told you too much already. Promise me you will not mention this to anyone, not even Orrin.'

Niclaus gave his word.

'Niclaus, all that I ask is that you trust me. And if you do, I will entrust you with my secrets.'

CHAPTER 22

IN THE YEAR 838 AD

Captain Morton cursed their luck. The season should have held for another three to four weeks. In the month since the outward journey, the island's picturesque landscape – its blossoming flowers and summer coastline – had disappeared beneath a blanket of snow. In all the years that they had been sailing to Svalbard, Morton had never seen the winter arrive so early. They needed to pick up their passenger and set sail immediately. Why was Vidar so late?

Standing on the snow-speckled shore of rounded stone and boulder, Morton felt the chill of the wind. The clear sky stretched far into the distance; it would be so easy to underestimate the freezing threat of this place. He rubbed at his stinging eyes, raw from exposure to the island's icy winds. His lips were chafed dry and his cheeks cheery-red in contrast to his mood. Finally, he spoke. 'I can't wait forever.'

'We aren't leaving him,' said first mate Rune.

The force of his words sent a jet of vapour into the air. Rune had never before disputed an order.

Morton did not tolerate anyone questioning his authority or

his judgement, especially not his first mate, but he decided to let the comment go unchecked. There were more pressing matters and he could reprimand Rune later. Morton's immediate concern was his missing passenger.

He looked inland, towards the snow-covered mountains to the northeast. Somewhere out there, the mangled land was tightening its freezing grip, choking the life from Vidar. He could feel it. Yet what could he do? As captain, his first duty was to ensure the safety of his crew and ship. He would soon have to give the order to set sail.

Pulling the collar of his tunic to his neck, he clasped his gloved hands together. 'The channel's nearly closed. It would be madness to wait any longer. He's already days overdue and I can't risk the ship.'

'One more day, that's all we are asking,' begged Anders.

Anders, tall and thin with a soft face, was the newest and youngest member of the crew. Morton had found him homeless and half-starving on one of his stopovers. Seeing something he liked in the boy, Morton had offered him a position. Anders had been aboard the *Ice Maiden* for almost nine years and thrived at sea, his natural appetite for hard work making him popular with the others.

'We know the risks, we're prepared to stay,' added Rune. 'Please, a little longer. He'll make it back.'

Morton looked seaward as he weighed up his options. The water before him was awash with floating debris. 'We'll wait 'til the evening tide, that's all we can afford.'

He lifted a stone from the shore and tossed it into the water, the ripples breaking the snowy landscape that was reflected in the glassy water surface. 'Look, it's already starting to freeze,' he said, pointing to the shoreline where ice was forming. He called his crew together. 'Listen, men, if we are going to wait, we'll continue to search the surrounding land. Jorun, you're with me. We'll search the south-east. Walrus, take Anders and head east. Torre and Rune, go north-east. Check for a possible route through the mountains. Remember to keep a sharp eye out for tracks or footprints. Vidar may be hurt and holed up somewhere. But – and this goes for all of you – I don't want any heroics out there. We are sailors, not explorers. We aren't equipped for this terrain. And Arne, make sure there's a something hot to eat ready for when we get back.'

Morton scanned the ridges and chasms. Vidar was out there somewhere. He had to find him.

CHAPTER 23

IN THE YEAR 802 AD

Damian opened the dark leather book. The font inside was heavy and, disappointingly, rather plain.

He read the foreword.

'This is the story of the people of Newgrange as told to me by Cado. I have no way of proving or disproving any of the information held within these pages. However, I can say with certainty that the narrator is honest and trustworthy. I hold Cado Boruc in the highest regard.'

    Brother Tomás, in the year of Our Lord 801

Underneath was a second piece.

'I wish to add that I have witnessed many things that I find impossible to explain. Cado claims these are merely examples of 'wisdom beyond belief'.'

    Brother Tomás, in the year of Our Lord 802

After the foreword, Damian found a few unattached pages

folded neatly inside. He opened them and read the heading – *Damian's Folly*. His heart raced. The writing had nothing to do with Newgrange. The pages were an accurate account of what had happened when he spilt the ink on the illustration of the Virgin and Child.

'*Damian hid the ripped parchment under the cupboard.*'

He was horrified. His mind swirled. No one else knew of the accident. How did Tomás learn of it? Somehow, the dwarf must have found out and told him. He had to retrieve the damaged page and destroy it, if it was still there. He dreaded to think what White Owl would do if he saw it. With the evidence destroyed, Damian could deny everything. He could pretend that the page had simply been lost. As the scriptorium was above the chapel, it would be impossible for him to retrieve the ripped parchment until the service was over. Given how effectively he had faked his sickness, he feared his sudden recovery would be greeted with suspicion.

Regaining his composure, he sat on his friend's bed and began reading the book of Newgrange.

The first chapter described the dwarfs' arrival in Erin and how they established their community. It continued, describing the leaders of the people and their ambitions. He discovered the work the villagers had undertaken to build their monuments. He turned the page to find a spectacular drawing, depicting lightning striking the great carved stone at Newgrange.

He read how the dwarfs had been able to collect such power and use it in many wondrous ways. His mouth dropped open as he read claims of special powers. His initial scepticism quickly waned. However fanciful the tale may have seemed, Damian believed it to be genuine. The potential of such ability excited him. If he could gain possession of it there would be no limit to what he could achieve. The thought excited him. He had a new purpose – one that would lead him away from Ceanannus Mór.

CHAPTER 24

IN THE YEAR 838 AD

Sticking his fingers into the socket, he ripped out the eyeball, sliced it open and sucked out its juicy contents. Then he carved a slice from the corpulent belly, and devoured it. He was ravenous. Gloved in blood, he wiped entrails off his painted beard.

Vidar's rations were low, so the energy-rich food tasted all the sweeter. It had been a stroke of luck to find the seal at the blowhole. About the size of an adolescent boy, it had proved harder to land than to lance. He had killed it on his first attempt, but getting a good foothold and grip of the dead animal at the same time had proved difficult.

His appetite sated, Vidar took enough meat to last him several days before setting off. Time was against him. He should have kept to his schedule and pushed westward to find the *Ice Maiden*, but he had a feeling that he was getting closer to the Vestibule and wanted to explore the mountains that lay ahead. Morton would be furious if he learned of his folly – but who was there to tell him?

Ahead, the ochre sun, shining from beyond the Blue Mountains, gave the bay the appearance of an amethyst road. Electrified by the beautiful setting and spurred on by a full belly and the belief that, having little of the island left to explore, he might be close to finding the Vestibule, Vidar stepped on to the frozen inlet. The mountains in front did not look overly challenging.

As he walked, he tapped the ice with his poles from time to time. He was able to gauge its thickness by the sound.

The rising snow-covered mountains blocked his line of sight. Unsure of the lie of the land, he hoped it offered a route to the west. He prayed that beyond was not cliffs or open sea. If the land was impassable, he would have to backtrack, costing him more time than he could afford. The wind grew stronger on the exposed bay as Vidar crossed the polished ice and climbed the gentle gradient. His hopes were high. Everything – the time away from Niclaus, the loneliness – would be worth it if he found the Vestibule.

As he made his ascent, Vidar found fresh ice bear tracks. He cursed his luck. Although ice bears populated the region, he had been fortunate not to come across any of them. The sight of the tracks unnerved him. He stepped into one of the huge paw-prints which dwarfed his foot. He recalled the beast that had killed Baggi. He knew that his spear and knife would be virtually useless if he came face to face with a bear – his survival depended on avoiding the animals altogether. Trudging between two scarred rock faces, he picked out another trail but found the paw-print of a second bear. Again, he tried to find a different route. He climbed a ridge only to find a hollowed snowy valley, but at its far end he saw a mother standing watch over her two cubs. Enjoying their first steps towards maturity, the two cubs spent their time in playful trysts, rolling down snow banks in a single bundle of fur. The sight cheered Vidar. They were the nearest thing to company that he would meet – the bears and a few reindeer were the only signs of life he had found during his treks. But at this time of year, the mother and cubs would be hungry. He knew to move away.

Unable to find a safe route over the mountains and running late, a dejected Vidar resigned himself to returning next summer. He found a path to the west, to the *Ice Maiden*.

The first clue to the changing weather conditions was the strengthening wind. Not only was it picking up, it was also icy cold. Ominously, a thickened purple canopy of cloud rolled across the sky. Although he needed to press on, Vidar, having reached the far side of the bay, took the decision to pitch his tent on the leeward side of the rock face and built a wall of snow to provide even better protection.

*

Vidar cursed his luck – the blizzard had held him captive in his sarcophagus for far too long. At times he could almost hear the roaring wind speak to him, goading him, daring him to venture out of his tent. Vidar drifted in and out of sleep, losing track of time.

With the temperature inside his tent below freezing, his breath reached the roof of the tent, condensed and froze as ice droplets. Vidar picked off a miniature stalactite and threw it out of the tent. He hurriedly resealed the opening before the last vestige of heat escaped. Outside, the wind howled loudly enough to hurt his ears, and blew so fiercely that he feared the tent would collapse under the barrage of driven snow. Yet the elements were more manageable than the boredom that came with his confinement. On earlier trips, he had amused himself by replaying conversations with ghosts of his past, re-enacting almost forgotten arguments, winning a lost one, or withholding a stinging remark. Ultimately, loneliness and despair would unite to embrace him. Now more experienced and mentally tougher, he fixed his mind on the future and blanked out any nagging doubts. If he failed in his search, there was always next year and the one after that, if need be. He would find the Vestibule, no matter how long it took.

Often when he walked, he talked aloud, having imaginary exchanges with his friends. Occasionally, he talked to Cado.

'No, Cado, I haven't found the damned ice cave. Yes, yes, I know I promised to find it. I just didn't say when. So far, all I have found is snow and more snow. Are you sure you've sent me to the right island? It would have been helpful if you had given me a little more information. Are you sure it's here? Yes, all right. I'll find it next year.'

He carried on chatting. It was only here in the wilderness that he dared to let his guard down and share his deepest secret with the world. It felt strange, silly even, but talking out loud about his search somehow eased the burden. He still had not seen anything that remotely resembled a vestibule.

The snowstorm abated and Vidar woke to an eerie silence. Believing he was already days behind schedule and still some way from the *Ice Maiden*, he had to get moving – his life depended on it. Relieved to be out of the putrid stench of his tent, to taste pure air, he punched his fists in the air and stretched his stiff back. He was getting old. He suspected that his leathery skin coupled with his greying hair made him look much older than his thirty-five years.

He checked his equipment and began packing provisions into the large leather sack attached to his sleigh. Disregarding his routine in favour of speed, he packed with the nearest items to hand. In went his sealskin suit, his poles, the bundle of leather and fur that formed his tent, an assortment of utensils and lastly his provisions.

It was pointless to worry over the rights and wrongs of his delay, of what he should have done – he needed to concentrate on what he was going to do. With the sun dispelling any lingering mist and the light easterly breeze blowing away the last of the cloud, the threat of further blizzards diminished. Journeying towards the coast, the ice and snow should have lightened but the early storm had put an end to that prospect. He cursed the deep snow. Pulling his sleigh, the unequal distribution of weight meant that his legs sank. He hated taking off his skis and walking. It was proving exhausting. His every step landed him knee-deep in snow and his sleigh continually clogged up. He persevered, stopping every thirty paces or so to remove the build up from the runners. It took a great effort to keep going. He refused to look back, afraid to see what little ground he had covered.

'Morton will wait, he won't leave without me,' he told himself.

Eventually a far-reaching ice plain replaced the thick snowfield. Vidar savoured the moment that he was able to put his skis back on. He felt jubilant to be clear of the deep snow. He skied for most of the morning and well into the afternoon, telling the time by the sun's position in the sky.

Instantly, Vidar recognised a change as one of his poles struck the ice. He wanted to hear the knocking sound of hard ice. There was definitely a weakness. Attentively, he watched and listened as his poles struck again. They sank deeper. He continued until one of his poles pierced the surface and water bubbled up. Vidar stopped. The ice was not sludge, but it did have an airy quality. He studied the contours before him, tracking a vein of slightly lighter-coloured ice. He speculated that there was water below the ice, perhaps a river. He considered following its course, trying to find a safer place to cross. He dismissed the notion. His deadline did not afford him the luxury and there was no guarantee that he would find anywhere better.

It was possible that the early return of winter might have covered the surface of a river with a thin membrane of ice. It would have been foolish to ignore the risk; there was every chance that it would not take his weight. Common sense and years of experience had taught Vidar how to gauge the strength of ice. He had a chart in his head. The safest was blue ice – he could march a herd of reindeer over it. After that, the whiter the ice the stronger it was. He did not mind the hard brown variety, usually smooth, which allowed for speed, but he hated the sludgy brown crushed sort, trusting it only for a quick dash.

The ice in front of him was definitely in the dangerous category. He contemplated stopping and putting on his sealskin suit that, being extra large, slipped over his clothes. It would allow him, if the ice broke, to half swim and half crawl to firmer ground. His sleigh, being buoyant, would float behind. He cursed his earlier haste. His suit was at the bottom of the sleigh, and he did not have time to unpack. Against his better judgement, he decided to continue.

At least the ice was flat, he told himself as he again removed his skis. He walked on through the sludge. It was wetter than he had thought, but it held. His tentative steps gave way to firmer ones as his confidence grew. Rather than keeping his pace constant, he increased his speed, believing his weight was better distributed.

A hiss of escaping air gave the first warning that the ice had yielded. A loud cracking noise followed. Its amplified echo made it sound as if the entire surface was giving way. Panicking and too far out to retrace his steps, Vidar raced on. Tension from the sleigh pulled at his harness. His mind was a whirl of activity.

The ice had given way behind. He tried to drive his poles into the ice but the sludge offered no support. With little traction, the harness hauled at him, dragging him backward. Taking up the strain, Vidar cursed as the realisation dawned: his sleigh was sinking. It should have floated. If he had kept to his routine and packed it correctly, it would have floated, not filled with water.

Vidar, hoping to pull the sleigh out of the water, tried to carry on walking. His shifting weight on the weakened surface proved disastrous – the ice cracked, plunging him into the freezing water. Instantly, the coldness sucked the air from his lungs and attacked his head, sending agonising prongs of pain into his temples. Vidar's priority changed from saving his sleigh to saving himself.

With the water pressure relieving much of the pull of the sleigh, he was able to release the harness and swim for the surface. His first attempts to get out of the water failed as the edge of the ice gave way. He was almost overcome by exhaustion when he finally secured a finger hold and clawed himself out.

Vidar fought to catch his breath, aware that to stay still would be as fatal as jumping back into the water. He crawled well away before he dared to stand. Forcing his trembling body upright, he was determined to walk. It was imperative to generate heat, dry from the inside out.

He estimated that he was still a few days walk from the *Ice Maiden* and would now have to complete the journey without food, water, or provisions.

His teeth were chattering, his body shivering, and the strong contractions of his cramping muscles sent spasms of pain all over his body. Although every step was excruciating, he forced himself to keep going.

The sunlight dazzled his eyes. In all the upheaval, he had lost his wooden visor. This was a disaster; the visor's tiny wooden slits protected his eyes from snow blindness. The northern hunters had warned of the condition caused by sunlight reflecting off the snow.

Vidar's clothes felt twice as heavy and ice had frozen on his beard, nostrils, and eyelids. He was beginning to lose feeling in his feet but still he carried on.

By reading simple signs, he was able to keep his bearings. In the Arctic sunshine, he walked without rest, taking the most direct route through a gap in the mountain range. He remembered a narrow path through its middle. Free of his sleigh, the route would be quicker. Vidar tried to ignore the first signs of a headache. He told himself it was just the cold irritating his temples, but the pain became more intense. His sight gradually deteriorated. Until now, he had followed his route easily. The easterly wind had shaped waves of ice sculptures along the way, making it a simple task to keep his course, but now he was almost blind, he had to rely on the wind on his cheek to know in which direction he was moving. He prayed that it would not ease up.

At first he walked hesitantly but gradually his confidence grew, as did the length of his stride. He tried to make himself laugh by imagining how he looked. Each exaggerated step began with a high lift and stretch, as if he was straddling a low wall. One boulder, catching him unprepared, sent Vidar sprawling. He suffered a bang to his already throbbing head. He felt nauseous, beads of sweat broke out on his brow, and he vomited. Too tired to move, he was sick down his cheek and into his furred hood.

Somehow, he managed to get on to all fours. Sheer willpower forced him to his feet. Every step was a challenge, each one more arduous than the last. His body was shutting down; the signs were evident, his arms were limp and it was becoming increasingly difficult to move his fingers. His ability to think clearly was lessening. Although he was fighting, he knew that he was losing the battle.

Vidar knew that if he collapsed now, he would die where he fell, but after a few steps, his left leg seized and he dropped to the ground in a heap. His greatest fear, death, became his greatest spur; it drove him on, forcing him to his feet again. He stumbled on until he walked into a jutting protuberance of ice. It pierced deeply into his thigh. The icy air instantly coagulated the flow of blood but the same air would quickly freeze the exposed flesh.

Another slight drop unbalanced him and his legs buckled. He landed on one knee. Again, he forced himself to his feet. He refused to bow. He refused to be beaten.

His headache eased. He recalled a tale Knutsen told. He claimed that before death came, a man's suffering would ease and inner heat warmed the body. Vidar believed him now.

Eventually his body refused to move and he keeled over. Lying on his frozen deathbed, he recalled an earlier conversation with Eve.

'Please, don't go, please,' she begged, standing by the waterside.

'I have to,' he replied, as he boarded the *Ice Maiden*.

'I have a bad feeling, please,' she repeated. She looked frightened.

'Don't fret, Eve. I'll be back before you miss me.'

'Do you promise?' she cried.

'I promise,' he said, solemnly.

He rolled on to his side and willed his body to stand. Spent, it did not respond. He had succumbed. His promise would be broken.

CHAPTER 25

IN THE YEAR 838 AD

Torre and Rune continued their search for Vidar. As they walked, the fresh wind blew the snow into their faces, causing them to drop their heads. Torre wondered how anyone could survive in the extreme conditions. 'We'll find him today, I feel it,' he said.

'I hope so,' whispered Rune, almost as if he was praying.

They persevered.

'I think I see something over there,' said Rune, pointing at a black spot to the side of an ice ridge.

'No, it looks like a seal sitting by a blowhole.'

They edged further to the right but Torre kept his eyes trained on the seal.

'Vidar would not have gone that way. He'd have come this way, around the ice. Besides there are no sleigh tracks,' pointed out Rune.

Torre was not convinced. 'I'll take a closer look.'

As he neared, the startled animal slithered into the water.

Torre caught up with Rune. 'He's never been late before,' he said.

'Don't worry. He'll make it back. It's just the weather. It's slowed him down.'

Torre's hands were beginning to freeze. He had lost feeling in them, and his feet felt worse. Ultimately, with Rune showing no sign of giving up, Torre called an end to the search. He had to; his companion looked to be struggling and was close to exhaustion. 'Come on, any further and they'll be looking for us as well.'

Rune kicked toe off heel, clearing the ice off his boot. 'Aye, lad, you're right. I'm at my limit. Hopefully one of the others will find him.'

As they broke from the pass, Torre spotted a dark shape, previously obscured by a high wall of ice. 'Wait, look over there.'

'Don't waste your time.'

'I'm going to take a closer look.'

Torre broke into a jog. The bundle before him took on human form. 'It's him! It's him!' he shouted excitedly, rushing towards the fallen man. Was he dead? Torre dropped to his knees to check. Although his breathing was desperately shallow, Vidar was alive.

Rune rushed to Torre's side. 'How is he?' he asked, pushing past Torre to begin his own examination.

'He's hanging on, just. He must have been disorientated to have come this way.'

'Aye, it was lucky you spotted him.'

Looking around, Torre could see no tracks in the snow. 'Even the wind conspired against us, covering Vidar's trail, hiding his footsteps.'

Rune clutched at Vidar's frozen limbs, rubbing them strenuously through his many layers, trying to encourage blood to flow through the lifeless body. Vidar's face had a waxy texture, which felt frozen to the touch. 'You are fitter. Make for the boat. Get help. I will keep him as warm as I can.'

Torre stripped off his outer coat.

'Don't be stupid.'

'I'll be warm running.'

Reinvigorated with hope, Torre raced off.

Luck was on Torre's side, he found Walrus and Anders, who were on their way back to the ship.

Walrus took it upon himself to carry Vidar. He scooped him up as a father would an infant and threw him over his shoulder like a rack of beef. Then he closed himself to the world and carried him without a word of complaint. Not once did Walrus show any discomfort or ask for assistance. He made the journey back his own personal mission.

CHAPTER 26

IN THE YEAR 802 AD

Since entering the chapel, Tomás' feeling of foreboding refused to lift. He had tried praying harder but he remained full of apprehension. The service seemed twice as long as normal. At one point, he considered walking out. One quick look at the abbot put an end to the idea.

At the end of the service, believing that White Owl would be eager to question him about Damian's absence, Tomás tried to sneak out unnoticed. He was almost away when he heard the call.

'Tomás.'

He pretended not to hear.

'Tomás,' repeated Monicurr.

'Yes, Father,' he reluctantly replied.

The sea of monks between them parted.

'Tomás, a word.'

'Yes, Father.'

'I did not see Damian in the chapel,' he said, waiting for the explanation.

'Ah, yes, Father, I should have told you earlier but I was running late. Damian has picked up a nasty ailment. He's been vomiting since last night.'

'Too ill to attend God's house?'

'You know Damian – he was determined to attend. That's why I was nearly late. I was helping him to the chapel but it's a bad sickness – any time he stands, he vomits. I'm going to check on him, will you join me?'

Prior Cinaed interrupted. 'Sorry to disturb you, Father, but one of the stonemasons has a query about the latest cross. And you know what they're like,' he said, raising his eyes heavenwards.

'I'll come straight away,' said the abbot, and then remembered Tomás. 'You go ahead and check on Damian. I will visit him shortly.'

The drizzle was cool on his face as Tomás hurried to Damian. He was surprised to find the whitewashed hut empty. His unsettled feeling intensified and he rushed to collect his book. Reaching the door of his tiny house, he heard movement. His suspicions were well founded. Damian was kneeling next to the bed, trying desperately to replace his book. Damian tried to explain, 'I, I was worried …'

Tomás exploded. In his fit of blind rage, he lunged at Damian, punching him in the face. Damian tried to scream but a kick to the stomach expelled the air from his lungs. A barrage of punches followed. Collapsing on to the bed, Damian curled himself into a protective ball. Tomás was unable to stop himself – he kicked Damian relentlessly until the sudden limpness of his opponent's body quelled his fury. Tomás lifted his book from where it had fallen and checked its pages before leaving.

*

Damian, having regained consciousness, pulled himself on to the bed. What should he do? He considered bringing the matter to Monicurr's attention. No, if he did so, Tomás would be expelled and the book confiscated. His own interests were best served by keeping all knowledge of the book to himself. If Damian wanted to get his hands on the book, and ultimately take possession of the power of Newgrange, he needed to mend bridges with Tomás.

CHAPTER 27

IN THE YEAR 838 AD

Morton and Jorun stood on the deck anxiously scanning the horizon for any sign of the crew or Vidar. Suddenly Morton spotted figures on the horizon.

With his bad eyesight, he could not make out how many people there were, and he could not see a sleigh. Anders, Torre, Rune and Walrus came into focus. They had not found him.

'Captain,' said Jorun.

'What?'

'I think Walrus is carrying something.'

But when Morton saw the limp motionless body of Vidar slumped over Walrus' shoulder his heart sank. He and Jorun ran across the gangplank to meet them.

'He's still breathing,' reassured Walrus, through heavy pants.

He gently lowered his weighty parcel before collapsing himself.

'Get him aboard,' ordered Morton.

Relieved to have Vidar on board, irrespective of his condition, Morton gave orders to sail. They had to catch the tide.

He gave Vidar a quick once-over. His breathing was shallow,

the rise and fall of his chest barely visible. 'Bring him to the forecastle, strip him, and wrap him in blankets. Wrap his head too. We have to warm him up,' Morton instructed.

He asked Arne, the cook, to heat some water, thinking that they would drop a little into Vidar's mouth, to try to warm him from the inside.

With Vidar made as comfortable as possible, the crew left him were he was for it took all of them to row the *Ice Maiden* out of the inlet. Morton stood by the steering oar watching his men at work. The disappearing oars reappearing in perfect symmetry, each one catching, and reflecting the sun's rays off its smooth ash.

Although they were perilous, Morton loved sailing along icy shorelines, admiring the carvings chiselled by the ocean. A dislodged ice block off the port side caught Morton's eye. It towered above the *Ice Maiden* and took on the form of a mother cradling an infant.

He lost interest, paying more attention to a narrow section of water. He watched the boat's sides, making sure they were clear of trouble. Looking back, the image was lost to the changing angle, and distorted the image into a grotesque hunching figure.

'Keep a sharp eye beneath the water line,' warned Morton. 'Anyone of those jutting pieces could rip the boat from prow to stern.'

Navigating the narrowing trench of silvery water, the *Ice Maiden* cowered beneath climbing walls of ice as it sailed towards safer waters. Gradually the channel widened and the threat diminished.

'Rune, come up here and take the rudder,' Morton called,

satisfied that they were beyond the most treacherous section of sea and anxious to see Vidar.

The *Ice Maiden*'s builders had prioritised her capacity for cargo over providing comfortable quarters for her crew. Vidar was in the forward section, a cramped hatch with sleeping room for three. Morton crawled in to see him. The hatch was in semidarkness. But enough light came through gaps in the panelled wood to allow him to look at Vidar. He seemed no better.

Arne tilted Vidar's head back before trickling a spoonful of lukewarm water into his mouth.

'How is he?'

Arne shrugged his shoulders, 'He's alive. Just.'

Arne, who doubled as the ship's doctor, was small and well rounded and was often ribbed for eating more than his share of the ship's provisions. He continued massaging the greyish flesh around Vidar's hands. The left hand had suffered a knock. He worked it strenuously, kneading the fingers, encouraging blood to flow. Finishing with the hands, Arne repeated the process on Vidar's blackened toes; the big toe on his right foot was like wood.

'There's a good chance he'll lose it,' said Morton, watching Arne.

'If he survives long enough for it to matter,' said a downcast Arne. 'It feels like I'm working on a corpse.'

'Don't say that,' Morton chided.

'The cold is too deep within. Like a thief, it steals his life. I see little hope.'

'Don't give up on him. Treat him as you would your own son.'

'Could you help me turn him over? I need to massage his body.'

Arne continued rubbing. Morton watched in silence hoping to catch the faintest movement, a twitch, or jerk, something that offered a glimmer of hope. Nothing stirred.

*

The days dragged – a headwind for part of the journey slowed down their progress.

Walrus joined Morton by the rudder. 'How is he?'

'No change. Arne thinks it is a good sign.'

Walrus frowned, not convinced.

'No, he really does. At first, Arne thought there was no chance of survival. He told me himself that it was like working on a corpse.'

'And now?'

'Now he believes there's a slim hope, says that the body shows signs of warmth.'

'Then why does he not wake?'

'He needs the rest. Arne says it's the body's way of mending itself. He thinks if we can get him back to shore, off the water, he'll have a chance.'

Torre joined the two men, ready to relieve Morton.

'As I was telling Walrus, if we can get him ashore, he'll have a better chance. Arne's afraid that he might become feverish. He says if he does it'll kill him.'

'Do you think he'll survive?' asked Torre, concern etched on his face.

Scanning the open sea ahead, Morton considered the question. He did not believe in offering false hope. He always spoke plainly and his men valued his words as a result.

'I really do not know. Like you, I pray he will. I will tell you this, though: if anyone can recover from this, it is Vidar.'

CHAPTER 28

IN THE YEAR 838 AD

Morton steered the *Ice Maiden* through the skerried waters, tracing the channels as easily as a villager follows a well-used path. He knew the sea as a husband knows his wife; he could read her moods and knew when to stay close to her slipstream and when to leave her to brood. She had a temper that could flare up and, in an instant, smash a boat to bits.

Familiar coastline came into view, rocks that had nursed Morton from child to boy and from boy to man. He could smell the scent of home, the aroma of the rockweed-coated shore.

On the far side of the fjord, clumps of scrawny grasses clung to the rock face. Along the fjord, he could make out his village, resting peacefully in front of a backdrop of snowy mountains.

*

Ealver and Ragnall, two of the three original judges at Niclaus' trial, sat at the water's edge. They were in high spirits. It would not be long before they broke into drunken song.

Ealver sat, looking over the water and resting his hands on his rounded belly. Extra muscle to keep warm, he claimed. Just like his many chins.

'Looks like a boat,' he slurred, rubbing his eyes in an attempt to see more clearly. 'I think its Morton's.'

'How can you see that far?' asked Ragnall.

Ragnall, not as rounded as Ealver, had a mop of thick curly hair, bushy eyebrows, and a long face with a pointed chin. 'My eyesight's never been good,' he said. 'I can just about make out the boat.'

*

'Go and get Gilder, quickly,' commanded Morton, as the *Ice Maiden* drew alongside Ealver and Ragnall, his urgency sparking the two into life.

When the boat docked, a worried-looking Gilder was waiting. 'What's happened? Is it Vidar?'

Morton jumped to the quay. 'He wasn't there when we went to pick him up.'

'Are you telling me, you left him?' he exploded

'Listen ...'

'I trusted you. You were supposed to keep him ...'

Morton gripped Gilder with powerful arms. 'Listen, you fool. He's on board.'

The words calmed Gilder. 'Where is he? Let me see him.'

Morton, still with a tight hold on, locked eyes with the furious village leader. 'Listen to me,' he said, in a whisper.

Gilder stopped struggling, relaxed his stiffened body and searched for hope in Morton's face.

'The weather turned early, he wasn't at the place where we had agreed to meet. We searched until we found him.'

In the background, Torre, Anders, and Walrus came into view, having carried Vidar from the hull. Walrus jumped to the shore allowing Torre and Anders to pass the dead weight of Vidar's body into his arms.

'Where shall we take him?' Walrus asked.

Gilder, shaken by the sight, did not reply.

'Where?' repeated Walrus.

'To Elwin's cabin,' Gilder stammered.

'I'll show you the way,' said Ealver.

'I'll go and warn Elwin,' said Gilder, breaking into a run.

Reaching the cabin, he banged on the door. 'Elwin,' he called, marching on in without invitation.

'Elwin,' he called again. 'Hurry, come quickly.'

'What's wrong?' asked an alarmed Elwin, hurrying into the room. She looked still half-asleep in her nightclothes. 'It's Vidar, isn't it? What's happened to him?'

'He looks bad – too long on the ice.'

'Where is he?' she cried.

'They're bringing him here now.'

The door opened and Walrus followed Morton, Ealver, and Ragnall into the room.

Elwin rushed to Vidar, horrified. Her legs trembled and she felt sick to the pit of her stomach. The sight brought a flood of buried memories, of the night she lost her husband.

Gilder threw logs on the smouldering fire.

'Place him there, on the rug in front of the fire,' she said.

Walrus lowered Vidar slowly onto the sheepskin and Elwin

covered him with a wool blanket. His job complete, Walrus excused himself, as did Rune and Ealver.

A door creaked open, revealing three sets of worried eyes. Fenja, Eve and Helga stood in the doorway, leaving only little Dylla asleep and unaware of the commotion.

'Girls, don't be alarmed. Everything will be all right,' said Elwin. 'Vidar's had an accident but he'll be fine.'

She crossed the floor to the girls. 'Now I need you all to wrap up. I want you to stay with Gilder. If that's all right with you?' she asked him.

'Yes, come on, girls. I'll leave you with Selina and then come back.'

'No, there's no need. There's not much to do. I will keep him by the fire. Get some sleep and come back in the morning.'

'Shall I wake Dylla and bring her with us?' asked Fenja.

'No, she'll be fine where she is.'

Gilder led the girls away, leaving only Morton, Elwin and Vidar in the room.

'What happened to him?' Elwin asked.

Morton told her how they had found Vidar, and explained how they had looked after him: 'We warmed him gently and massaged the cold out of him as best we could.'

'Has he shivered?'

'No.'

'And has he had a fever, been delirious?'

'No, he hasn't stirred, not moved a muscle, nor uttered a word.'

Morton dropped his head, almost ashamed, 'It's like his body doesn't know to give up.'

'He hasn't given up, so we mustn't either,' said Elwin. 'You leave him to me. I'll make him better. Just wait and see.'

'I hope so,' replied Morton.

'It's late. I'm sure you are exhausted. Go, get some sleep.'

'Are you sure?'

Elwin escorted Morton to the door. 'Yes. Thank you for bringing him home to me.'

Home. Even as she said it the word struck Elwin like a thunderbolt. Here was Vidar's home, their home. He had become so important, not only to her but also to her daughters. She fought to hold back tears. Since Vidar's arrival, so absorbed in her own grief, she had shown little interest in him. She felt ashamed but more than that, incredibly sad. Now she wanted to know everything, wanted to learn all she could about him. All in good time, she told herself. For the present, Vidar's health was all that mattered.

Elwin lifted Vidar's head on to her lap and stroked his wild hair into some semblance of a shape.

Usually frozen meat did not smell, she thought. His clothes reeked, the odour overpowering. With difficulty, she removed the offensive-smelling garments and spotted the large scar on Vidar's back. The wound was old. She ran her fingers over the damaged tissue wondering, worrying, how the injury had happened. She spotted faded claw marks on his side, lower back, buttocks and the back of his thigh.

Elwin knew the importance of warming Vidar gradually. To do otherwise risked after drop, a condition caused by warming frozen limbs too quickly in which the freezing blood circulated too rapidly, attacked the heart and caused death. She began by warming cloths and applying them to Vidar's chest. She then massaged his body, working at the parts that looked the worst. She could see that some of the skin had blistered. It was a good sign.

For the rest of the night, she covered his body with lukewarm cloths, reapplying them in a clockwork system, slowly increasing their heat. After kneading her hands sore, she undressed and slipped beneath the blankets.

To Elwin, given the circumstances, lying beside another man felt strange, uncomfortable in fact. She felt disloyal to Magnus. Tossing the predicament around in her head, she scolded herself for being overdramatic. Yes, she had had a life with Magnus but that was in the past and she knew that shared body heat was a route back to health for Vidar.

CHAPTER 29

IN THE YEAR 802 AD

Tomás came away from the abbot's room feeling downhearted. He knew that he could not reveal any details of his fight with Damian. He knelt at the altar, signed the cross, clasped his hands, bowed his head, and prayed, hoping to find solace. His lips mumbled prayers that his wandering mind did not hear. He was still struggling to come to terms with his violence towards Damian. He felt so ashamed. And now his loyalties were being torn between the abbot and Cado. Tomás had to find a solution that satisfied his duty to the Lord and his responsibility to Cado.

Suspecting that Damian already had doubts over his holy calling, and remembering Cado's words, Tomás believed that he now posed a serious threat. Newgrange was in danger. Now that Damian had read the book, Tomás was sure that he would stop at nothing to gain knowledge of the dwarfs' world. Tomás had to act and act swiftly. Somehow, he had to convince Damian of the need for secrecy. Cado had warned of terrifying consequences if the wisdom of Newgrange fell into the wrong hands.

Outside, the weather had not improved. The sun remained hidden behind an overcast sky. Tomás shivered involuntarily as he passed the graveyard. Not normally superstitious, he prayed that the dark day was not an omen of things to come.

He hesitated at Damian's door. In the past, before the fight, he would have walked straight in. Tomás' anger had been replaced by trepidation as he knocked and waited.

'Who is it?'

'It's Tomás. Can I speak to you?'

'Come in,' shouted Damian

The sight of Damian's injuries sickened Tomás; he found it hard to believe that he had acted in such a savage manner.

Surprisingly, Damian attempted to apologise first. 'Tomás, I am sorry. I should have respected your privacy. I should have known better than to pry in your room. I would like to explain my reasons for doing so. I was, at first, acting out of genuine concern for you.'

Although Damian's words were conciliatory, Tomás could tell by his demeanour that his temper was simmering. Under the circumstances, he was showing remarkable restraint. But, in all probability, he was probably itching for revenge.

'No,' Tomás interrupted. 'I owe you an apology. I acted abysmally. Please forgive me.'

'It was just that you have been behaving so strangely. I feared that you were in trouble. I thought that the dwarf was somehow going to use you to steal our book. The more secretive you were, the more resolute I became. I was determined to help you. And now having read your book ...'

'You must tell no one of it.'

'We have to learn their secrets.'

'I have sworn to protect these secrets. We are not nearly ready to possess them,' Tomás appealed.

Damian's temper and voice were rising. 'We have a duty to discover their power and I have as much right as you to learn of their ways.'

Looking into his friend's penetrating eyes, Tomás could see the darkness that Cado had warned of long ago. Tomás' head was beginning to ache with tension. He had to placate Damian. 'Listen, Damian, let us not fight. What you say is true. Together we will learn their secrets.'

'Then why…'

'I was wrong to keep this from you. Knowing how strong your faith is, I was worried that you might disapprove of me working on such a book. I was afraid that you would tell Monicurr and that all this wondrous knowledge would be lost.'

Damian's eyes narrowed as he listened. Tomás knew he would be sceptical.

'And Cado is extremely suspicious. I wanted to gain his confidence before I told you.'

'Why the change of heart?' asked Damian, his mistrust obvious.

'Damian, I had always planned, when the time was right, to share all that I know with you. Who else would I share it with?'

'Then why did you attack me?'

'I don't know. I panicked … I was afraid you would jeopardise all my hard work. I am sorry. I should have brought you into my confidence long ago.'

'So, we do this together?'

'Of course we do,' answered Tomás, assuaging him.

'Do you give me your word before God?'

'Yes, I promise,' Tomas lied, reluctantly. He could see Damian relax. 'But if we are to do so we must be extremely careful. No one else must know of the book.'

Tomás' mind worked on a plan. Perhaps there was a way to limit the damage. 'Damn,' he cursed.

'What?'

'White Owl.'

'What about him?'

'How are we going to appease him?'

Both stood pensive pondering their dilemma.

'Leave him to me,' said Damian.

'And how do you propose to…'

'I'll seek his counsel. I'll tell him that we were exercising, wrestling. I'll tell him that I lost my temper, and that I attacked you. I'll tell him you tried to stop me.'

'He'll not believe you, he's not that gullible.'

Damian smiled. 'Oh, but he is. I'll tell him how I lost control and attacked you. I'll ask for absolution. Monicurr's weakness – the penitent man. Besides, what choice has he? He needs us to continue working on his manuscript. When he sees us as friends, he will gladly put the incident to bed.'

Tomás could see the wisdom of this plan.

'But there's still the problem of the ripped manuscript,' Damian said, thinking aloud.

'We could pretend it got lost.'

'No, that won't work. White Owl would tear the monastery

apart to find it. And when it didn't show up, everyone would suffer.'

'Especially Cal,' agreed Tomás. 'Perhaps we could redo the page without the Abbot's knowledge. It would take some effort, but so long as Cal did not discover it, we might get away with it.'

They agreed to try.

'Can I read your book now?' asked Damian, making plain his overriding interest.

'Not now. I have to bring it with me when I meet Cado this afternoon. He's taking it away with him to check. Once he brings it back, I shall give it to you.'

Tomás, who had walked to the door, turned back to face Damian. 'I truly am sorry,' he said, knowing that he was, in fact, apologising for what he was about to do, rather than for anything he had done.

CHAPTER 30

IN THE YEAR 838 AD

In the first in a series of vivid dreams he had had, Niclaus watched in horror as ice gave way under Vidar's weight and he fell into dark water. It was so vivid – he could feel the chill, could see light through the ice ceiling, and could almost reach out of the dark recesses into the brighter water, closer to the surface. Niclaus screamed encouragement to Vidar as he fought his way upwards, as he dragged himself out of the water, and as he started to walk. When Vidar fell, Niclaus shouted louder. He whooped and cheered each time the older man forced himself to his feet and restarted walking. It was as if Vidar was responding to him. Where Vidar found the courage or reserves of energy from, Niclaus did not know. He watched terrified as Vidar fell a last time, and cried as he succumbed to the Arctic.

Niclaus had woken, sobbing. He had gone to Eve and told her of his dream. She, in turn, had tried to persuade Vidar not to take the voyage but he would not listen and promised her that he would come back safely.

*

His body clammy, Niclaus twisted and turned. He was having another restless night. In his latest dream, he watched as Jorun and Anders manhandled Vidar to the forecastle. As they jostled him into the forward section a silver locket around Vidar's neck caught on Jorun's belt. The chain snapped and the locket fell. It landed between joints in the floor. Niclaus had seen the locket before. He could not quite place where or when; he just knew he had. It was made of silver and the inscription said 'Father to Every Child'.

'Come on, you two, wake up. Your beds are needed,' said Gilder.

'What's up?' asked Orrin.

It took Niclaus a moment to waken. He recalled the dream; he was certain it had been important.

'There's been an accident. Vidar's been injured.'

'What happened? Is he all right?' asked a startled Niclaus.

'He's in a bad way; he was found frozen in the ice.'

The colour drained from Niclaus' face. He did not dare tell his father of his dreams.

'Elwin has asked if the girls can stay here while she attends to Vidar. That means you two lose your beds. The girls will be sleeping here,' said Gilder.

'No, that's fine,' said Orrin. 'We'll be happy to sleep in the barn.'

Once out of the house, Niclaus steered Orrin towards the shore.

'It's late,' moaned Orrin, 'Where are you taking me?'

'To Morton's boat.'

'What for? Can't it wait until morning?'

'No, we need to find something.'

'What's so urgent that it can't wait?'

'You'll see,' said Niclaus, as he broke into a run.

'Arne won't let you on his boat, you know – not until morning,' Orrin called after him.

Arne was the only member of the crew still on board – all the others were staying on the land, with family or in the main barn.

'Can we come aboard?' called Niclaus, announcing their arrival.

'So, it's you pair that scare an old sailor witless? It's late. You two should be in bed,' said a blurry-eyed Arne, as he struggled with his breeches.

'We haven't got one,' explained Orrin. 'Vidar's been taken to Elwin's house and the girls have been moved to our beds.'

'So you're homeless, are you?'

'We were kind of hoping you'd let us stay on board,' said Niclaus.

'Well not tonight. We haven't unloaded. You can come back and help me in the morning if you like.'

'We'll be here first thing,' agreed Orrin.

Not prepared to wait, Niclaus jumped on to the boat. 'I just want to check were Vidar was lying, I think he dropped something.'

'You can look if you like,' said Arne. 'What is it you think he might have lost?'

'It's a silver locket, his lucky charm.'

'Then find it, young man. He needs all the help he can get.'

Niclaus scurried down the hatch into the forward section of the hull. The light was poor. He used his hands to feel around, tracing his fingers along the grooves in the wood, desperate to find the locket.

Above, Arne lit an oil lamp and gave it to Orrin.

'If there's something down there that you think can help Vidar, you better find it. But don't set fire to my boat, nor tell anyone I let you on board with a torch,' he said, with a wink.

The boards creaked as Orrin jumped from the deck, landing next to Niclaus. 'How do you know there's something here?' he asked.

'Before he sailed, Vidar told me he dropped a lucky charm here. He said his fingers were too big to reach it, and asked me to get it for him at the next chance I got.'

Arne looked at him with suspicion. He began to speak, 'But the ...' He stopped himself. 'It's late. Hurry up.'

Standing over Niclaus, Orrin caught a glint of metal as it reflected the lamplight.

'To your left, at the very edge,' said Orrin, guiding Niclaus to the spot. Niclaus found the locket between two panels. His heart fluttered. Could it be as he had dreamed? The thought was unnerving.

He pried it loose. It was damaged and dented but he could still make out the impression of a heavyset man carrying a sack over his shoulder. Turning the locket over, he could see an inscription, but the light was poor and he could not read it.

Niclaus spat on it and rubbed it clean. 'Shine the light over here – I want to read the inscription.'

It read, as he knew it would, 'Father to Every Child'.

'Well, is it his?' enquired Arne from above.

'Yes, no doubt about it.'

'Well then, what you waiting for? Vidar'll need that, won't he?'

The boys were off as swiftly as hares.

CHAPTER 31

IN THE YEAR 838 AD

Downcast, Niclaus made his way to the shore to say farewell to Morton and his crew. They had stayed in Folda too long, waiting for a miraculous recovery from Vidar that failed to materialise. As usual, a good crowd gathered to see the *Ice Maiden* off. To Niclaus, their sailing confirmed his worst fear. They were giving up on Vidar.

Arne stepped off the boat and walked over to him. 'Are you all right?' he asked.

Niclaus smiled back, 'Just sorry to see you all go. Sort of hoped that Vidar would be well before you left.'

'Well, at least you found his lucky charm.'

'Some good that turned out to be. I thought putting it around his neck would somehow cure him. How stupid am I?'

'You know, I always meant to ask you about that night.'

'What?' said Niclaus, caught unaware.

'How did you know the charm was on the boat? Vidar always wore that locket around his neck for good luck. I remember seeing him kiss it before he set off. Now, that being the case, there's no way you could have known the locket was in the hull. Is there something you want to tell me?'

'You'll not believe me.'

'Try me.'

Niclaus remained silent, not knowing how to begin. 'I had a dream, I, I …' he stammered.

'Go on, boy.'

'I had a dream of a holy man dressed in a brown hooded robe that was tied with a cord rope, and a little man, dressed in grey, with friendly eyes. I can hear the little man's voice in my head: he said, "Tomás, I want you to take this and wear it always." '

Arne stood, mouth open. Niclaus could tell by the reaction that his words were registering, that Arne believed him.

'And how did you know the charm was in the hull?'

'In another dream, I saw Vidar being carried to the ship and then to the forward hatch. The locket got caught and fell where I found it.'

Arne called the captain.

Morton, in his woollen tunic, looked more intimidating than usual as he towered over Niclaus.

'Speak, boy. What is it you want to tell me?'

Niclaus repeated what he had told Arne.

'Is there anything else you remember?'

'No.'

'Are you sure? It's important.'

'Absolutely.'

'What of this little man and the holy man, who are they?' Niclaus asked.

Morton sighed, 'The little man is called Cado. He's … well he's complicated. I don't think it'll be too long before you meet him.'

'And Tomás?' asked Niclaus, recalling the name.

'Ah, Brother Tomás, now he's not so complicated. He's a monk from Ceanannus Mór, on the island of Erin. It's his charm that Vidar wears and that you found. I really don't know how much I am allowed to tell you but ...'

'If it concerns me, I think I have a right to know.'

'Aye, lad, I reckon you do.'

Morton told Niclaus of Cado, of the strange little man who had paid handsomely for many voyages, and of Vidar's quest.

'What is it that Vidar searches for?' asked Niclaus.

'I don't know, he's never told me. Look, my next trip takes me to Erin. I'll see Cado there. When I do, I'll seek his counsel. And I'll speak to Tomás,' Morton paused, 'see what he can tell us about this locket.'

*

Niclaus continued to deputise for Vidar, carrying out his duties without a word of complaint. Orrin had offered to help but Niclaus declined.

It was a fresh morning as Trost pulled the empty cart to the nearby forest. Another day chopping wood lay ahead and it would be sunset before they got home. Not that Niclaus minded. He enjoyed being with Eve and the satisfaction that came with finishing each hard day's work.

Three weeks had passed since the *Ice Maiden* had sailed and it would be several more before she made it back to Folda. Niclaus had grown over the summer months, another spurt towards adulthood. Gilder had told him that he would not grow much more; he was already slightly taller than his father was and stood half a head above Orrin, who, he believed, had some stretch left. Niclaus had also broadened out although he was still thinner than Gilder. He felt the evidence of his physical maturity in his work; his axe cut deeper and he was able to get through a heavier toil.

Working in the forest was all about economy, getting the maximum yield for the minimum amount of effort. Niclaus swung his axe into a stump. It buried deep. Turning the axe in his hand, his next stroke brought the the axe head crashing onto the bough of the felled tree, causing the block to split in two. Niclaus bent to readjust the trunk.

As he worked, he thought of the locket. Why had he dreamt of it? There had to be something about it. 'Eve, the locket we put on Vidar. When we get back, will you bring it to me?' he asked.

'Why?'

'There's something about it.'

'There's not, Niclaus. We've checked it already.'

Both stopped.

'Did you hear something?'

Eve nodded.

Again, they heard it, only clearer.

'Niclaus. Eve. Where are you?' It was Orrin.

'Over here,' called Niclaus. 'What do you want?'

'Come quick. You have to get home. It's Vidar.'

Eve blanched as tears came to her eyes.

Orrin broke from the undergrowth, Helga by his side. The sight of Helga was too much.

'Elwin sent me to …' said Helga.

'Spit it out,' Niclaus said, cutting her mid-sentence.

'He's awake,' she exclaimed, beaming with delight. 'I've been sent to get you.'

Eve broke down, relief etched across her face.

'Come on, what are you waiting for? He's asking for you,' said Helga.

'What, he's talking already? Have you seen him?' Eve asked, excitedly.

'Yes, he's sitting up. Dylla's on his lap.'

'And he's fine, I mean he's …?'

'Yes, he's sitting up, talking. He was eating when I left.'

'I'll help Niclaus finish up here and be back soon.'

'Don't be silly, I can finish off here,' said Niclaus. 'I'll hitch Trost and see you back at the house. Go on, get going.'

CHAPTER 32

IN THE YEAR 802 AD

Monicurr usually only officiated at the more significant occasions in the church's calendar, but today – just an ordinary day – he stood before his congregation. Tomás had long ago realised that, when necessary, White Owl used the homily to guide those whom he believed were in need of spiritual direction. Today was one of those days. He delivered his sermon with life and warmth, convincing his listeners of his point of view.

The abbot stood to the side of the lectern. Tomás could feel his stare. It was clear who the sermon was aimed at.

'"… *aleph beatus vir qui timet Dominum beth in mandatis eius volet nimis*," said Monicurr, quoting scripture to support his message.

'What did he say?' Brother Anton asked Damian.

Rheumy Anton was old and his health poor, he barely heard the abbot. Even if he had, he would still have been at a loss. It was common knowledge that Anton had made no effort to learn Latin and knew only the words of the services.

'Blessed is the man that feareth the Lord: he shall delight exceedingly in his commandments,' translated Damian.

Monicurr continued his address, quoting more scripture,

'... but if one strike thee on thy right cheek, turn to him also the other.'

Tomás was struggling with his conscience, not comfortable about what he was going to do.

'*Dóminus vobíscum*,' said Monicurr

'*Et cum spíritu tuo*,' muffled the congregation.

'*Benedicámus Dómino*.'

'*Deo grátias*,' responded the worshippers.

Monicurr kissed the altar, raised his eyes to heaven, and brought his arms in a wide arc to join hands above his head.

'*Benedícat vos omnípotens Deus Pater, et Fílius et Spíritus sanctus*,' he said, blessing the monks.

'Amen,' they replied.

The service complete, Tomás knelt in reverence at the altar before heading towards the chancel.

'Where are you going?' whispered Damian.

'I'm going to see Monicurr. Wish me luck.'

'Good luck.'

'Now, off to the tannery. I promised Vincent that you would help him,' whispered Tomás, raising his eyes, feigning despair.

'Do I have to?'

'Yes.'

Brother Gerard, who normally cut the sheets for the manuscripts, was not well and had delegated his duty to his understudy. Vincent's first attempt had ended with the parchment being thin and translucent in parts and Cal had berated the novice. Tomás had explained to him that it had been unfair since this was a recurring problem, which was more to do with imperfections in the calfskin. The novice's confidence knocked, Tomás had promised to have Damian help him with his latest efforts, Damian having carried out the process many times.

Tomás crossed the altar towards the sacristy, very much regretting what he was about to do. 'O God, be merciful to me a sinner,' he prayed.

He inhaled deeply, knocked gently on the door and slipped into the sacristy.

Monicurr was engaged in quiet prayer.

'Excuse me, Father; I have a most pressing matter.'

'Now, Tomás, what is so urgent as to break my devotion?'

'I need your guidance.'

He hoped to lure the abbot into a paternal mode, a role in which he revelled.

'Come, walk with me,' said Monicurr, leading Tomás over the chancel, along the aisle and out of the chapel. They continued walking, passing the monastery's large vegetable patch.

'Your actions of late have troubled me greatly,' said White Owl.

A few of the monks, busy attending to their vegetables, bowed reverently to their abbot as he passed.

'I wish to explain myself and hope you will forgive me,' Tomás replied, remorsefully. 'I was unable to speak truthfully in front of Damian. I ask for your patience as I relate the circumstances that resulted in my disagreement with him. I am only speaking out of my great respect for you. Damian is very troubled. I think that it might be good for him to get away from here. Perhaps he needs to go back to a more familiar setting, like Iona. There, surrounded by old friends, he could recuperate. Then, when he is feeling himself, you could allow him to return and take up his position.'

'Tell me, what is wrong with Damian?'

Tomás began. 'He hasn't been himself lately. He has been questioning himself, even questioning his belief in God. His work has suffered.'

'What do you mean? I find this hard to believe. Only recently Cal told me how exquisite his latest illustrations have been.'

Tomás dropped his head. 'If you speak to Cal, he can confirm it all. He has heard Damian's talk. I am tired of trying to cover for him. Some days, he's like his normal self – he works hard and seems contented, like the Damian of old, and then other days, he seems confused. He does not remember conversations or worse, he makes things up. Lately, he claims he does not want to be a monk any more, says that he does not want to rot away in the scriptorium. I have tried to reason with him. I have asked him to pray with me, but he refuses. I offered to speak to you for him. He just laughed in my face. I should have come to you sooner. If I had known that he was capable of making deliberate mistakes and causing damage to the book, I would have told you immediately.'

The abbot's face whitened. 'What damage?'

'I was reflecting on our achievements and admiring the beauty of our work when, to my horror, I noticed the mistake. I had duplicated a section of text. I told Damian straight away. Imagine my dismay when he boasted that it was all his doing. He had turned the pages that I was copying deliberately. He thought it funny.'

'Surely Brother Cal would have noticed?'

Tomás shook his head.

'I need to see this,' said Monicurr, almost breaking into a sprint as he covered the ground to the scriptorium. Tomás followed. Inside, they marched up the spiral staircase between the altar and the sacristy. Once inside, he opened the book and hastily found the passage. 'If it was only one error, I'm sure you could have forgiven him,' said Tomás.

'There's more?'

Tomás slid the ruined vellum from under the cupboard and handed it to Monicurr.

'No,' Monicurr mumbled, appalled. Only recently, he had voiced his admiration of the picture. He sat down and rubbed at his temples.

'I confronted him in the scriptorium about the duplicated text. I told him that we had to inform you, that you would forgive him. Again, he laughed in my face, telling me that you were an old fool.'

Tomás was choosing his words carefully. 'Damian screeched at me, told me to mind my own business. He was ranting. Said he did not give a damn about the Holy Book. Then, in a fit of temper, he grabbed the cow horn filled with ink and poured it over the illustration. I tried to stop him, but before I could, he ripped the vellum in half.'

Monicurr clearly believed every word as Tomás built his story to a crescendo. 'I told Damian that I would speak to you, that we would sort it out together, and that everything would be fine. Father, I did not realise how sick Damian was. As I was leaving, he lunged at me, striking with the nearest thing that came to hand. The metal rod missed me by a hair's length. Father, I am mortified for fighting back but he was like a wild beast. Please forgive me?'

Monicurr swallowed the tale whole, not once doubting Tomás' integrity.

Tomás' ruse was working exactly as planned. Monicurr's concern for the manuscript far outweighed his interest in the brothers' fight.

'I need to contemplate what course of action to follow. We shall speak again later,' said Monicurr.

Tomás walked to the door of the scriptorium, not at all proud of himself.

'Tomás?'

'Yes, Father,' he replied, nervously facing the abbot.

'Thank you for confiding in me. I can only imagine how painful this must have been for you. This conversation will remain private.'

Making his way to the chapel, Tomás knelt before the statue of his Lord Jesus and prayed. He asked God to forgive him his transgression. He felt totally torn. He was putting all his trust in Cado. If the faith he placed in Cado was unfounded, Tomás would have a lot of explaining to do. And yet, even allowing for what he had done, in his heart he knew that his actions had been right. He was prepared to help Cado write the book of Newgrange if, most importantly, it helped lead him and his people to the Lord.

*

Abbot Monicurr had slept little as he deliberated his course of action. Repairing the duplicated section of the book would be time-consuming, but this error paled into insignificance when he compared it to the matter of the ripped illustration. The page was irreplaceable. And then there was Damian, who was clearly troubled. How could he help him? Sitting at his carrel and looking for inspiration, he casually opened the Bible in front of him. He read the passage.

'Nor shall he return any more into his house, neither shall his place know him any more.'

Monicurr saw the verse as a sign. The Lord had shown him the way.

Not one to procrastinate, he called his trusted deputy, Prior Cinead. Upon his arrival, Monicurr conveyed his instructions without giving the reason for his decision. He had decided to send Damian to Iona. He could recuperate there.

*

Cinead did not relish the task assigned to him by Monicurr, but he was powerless to intercede. He would carry out his duty irrespective of how much he did not want to. 'Damian, I have some grave news,' he said. 'The abbot has given me instructions.'

Damian paled.

'You are to leave for Iona immediately.'

'What? Why?'

'Abbot Father did not give a reason.'

'I can say goodbye to my friends?'

'I'm afraid not,' said Cinead, apologetically. 'Brother Colm and

Eoghan are busily preparing. They will escort you to Iona.'

'I will go and pack.'

Cinaed nodded. 'I'll meet you at the gate.'

Gathering his belongings, Damian hurried to look for Tomás, but could not find him. He arrived at the gate to find Cinaed waiting with Colm and Eoghan. Cinaed gave Eoghan a sealed letter addressed to Connachtach, Abbot of Iona.

*

The abbot's mood lightened as Cal and Tomás tried to find a way to mend the duplicated text. In the end, Monicurr made the surprise decision to leave it be for now, realising that it was not as serious as he had first thought. The scribes added red crosses around the text to highlight it – it would be a simple task to repair it after they had completed their work.

On the downside, Ceanannus Mór was now short of two skilled scribes. Connachtach's position remained unfilled and it would take years to train someone to the same high standard as Damian. Monicurr had acted quickly, but even after a period of reflection, he still believed his decision had been the right one. He was just thankful that it had been Damian and not Tomás. Monicurr could never have banished Tomás – he was too skilled a copyist.

'We will manage,' Monicurr said to Tomás as they discussed the layout of the next page.

CHAPTER 33

IN THE YEAR 839 AD

Vidar's recovery was taking longer than he had hoped. Being proudly independent, he struggled with his incapacity. He despaired, doubting that he would ever regain his fitness.

Elwin stood behind Vidar as he wrestled logs into the fire. His pent-up frustration was noticeable as he struggled under the exertion.

'You're doing too much,' she whispered. 'Please, Vidar, take it easy.' She held his cheek in her hand. 'You're getting stronger by the day. Just be patient.'

Vidar smiled as he took his seat by the window. She was right, of course.

Slowly, Vidar's body re-emerged from its long winter sleep, and gradually his energy and stamina grew. He pushed hard to get back to full fitness. By the summer, he had improved, but he was nowhere near ready to undertake his annual trip to Svalbard.

'I think we'll have to call off this year's trek,' he told Morton when the *Ice Maiden* arrived in Folda.

Morton laughed.

'What's so funny?'

'Sure there'll be no trip this summer.'

'And why not?' asked Vidar in annoyance.

'Cado didn't pay for one,' smirked Morton. 'You know him; he'll not pay more than he has to.'

Vidar tried to laugh. The news should have been a relief but in truth, it galled him. Cado should have told him.

He sighed. 'Well, at least I have plenty to do this summer. The old barn is in bad shape. I suppose I'll have to fix it.'

Summer came and went and by the beginning of the autumn Vidar had resumed all of his duties. Vidar and Elwin married the following spring.

*

Vidar's return to health meant that he could once more take on Niclaus' and Orrin's training. 'Come on you two, we have to make up for lost time,' he shouted, as they ran through the forest.

Niclaus lengthened his stride, leaving Orrin and Vidar behind. He felt strong. Last spring he would have been trailing behind Vidar. Even allowing for his illness, Niclaus believed that Vidar could not have kept pace with him. He was reaching his physical peak while Vidar had passed that summit many years before.

'Hurry up, old man,' called Orrin, who had also opened a lead on Vidar.

Vidar trailed into the village quite a while behind the boys. Expecting to see them collapsed in a heap, he instead found them giddy with excitement. 'What's got into you?' he asked, seeing their animated faces.

'Gunnar has just announced it,' said Orrin.

'The Trial – it's to take place before the end of the year,' said Niclaus, ecstatically. 'They are meeting tonight to select the competitors.'

'Tell me something I didn't know,' laughed Vidar.

'What? You knew already?'

'Of course I knew. What do you think us old men talk about when we're not chasing you around the countryside?'

'So, how long have you known?'

'Oh, Gilder mentioned something, back at the …' he paused, 'at the start of last summer.'

'Last summer!' exclaimed both boys.

'And you didn't think to mention it to us,' said Niclaus.

'Oh, it must have slipped my mind.'

The two boys could hardly contain themselves. The process was under way.

*

Unsure of how he would be received, Vidar erred on the side of caution and stayed away from the selection. To many – no matter how fond they had become of him – he would always be an outsider, not welcome at any village meeting. He would wait for the boys to arrive for their morning training. They would tell him all about it then.

*

The wind howled as Gilder, flanked by Olaf and Gunnar joined the men of the village in the main barn. Entering last, they took their places at the table in the centre. All three had completed earlier Trials. Gilder had pipped Olaf at the finish in the last race, and elderly Gunnar had taken part in the one prior to that.

'It seems like only yesterday it was us standing there,' Olaf remarked to Gilder.

'Aye. I thought I wasn't going to be selected. Do you remember they picked me last?'

Olaf rose to his feet. 'Friends, we are here to select the young men who shall compete in the Trial. Selection is in itself an honour. For the winner, the one who raises the red flag, this is not merely a victory. It is much more. It means we are entrusting the future of the village into your hands. The real challenge begins then, when you learn how to be a leader. You know, the last race was very, very close. Gilder beat me by a hand's grasp.' He masked his anger well. 'It broke my heart but it also made me stronger. I was too full of myself. I thought I would make the greatest leader. I was wrong and the Trial produced a deserving successor.' He pointed at Gilder. 'He has proved himself most worthy.'

The hall resounded to applause as Gilder stood to speak. 'It is true that I did sneak the victory that day. There was but a hair's breadth between us. But what that margin taught me was that I was not a leader of the village but an equal among many.'

'We wish,' retorted someone, to everyone's amusement.

'From that day Olaf has stood shoulder to shoulder with me, guiding me, helping me with many of the tough decisions we have had to make, as have you all.'

The crowd murmured knowingly.

Gilder stretched his arm and waved a finger in a circle at the group. 'A leader only gently steers us where we all want to go. I am merely the voice.'

Gunnar stood. 'Now for the best part,' he said to further cheers.

The selection process was straightforward: there were to be five competitors. Niclaus, Orrin, Ludin, and Aslak were considered to be definites. They were lucky enough to be young men who were coming into their prime at the time of the Trial. It was really only the name for the final place that was in question. With Gunnar on the panel, many fancied his son, Thorsfied, to take the last place. The only other possible candidate was Magnus, son of Ragnall. He would have made a worthy opponent to Thorsfied but they were both too young to offer a serious challenge to the older boys.

'Who would like to be first to propose?' asked Gunnar.

Custom dictated that the current leader went first.

Gilder coughed, clearing his throat. 'I was expecting Vidar here tonight. As Niclaus helps him every year, I was hoping he would have offered to select one of my sons. With only one vote, I cannot choose one over another.'

'May I be permitted to speak?' asked Ealver. 'As one of the judges who sentenced Niclaus to his whipping all those years ago, I would like to nominate Niclaus as my way of … well, of showing how much I regret that night and of how proud I am of him. If he didn't mind that is.'

'Well, what do you say, Niclaus?' asked Gunnar.

'I would be honoured.'

Gilder followed, naming Orrin. Olaf and Lars put forward their sons Ludin and Aslak. Gunnar proposed Thorsfied and finally Ragnall put forward his boy Magnus. Six names for five places.

The panel conferred briefly.

Gilder stood. 'It has been agreed that Niclaus, Orrin, Ludin and Aslak shall take part. This leaves one for either ...'

Just as Gilder was about to discuss the last possible contenders, the main door swung open, and in strode Berit, the herder. He stood menacingly at the threshold.

'I hear you are selecting for the Trial,' he said.

'Come on in, don't just stand there,' said Gilder. 'Join us.'

Berit motioned to someone outside.

In stepped Henik, Niclaus' old foe. He was formidable looking, like his father. Niclaus had not seen much of him over the years.

Berit moved to the centre of the room.

'I would like to propose Henik for the Trial.'

Gilder looked to Gunnar for his lead; he would know what custom dictated.

Gunnar spoke directly to Berit. 'Only those living in the village are allowed to raise the flag at the end of the Trial.'

Berit nodded. 'Henik's mother is from here, is she not?'

'Yes, but Henik ...'

'As of today he lives with her.'

'Is this true?' asked Gilder.

Henik nodded.

Olaf's expression mirrored his words. 'Only those invited can compete in the challenge and we have already made ...'

'Are you afraid of Henik?' interrupted Berit.

Gilder stood up, putting a hand on Olaf's broad shoulder. 'We set this Trial to find the best possible leader for the village. Henik is the right age, strong and fit. As this is the case, I believe it is only right that we allow him to enter.'

Acknowledging Thorsfied and Ragnall's disappointment, Gilder explained his decision. 'Boys, I am sorry. Age is against you. Henik is that bit older. Another few years and you would have been selected.'

Likewise, Gunnar reluctantly concurred. 'It's agreed. Henik will take the last place.'

CHAPTER 34

IN THE YEAR 840 AD

Niclaus, rising early, made for the barn where he expected Vidar
to have already started his morning routine. He knew that Vidar
would be delighted for him and Orrin.

'Vidar, it's me,' he called out.

There was no reply. Niclaus decided to muck out until Vidar
arrived. He picked up the pitchfork from where it rested against
a stall. Shortly after, the barn door opened and, catching in a gust
of wind, slammed shut. Again the door opened, and in stepped
Eve.

'Well, were you selected?' she asked.

'Of course I was,' Niclaus grinned.

'And Orrin?'

'Orrin, Ludin, Aslak and ...'

'And who?'

'Guess?'

'It was Thorsfied wasn't it? I knew Gunnar would pick him.'

'No, it wasn't Thorsfied.'

'Magnus then. I'm sure Gunnar's furious.'

'No, it wasn't Magnus either.'

'Then who? Stop teasing me.' She was starting to get annoyed.

'You won't believe it. They chose Henik.'

'Henik. Why him?' she asked. 'He hasn't been in the village for years. Can you beat him?'

Her concern was clear. He loved that her loyalty lay with him. Without realising what he was doing, he stared at her. She caught him and embarrassed, he looked away. He looked back, deliberately not flinching. She held his stare, challenging him. Eve edged closer. He put a hand to her waist and pulled her tight.

'Niclaus, are you there?' shouted Vidar, as he opened the stable door.

Niclaus and Eve jumped apart.

'I was here looking for you,' replied Niclaus.

'Well, how did last night go? I take it you were selected?'

'Of course, he was,' said Eve, as she stormed out, slamming the door on the way.

'What's wrong with Eve?'

'I don't know. She was in good form until you came in.'

Vidar did not look too concerned. 'So you and Orrin were both picked?'

'Yes, that's what I came to talk to you about.'

'What about?' asked Vidar.

Niclaus felt awkward. Looking down at his feet, he blurted out his dilemma. 'With the Trial set for the autumn, I won't be able to carry out your work this summer. I'll need to train. I need to catch up with the others. I've missed out on a lot of practice these past few years.'

'And what of my treks?'

'You didn't go last year. One more postponement won't matter that much,' said Niclaus, sure that Vidar would agree.

'I'm sorry Niclaus but I need you here. I have to make up for last year. I've wasted one year and I can't afford to lose another.'

'But, but I need ... you promised me that you would have me ready.'

'I did, lad, and you shall. I haven't much more to teach you.'

Niclaus felt his temper rise. 'So you expect me to sacrifice my chances of winning the Trial to take on your responsibilities while you run off to some island, looking for who knows what?' Niclaus was shouting now. 'And how have you stuck to our agreement? You haven't. The deal's off. I'll train myself. And you, you can look after your own problems.'

'We have an agreement, you gave your word.'

'Damn your agreement,' said Niclaus.

Throwing down the pitchfork, he marched out of the barn.

*

Eve sat eating her breakfast, thinking of Niclaus who had not come near her since the encounter in the barn. Unaware of his argument with Vidar, she thought that he was avoiding her and could not understand why. He had such an effect on her; he could infuriate her like no other, and yet in a flash could have her laughing heartily. They had been close to kissing, she was sure of it. Perhaps that was it. He was regretting it. Like most girls her age she doubted her own looks and worried that he might find her sister, Fenja, more attractive. Her pride was hurt, he should have had the decency to face her and tell her. She deserved at least that. To Eve, at an age where any minor hiccup was a catastrophe, the falling out was absolute. There was no way she would make up with him, not now. She tried to convince herself that she did not like him, pretended that she hated him. What could she do? What would she do? Nothing, she thought, resignedly. If Niclaus did not want to see her, she would not lower herself to chase after him.

She sensed a bit of an atmosphere between her mother and Vidar. 'What's wrong?' she whispered.

'It's nothing,' answered Elwin.

Her mother was not a good liar. Eve gave her a look that asked for a truthful answer.

'I'm just not happy with him going off on his trek.'

The news of Vidar's intended trek should not have been the surprise that Eve found it to be. The telltale signs had been there for all to see. Eve had believed that it would be next spring at the earliest before he would have been ready to go again. 'Are you really going?' she asked, her anger growing.

'He's leaving at the end of the week,' confirmed Elwin.

Vidar ran his spoon around his bowl scraping up the last of his oats. 'I have to go. I made a promise. I have to keep it.'

Eve unleashed a tirade. 'You made a promise to me. You promised you'd come home.'

'And I did.'

'Through good fortune, you were lucky. You were finished when they found you,' Eve said, her words cutting in their truthfulness.

He gave no reply. He did not have one.

Vidar stood up from the table.

Eve, with anger in her heart and a spitting tongue, was not prepared to let him off lightly. 'So you really are going to go?'

'A man is only as ...'

'Damn you.'

'Eve, that's enough,' interrupted Elwin.

Eve did not have to say any more, she had made her point. She grabbed a shawl and rushed out into the wet day. In hindsight, she should have cooled off but tearful and emotional she hurried to find Niclaus.

She passed Orrin, who was carrying a bucket of water towards his house.

'Have you seen Niclaus?' she asked him.

'He's feeding Trovil.'

Eve's step was quick.

'Go easy on him,' Orrin called after her.

Reaching the barn, Eve stormed in.

Niclaus smiled weakly.

It was obvious that she was seething.

'What sort of ...' she began, but Niclaus stopped her mid-sentence, planting a kiss on her lips.

However, with Eve's temper still boiling, she needed to speak. 'Who do ...?'

He kissed her again.

'Why have you been avoiding me?' she sobbed.

Niclaus pulled her close and kissed her a third time. She responded. Tears ran down her face and on to their lips, making their kiss wetter and more passionate, better than Eve could have imagined.

'I wasn't avoiding you. I was avoiding Vidar. We had a fight.'

Eve was relieved. So excited, she did not inquire about the fight. Not only had Niclaus not been avoiding her but also he had kissed her. At last!

'So,' said Niclaus, 'what has got you into such a state?'

'Nothing,' she whispered as she kissed him again. 'I've waited forever and a day for this,' she giggled.

Putting his arms around Eve's waist, he squeezed her as he picked her up. They fell on to the straw and continued kissing.

*

Vidar brooded before deciding to go and speak to Eve. He would calm the waters before he sailed. Walking towards the main body of the village, he met Orrin.

'Have you seen Eve?'

'She went to speak to Niclaus in the barn. I wouldn't want to be him, she looked mightily angry when I saw her.'

Vidar grunted and marched on.

The barn door was open.

The sight that greeted Vidar looked anything but innocent. Eve's skirt had risen to expose a thigh. Moreover, from the angle of approach, Niclaus looked to have his head in her bosom. Vidar exploded. He grabbed Niclaus, pulling him to his feet before backhanding him across the face.

'Stop it,' screamed Eve.

A mist of anger descended on Vidar. All he could see was his son and daughter kissing.

Niclaus tried to reason. 'It's not how …'

Vidar threw a punch which sent Niclaus sprawling to the ground.

Eve jumped between the two. 'Stop it,' she screeched.

Behind, Trovil whinnied, spooked by the disturbance.

Vidar took a step back. He exhaled deeply in an effort to calm himself. He spoke in a low, measured voice. 'You made me a promise. Make sure you keep it. And stay away from my daughter.'

CHAPTER 35

IN THE YEAR 802 AD

'I have something I need to tell you,' said Tomás.

The little man's eyes narrowed. 'What's troubling you?'

Cado and Tomás were sitting in the sun, on the gently sloping hill, where they had first met. Tomás absentmindedly pulled the head off a buttercup, trying to mask his unease. He could feel Cado's stare. Hesitantly, he outlined the events of recent days, explaining how Damian had taken and read the book of Newgrange. He finished by apologising for failing to stop him. He waited anxiously for Cado's reaction.

Cado was silent for what seemed an eternity, thinking deeply before he spoke. 'Why did you feel the need to have Damian removed to Iona?'

'I saw a hunger in Damian. I believed his desires to be selfish, worldly. He wanted the power of Newgrange for himself.' He continued telling his story, telling of his meeting with Monicurr, how he had lied to protect Cado and his people, and how his dishonesty ate at his conscience.

Cado apologised for putting his friend in such a predicament and promised to do all he could to ensure that Tomás never had to do the same again. He also warned Tomás about Damian. 'Tomás, you have made an enemy, one who may someday seek his revenge. Be wary of Damian. I fear his blackened heart. He will fester in that faraway place until he snaps. Guard against him well.'

Although Tomás knew not to doubt Cado or his words, he refused to believe that Damian would not find the right path. No, Tomás would not give up on Damian. He would mellow.

'I am truly sorry. You have lost a friend on my account.'

'No, Cado, Damian shall always be my friend.'

'Perhaps,' sighed Cado. 'Tomás, you may cherish him as a friend but soon Damian will become unrecognisable to you.'

'Shall we write for a while?' suggested Tomás, changing the subject.

The two were soon engrossed in their work.

'At least we won't have to worry about Damian spying on us. We'll maybe get more of our own project done,' said Cado.

Tomás explained his predicament. 'With Damian gone, I will have to double my workload on the manuscript. I doubt I'll have anywhere near as much time.'

Cado looked pensive.

'Don't worry, I'll find a way,' said Tomás.

'Tomás, we have to get as much done as possible. I have not got long.'

'What do you mean?'

'I am needed elsewhere. I shall be leaving soon and we will not get a chance to work on our book for a while.'

'What? Where are you going?'

'I have a sailing to undertake. If it's successful, it will be a rewarding venture. I will tell you about it upon my return.'

'When are you leaving?'

'Within a few days. Events are unfolding quicker than I envisaged. I told you before of the division within my village, and of my adversary, Bram. I fear he is more powerful than I first imagined. He will stop at nothing until he destroys our way of life.'

'I don't follow. How can one man do so much?'

'By breeding mistrust and scaremongering. Do you remember the Orb I spoke of?'

'Yes.'

'Well, Bram believes that if he can possess the Orb, he can use its power against you and your people. You remember the dust I showed you?'

'Yes.'

'Well, the Orb creates the dust.'

Tomás was confused. 'Why would he use it against us?'

'You need to understand that many in Newgrange still harbour ill feeling towards your kind. In the past, my people suffered great persecution from tall walkers. This was the reason why we chose to live in isolation. It would not take much to inflame old hatred. If Bram can create an atmosphere of fear, and make people believe that Newgrange is under threat from tall walkers, then he can persuade a majority to follow him. If he is successful, I will be powerless to stop him. As leader of Newgrange, he will be free to use the power of the Orb as he wishes.'

'And how will he create such an atmosphere?'

'I fear he is already gathering outsiders to do his bidding.

Somehow, I have to find a way to stop him.'

Cado sighed as he stood. 'Tomás, the burden I spoke of will soon come to visit us.'

Tomás got to his feet. 'Do not fret, when the time comes, we will face it together. Now,' he said, trying to lighten the mood, 'how long will you be away?'

'Not too long, three weeks at most. I only hope you will be glad to see me on my return.'

Tomás' spirits rose with Cado's reassurance that they would meet again soon.

'I have something for you,' said Cado, taking a piece of jewellery, a silver locket, from his pocket. The front depicted a heavyset man carrying a sack over his shoulder. On the back was the inscription 'Father to Every Child'.

'Thank you, but I cannot take this. I am sworn to a life of poverty.'

Cado smiled. 'It is not a gift, as it is not mine to give. I ask that you keep it safe until the rightful owner claims it.'

Cado placed it in Tomás' hand and wrapped his fingers around it.

'I will guard it well,' said Tomás, putting it on.

'Don't open the locket, but always keep it close,' said Cado.

CHAPTER 36

IN THE YEAR 840 AD

Vidar, much to their annoyance, had volunteered Niclaus and Orrin to break up the sods of the recently ploughed land. To make matters worse, he had excused all the other young men from the arduous task, explaining that it was another training exercise.

'I'm not doing this,' said Niclaus, who, excluding training, had still not spoken to Vidar. 'It's not fair.'

'Stop complaining and get on with it.'

'I'm going to see Father.'

Orrin laughed. 'What good will that do? I can't see him overruling Vidar.'

From early afternoon, the two spaded the soil, breaking up the mounds of earth along the deep rutted lines. They worked in silence.

Orrin had found the best way to get the job done was by gritting his teeth and getting on with it. It was slow and laborious and seemed to take forever but, with a dogged determination, the two slowly broke the back of the work.

'Can't blame him really, can you?' said Orrin.

Niclaus did not answer.

'Can you imagine what you'd have done if you'd caught someone like me, in the barn with your daughter?'

Deliberately pitched, the question was a subtle attempt to soften Niclaus' anger. If he could get Niclaus to view the incident from Vidar's perspective, then perhaps the pair of them could find a way to settle their differences.

Niclaus' face broke into a huge smile.

'I'd kill you,' he said, grabbing a handful of soil and throwing it at Orrin.

Twisting and ducking, Orrin avoided the first clod. However, the second caught him in the small of his back. It hurt. Orrin yelled as he delivered two well-placed shots of his own. Both landed, one square on Niclaus' chest, the second right in the mouth.

The brothers laughed. Niclaus spat out the soil.

'Truce, truce, I call truce,' declared Orrin.

'All right,' agreed Niclaus. 'But I owe you.'

They lifted their spades and resumed working in a now companionable silence.

Orrin, a few paces in front with his back to Niclaus, eventually spoke. 'Well, the way I see it, the only thing Vidar did wrong was not to hit you hard enough.'

'The way you see it,' repeated Niclaus as he bent and grabbed another clod and tossed it, thwacking the unsuspecting Orrin on the back of the head. 'Well, the way I see it, we're even,' he smirked.

Orrin rubbed his head. 'I suppose I deserved that. Look, Niclaus, Vidar sails tomorrow, if you don't make peace with him I'll have to do his work and I don't want that.'

'That's not such a bad idea,' said Niclaus.

'And where would that leave you? It won't be good if you and he haven't patched things up.'

'It's up to him, he owes me an apology.'

'And have you considered Eve? If Vidar leaves and you two aren't talking, it'll kill her. What if something happens to Vidar when he's gone?'

Orrin let the question hang, allowing Niclaus to mull it over as they continued their toil.

'I probably would have done the same thing,' agreed Niclaus, after a time.

Orrin knew not to reply.

'Damn you.'

'Me, what have I done?' replied Orrin, a look of wounded indignation on his face.

Orrin's gentle persuasion had worked.

*

Standing at the water's edge, a tearful Elwin gripped Vidar tightly, pulling at his tunic. 'Vidar, don't take any chances like the last time. Find whatever it is that you are looking for, for I can't stand this anymore.'

Vidar wanted nothing more. He squeezed her tight and kissed her. Then he scooped Helga and little Dylla. He kissed them both and they recoiled trying to avoid his scraggly beard.

'Will you bring me another present?' Dylla asked.

'I'm afraid not, there's not much of anything where I'm going this time.'

'Then why are you going?' Dylla asked, simply.

Vidar laughed.

'May God keep you close,' Fenja whispered, kissing him on the cheek. It was a saying he himself often used.

Vidar looked at Eve. Although they were talking, they still had not made peace since the incident in the barn. To his surprise, she hugged him. 'Come home to us,' she sobbed.

He swallowed hard. 'I will,' he said. He began to board, then paused. He faced Eve and whispered in her ear. 'I'm sorry. I shouldn't have behaved so rashly in the barn.'

'Thank you,' she replied.

Gilder, along with Selina, Orrin and a few of the villagers had gathered to wave the boat off.

Gilder patted Vidar on the back. 'Like a bad smell, you'll be back before we've missed you,' he joked.

'Keep your training up,' Vidar said to Orrin.

'Of course I shall.'

'And Niclaus?' Not a word had passed between them since they argued and the thought of leaving without being reconciled pained him.

'Why don't you speak to him yourself, he's on board talking to Arne.'

'Aye,' said Vidar, surprised. 'I suppose I will. I should have done so before now.'

'I think he's waiting for you.'

Niclaus came into view, somewhat to the surprise of Eve who was watching by the water's edge.

'I came to tell you that I will act for you when you are gone,' said Niclaus.

'I knew you'd keep your word,' Vidar hesitated. 'Niclaus, I am sorry.'

'No,' said Niclaus. 'It is I who should apologise. A father shouldn't see his daughter in that kind of situation.' He continued his rehearsed words. 'It was very innocent. It was actually our first kiss.'

Vidar grunted.

'She means a lot to me,' Niclaus explained.

Vidar sighed, uncomfortable with the subject. Yet, he was not so old that he could not remember his first tryst with Fiona in Magority. Was it so long ago? It felt like only yesterday. 'It'll take a lot of getting used to.'

Niclaus offered Vidar his hand. 'Good journey to you.' he said, with a firm grip.

'Thank you,' replied Vidar.

'Off my boat, Niclaus, or I'll take you with me,' shouted Morton.

'Wait, one last thing,' said Vidar.

'Yes?'

'Take this,' he said, as he unclasped the locket from around his neck.

'No, you don't have to.'

'Consider it as my apology. It's yours,' he said, handing it over.

Niclaus eyed the inscription, 'Father to Every Child'.

'What does it mean?' he asked, curiously. He had meant to ask Vidar about the locket when his health improved but had forgotten all about it. He still had not spoken to Vidar of his dreams.

'I was hoping you'd tell me,' said Vidar.

'It's yours by right,' said Morton, joining the conversation. 'I meant to tell you. Cado says it belongs to you. And the dream was just a way to let you know.'

Niclaus looked confused.

Vidar laughed. 'I was giving him a present and you go and spoil it. It seems I was only minding the locket for you.'

'Just passing on a message,' puffed Morton, as Niclaus got off the boat.

'And so my boy wakes from his slumber,' Vidar whispered under his breath as the *Ice Maiden* pulled away from the shore.

CHAPTER 37

IN THE YEAR 840 AD

Morton rolled out the old parchment, its edges frayed and its vellum cracked. Upon it, built up painstakingly over many years, was a map of the island, the ink lines outlining each previous journey. He could no longer differentiate between the points where one voyage ended and another began; his eyes could barely bring the folio into focus.

In truth, Morton felt as old and worn out as the page itself. He rubbed his tired eyes with the palms of his hands. Yes, Cado had promised to negotiate further sailings for the *Ice Maiden*, but Morton felt he was getting too old. He had made up his mind. This would be his last sailing to the frozen north. After that, one more trip to Erin would release him of his undertaking, and he planned to retire to Folda. He hoped to persuade Rune and Torre to join him. They would keep him company and help make life on land bearable. The plan was straightforward: to sell his vessel and trading routes to Jorun, who was young and ambitious and who would make a fine captain. He and Morton would come to a financial arrangement. Jorun would not be able to raise enough money to pay Morton outright, and so would agree to a slightly inflated price. Then he would be obliged to work off the debt. Jorun was honest and of sound character and Morton had every faith in him honouring the agreement.

Feeling stiff, Morton stretched. The tension mirrored the apprehension he felt about the final voyage to Svalbard. He had good reason to feel nervous because Cado had confided to him that he was uncertain about the outcome of the journey. Cado would never send Vidar to his death, Morton repeated to himself, trying to banish his concerns. Still, worry gnawed at him. When Vidar had gone missing on his last trek, he had taken solace from the knowledge that Cado had paid for one final trip. He had no such safety net now.

Vidar placed his knife on the parchment to keep it from curling. 'What sort of map maker do you call yourself?' he teased, pointing to the parts of the map he had covered on his previous trek.

'Fix it then, boy,' Morton said, irritably, as Vidar drew an inlet, reshaping the lie of the land yet again.

'It fooled you because it's always frozen.'

Vidar placed a finger on the map, 'It was about here that I fell through the ice.'

Morton was surprised. The distance Vidar had covered on his last trek was much greater than he had believed. 'We should have left you,' he grumbled.

Vidar slapped the captain on the back. 'And I'm grateful you didn't. Here's where I need to get to,' he said, indicating the most northerly area.

Vidar's latest editing had cut a chunk off Morton's original sketch, dissecting the northern section into an island. Over the years, Vidar had altered the map to include inlets, coves and many smaller isles that littered the coast. In truth, it was now a much more accurate representation of the archipelago.

Morton sighed his disapproval: the further north, the greater the exposure to the ice. 'I'll take you as far round the top of the island as I can. Mind you, I can't guarantee how far that will be,' he said. 'We passed the Rock early this morning while you were sleeping.'

Rock Island, situated halfway between the mainland and Svalbard, gave Morton an indication of the conditions that lay ahead.

'And what's wrong with that?'

'A freezing mist hung over her. I am afraid Svalbard may be still frozen. If she is, then this year's trek could be a lost cause already.'

'Don't fret, Morton. I have a good feeling about this one.'

'I wish I shared your optimism.'

'Then do, for I know where I'm going and I'm well prepared.'

Morton's frown eased. 'I hope so, lad.'

*

Morton had been first to spot the signs of the brewing storm. 'Furl the sail,' he commanded. 'Drop the mast. It's going to be a bad one.'

Vidar watched the crew loosen the mast from the keel as the storm threw wind, rain, and sea over the ship's bow.

'Come on, give me a hand,' Rune called to Vidar. 'Help me tie the mast to the deck.'

'Make it doubly tight,' called Morton. 'We lose her and it'll be a long row to land.'

Monstrous waves threatened to swamp the boat. So ferocious was the squall that the crew members tied themselves to the hull. The *Ice Maiden* rode high on mountainous waves only to plummet violently as though falling off cliffs of water. Vidar feared the vessel would be lost, and the sight of Rune clutching a Norse amulet around his neck and praying to Njord the god of the sea did little to allay his fears, especially as Rune had converted to Christianity years before.

Eventually the storm passed, the waters calmed and the sky cleared from the south. To Vidar the experience had been one of the most frightening of his life. He smiled as he remembered Morton at the height of it. He had stridden across the deck, the only man not to tie himself to the boat, bellowing orders as he went. He had looked indestructible.

On the positive side, the storm carried the boat in a north-easterly direction, meaning that the *Ice Maiden* was well ahead of schedule when she reached icy water. No matter how often Vidar had travelled north, the beautiful landscape always left him breathless. He found the contrast of the white sculptures against the black water mesmerising. Below the waterline, the ice fused with the water to turn the bases a majestic jade colour.

Soon a jigsaw of jagged ice replaced the translucent water.

As they neared the island, the ice thickened on either side, leaving a narrow canal of clear water, kept free by a warmer undercurrent. To either side the ice rose up to dwarf the *Ice Maiden*, casting long shadows over the boat. Off the port bow, a huge berg creaked and shattered. A large section calved into the water causing a wave that flooded the deck. Jorun, although soaked, laughed with relief as the water settled.

The Devil's Graveyard, as Rune had named the stretch, was always treacherous and Morton made sure his crew remained vigilant as they crawled through it. It remained constant in width allowing the boat to reach Svalbard's southern tip. Morton could not disguise his relief when he saw the southern parts of the island in the early stage of summer. Likewise, Vidar could not hide his delight as Morton pushed the *Ice Maiden* further north along the island's west coast.

Morton continued to shout out instructions to his men, keeping them alert as they went.

They cleared the head of the island and sailed around glacier tongues that thrust out of folds in the coastline. They passed animals and seabirds too numerous to name.

Morton, more adventurous than normal and determined to give Vidar as much of an advantage as possible, sailed the *Ice Maiden* around the top of the island before navigating a south-easterly channel between the isles.

'Drop the anchor,' Morton ordered.

'It looks like you've got me to the very spot I pointed to on the map,' said Vidar.

To the stern, a seal popped its head out of a small blow hole. It looked inquisitively at the interlopers before slipping back into the water to the safety below.

The inlet was ice-free. They landed and set up camp. Two reindeer caught Morton's eye.

The reindeer did not seem bothered by their intrusion. Curious, they walked towards the party, searching for food. Lichen, their main source, was plentiful but the camp offered new aromas.

Morton approached the beasts. 'They look funny.'

Anders agreed. 'Their legs are small and too muscular. Back home, they wouldn't let mongrels like these into the main herd. They would weaken the bloodline.'

Morton reached into a sack, took out an apple and a carrot, and offered them to the nearest animal. Picking up the scent, it strolled over and ate the carrot from his hand. The second, following a step behind, nuzzled in, her dreamy eyes asking the question, where was her food? Morton petted her.

'Easy, lady,' he said, pulling out a few carrots.

Vidar believed that this was his last chance to find the Vestibule. He was getting older, his body was not as strong as it had once been. On the plus side, he had experience of the terrain and his years of failure had made him mentally strong. He had braved the worst conditions and had not been beaten.

He decided to cut down on the provisions he would take. It was a risky decision. If his hunch was wrong, he would be in no position to carry on. Weighing up the pros and cons, he decided to chance the short trek. 'Morton, I'm going to cut my trip.'

Morton gave him a look of bewilderment.

'With you sailing so far inland I believe you have knocked over a week off my search. Add this to the time I'll save on the way back and, by travelling light, I believe I can be back in less than two weeks.'

Morton rolled his eyes. 'And you'd like me to stay?'

'I was hoping … I just thought it might be an idea.'

Vidar knew that Morton would hate the suggestion – the slightest drop in temperature could close the open channel and trap the ship and its crew – but he thought the captain would also see the sense in it.

'I'll wait as best as I can, but at the first sign of any deterioration in the weather, I'm sailing. You'll have to catch me on the far side of the island, where the water's better.'

CHAPTER 38

IN THE YEAR 802 AD

The dragonboats cut through the sea with easy speed, their sleekness allowing them almost to glide on the water. Onward they pushed, carrying their cargoes of fighting men on another raid to strike fear into the White Cross Followers. The marauders, as was their custom, planned to arrive shortly before the rising sun. Hakon believed that this increased the element of surprise and lessened the chances of meeting any organised resistance.

It irked Hakon that the White Cross Followers still inhabited the island they were travelling towards, given that his men had plundered and ransacked it before. Tonight he would see the settlement razed.

Hakon ruled without mercy. Not one voice had dissented against his leadership since his scuffle with Barid. Moreover, that altercation had worked to his advantage, with Barid now standing by his side as comrade, brother and trusted friend. Hakon was not stupid – the inevitable challenge would come, but not in the immediate future.

Hakon's only weakness was that he had not fathered an heir. He believed a son would ensure his legacy.

The island was before him.

Oto stood to his side, sharpening his axe on a whetstone.

Hakon watched the ripples made from his boat as it cut through the freezing waters. Another two dragonboats followed, each one made to the same specification. Built from strong oak planks, each measured eighty steps in length and seven steps in width. Sixteen pairs of oars drove the boat when rowing, and a starboard side rudder rose easily to allow quick beaching. To Hakon, his men were the finest men in the world. Each ship carried seventy men –half were crew and half were warriors – giving him two hundred and ten men at his disposal, a small army.

Standing at the back, Hakon drank up the atmosphere: it was electric. The nearer they came to shore, the more the men's anticipation grew. Some wore smiles, others deep scowls, but Hakon ignored their false faces. He looked into their eyes. He swore he could tell the bravery of a man by his eyes.

Hakon made a point of being first ashore, believing it showed leadership. Barid was always last off, his role to discourage anyone from being less than eager. Barid had pleaded for a position at the front, believing that being at the back made him look cowardly.

'The crew think you're soft, think Bera is telling you what to do,' said Barid, trying to rile Hakon.

Hakon laughed. 'Barid, my decision's final. I need your eyes and ears at the back. Others would shirk the responsibility of weeding out the cowardly. Not you – you are no man to turn a blind eye. That is why I need you.'

Although what he said was true, all the men understood his real reasoning. Hakon did not intend to bring home a dead brother to his wife.

'Furl the sail,' he ordered.

Although the risk was slight, he could not afford to have it damaged by a flaming arrow.

'Banners,' ordered Hakon.

Three large identical banners were unfurled, each displaying a black raven on a red background.

'Remember, leave one alive,' Hakon warned, keen to have one survivor to spread news of the raids.

'Weapons ready,' he shouted, as he jumped on the forward gunnel and stood next to the winged serpent figurehead. 'Untie shields,' he commanded.

Uniformly the men took their shields from the strake.

'Thor's strength,' shouted Barid for good luck, as he handed Hakon his metal-rimmed shield.

Hakon adjusted the shield's straps. Painted blue, it had a large metal boss. 'Let the Valkyrie be asleep,' he shouted, beginning the war cry.

'Maidens of Odin keep your eyes off our battlefield,' responded the warriors, building themselves into frenzy.

'Dead men can't fight,' Hakon roared.

'Keep Valhalla's great doors closed,' they all roared in unison.

Hakon smiled. Although it was a great honour to die in battle, each man had a duty to stay alive. His companions needed him.

Hakon landed in waist-high water and waded. His men followed, careful not to beat him ashore. A path led from the pebbled beach to the settlement. The monastery would offer minor resistance. From experience, Hakon knew that the White

Cross Followers had a soft underbelly. He had disembowelled many.

CHAPTER 39

IN THE YEAR 840 AD

Vidar made a final check, running his hands over the sleigh's runners and frame. It was, as he had learned to his cost, his most vital piece of equipment.

'Are you sure about this?' asked Morton. 'You've taken out most of the wood.'

'With you shortening my journey, I won't need anywhere near as much. I'm going to limit my cooking, not light as many fires.'

'If the weather changes you'll be in trouble. You'll find no wood inland. I'd be happier if you packed extra,' said Morton, handing Vidar a bundle.

'All eventualities,' agreed Vidar.

Morton escorted Vidar out of camp. 'Godspeed.'

His parting words would be the last that Vidar would hear for a time.

He set off purposefully, knowing where he was heading – the Blue Mountains. Setting a gruelling pace, Vidar was keen to make the most of the good weather. Behind, the two friendly reindeer followed – he thought they must have picked up the scent of his food. Vidar soon found himself stripping off a layer of clothes.

It was a tedious but essential task, dressing and undressing, continually adjusting his clothing so that he neither sweated nor froze. The dryness of the air made the temperature much more bearable than the same temperature would have been in Folda.

Having skied for two-thirds of the day, Vidar stopped to set up camp.

Fed, and with his camp established, Vidar collapsed, exhausted, into his tent. It took a few days to acclimatise on each trip.

By the end of the second day, Vidar had covered more ground than he could have imagined. It seemed that his luck, which had deserted him on his last trek, had returned. His body and equipment were holding up well. The weather was fine and he was finding plenty of fresh melt water. But for one deviation – when he'd tried unsuccessfully to take a short cut through a tricky gap – he could not have wished for a better start.

On the third day Vidar came across a jagged landscape, one where the ice had crashed, pushing up miniature ridges that were extremely difficult to pass. The reindeer, losing interest in Vidar, took a different path, leaving him to the solitude of the Arctic. His skis packed away, Vidar fought through the seemingly never-ending rutted land for most of the following day. Dogged persistence drove him over each barrier. Eventually the ridges petered out. He felt his spirits lift. The land in front dropped to reveal the frozen bay, the scene of his fall. Beyond, the cobalt slate ridges towered into the sky, just as he remembered. Sheets of ice ate the land on either side of the mountains.

Vidar crossed the frozen bay. He skied confidently. Although the memory of his last attempt was fresh, he was pragmatic enough to ignore niggling doubts. He told himself that it was early in the season and that the ice was sound. Reaching the far side of the frozen sea, he forced his sleigh over the raised protuberance of brown foam, twisted to ice. Ahead, a group of rocks offered a good place to set up camp. He toyed with the idea of pushing on further, but opted to rest, believing it better to start his climb fresh.

After a long sleep and a hearty meal, he packed a light bag and set off, leaving most of his belongings at the mountain's base. He was confident of finding shelter if he needed to. Liberated from his sleigh, Vidar found the increasing gradient manageable. After five days of walking, skiing, and climbing, he reached the Blue Mountains. He was soon scaling it. Apart from a minor scrape or two, everything was going to plan. Even the sight of bear tracks failed to worry him – he could tell they were old.

Shielding his eyes from the sun's glare, Vidar inspected the final section of the mountain. Cloaked in snow, it was formidable – vertical in parts, with every crack and crevice glued shut with hardened ice, and every overhang protected by glacial stalactites. A swirling wind lifted snow off the summit, carrying it on upward eddies. The fine powder would cover him as he progressed. One indent in the face offered hope: Vidar memorised its position.

The snow crumbled under his feet as he walked to the rock face to begin his ascent. Adjusting his bag on his back, he took a deep breath, and pulled himself over the first large boulder. Advice from his father, given a lifetime ago, filled his head. 'Vidar, it's the quality of the life we lead that is important, not the length of it.'

Perhaps not the most inspiring words. It was peculiar to think of his father now, given that he had not for such a long time. He put it down to nerves – that and the fact that his father had always been there when he needed help.

As the climb increased in severity, Vidar stopped to plot the next stage. He searched for cracks and footholds to exploit. It looked more daunting than he had first reckoned. It would test his skill to the limits.

His senses keenly honed, and moving with a confidence that belied any trace of fear, Vidar continued. Although his hands were cold and his sleeves wet, his strong fingers found nooks in the uncooperative rock and he continued to haul his frame up the face. His feet, working in unison, remained balanced and sure, even on the most precarious surfaces. Vidar felt comfortable, but not enough to be complacent – he was wise enough to know the dangers of over-confidence. He followed one particular cleft in the rock until the point that the crack was filled with ice. Balancing, he rocked forward and back, gaining momentum before he sprang to his right to a narrow ledge. Pivoting on his supporting foot, his weight shifting, he felt his foot lodge. Pulling out of the jump, he clawed at the rock to stop himself, scraping a few knuckles and taking a painful knock to his knee in the process.

He found himself stuck halfway up a rock face, one foot dangling and the other lodged in a cavity, his chin resting on the knee of the trapped leg and his two hands clinging, cat-like, to minute finger holds. Keep calm, he told himself. It could have been a lot worse. He could have broken an ankle or fallen to his death. If he could jump to the ledge as he had originally intended, he could stretch and pull himself to the large fissure above, which looked wide enough to afford him a rest. From there, the climb eased. None of this would be possible without freeing his foot.

Vidar forced his bent knee to straighten, all the while clinging to the rock face. His left leg shook with relief as the right took up the strain. He gulped air and held his breath as another sparging of snow blew into his face.

Gently, he tried to ease his foot loose. It did not budge. He applied extra pressure. There was high probability that the force he would need to dislodge his foot would also carry him off the mountain.

Vidar eased his axe from his belt, intent on loosening the rock and ice around his foot. It was not possible to take a swing, standing as he was. He would have to edge his way back into his original crouching position and then scrape away at the rock.

Vidar was tiring and starting to feel the cold. He scanned the russet land. It was late in the day and the weakening sun hung above, casting shadows over the mountain. It would not be long before his position fell into shade and the temperature plummeted.

He was getting desperate. He had to do something. Not prepared to wait for the inevitable, Vidar dropped his good foot from its perch, his fingers sliding down the rock face. He was back to his original position, with his knee under his chin, but he now had his axe. He was still unable to get a full swing; instead he picked away at the crevice. The rock loosened. Next, he forced his aching left leg to straighten, all the while terrified that the weakened foothold would give way. It held. He forced his foot free.

He let the blood circulate to his leg. Again, he rolled back and forward before springing to the ledge to his right. Vidar hauled himself to the fissure overhead. He had survived.

CHAPTER 40

IN THE YEAR 802 AD

Abbot Connachtach held Monicurr's letter in his hand. Damian was sure it explained the reason for his expulsion. Brother Eoghan, who had escorted him to Iona, had been given the responsibility of delivering the letter. Damian had been back on Iona for nearly a month and the abbot had spoken little to him, but his greetings had been warm.

'Damian, I thought it best to let you reacquaint yourself before we had this talk.'

'Thank you,' he replied, keeping his eyes reverently downward.

There was kindness in Connachtach's tone. 'What happened? You look so despondent.'

'What does Abbot Monicurr's letter say?'

'It's what it doesn't say that bothers me. It offers no insight into the reason behind your transfer.'

Damian breathed a sigh of relief.

'Perhaps you would like to tell me what happened?' The abbot's words were more of a command than a request.

'I accidentally damaged the manuscript.'

Connachtach's dilating eyes belied his outward composure. He waited for Damian to elaborate.

'I damaged an illustration, a picture of the Virgin and Child.'

'Oh, Damian, I'm sure it was an accident.'

'I knocked over an inkwell, ruined the picture. I panicked, tore it up, and tried to hide it. It was stupid of me.'

'Damian, we all make mistakes. I'm sure, given time, Monicurr will forgive you this transgression. His letter states that you have been under a great strain. He asks that we allow you time to recuperate. In the meantime, you could duplicate the damaged picture, working in my library rather than in the scriptorium. Then, when it is completed, we could present it to Monicurr.'

Damian left the abbot's company feeling deflated. He was trapped on Iona and needed to return to Ceanannus Mór and more importantly to Newgrange. He cared not for the religious life that once had been so important to him. All that mattered was gaining possession of the dwarf's book.

*

To an untrained eye his reproduction of the Virgin and Child would have been a masterpiece, of that Damian was certain. It was by no means the equal of the original. Unknown to the ailing abbot, the illustration would not have passed Monicurr or Cal's scrutiny – but then Damian had not meant that it should.

Damian's work lacked conviction and contained deliberate errors. The symmetry of the original piece was lost. Mary sat off centre. One angel was without its ornate fan, another had two left hands while the last two gazed upward rather than at Mother and

Child. As a final insult, Damian had inserted a miniature picture depicting six men at the right-hand side, towards the bottom. All six men turned their back on Christ – like him, they were renouncing the Lord.

Unknown to Connachtach, Damian had been using his time in the library to learn all he could of the stars in the sky. Having read snippets of the book of Newgrange, he knew how important the sky and languages were to the dwarfs – he just did not know why. He also reacquainted himself with Osgar, an elderly missionary, who had travelled widely and could converse in many tongues. Damian became his most conscientious student. He closed the latest volume he had been reading and rubbed at his tired eyes. He would suffer the abbot's wrath. Deliberately missing a service was reprehensible. He did not care. His festering mind could not put into words the desire at his core. It poisoned his very being. All that mattered to him was Newgrange and possession of its mystical power.

The weeks had turned to months and the lack of contact from Ceanannus Mór added weight to Damian's suspicions – he now believed that Tomás had been the instigator of his expulsion. Two monks had been and gone and neither brought any word, and his own letters to Tomás had gone unanswered. He knew that his departure would mean that there was one less scribe working on the book. Monicurr would not have taken the decision to send him away lightly. He could only think that Tomás had concocted some story to get him away and keep the power of Newgrange to himself.

The monks would soon be awake, preparing for the service

that heralded the arrival of a new day. Thankfully, the abbot had not yet come looking for him, but it would be only a matter of time before he did. Damian walked towards his hut. He would regret his late night during morning prayers, if he went at all.

He glanced out to sea and was shocked to see the silhouettes of ships on the horizon. Doubting his eyes, he looked again. He was not mistaken – three raiding ships were closing, carried on the black water. Dragonboats: he recognised them from the descriptions given by older monks.

Damian knew what he should have done. He should have raced to the warning bell in the centre of the monastery's courtyard and sounded it as loudly as he could. Instead, he watched, mesmerised, as the dragonboats neared. Damian thought about the martyrs of Iona. No, he told himself, he was not prepared to add his name to their list, especially now. The prow of the first vessel rose out of the water like the head of a sea serpent. He knew that the raid would mean death for him and the monks. Unless … perhaps there was a way to stop the carnage. Could he possibly use the Norsemen to his advantage? It was worth a try. Besides, he had already made up his mind. He would leave Iona, and more importantly, he would leave the Holy Orders.

Feeling extremely calm, Damian crossed to the church. Opening the tabernacle, he lifted the chalice and poured the blood of the Lord into a metal cup. Next, he lifted the ciborium and emptied the communion out. Replacing the chalice and ciborium, he carried the heavy gold tabernacle down the aisle, under the portico and out beyond the gate of the monastery. Next, he collected two brass candlesticks tinged green with verdigris and a silver crucifix statue from the altar and placed them next to the tabernacle. Finally, he went to the abbot's library. All the monks knew that Connachtach had a hoard of gold and silver. Whilst using the abbot's private library Damian had stumbled upon the cache. It was too noticeable to miss, sticking out as clearly as a lighted candle in the dark. Connachtach hid it behind a small bookcase in the corner of his cluttered room. Repeatedly pulling the bookcase out had etched a clean groove in the flooring. Damian removed the strong box. Taking one last look around the room, he spotted his illustration. He rolled it up carefully and put it inside his habit. Damian crossed the grass to the gate and unbarred it. Marching along the stony path, he prepared to greet the Norsemen.

*

'Let me speak with your leader,' said Damian.

Hakon stood before his men, towering over Damian.

'What do you want with me, Cross Follower?' asked Hakon, surprised that the monk conversed in his native tongue.

'I wish to bargain,' he said, handing over gold and silver coins. 'This is just a token.'

'I would have found it anyway,' said Hakon.

'Perhaps, perhaps not. Only I and the Abbot knew its location,' he lied. 'Your boats have sailed away empty-handed before.'

Hakon studied Damian. All the White Cross Followers he met must have been runts, or else this Christ God made them weak. The one standing before him was not worth dirtying his blade on.

'I have stacked the monastery's valuables at the open gate. I could not carry them all.'

'And where are the rest of you?'

'Still asleep. I saw your boats on the water and collected anything of value.'

'Is this a trap?' asked Hakon.

'A trap I would die in. No, I assure you, I very much wish to live. And I have an offer that I hope will interest you.'

'You have staked your life on this offer?'

'I have.'

'By Loki, I fear I have a troublemaker in my midst,' said Hakon. 'What do you offer? What could be worth so much that I would think of sparing you?'

Hakon drew his sword from its scabbard and positioned its glistening point at the monk's throat. He pressed too hard, drawing blood. 'Pray it is a good offer or I will run you through.' Hakon was warming to the little monk who had not so much as flinched. He had not hidden or recoiled like the snivelling White Cross Followers he had encountered before. At least he was brave enough to face his fate.

Damian bargained for his life. 'I, I offer you the richest treasure, hidden not far from here. If you agree, I shall lead you to it in exchange for sparing both my life and the lives of the brothers. If you refuse and strike me down, you will find the doors to the monastery already open.'

'What treasure do you speak of?' asked Hakon.

'When we have a deal I will share my knowledge. I promise you, we will both become rich and powerful.'

Something in the monk's manner fascinated Hakon. The fact that he staked his life impressed Hakon – there was a confidence about him. What could be so precious? What harm could it do to listen to the monk's offer?

Hakon addressed his men. 'We'll strike this bargain. Let the White Cross Followers live.'

The raiders gave a collective groan.

Hakon laughed. 'That does not mean that they should be comfortable. Burn the place.'

CHAPTER 41

IN THE YEAR 840 AD

After his scare, Vidar kept climbing. It not only kept the chill from his bones, it also took his mind off any lingering doubts about the climb. It was imperative not to lose his nerve – a nervous climber was a dangerous climber. Throughout the day, the wind strengthened, clearing the sky of cloud.

Vidar found the remainder of the ascent easier. As he cleared the summit, a welcoming sun greeted his arrival. It was much warmer now that he was out of the shade of the mountainside. He stood peering into a huge crater, its shingled slopes running down to a glittering ice lake, its shore peppered with boulders and debris. More rocks lay upon the ice, half-buried in thawed and refrozen water, they looked as though they were sinking into the frozen lake. His eyes were drawn to a frozen waterfall, its enchanted water suspended in midair as if by magic.

A light mist rolled off one particularly pointed peak. Vidar was surprised to see a waterfall of melted water trickling down its slopes. The water seemed to dissolve into the edge of the lake, disappearing to where? He did not know.

Jumping a few small overhangs, Vidar made his way to the

edge of the lake. The shingle, giving way beneath his weight, made it difficult for him not to break into a run, forcing him to check himself every few strides. At times, going downhill was more difficult than walking uphill.

Crossing the lake, he straddled a few rocks and jumped from boulder to boulder to reach the waterfall. The melted water had etched out a shaft. Where did it lead? Vidar could not be sure. Standing in the hollow, he believed he had found the Vestibule.

Vidar began to walk the perimeter of the lake. He was close, he was sure of it. His sense of anticipation grew.

The day dragged on and Vidar's spirits dipped. Perhaps he was wrong. Perhaps the Vestibule was not here. No, he chastised himself. This was definitely the place. He walked to the centre of the lake and ran a careful eye over the ridges of snow and rock that surrounded the crater. He contemplated beginning his descent as he walked towards the original trickling waterfall.

Above, a few stars were visible in the daylight. He could make out the ones he used to guide himself. As he lowered his head, he caught sight of a reflection in the waterfall. Excitedly he hurried to the spot. The rainbow became visible. Vidar stood, mouth agape, his heart pounding.

'Yes,' he yelled, punching the air in celebration.

Partially obscured by the falling water, the entrance of the Vestibule was exactly as Cado had described. Sunlight reflected off the iridescent ice walls throwing spectres of colour along the chamber. It was a fabulous sight.

Vidar entered, giddy with excitement. Under his feet was a spectacular rainbow of ice. Half-sliding and half-walking, he descended further and further into the widening Vestibule. Surprisingly the passageway was bright. The rainbow died away, replaced by steel-blue ice. Massive incisor-like stalactites and thick stalagmites, created over centuries, clung to the roof and rose from the ground, slowing his progress. Although the air tasted fresh, the magical ambience overwhelmed Vidar, leaving him breathless. He was entering a wonderland.

A little further along, the cave opened out into a snowy valley, bright as a summer's day. The lake above had remained frozen overhead yet thawed underneath. There was enough light to sustain life. He danced on the snowy ground, ecstatic with his discovery.

Vidar planned not to waste a moment. He was bound for Erin, to the ghosts of his past.

From the Vestibule, he had one last look back at the wonderland beneath the ice, the most fantastic of places. He felt privileged to have found it. Bending down, he picked up a pointed stone and scraped a message on a rock. It was only fitting that he should be the one to give the place a name.

He scraped a P followed by O and L. He added an A and an R and finished off with the letters I and S. Vidar stepped back to admire his work. No, that was not personal enough. He wanted Niclaus to know he had found it first. He scraped more letters: N, O, R, T, and a H. Polaris for Niclaus, North for Orrin. There would be no mistaking who had named it.

A tinge of sadness replaced his euphoria. Somehow, he suspected that this would be his only visit to the magical place. He could now understand Cado's insistence that he journeyed alone – the fewer who knew of its existence the better.

Vidar found his descent easier than his climb. 'Don't rush,' he reminded himself on numerous occasions. It would have been easy to allow his exhilaration to overcome him – a moment's carelessness could have been disastrous. Reaching his camp, it took a massive amount of restraint to keep from packing and rushing back to the *Ice Maiden*.

All the feelings of bitter disappointment and frustration, the years of punishing toil and effort, had been worth it. Snuggled up in his tent for the night, Vidar thought that he would have trouble sleeping. He need not to have worried – he soon fell into a deep slumber.

Waking suddenly, disorientated, Vidar sat up. An animal was rummaging outside. Blade and axe in hand, he readied himself for an attack. What chance would he have against a bear?

He sat, almost afraid to breathe, for what felt like an eternity until a familiar bleating broke the silence.

Poking his head out, he breathed a sigh of relief.

He laughed heartily and the reindeer outside brayed back. His two friendly reindeer stood before him, wide-eyed and looking for food.

On the way back, Vidar followed the animals as they led him around the broken ice field. They met a stretch of ground, deep with drift snow. Normally Vidar would have avoided it as the sleigh would have iced up and become too heavy to move. He had an idea. He made a harness out of rope which he attached to the reindeer. Without much argument, the animals started to pull the sleigh. Their legs powered through the deep snow better than any reindeer Vidar had ever seen.

Early on the twelfth day, Vidar came into view, riding proudly on the back of one of the reindeer, the other by his side.

'Well I'll be …,' said Anders.

'What?' Morton said, straining to get a look.

'Looks like Vidar's back already.'

'Arne, Arne where are you?' Morton called.

When he did not answer, Morton sent Walrus with instructions for Arne to prepare something for Vidar.

Morton, walking to the edge of camp, chuckled at the sight of Vidar on the reindeer. 'I see you've tamed them.'

'Easy, when you know how,' Vidar called as he dismounted.

Morton looked at him expectantly.

'Yes, yes, I found it.'

An awkward pause ensued. Vidar felt uncomfortable not being able to elaborate. He knew Morton would have loved to ask what it was that he had found. 'I'm sorry …' he said.

Morton understood. 'All that matters is that you have found it and made it back safely. We are finished here, aren't we?'

'We are.'

Morton clasped him in celebration, 'I knew it. I knew you'd do it.'

'Your debt is clear also?'

Morton's lips broke into the largest smile, 'Aye, lad, one round trip to Erin and I'm free.'

Hugging Morton tightly, Vidar thanked him. 'I couldn't have done it without you.'

At camp, the crew greeted Vidar's success with loud cheers. They were ecstatic, although curious to know what exactly he had found.

'Is there anything else I can do for you before we leave this damned island?' asked Morton.

Vidar grinned. 'There is one thing.'

*

With a lot of coaxing, the two unusual reindeer were loaded on to the boat, much to the dismay of Walrus, who preferred the idea of a meal.

The ship was soon under sail.

Vidar's gaze remained on the rugged island, his eyes drinking in the vision of snowy mountains in the sun. The view was a memory that might have to last him his lifetime. It mattered little – he left behind a conquered land, one that had yielded its secret. He had kept his word. His search was over. Now he could settle in Folda with Elwin, the girls and Niclaus.

Once they had set sail, Morton joined Vidar at the back of the boat. 'I have a present for you. Courtesy of a certain Gilder, his instructions clear. "Bring my brother home and celebrate his safe return with this."'

Morton produced a large keg of ale. 'We toast your safety and your success.'

It was the perfect gesture. Gilder was as close to a brother as Vidar would ever have.

Morton bellowed out orders, his mood fiery. 'Rune, watch the ship, sail the course. The rest of you come here,' he said, ushering them into the centre of the deck.

They assembled as instructed. 'Tonight we celebrate Vidar's success.'

The men cheered loudly.

Morton brought a tankard of ale to Rune at the side rudder. 'Here, you deserve this.'

Smiling, Rune took his drink as Morton gestured for Torre to join them. The three men had sailed the sea together for a lifetime.

'Jorun, he'll make a good captain?' asked Torre.

'Aye, I think it's time we left the sailing to younger men,' agreed Morton.

They looked at one and another.

'To retirement,' toasted Morton.

*

A small crowd had gathered to greet the *Ice Maiden*. Elwin felt all eyes upon her as she took her place next to Selina. She and her daughters had been last to arrive. She watched nervously as Niclaus and Orrin raced along the water's edge to get word from the boat.

'He'll be fine,' said Selina, embracing Elwin.

The boat was much too early, not being due for near on another month. Dread filled Elwin. She could not bear to live her life without Vidar.

The boys saw Vidar and waved.

Their greeting was not lost to those waiting.

The cheers grew. Elwin breathed, as if for the first time. Excitement replaced the sickness in her stomach. Her husband was back. She swore that she would not let him venture off again. Her four daughters hugged each other, crying and laughing at the same time.

Nearing the quay, Vidar jumped from the boat, splashing into the deep water to further cheers. He swam back to shore and ran to Elwin and the girls.

'You're soaking,' cried Elwin, as she hugged and kissed him.

Fenja, Helga and Dylla joined in the embrace, only Eve held back.

Vidar broke free of his family hug. 'Aren't you glad to see me?' he asked her.

'No, I am not. You going to stop these journeys, they're too dangerous. Your place is at home with us.'

'You are right,' he agreed. 'I'm finished. I'm too old for this foolhardy business.'

Vidar felt Eve's doubtful eyes, 'I promise you I have finished what I set out to do. I'm finished with the far north. I only have one final sailing to Erin and I'm done.'

Elwin cried with delight, 'Is it true?'

'Yes,' he confirmed as he lifted her off the ground and kissed her.

*

Morton brought the reindeer ashore and led them to Niclaus, who had volunteered to see them fed, watered, and settled in the barn.

'They look unusual,' said Niclaus, eyeing the reindeer.

'Don't let their looks deceive you. They are the strongest and fittest deer.'

Niclaus shrugged his shoulders. 'Well they don't look it; they look odd, too small, legs too fat.'

'They're perfect. Vidar says they are from the greatest breed of all,' disagreed little Dylla, who had only just finished quizzing Vidar about them, and who was impatient to get a proper look at her new pets.

'With Vidar, nothing would surprise me. Do you want to help me take them to the barn and give them a feed?' asked Niclaus.

'Yes,' replied Dylla, excitedly.

CHAPTER 42

IN THE YEAR 840 AD

'What do you think he wants us for?' asked Niclaus.

'I don't know,' replied Eve, linking his arm.

The day was bright and the breeze was surprisingly warm as they walked towards Elwin's cabin.

Eve's face blanched. Vidar was dressed for sailing.

'You promised,' she said, struggling to keep her composure.

'Now, Eve, it's not like that. I am not going on a trek.'

Eve visibly relaxed.

'I have one last trip to Erin – the one that I told you about. I had not intended to make the trip until after the Trial. I only realised last night that I would have to go so soon.'

'Morton?' she said, aware of his arrival the previous day.

Vidar nodded. 'Would you like to come with me?'

Eve softened. 'Would you really take me?'

'Of course I would. I wouldn't ask unless I meant it. The only thing is …'

'What?'

'You'll not be back in time for the Trial.'

Eve smiled. 'You know I can't miss that.'

'What? When are you going?' asked Niclaus.

Vidar lifted the large sack he had prepared for the journey.

'Today, I'm sorry. I had hoped that I would have been here to cheer you and Orrin on.'

Digging into the sack, Vidar pulled out two crystals the size of his palm and handed them to Niclaus.

'Sunstones – one for you and one for Orrin, as promised.'

'Thank you,' said Niclaus, slipping the crystals into his pocket. 'You said you were going to Erin. Is it to meet the monk and the dwarf I dreamt of?'

'It is.'

'Does your trip concern me?'

'I don't think so,' said Vidar, honestly.

'Eve, will you go and see what's keeping your mother?' Vidar asked.

'Why do you think I dreamt of them?' Niclaus asked, once Eve had left.

Vidar frowned.

'Why do you freeze up when I try to discuss this with you? You know more than you are letting on. What is it that you won't tell me?'

Elwin, accompanied by her daughters, came out of the house.

'Niclaus, not now. When I get back I shall tell you all that I know.'

Elwin took Vidar by the hand. 'And what was that about?' she asked, as Niclaus dropped behind to walk with Eve.

Vidar sighed. 'I can't keep it from him much longer. We'll have to tell him soon.'

'It'll work out fine,' she said, reassuringly.

'I don't know. This is the first time that Cado has summoned me. I think this could be the beginning of a great upheaval for us all.'

Vidar and Elwin had discussed Vidar's trip in detail. He had promised that this was his last one. Together they had made plans for the future. The only problem was that they did not know for how long Vidar would be gone.

CHAPTER 43

IN THE YEAR 840 AD

A mixture of nervous excitement and apprehension kept Orrin from sleeping. Tomorrow was the eve of the Trial and the day would be spent selecting animals and equipment. He had visualised how he would achieve his victory. He could taste the sweetness of success, could feel his jubilation as he hoisted the red flag high above his head and waved it frantically in front of his proud father – nothing would please him more. Eventually the well-worn dream, that had changed little over the years, played its last scene and Orrin slipped into unconsciousness.

*

Niclaus drifted off to sleep the moment his head touched the pillow. However, unlike Orrin, a scattering of mixed-up dreams interrupted his rest. He was relieved to wake from one particularly unpleasant one – of snarling wolves, bloodied from their hunt. As it was still early, he forced himself back to sleep but continued flitting in and out of slumber until he finally woke, sweaty and fatigued. He was unable to recall the specifics of his dreams, retaining only fragments. He did remember riding his sleigh with

Vidar's ungainly reindeer pulling. In another, he could see the same two animals leading a train across a frozen lake.

*

The boys shared a laugh over breakfast as Niclaus recounted his dreams and Selina fussed over them.

'I'm telling you it was the funniest thing, seeing those two animals with their short legs, trying to keep up in the snow.'

Orrin was laughing, tears in his eyes. 'I take it you didn't want to win the challenge then.'

Niclaus' face turned serious. He sat up straight, 'I have had other dreams that came true.'

'You wouldn't dare. Don't even think …' said Orrin, aghast.

Instinctively, Niclaus clasped the locket that he wore around his neck. The beasts may not have looked fit for a sleigh ride but he could hear Vidar's words in his head, describing them as 'the strongest and fittest deer.' Moreover, Dylla claimed that Vidar had told her that they were descendants of the greatest reindeer breed.

Selina scooped yet more pancakes on to the boys' plates. She had made them because they were their favourite. She looked close to tears.

'Don't worry, we'll be fine,' said Niclaus, trying to reassure her.

She tried to muster a smile. 'I know you will.'

'Who do you think is going to win?' asked Orrin.

'I don't care who wins. I'd rather Henik won if it meant neither of you had to lose. I couldn't stand to see either one of you disappointed,' snapped Selina, before rushing out of the room.

'See what you've gone and done,' Niclaus sighed.

'All I said ...'

'She is right you know. Things will change,' said Niclaus.

'They don't have to.'

'You're kidding. One of us will be Ugter. The other will have his dream shattered.'

'No, Niclaus you are wrong. Nothing changes. If you think it does then you're not the brother I have known all these years. If I win ... or should I say *when* I win ... ' he said, lightening the mood, '... I will need my brother at my side to guide me in difficult times.'

Niclaus accepted the scolding. It cheered him. Orrin was right as usual. It was only a race – but one he would not lose.

'Besides, our responsibility is to the village. Remember, Niclaus, that its welfare comes before all else.'

Niclaus laughed, 'You'd be a tough taskmaster.'

'In case I forget, good luck out there,' said Orrin.

'You too,' replied Niclaus.

*

On the eve of the Trial, the villagers gathered by the water's edge offering blessings to the competitors, and prayers that everyone would return safely.

The increasingly thin-looking Gunnar took centre stage. Gaunt and haggard, he was paler than ever. Illness was ravishing his once well-honed body.

'I call forward Niclaus. I call forward Orrin. I call forward Henik. I call forward Aslak. And finally I call forward Ludin,' he said.

Cheers greeted each name.

'The Trial shall start on Lofoten Island. All five competitors shall row from there to the fjord,' said Gunnar. 'Next, the boys will climb to the top of the fjord, following the route selected by Olaf.'

Again, the crowd cheered as the muscular Olaf, the best climber in the village, took a bow. Orrin and Niclaus had already discussed whether Olaf would have given Ludin an advantage by telling him the route, but decided that Olaf was too honourable.

Gunnar hushed the crowd with a wave of his hand. 'After the ascent, the boys will have a night's rest. The following morning, they will ski the glacier track through the gap between the mountains of Akkavare and Kebnekaise. It is a full day's skiing. After another night's rest, the racers will race their sleighs through the forest of Slarin. They will be given the choice of either a dagger or a staff for, as you know, bears and wolves inhabit the forest. Hopefully they won't be needed.'

'Some use they would be be against a bear or a pack of wolves,' whispered Aslak.

'Don't worry. There's never been an attack during any Trial. They only do it for show,' replied Niclaus.

Gunnar continued. 'Clearing the forest, they reach a final checkpoint. From there, it is a race to the finish at Valirth on the far side of Lake Torne. Remember, each challenger must bring a sleigh to the finish. Without it you will have failed and will not be permitted to raise a flag.'

Niclaus recalled a tale told by Gunnar. During his Trial, one of the competitors, knowing the frozen lake would not hold the weight of a sleigh, left his team and crossed on foot. He thought he was in with a chance of winning. Gunnar always laughed at the part of the story where the man was sent back to retrieve his sleigh.

'I wish he'd hurry up,' Ludin whispered to Niclaus, putting a hand to his mouth and pretending to yawn.

Gunnar gave the two boys a glare. 'At the finish shall be five flags, four blue and one red. The first to raise the red flag shall be the new Ugter. All others who raise a blue flag shall have completed the Trial. Remember, to complete the Trial is a great honour. Never in our history, have all five competitors done so. It just leaves me to wish you all good luck and a safe journey.'

Applause greeted the end of his speech.

'Thank God,' grumbled Henik.

Niclaus eyed his old foe. He looked bored with the ceremony. The years had changed him little – if anything Henik looked more sullen and menacing than Niclaus remembered.

Eve gave a loud wolf whistle aimed at Niclaus, one to make any boy proud.

'Come on,' said Reseth.

He revelled in his role as marshal. It was his duty to preside over the selection of the reindeer. Reseth led the group, which included Olaf, out of the village. They walked to where the herders waited with the best of their animals, sixteen in total. The herders loved the Trial, the hardened men betting heavily on the outcome.

'We shall draw lots to decide who has first choice,' explained Reseth. Olaf held out five strands of straw.

'Watch me win,' said Orrin as he picked first.

Aslak followed. 'Damn it,' he moaned, his strand smaller than Orrin's.

Henik's straw placed him between Orrin and Aslak. Niclaus took his.

While all eyes were on Niclaus, Olaf pulled a longer straw out of his pocket, discarding the one in his hand. The trick went unnoticed by all but Ludin.

*

Olaf smiled; his plan was falling into place. Outwardly, he gave the impression that he had graciously accepted defeat when he had been a competitor in the Trial. In reality, the pain of losing was as fresh today as it had been all those years ago. The overwhelming favourite to win, he had gained a lead in the final section. If Gilder was to have stood any chance of winning, he would have had to catch and pass Olaf, which was pretty much impossible. Hurtling over the snow, his reindeer pulled him on toward the finish. And then suddenly Gilder veered off, steering his sleigh up the hill. At first, Olaf thought that his challenger was conceding defeat. The thought did not last for very long as the snow below his sleigh turned to slush. Olaf cursed his luck. Either he was crossing a river that ran into Lake Torne or he had steered over a section of the lake. His team pulled valiantly but the sludge slowed their progress. Gilder's route was longer but he covered the ground quickly. Olaf's sleigh reached harder ground. Converging on the finishing flag, Gilder held Olaf off, winning by a hand's breadth.

Olaf had never been able to put into words the pain that he felt at having the win snatched from his grasp. Replaying the race in his mind, he could not understand how Gilder had known the lie of the land. Olaf convinced himself that Gilder had somehow gained knowledge of the course in advance.

Over the years, pain and bitterness festered and he determined that Ludin would avenge his defeat. Together they had planned for every eventuality, plotted every stage of the Trial, and worked out every conceivable, fair or unfair advantage they could attain. If Gilder could cheat so could Ludin.

*

'Yours is longest so far,' confirmed a disappointed Orrin to Niclaus.

Henik double-checked.

Ludin was last to pick. He pulled the longest straw, much to Orrin's consternation.

Having the advantage, Ludin selected the herders' most prized animals. Olaf could barely contain his delight.

Niclaus was next. He took his time, studying the posture and muscle tone of the beasts. Two reindeer stood out from the rest. He checked their eyes, they were clear, a good sign of health.

Orrin muttered something under his breath. Niclaus suspected he had fancied the pair himself. They were reaching their prime and would soon replace Ludin's as lead reindeers of the herd.

'Can I select reindeer that are not here?' he asked Reseth.

'You can if you want,' said Reseth.

'But these are the top animals,' said Jakob, the head herdsman, surprised by the question.

'I pick Vidar's reindeer.'

A chorus of laughter greeted Niclaus' decision.

'You're not serious? Those two animals are runts. Even the

main herd do not recognise them. Surely you should reconsider?' said Reseth.

'I choose Vidar's two reindeer.'

'Very well,' confirmed Reseth. 'Who's next?'

Orrin stepped forward and promptly chose the pair he wanted.

Henik did not look too bothered – if anything, he looked extremely confident.

'I have trained these animals myself,' he said, pointing to his preferred pair. Having spent the last ten years working with the herd, there could be no denying that he knew a good animal from a bad one. 'I can win with these.'

Niclaus believed him. If Henik was anywhere close to the front coming into the sleigh ride there was a high probability that he would win.

Aslak followed Henik, completing the process.

Ludin took Niclaus to the side. 'During the trial, our friendship ceases.'

'Don't be so serious. We are friends always,' said Niclaus.

'No, Niclaus, during the Trial you are the same as Henik. You are my enemy.'

CHAPTER 44

IN THE YEAR 840 AD

A brewing storm ensured that the black and white puffins had not ventured far from their nests and the snow-white kittiwakes had retreated to the clifftop. The wind blew with icy breath, warning the young men of what lay ahead. The protection offered by the mountainous island would be lost as soon as the racers cleared the shore. The crossing was going to be hard and dangerous – anyone who capsized could die from the cold alone.

The five boys stood nervously waiting for their destiny to unfold. There would be no comfort in coming second: all the spoils went to the winner. Orrin stretched, easing a slightly stiff back, and rubbed at his tight jaw, a telltale sign of the tension he was feeling. Driven by a belief that he was most suited to protect the tradition and customs of his people, he was desperate to succeed his father. He knew it would be difficult to prevail against the power of Henik or the ability of Niclaus.

Orrin contemplated his chances. He needed to force the pace and open a good lead at the start. It was a tall order, especially as Niclaus had always got the better of him during their training. Orrin was stockier and, given his weight advantage, should have been stronger. But Niclaus had the edge, both mentally and physically. His leanness hid the strength of a bear and the agility of a deer.

Appraising all their talents, Orrin knew that he would be quickest in the boat, Ludin the climb, Niclaus the skiing, and Henik would easily be the best on the sleigh. Orrin shook his head as he thought of Niclaus and his team of reindeer. He should not have picked Vidar's silly creatures. They would cost him the race. If Orrin was ahead at that stage, he could see no way back for Niclaus. Then there was Henik. He was the unknown quantity. One thing was for sure, Orrin needed to be ahead of Henik going into the sleigh ride.

*

Henik stood with his father, Berit, who was gesticulating wildly, demonstrating how to paddle. Henik, standing half a head taller than Niclaus, had filled out over the years. He was strong and, Niclaus suspected, would not be afraid to use rough tactics given the opportunity.

A huge slap on his back interrupted Niclaus' thoughts; a great bear hug followed as Ludin lifted him off his feet and slammed him to the ground.

'I'll kill you now, before the race,' he sneered

Niclaus looked at him, not knowing if he was serious.

'Remember what I told you. During the race our friendship stops,' Ludin warned. 'But after I win you can be my friend again.'

Taken by surprise and totally winded, Niclaus lay prostrate. 'I get the message, you oaf. Anyway when I'm Ugter, I'll send you to the northern fjord,' replied Niclaus, threatening Ludin with the worst duty in the village.

Niclaus considered Ludin's prospects. He was big and powerful, and his strong arms could give him the edge in both the kayaking and the climb. Practice on the mountains with his father would have undoubtedly honed his skill. He would be a formidable opponent for the first two parts of the Trial but he was a poor skier and a worse sleigh rider. In fact, of all the competitors, Niclaus felt that Ludin might struggle most to complete the course.

Niclaus' thoughts turned to Aslak. He was something of an enigma who was always on the periphery. He might just surprise a few people. One mishap and Aslak could possibly nick the race. Niclaus would keep a close eye on his lanky friend.

Orrin went back to his kayak, checking it for the umpteenth time. Niclaus watched him. Yes, Orrin would be a big threat. He had a sharp mind and most of the villagers, Niclaus included, believed he would make an excellent leader. No one had his heart.

The wind whistled hard forcing Ragnall to raise his voice. He ordered the boys to their positions. With a simple call the race was on.

In the early stages of the crossing, the five kayakers kept close. No one ventured to create a lead. Ludin slowly fell behind. Henik too was finding it hard going.

Orrin's strokes lengthened causing both Niclaus and Aslak to lose ground.

Aslak looked comfortable, however. He had not broken sweat while Niclaus was drenched from the exertion, and Aslak soon pulled ahead of him, leading by about a length. Henik followed with Ludin further back.

Ludin found a bit of rhythm and overtook Henik. Orrin's lead over Aslak remained constant but, to Niclaus' surprise, Aslak was getting further and further ahead of him.

Niclaus swore as he suddenly felt water inside his boat. At the same time, he realised how low his kayak was sitting in the water. He was too far from shore. Panic was beginning to take hold.

'What is it?' shouted Aslak.

'My kayak is letting in water. I don't think it'll make the crossing.'

The leak explained why he had slipped so far behind.

'Grab on to my kayak,' instructed Aslak.

'No, go ahead, I'll swim in.'

'Don't be daft. You wouldn't make it.'

Niclaus pulled himself out of his sinking kayak and gripped the rim of Aslak's.

Ludin and then Henik passed, neither speaking. Orrin rowed back.

'What are you doing, you fool?' shouted Niclaus.

'Do you remember our first training? We had to swim across the fjord.'

'Yes.'

'You promised not to leave me. Well, I made the same promise. Besides, father would kill me if I left you out here.'

'Come on,' said Aslak. 'Two of us rowing with you holding the boats steady will be a lot faster than one. We'll be a bit behind but we'll catch it up.'

Aslak and Orrin rowed side by side, as Niclaus gripped the

back of their boats tightly.

Niclaus was astonished by Orrin and Aslak's generosity. Here, in the most important race of their lives, they had both jeopardised their chances of winning to help him. By contrast, Ludin – who he had saved from the wolves on the ice – had ignored him.

Ludin, first ashore, climbed out of his kayak and rushed to the first checkpoint which was situated in the centre of the village. Olaf gave his son a clenched salute and whistled wildly. Standing by his side, his red-haired wife Rula, who barely reached her husband's shoulder, applauded also. Rula handed her boy a ladle of water. Ludin quaffed it, refilled the ladle and gulped that down as well. He wiped his mouth with the back of his hand and grabbed a few choice apples before breaking into a jog. Following the main stream, Ludin had already cleared the low fields and was entering a thicket as Henik came ashore.

'Good on you,' encouraged Berit, his delighted father. 'You have a good start on the others. Now, go catch Ludin.'

The trailing trio had lost a lot of time. A subdued crowd greeted their arrival. Gilder's blank expression gave little away while Selina looked relieved that both boys were safe.

'What happened out there?' asked Gilder.

Niclaus told him, praising both Aslak's and Orrin's selflessness.

Eve broke through the ranks to offer words of encouragement to Niclaus.

Gilder wished his boys good luck. It was his last chance to see them until after the final. His main responsibility was to ensure the safety of the village – with so many men away, either following or marshalling the race, Gilder was obliged to remain behind.

Taking a quick drink, the three were off at full speed. They had a lot of catching up to do. Ludin, already clear of the tree line, was starting his ascent of the fjord.

CHAPTER 45

IN THE YEAR 802 AD

Laden with their booty, the horde retreated, many dissatisfied that their incursion had ended without bloodshed.

'It's a bad omen,' said Steapa.

'Nonsense, lad, Hakon's only delaying our raid,' explained Oto.

Steapa spat. 'Why would he spare the White Cross Followers?'

'He made a deal: their lives in return for a great treasure.'

A few of the men nearby muttered disapproval, although none was foolish enough to voice their opinion openly.

Reaching the beached dragonboats, Hakon blew on his horn. 'I have by my side he that was once a White Cross Follower,' he announced.

The crews looked on in surprise.

'He has said that he wants to follow Odin.'

'Is this true?' asked Oto.

'He only does it to save his neck,' countered someone from the back.

'Listen, men. I know you are sceptical but how many White

Cross Followers have renounced their faith?' asked Hakon.

'None,' said Envik, leader of the second boat.

'We never asked any to,' added Oto, to a cackle of laughter.

'Do you renounce the one you call the Christ?' asked Hakon.

'I do, gladly. He is a weak god in comparison to your mighty Odin,' cried Damian, his apostasy absolute.

'This one claims that he knows the resting place of a great treasure. What do you say?' Hakon asked of his men.

Barid eyed the monk. 'If he delivers it to us, Odin will have shown his pleasure. If not …'

'Agreed,' said Hakon. 'We sail not for home but for this place that holds the great prize.'

Under sail, Hakon sensed unease, all being unusually quiet. The company of the White Cross Follower made more than a few of the men uncomfortable.

Envik sailed his boat closer to Hakon's *Sea Dragon*.

'Can I have a word?' he called to his leader.

Hakon waved him over.

The two boats narrowed the water between them as the crews raised their oars. Thrown grapnels pulled the vessels together. When the ships were close enough, a rower dropped his oar to span the gap between the two. Tucking the oar under his arm, the rower took the strain as Envik sprang nimbly along it before leaping aboard the *Sea Dragon*.

Hakon took Envik aside.

Behind, the two crews threw good-natured insults at each other.

'What if it's a trap?' Envik asked his young leader, learning that the intended target was upstream, away from the coast.

'We shall prepare for one. Alsed in the third boat shall anchor away from the place and take his men over land. They will blow their horns if they spot any danger. Meanwhile you and I shall follow behind at a safe distance. We'll leave plenty of men to protect the boats.'

Raucous cries rang out behind them.

'Hakon,' shouted Oto. 'Steapa has thrown a challenge to anyone on the *Seahorse* for a race along the oars.'

Hakon laughed. 'Well, Envik, any of your lot want to beat him?'

'Gladly,' said Envik, turning to his men. 'Who accepts the challenge?'

There were a number of volunteers, all being eager to teach the upstart a lesson.

With much betting taking place, Envik picked his most experienced man. Sturla was tall and surprisingly thin.

'Loosen the grapnels,' ordered Envik. 'Would you like a wager?' he offered Hakon, as the boats separated and the rowers lowered their oars.

'I think young Steapa might get wet,' declined Hakon, turning away from the entertainment.

Envik followed. Despite approving of Hakon's plan, he voiced his main concern. 'My lord, I trust you fully and will follow you to Odin's gate but I have a bad feeling over that stranger,' he said, pointing to Damian, who stood at the front of the craft.

'Envik, we'll let Barid captain your boat. I want you to stay close. Be my eyes and ears. If you find the newcomer treacherous, I trust you will enjoy disposing of him. And if he is telling the truth … well, then we shall have our reward. There is something about him. I think he will be useful to us.'

'I will watch him like a hawk.'

'Of that, I have no doubt. That is why, like my father, I always entrust you with my most important duties. Oh and, Envik, get him more fitting clothing. The men find his dress unsettling.'

A roar erupted. Hakon turned to see the triumphant Sturla standing on the last oar. He had completed the race by jumping from oar to oar down the entire length of the boat. Steapa was nowhere in sight.

'Leave him in the water,' demanded Oto, having bet heavily on the boy.

Hakon finished by asking Envik to pass on instructions to Barid, who was to take command of the *Seahorse* and to Alsed, leader of the final boat.

With Steapa pulled back on board, the ships resumed their voyage.

A strong wind pushed the flotilla eastward, towards Erin.

Following Damian's directions, it took another day and a half of sailing before the boats reached an inlet between two headlands. To the south, gentle hills climbed into the distance. They had already passed the high mountains of the northern headland, and marvelled at the climbing heather and forested land.

Oars replaced sail as they entered the embouchure. From the bay, the raiders rowed into the sandy estuary of the Boyne. To either side, great mud flats threatened to swamp the lazy river.

Beyond, the wide marsh was alive with the sound of summer birds and animals.

*

Unlike the Norsemen, who slept soundly, Damian lay awake at night. There was hardly any space for sleeping – the Norsemen stored their personal belongings in chests, which slotted perfectly into grooves on the deck. These doubled as seats for the oarsmen, leaving little space for sleeping. But it was more than the cramped quarters that was troubling him: he spent the nights fighting with his conscience, for although the deal he had struck with Hakon spared the lives of those on Iona, he had not thought to include the monks of Ceanannus Mór. His mind raced constantly as the names and faces of his brothers danced before him. He thought of old Anton, he could see him vividly, nodding off during Mass; of kindly Brother Ciaran with his cherubic grin; and of Conor, who joined the Order in the same week as Damian had.

As well as worrying about the monks, he was also terrified that he would incur Hakon's wrath. He had taken a huge risk; he had not been forthcoming with all that he knew. Yes, he had mentioned the Bible and its jewel-encrusted case and, yes, he told Hakon about Newgrange and the mysterious little folk. He also told of the book of Newgrange and explained that he needed to decipher it before they could hope to learn their secrets. Damian had been surprised by how eager Hakon had been to believe his story.

Now, ahead, around the bend in the river, was the village of Newgrange. He had never approached it by water before and hoped that it remained obscured by the tree-lined bank. If not, if the dwarfs were visible, Damian would have a lot of explaining to do. He had deliberately kept back the fact that they passed the village on the way to Ceanannus Mór. He knew that Hakon would have insisted on raiding the village and Damian needed to learn all he could before risking such an attack.

*

Luck was with him: the boats sailed past Newgrange without incident.

At one stage, Damian toyed with the idea of jumping ship. A futile notion – they would have caught him in no time and, besides, his overriding ambition was still to possess the secrets of Newgrange. If that meant sacrificing Tomás and his fellow brethren, then so be it. He felt his temper boil as he remembered the humiliating months waiting for word from Tomás, word that failed to arrive. Damian steeled himself, letting his anger grow. He recalled the beating he suffered at Tomás' hand and the embarrassment of his expulsion. He would shed few tears for Monicurr.

Damian was succumbing to greed and ambition as surely as a huge wave would overwhelm a sailboat, sending it to the bottom of the ocean. Nothing but the black leather book mattered, he told himself, as he prepared to join the raiding party.

*

Hakon walked to the front of the boat to speak to Damian. 'What is the route like ahead?' he asked.

All the while, he kept a keen eye on either side of the river, watching for signs of movement or threat of attack. To the right, the water's edge was rush-lined and to the left, it was thick with overhanging willows that dipped their tendrils into the water.

'Ahead is a long sweep to the right. From there, the river rises. From that point, we will have to travel on foot.'

'Why have they not made a lock for it?' enquired Oto, who stood within listening range.

'There are a few families who make a good living loading and unloading boats.'

'How big a settlement?' Oto asked.

'You have nothing to fear. They are simple folk and number no more than fifteen at most.'

'Shall we send a forward party to scout the land?' asked the ever-cautious Envik.

'No, I believe him. First sign of trouble and we'll sail away, with one less of a crew,' Hakon replied.

As they neared the settlement, Hakon was pleased to see that it was just as Damian had described.

'I don't like this,' said Oto. 'We could be hemmed in too easily. Are there any more rises in the river we should know about?'

'No, it's the only one.'

'Oto, call Barid and Alsed,' commanded Hakon.

Quickly both men joined Hakon, Envik, and Oto.

'What do you think about leaving a boat and crew here, old man?' Hakon asked Envik, deliberately keeping the mood light.

'It's a smart idea. So long as it's not my boat. My men are too pent up. They need a good raid.'

Hakon's mood darkened. He expected his men to follow orders not give them. 'Your boat stays.'

Envik's face turned to thunder.

'But that doesn't mean you are not welcome to join my boat.' Hakon's offer spared Envik any embarrassment. 'Twenty men from each crew will stay. Let them throw dice for the duty.'

Envik's smile returned but Hakon knew the lesson had not been lost on him. Envik would think long and hard before he made the same mistake again.

'I will stay if you wish,' offered Envik, by way of apology.

'Thank you, but I have someone else in mind. Barid, you will command the boat.' This way Barid would remain out of harm's way.

Barid grinned at him. 'That's a great idea. If it is a trap and trouble comes our way, it'll surely start here. Ahead, the monastery will be easy picking. I might get some real fighting. Up-close kind.'

'On second thoughts, Barid, perhaps it would be better if you accompanied me to the monastery. Alsed you stay.'

'It's not too far a walk from here,' said Damian to Oto.

The sight of the monk trying to strike up a conversation with Oto amused Hakon. Bar himself, Oto entertained no other as a friend.

'Walk – he thinks we walk,' Oto sneered. 'Did you not know that dragonboats fly?'

'Two boats,' commanded Hakon.

'Let's show our latest recruit how it's done,' shouted Oto.

Damian watched as the Norsemen hauled the boats out of the

water and carried them at shoulder height upon their oars. They were soon rowing upriver.

'We are very close, just around the bend,' Damian said.

'Oto, lead the first group over land,' said Hakon. 'Scout well. Use your horn to sound a warning if you have any doubt.'

They stopped briefly to put Oto and his men ashore.

A little further along, Damian pointed to a well-used bank. 'If we pull up here, it is only a short distance through the woods to the open fields below the monastery.'

Hakon gave the orders to disembark and prepare to attack.

The unprotected monastery came into view, oblivious to the approaching threat. The strong oak doors were wide open, offering a welcome to all. Years of uninterrupted tranquillity were about to be shattered.

'I want Oto to lead the charge,' Hakon said, much to the surprise of his men.

Usually Hakon led the initial charge but today, he kept Damian by his side, closely watched by Envik.

'Remember, I am looking for one monk in particular,' he said, and went on to describe Tomás in detail. 'Bring all who fit the description to me.'

CHAPTER 46

IN THE YEAR 840 AD

Niclaus, Orrin, and Aslak instinctively began working as a team, taking turns to lead. They had to climb via the red cloths that Olaf had attached to the rock face as markers, each one visible to the marshals who were positioned at stations along the route.

They kept a keen eye on Ludin, trying to commit his route to memory. Pushing hard, they were beginning to gain ground on second-placed Henik, but Ludin was far ahead and looked to be climbing with consummate ease. He looked so comfortable – every step was sure, almost rehearsed.

'He seems to know the route,' said Aslak. 'Do you think that Olaf might have taught him it?'

'No,' said Orrin. 'Olaf is much too honourable. Ludin has just learned to climb as well as his father.'

*

Ludin could not have asked for a better start to the Trial. Fate walked with him, he told himself. He was determined to avenge his father. He would be Ugter, no matter the cost.

Although the ascent was steep and treacherous in places, the only problem he had encountered was remembering the route he and his father had chosen. They had spent hours deciding on the best way to the summit, picking a route that optimised Ludin's muscular physique.

Ludin was setting an almighty pace as he climbed. Frequently, he looked to be clinging vertically as he punched and kicked fingers and toes into nooks and crevices. At other times, he hung from the lips of overhangs, oblivious to the precarious height or the wind that threatened to carry him off. One slip or misjudgement would have sent him hurtling to his end. Tracking a rupture in the rock, he reached above his head and gripped a plant. It felt sturdy. Pulling himself up, his stomach churned as the plant came away in his hand, closely followed by several rocks. Ludin, with his years of climbing experience, dropped back to his previous position and waited until it was safe to continue. Ludin loved to climb; he felt exhilarated as he rose to the challenge. Adrenalin coursed his veins as he stretched to reach another red cloth. He lifted it and kissed it for good measure. Up here, Ludin's world narrowed to the length of an arm, beyond was in the realm of make-believe. Although supremely self-assured, Ludin was not stupid. It was one thing to climb daringly and another to climb recklessly. The words of his father came into his head, 'Foolishness and overconfidence always make for the quickest descent.'

He soon completed the climb. A run over a few fissures and Ludin would have earned his first rest. He paused on a huge boulder, lodged ominously over a gaping fracture in the rock. Below, the fjord stretched majestically to the sea. Swivelling his head, Ludin got his first view of the tangle of rock pinnacles, crowning snowfields and glaciers that soared to the top of the world.

A gust of wind caught him unaware, nearly carrying him off. He moved away from the edge and ran into the first camp, where the surprised-looking Hogst and Jord waited at the first of the two overnight stops of the trial. Hogst started to say something but Jord, pulling on his sleeve, hushed him. 'We're to stay impartial, remember?' he said, putting a log on the fire. He would estimate each competitor's time by the log's condition. It was a crude but effective way of measuring the time differences.

Hogst nodded and resumed stirring his cooking pot. Jord spooned meat and vegetables on to a plate and offered them to a ravenous Ludin. Jord normally had a pleasant manner but today he was abrupt. Ludin supposed his sharpness stemmed from being too old to enter the competition himself. Born between Trials, Jord made no secret of his resentment, telling all he would have won if he had had the chance.

*

The stones loosened by Ludin gathered pace as they fell. Henik, following a diagonal fracture in the rock, was far to the left and out of danger. He had started the climb confidently, having spent many a childhood day fooling around on the very same rock face. But climbing at breakneck speed was tricky, especially when there was a swirling wind, which grew in strength the higher he climbed. As the gap between him and Ludin increased, Henik fretted over the group climbing behind him. He needed to know if they were gaining on him. Finding secure footing and handgrips, he risked a quick glance down. Seeing the group below raised his spirit. Yes, they had narrowed the gap, but not nearly as much as he had feared. Ludin might have been extending his lead but the group below was still some way off. Henik's plan changed. He stopped worrying about catching Ludin – he was simply too good a climber. He decided instead to consolidate his position during this stage, and concentrate on catching Ludin later.

Before long, Henik cleared the top of the fjord and arrived at the camp. He could barely lift his spent arms, his calves ached, and his fingers were raw. To make matters worse, he had lost a considerable amount of time to Ludin. Reaching the checkpoint, he stood by the campfire to warm up.

*

Niclaus and his group were directly under the rockslide. A rumbling above warned the group and in panic, they clung to whatever they could. Orrin and Aslak had been under a ledge and avoided the barrage. Niclaus was not so lucky. Out in front, he had cleared the ledge and took the brunt of the slide. One particularly sharp rock hit the side of his head, opening a nasty gash behind his ear. Another smashed into his collarbone with such force that he was lucky to stay upright. It had been a narrow escape. Niclaus ended up with a throbbing headache, a bloody nose, a welt on his forehead and an aching shoulder, not to mention a few cuts and scrapes to his arms and legs.

'Are you all right?' asked Orrin.

'I'll live.'

'Well then, hurry up,' urged Aslak.

Despite their setbacks, the three boys entered the camp shortly after Henik.

'Good to see you got here at last,' taunted Henik.

Niclaus, rising to the bait, rushed at Henik. He suspected him of sabotaging his kayak.

Jord and Hogst held the boys back.

'What's your problem?' shouted Henik.

'You slashed my boat. Afraid I'd beat you.'

Henik looked stunned. 'You think I did that? Are you mad?'

'It was you,' roared Niclaus, lunging at Henik.

Orrin and Aslak held him back.

'I don't need to cheat to beat you.'

Jord and Hogst stood between the pair.

'Stop this,' Hogst interceded, with enough authority to calm the situation. 'Have you proof that he damaged your …'

'Of course I don't. He's too sneaky for …'

'Well then, be careful who you accuse.'

Jord tried to defuse the tension. 'Right, boys, I have already dressed Ludin's cut knuckles. Is there anything I can help you with?'

'I've had enough of this,' said Henik, storming off to his tent.

Jord began cleaning out Niclaus' cut.

All of the boys, with the exception of Aslak, had some ailment or discomfort. Niclaus' head injury was probably the worst. Orrin complained of a strain in his lower back and blisters on his right foot, nothing too serious.

That night, when sleep did not arrive, Niclaus replayed the incident on the water in his mind. The lengths that Henik was prepared to go to frightened him. Niclaus could so easily have been killed.

CHAPTER 47

IN THE YEAR 840 AD

As sailings went, the voyage from Folda to Newgrange had been straightforward, which added to Vidar's jubilant mood. He was returning triumphant. He had found the Vestibule.

'Not long to go now,' said Morton, as the ship sailed into the Boyne estuary. The river was free flowing, and the grasses beyond its banks were dark and rich, after much rain. Many of the trees along their route were succumbing to the onset of autumn.

The *Ice Maiden* sailed past Newgrange, a deep thicket obscuring it from view.

'You won't be stopping for long,' said Morton.

'What? Why?' asked Vidar, clearly surprised.

'I've to set sail within the day.'

'But you always come back for me.'

'Not this time. I've to drop off the supplies and sail back to Folda with you. You are my final cargo.'

'But you told me that I was to meet Cado?'

Morton looked puzzled. 'Cado did say that I was to take you to the monastery as usual. And set sail the very same day, taking you with me.'

'There's no way that I can visit both places in a day. Perhaps you were meant to drop me off close to Newgrange on the way past.'

'Unless Cado is already at Ceanannus Mór,' suggested Morton.

Reaching the rise in the river, Rune steered as close to the bank as possible. Anders jumped from the boat with mooring rope. He landed knee-high in water, to cheers from Walrus and Torre. A few of the villagers greeted the boat, hoping for work unloading its cargo onto waiting crafts on the higher stretch of water.

With the dyes and inks that made up most of Morton's consignment on board, Morton and Vidar were soon rowing upstream in a long riverboat that they had hired from the locals.

By late afternoon, they were disembarking, ready to walk up the incline to the monastery.

'Vidar, you go ahead. Tell the brothers that I am here. They usually send a few bodies to help me unload.'

A young, curly-haired monk, seeing Vidar approach, unlocked the main gate. 'It is good to see you,' he called.

Vidar struggled to recall his name. 'And you too ... Ronan,' he remembered just in time.

'They are expecting you.'

'Who?'

'The abbot, Tomás, and Cado – they are in the scriptorium. Would you like me to escort you?'

'No, thank you,' said Vidar, taking his leave. He could not wait to tell Cado his good news.

Entering the chapel, he dipped his hand in the stoup of holy water, signed the cross, genuflected and walked up the aisle towards the altar. The church looked exactly as he remembered. The scent of candle wax and incense filled the air. The ambience, as he recalled, created a feeling of closeness to God.

The chapel had played such a pivotal part in his life. Memories flooded back. He had taken his marriage vows at the very spot where he now knelt and Brother Dermot had christened him at the font to the side of the altar.

Filled with nostalgia, he knelt and offered prayers for Fiona and her family as well as Elwin and the girls. Finishing his private reflections, Vidar climbed the spiral stairs that led to the workshop.

CHAPTER 48

IN THE YEAR 840 AD

The strained atmosphere in the camp continued the following morning.

Niclaus should have been looking forward to this part of the trial – he was the most accomplished skier. He should have been able to close the gap on the two in front. Instead, because of everything that had happened, he would ski with Orrin and Aslak and try to guide them back into contention.

An ebullient Ludin stood to Niclaus' side rubbing his skis. His smugness did nothing to endear him to Niclaus.

'I thought you'd have helped me out there,' said Niclaus.

'Why?'

'I thought that, well I thought maybe …' Niclaus stammered. 'I just thought that as my friend you would have helped me in the water.'

Niclaus did not mention the fact that he had once saved his friend's life, but he was sure that Ludin knew what he was thinking of.

Ludin laughed, irking Niclaus further. 'I knew you'd be fine.'

'Ludin, come on, let's get you started,' said Jord, getting to his feet.

'But I thought we were going to wait until the mist had cleared?'

'The temperature in camp is beginning to boil,' explained Jord. 'I think it's better if you get going.'

Having camped in a hollow at the top of the fjord, it took just a few steps for the group to crunch their way on to the edge of the snowy wilderness.

'A day and night on the snow will soon calm those fiery tempers,' added Hogst.

'Go,' shouted Jord, giving Ludin a push off.

A couple of thrusts with his poles and momentum sent Ludin gliding down the majestic pass. Gaining speed, Ludin hunkered down into a crouch, bending his knees to absorb the vibrations and impact.

'Look at him go. A goat on skis,' laughed Orrin.

There was no denying that skiing was Ludin's weakest discipline. The others watched him flit in and out of the mountain shadows until he was lost to the mist.

*

'Come on, surely that's enough,' entreated Henik.

'Not long now,' said Jord.

Jord looked to Hogst, who sat watching the fire. Eventually, he raised a thumb, giving Henik the signal to begin. They all watched until Henik was lost to the mist.

Niclaus, Orrin, and Aslak took their places. It would be a while before they were allowed to start. 'At least we'll be able to follow their tracks,' said Aslak.

'It can't be much more,' pleaded Niclaus, the gap between them being greater than the boys had estimated.

'We'll never catch them,' complained Orrin.

'You have a full day's skiing ahead of you. You'll have plenty of opportunity,' said Jord. 'Go. Catch them.'

Restrained by the invisible leash of conscience, Niclaus resigned himself to a slower ski than he would have liked. Slower, however, did not mean slowly, and Niclaus was about to show Orrin and Aslak how strenuous a day spent on the snow could be. Setting an uncomfortable pace had its risks – there was a fine line between pushing them to their full potential and driving them beyond their abilities.

Balanced and supple, Niclaus glided through the snow. Orrin and Aslak tried to replicate his movements, rolling their shoulders and twisting their hips into turns. At times, Niclaus had to rein himself back and stop attacking the racing line so vigorously. Skiing took not only skill and balance, it also required confidence, and although they were competent skiers, Orrin and Aslak lacked self-belief. At one sharp corner, Niclaus forgot himself and took a tight line. Hurtling on, Orrin failed to hold the turn, lost control, and ploughed headfirst into a bank.

Aslak, seeing Orrin crash, corrected his angle and sailed past, sideslipping to a long stop. Niclaus skied back to check on Orrin. 'Are you all right?'

Orrin laughed. 'Yes, I'm fine.'

Big ugly scars cut into the snow, spoiling the beauty of the wilderness, but showing them Ludin's and Henik's routes.

On their heels, Niclaus could see where one had turned widely or too sharply. On other stretches, he could see where they had run into deep powdery snow, one of the hazards that came with being out in front. Although he believed he was making inroads into their leads, he doubted it was of any significance. It would take a few big mistakes from Ludin and Henik before his group could hope to catch up. No, they needed another way to make up the distance and the only plan formulating in Niclaus' head was a foolhardy one. He kept it to himself.

The high mountain range of Kebnekaise blocked the straightest route, forcing the racers to make a detour through a tight pass between Kebnekaise and the Akkavare mountains. From there, they would proceed to the stopping point at the edge of Slarin, the large conifer forest.

'Niclaus, we should be heading that way,' said Orrin, pointing toward the tracks made by Ludin and Henik.

Niclaus gave a mischievous grin. 'Don't you trust me?'

'No, not if you keep skiing that way.'

Aslak looked at Orrin nervously.

'We're gonna skim over Kebnekaise. It'll save us heaps of time and we'll come out ahead of Ludin and Henik.'

Orrin pulled to a halt. 'No way, it's too dangerous.'

'We've done it before, remember?'

'How lucky were we then?' Orrin shuddered at the memory of their folly. 'And that was not at the height of the thaw. It's too risky.'

Niclaus cursed Orrin for his good sense. He was right: the thaw was well underway.

'What do you think?' he asked Aslak.

'I'm pretty much undecided,' said Aslak, looking at the ground, not prepared to side with one brother over the other.

'We'll go over Kebnekaise,' said Orrin

Niclaus did not expect this. It was unlike Orrin to back down.

'Are you sure?' asked Aslak.

'What choices have we? Their lead is too big. Crossing Kebnekaise offers us a chance of beating Henik. It's worth a shot.'

'Just make sure you get me through this,' Aslak said to Niclaus.

It would take all Niclaus' skill to lead Orrin and Aslak. Bordered on all sides by razor-sharp ravines and deep gullies, its paths at times were barely the width of a single man. The region suffered from avalanches and cascading rivers of melted ice, as well as exploding jets of pressurised water that wiped out large sections of the path. If they were successful, they could expect to be on a par with Ludin and Henik, at the very least.

They skied through the rest of the morning and were already ascending Kebnekaise when Aslak asked to stop. 'We should take a rest.'

Niclaus was glad – they would have waited an eternity before either he or Orrin had made the suggestion.

'Come on, let's get going,' said Niclaus, after a short time.

'Do you think we could hold up a little longer?' Aslak asked, sheepishly.

Niclaus looked to his brother, but Orrin dropped his head and Niclaus was sure he saw a smirk at the corner of his mouth.

'Yes, let's wait. There's no point pushing ourselves to exhaustion is there?'

Orrin lifted his head and nodded approvingly, there was a long way to go and it made sense to take breaks.

Niclaus studied the route ahead. 'If my memory is right, from here the path begins to narrow. We might have to carry our skis.'

'Yes, and the way down the far side is hair-raising too,' added Orrin. 'You'll be fine. We'll keep you safe,' Niclaus said to Aslak.

They pushed on. At times, when the climb was especially arduous, they had to remove their skis and walk.

'I need another rest,' said Aslak.

He looked to be in a lot of discomfort. Niclaus was about to stop when Orrin intervened. 'Not yet. Keep going.'

'I have a bad stitch.'

'Breathe in through your nose. Hold your breath and then exhale, slowly, out through your mouth. You can beat a stitch. I know you can.' Orrin added further words of encouragement, 'Don't listen to your head. Listen to your heart.'

Aslak gritted his teeth and kept on going.

'Why didn't you let him stop?' whispered Niclaus.

'If he stops now, he'll stop again. If he perseveres he will take pride from his effort and he will climb.'

Niclaus was also struggling with the cruel climb although he would not admit to it. His head was light and pressure was building in his ears. At first, popping them gave relief but by halfway up, he could not force enough pressure to do so. He hoped his discomfort did not show.

'Can you see anyone?' asked Aslak as he rounded the path. It was the first clear view they had of the pass and valley below.

'No, we're still too far away,' replied Orrin.

Eventually the route opened out, enabling the boys to see the snow-crowned summit. They soon reached it. The vista was dramatic; they could see the forest of Slarin and the frozen wilderness beyond. Looking back towards their village, they could make out the top of the fjord and the dark sea beyond.

Orrin pushed off. 'Come on. We'll freeze to death if we hang about here.'

'Going up was the easy bit. Be careful not to build up too much speed,' warned Niclaus, as he started his descent. He was looking forward to getting off the mountainside.

Their route zigzagged, sometimes so sharply that Niclaus feared they would fall off. Aslak, to Niclaus' surprise, was managing extremely well. At certain points, it was possible to kickturn on to the track as it crossed below. Niclaus showed the best way to do it. Jumping and swivelling, he twisted his skis through a half turn, landing on the path about face. An apprehensive Aslak followed, his confidence growing with each landing, but for a few wobbles, he mastered it relatively easily.

Below, halfway down the mountainside, a beautiful lake glistened in the sunlight. The apex and top section of the mountain's inverted reflection shone off the surface. The lake was much smaller than Niclaus remembered, but he still recognised the danger it posed. They would cross beside the wall of hardened ice that held the lake in place and then they would drop below it. The pressure on the wall was immense. During the day, the icy water's temperature would rise slightly and the wall would melt a little. Nightfall would see the reverse with the wall hardening and the water cooling. One rupture in the wall's defences and the lake would empty down the mountainside. There would be no chance of survival. Niclaus and Orrin had seen its destructive powers at first hand on a previous visit to the mountain.

'Wait here,' whispered Niclaus, as he crept along the side of the lake.

About thirty paces on, he motioned for Orrin to follow.

'From here on it gets nasty. Keep the same space between us as I keep from Niclaus.' Orrin warned Aslak. 'And if you hear a rumble, ski. Don't stop.'

Niclaus moved slowly, his eyes fixed on the snow directly in front of him, studying its texture and thickness, detecting subtle changes, small variants that warned of danger underfoot. Little escaped his attention. A little further along, the path narrowed and dropped abruptly.

Ahead, Niclaus stood looking at a gentle waterfall. It splashed on to the carapace of ice covering the path before spilling into a bottomless ravine. Stamping his skis to get purchase, Niclaus gave a thrust of his poles and skied through the freezing water. He fought the urge to scream as the ice-cold water coursed over his head and body. Orrin followed.

Aslak gave a squeal as he passed under the waterfall to the consternation of the brothers.

'Hush,' warned Orrin.

Niclaus froze in anticipation. Orrin and Aslak did the same. Anxiously, they waited. The ice creaked, chastising Aslak for his noisy outburst. Niclaus held his breath, afraid to exhale.

CHAPTER 49

IN THE YEAR 840 AD

Vidar pushed the door open. Its creaking alerted the room's occupants to his arrival.

At the far side, Father Abbot, Tomás, and Cado were deep in discussion. The wooden boards groaned as Tomás crossed the ink-stained floor to welcome his guest. 'Ah, Vidar it's great to see you. It has been too long.'

Tomás looked older and thinner.

The smell of the scriptorium greeted Vidar as warmly as his old friend's embrace. To either side of the doorway, ran two bookcases filled with ancient manuscripts and books. Their mustiness blended with the aroma of fresh ink, adding atmosphere to the air.

After welcoming Vidar, Abbot Finntoin excused himself. 'I have to prepare my sermon,' he explained. 'I hope I'll see you in chapel later.'

'I'm afraid I don't think I'll be staying.'

'But you've come all this way.'

'I know, Father. I had intended to stay but I have only just learned of pressing matters that I must attend to.' He shot a glance at Cado.

'Then, come back to us soon,' said Abbot Finntoin.

Vidar tried to whisper his news to Cado.

'Would you like me to leave too?' asked Tomás.

Cado shook his head. 'Certainly not. Remember, you have been chosen to select Newgrange's next leader. It's a big responsibility.'

'I don't think that I am suited to make such a decision.'

'Tomás, there is no one more suited. You have undertaken the writing of the book of Newgrange.' Cado pointed to the tome on the table in front of them. 'Excluding me, you know more of my people's ways than anyone. You will give this book to the man who has the greatest need of it.'

Cado turned to include Vidar in the conversation. 'We three are about to take our most important voyage.'

'When do you expect us to leave?' asked Tomás.

'Now.'

'Oh,' exclaimed Tomás, startled by the suddenness. 'I will need to seek my abbot's permission.'

'We'll meet you at the boat,' said Cado.

Vidar, beaming with pride, told Cado how he had found the Vestibule. 'It's beyond the Blue Mountains …'

'I knew you'd do it. But now we have to undertake a new challenge.'

Vidar's head dropped. 'I'm sorry, Cado, I cannot go with you. I promised my family in Folda. No more voyages. I cannot break my word.'

'This is not for my benefit.'

'What do you mean?'

'The boys are in trouble.'

Vidar felt sick to the pit of his stomach. 'They're about to do the Trial. Tell me what you know.'

'I have seen things. If we do not reach them, there will be injury and death. We have to sail immediately.'

Vidar calculated the timescale. Even with calm seas and a favourable wind, the Trial would be underway before they reached Folda. 'We'll not make it.'

'We have to.'

CHAPTER 50

IN THE YEAR 840 AD

Having pushed himself hard on the last uphill stretch, Ludin was enjoying the rewards of a downhill run. The wind gushed into invisible gaps in his clothes, cooling his sweating body, and tears streamed from the corners of his eyes. Weaving around a small pine, he skied into another cloud of hovering mist. Rising temperatures and melting ice created the perfect conditions for the mist and icy fog but Ludin – convinced it would not stretch too far – believed that he could ski on easily enough.

The mist was much thicker than he had anticipated as he entered the hollow. Ludin was virtually blind. Travelling at speed was dangerous at the best of times, but now it was idiotic. Ludin, determined to hold his lead, abandoned good sense and refused to slow. The fog became disorientating. All he could see was white in every direction. Suddenly, he felt lightness in his stomach.

The sudden impact, when it happened, sent him hurtling head-over-heels for what felt like an age. He realised that the lightness that he had felt was the exact moment that he careered off the ledge. Getting to his feet, and looking up to the mist-covered ledge, he was shocked to see just how far he had fallen. The cliff in front stood half the height of the fjord of his home. He had been fortunate to survive – the deep snow had broken his fall. A few anxious moments passed as he searched for his skis. He planted kisses on each one as he found them. His luck was holding. There was little chance of anyone replicating his jump. Shaking off the loose snow, Ludin attempted to repair his shredded boot. The leather had ripped as the ski tore itself free during the impact. Using the straps, he was able to tie the boot into a semblance of shape before reattaching it. Good enough to hold until the finish, he told himself as he set off again.

Gradually the effects of his fall became evident. Aches, which had felt minor, flared up. The tiniest movement sent spasms through his neck, and his left ankle, wrenched in the fall, was unable to bear his full weight. Soldiering on, he kept most of his weight on his good foot and tried to limit his movements. Turning was proving excruciating and every bump exacerbated the pain. Ludin was losing time. How much, he could not gauge.

*

A combination of factors saved Henik from sharing Ludin's fate, sense and luck playing their parts. The good sense was that he slowed down; the luck was that the mist had partially lifted by the time he arrived at the edge. Seeing the disappearing ski tracks, Henik reacted with lightning speed. He leaned forward on his skis, forcing his poles into the snow as far in front as was possible. Then he sprang into the air and twisted his hips. He landed face forward with his skis at right angles. It had worked. He had stopped short of the ledge. Just. Looking over, he expected to see

Ludin's body below, but there was no sign, although it was hard to see anything clearly on the whitened valley floor.

He scanned his route. He had to continue northward before he found a path to the valley below. Then he would circle back to end up below where he now stood.

Finishing his descent, he entered a clear field of snow that stretched far into the distance. Heading southeast, he soon passed the side of Kebnekaise and veered northeast through the gap between it and the Akkavare Mountains. To the west was the cliff where Ludin had fallen.

It was late in the afternoon when Henik came across fresh tracks. He swore. Ludin had survived the fall. It was the only explanation. The others were too far behind. Ludin was proving to be a more worthy adversary than he had ever imagined. Although downhearted, he resolved to push harder. It was not long before Henik realised that Ludin hadn't survived the fall unscathed. The tracks of Ludin's skis merged into one. On downhill sections, Ludin was skiing on one leg. He must have hurt himself in the fall. Henik stepped up his pace. His spirits rose and his discomfort was forgotten as he caught sight of Ludin. He was alive to the chase. Henik was still some way off but he was closing.

*

Looking over his shoulder, Ludin could make out the silhouette of a solitary figure. He suspected that it was Henik, believing the other three would stick together.

To either side, the Kebnekaise and the Akkavare Mountains towered. The way ahead, described by Gunnar, was of a pass between the two ranges. His description was not exactly accurate. He forgot to mention that Kebnekaise's base split into massive talons of rock and stretched to touch the sharp face of Akkavare. Each one was like a miniature mountain. As Ludin reached the first hurdle of snow-covered rock, he recalled what his father had told him of the snow on the prongs.

'Wind from the plain carries snow on to the hard rock. Over time, it freezes and fresh snow accumulates, building up a sandwich of frozen slabs. It's a wonderful spectacle to see it when it crashes down.'

'Have you seen it?'

'Yes, I've caused it.'

'What? How?'

Olaf had smirked as he answered. 'The snow is so heavy. All it takes is for you to ski across the top of the prong. Oh, you can ski up and over it safe enough but ski across the top ledge and you'll send slab after slab of frozen snow tumbling down. One misplaced step, that's all it takes.'

There were tracks in the snow, a caravan of sleighs and reindeer travelling from the south. Men from his village and reindeer herders, no doubt bringing sleighs to the forest for the last stage of the race. From the footprints and animal droppings, he guessed they had stopped at the bottom of the slopes. He could see the sense of this: they probably had not wanted too many on the dangerous surface at once and had staggered their ascent.

Ludin was beginning to panic: with a damaged ankle, there was no conceivable way to maintain his lead unless he could somehow thwart the others and with the next stage of the Trial being his weakest discipline, he needed some sort of lead. He had to do something. What if he started an avalanche? The dangers were obvious. There was no way of knowing the outcome of a snow slide. He did not care. All that mattered was winning the Trial. If he could disturb one of the overhanging snow slopes, he could delay his opponents, perhaps gain a large lead. This would give him the advantage for the sleigh ride. With a healthy lead and having, in his mind, the best reindeer, he might be able to hold on to the finish.

So Ludin, having reached the top of the tallest prong, skied along its crest, deliberately triggering a split in the slope, ripping a deep fissure along the ledge. Although the rent was visible, the mountain of snow refused to budge.

A moment passed. And then a deep rumble roared out. Slab after slab charged down, sending a billowing cloud of snow skyward, obscuring Ludin's view.

CHAPTER 51

IN THE YEAR 802 AD

The tentacles of mist stretched all the way from the river to the hilltop monastery. To Hakon, it looked as though it was preparing an attack of its own. It was an eerie scene.

Hakon led his men out of the mist. 'It's exactly as the White Cross Follower described.'

Envik eyed the open gateway. 'It could still be a trap.'

'It would be a foolish one. With open gates, no one can stop us. No, I think we have found some easy pickings.'

The first to die did not waken, executed where they slept. The next were a few brothers stirred by the growing commotion. The monks were generally gentle men who offered little resistance.

Oto reached the church first. Finntoin, Sean and Brendan, sealed the tower, hoping to find sanctuary. Inside the three young monks bolted the door and climbed the ladder to the steps. The tower's design meant that the inside steps stopped short of the ground. The only way to reach them was by way of the long ladder, which the monks had pulled up behind them. The door to the tower, although strong, would yield, and it would not take the raiders long to reach them. The three monks' prayed that the raiders would not bother with them, but knew that if the raiders believed there was anything of value in the tower, their chances of survival were slim.

Abbot Monicurr, having worked long into the night, had fallen asleep on an improvised bed in a corner of his workshop, where he had been spending too many nights of late. Hearing the disturbance, he put the Holy Book inside its case and covered it with an old cloth recently removed from the back of the altar, praying that the raiders would not find it. Then he hurtled down the winding stairs into the sacristy. Grabbing the processional cross, he rushed out of the side door of the chapel. Lifting the cross, he twirled it round his head and brought it crashing into Oto's leg, its metal arm piercing deeply into his thigh. In the same instant, Oto thrust his blade into his attacker. It sliced through the abbot's cassock, through the softness of his stomach, and punctured a lung. The abbot collapsed.

'Nunc dimittis servum tuum Domine secundum verbum tuum in pace.' he murmured, before slipping into unconsciousness, never to awaken.

The raiding party worked swiftly through the houses, ransacking everything.

Tomás heard the raiders and rushed from his hut to the nearby barn, hoping to find refuge. It was empty but for one lame horse. He searched frantically for a hiding place for the book of Newgrange, desperate to keep it out of Norse hands. He hid it under some straw, praying that the intruders would not be thorough in their search. Although he agonised over the screams and cries of the dying and felt ashamed and cowardly, he was wise enough to know that it would have been futile to try to fight. Instead he cowered in the corner of an empty stall, praying for his dying brothers.

The horse was braying and whinnying, spooked by the furore outside. The barn door creaked open.

'There's a horse in here,' shouted Ralla, the first through the door.

Peeping through a gap in the wooden slots of the stall, Tomás counted three soldiers.

Ralla moved closer. He was so close that Tomás could see the scattering of scars on his forearms.

The Norsemen began to search the barn, kicking straw, and overturning buckets, before – inevitably – they found Tomás.

'What have we here?' teased Baldo, last of the three.

'It's the biggest rat I've ever seen,' laughed Kjarton.

'Let me have him,' implored Baldo.

Kjarton acceded.

Baldo tossed his axe from one hand to the other. He swiped at Tomás, who rolled out of the way, the blade swishing past his shoulder. Tomás tried to edge away but had nowhere to go.

Kjarton and Ralla circled from the side, boxing Tomás in more tightly. Baldo stepped forward and swung his axe again, and this time he did not miss. Tomás raised his arm to deflect the blow. The sheer power of the strike smashed his forearm. Tomás realised with horror that he was about to die.

'Wait,' called Kjarton. 'We're supposed to bring all the younger monks to Hakon.'

'He'll not miss one,' said Baldo.

'We've one in here,' shouted Ralla, walking to the barn door.

Hearing the call, Damian led Hakon towards the barn. 'It'll more than likely be him in there,' he explained. He knew that the barn was near Tomás' hut. They entered, finding Baldo kicking viciously at Tomás.

'It's him,' whispered Damian, who had changed out of his cassock and was now wearing a hooded cloak.

'Stop. He has something I want,' declared Hakon, marching to the monk.

'Give me the book and I shall let you live.'

Tomás was in severe pain but forced himself to stand before Hakon. He did not understand what the raider was saying.

Damian came into view.

'And a man's enemies shall be they of his own household,' Tomás mumbled. Cado had been right: Damian had returned.

'He asks for the book,' explained Damian.

The realisation dawned. 'You brought them here,' he shouted. 'Did you have them all killed for the book? What have you become?'

Damian looked away, saying nothing.

Hakon hit Tomás with the back of his hand, sending him sprawling to the ground. Pulling him to his feet, Hakon struck him again, full in the mouth, sending teeth and blood splattering. Hakon continued without mercy, beating Tomás until he curled up into a ball. Hakon unleashed a fury of punches to the back of Tomás' head. Finally, he pulled him up by the hair and laced three powerful kicks into his midriff.

'Tell him where the book is,' shouted Damian.

Hakon screamed words that he did not understand, all traces of humanity gone from his twisted face.

Tomás found courage and refused to speak. He was not foolish enough to believe that he would live in any case.

'Have it your way. Round up any White Cross Followers who still live and bring them to me.'

Tomás heard the screams long before the three monks stood before him.

'Now watch carefully,' Hakon said, taking a dagger from his belt. Transfixed by the horror that was about to unfold, Tomás whimpered for mercy.

'Give him what he wants,' pleaded Brother Feargal, realising that his fate now rested with Tomás. Tears were streaming down Feargal's angry face. 'Tell him.'

'I'll tell you what you want to know.'

His words came too late. In one swooping motion, Hakon brought the knife across Feargal's throat, slicing him from ear to ear. Death was instant.

'Let them go and I'll hand it over,' cried Tomás, rushing to get the book.

'Tell him that he has no bargaining rights here,' said Hakon to Damian.

Hakon pushed his wet blade into the stomach of Brother Conor. Conor gasped and crumpled as Hakon spilled his bowels and entrails on to the floor.

Damian took a step forward and grabbed the book out of Tomás' hand as more Norsemen entered the barn.

His work accomplished, he callously left his friend to the

mercy of the raiders.

A step behind Damian, Hakon gave his order: 'Kill them all. I have what I came for.'

Brother Darragh's futile attempt to flee was all too brief; Ralla butchered him where he stood.

'I have a rat to kill,' exclaimed Baldo, approaching Tomás, who looked around desperately for a weapon. There was a spade resting against the barn wall. Lunging, he managed to get to it before Baldo cut him off. Beaten and with a broken forearm, Tomás was in no condition to defend himself. He jabbed at the Norseman with the spade, using his one good arm. The Norseman looked away, feigning boredom.

'Look, the rat, he tries to fight.'

'The children back home fight better. He's pathetic. Finish him quickly,' ordered Kjarton.

Baldo used his sword to knock the spade from the monk's feeble grasp. His first blow was delivered with such force that it sent Tomás sprawling.

Tomás' screams for mercy went unanswered as Baldo carried on his savage assault. The final stroke was delivered with such ferocity that the blade sank deep into Tomás' chest, forcing Baldo to rest a foot on Tomás' trunk to pull the blade free. Whilst bending down, Baldo spotted the silver locket around the monk's neck. Its clasp broke, its contents spilt. Baldo snatched the locket and hid it in his pocket. One piece of booty he would keep for himself.

As Tomás felt his life ebbing away, he thought of his brothers and the suffering they had endured. He cursed Damian. How could he inflict such wickedness? He thought of Cado and how

Tomás had failed him. The book of Newgrange was lost. He knew he would not survive much longer and yet he felt no urgency in praying to his God. He felt abandoned, just like the Lord Jesus. If God would not save his own son what chance had he?

He was choking on his own blood. A warming sensation spread through his body as he slipped into unconsciousness.

The Norsemen retreated, carrying Oto with them. He was the only one to suffer any injury.

Soon Hakon and the raiders – along with their spoils, including the book of Ceanannus Mór and the book of Newgrange – were sailing homeward.

'We have what we came for,' said Envik. 'Shall I kill the White Cross Follower now?'

'Patience. He is still of use to me,' explained Hakon, who had not shared the knowledge of the book with his men.

With a wave of his hand, Hakon dismissed Envik, leaving him alone with Damian. 'It seems you spoke the truth of the wealth of this monastery. Have you also told me the truth about the book?' he asked, stretching out a hand to take it from Damian.

'I have, my lord.'

'Good. You will read it to me on our return.'

Hakon walked to Envik. 'Protect this with your life,' he said, entrusting him with the safety of the book of Newgrange.

CHAPTER 52

IN THE YEAR 840 AD

'I think it's safe to continue,' Niclaus whispered, after a time.

Unknown to Ludin or Henik, Niclaus, Orrin, and Aslak were coming down the mountain. They were a lot closer than Ludin could have imagined. Being higher up, they clearly saw Ludin's actions, and watched in horror as Henik was enveloped by snow and swept away.

Niclaus also knew that there was a high probability that the lower avalanche would trigger secondary ones higher up the mountain. Above them was a thousand times the amount of snow that had fallen in the recent disturbance. 'Get going,' he whispered.

Aslak looked unconvinced. 'Shouldn't we wait?'

'There's little point. The lower down the mountain we are, the greater chance we stand.'

'He's right,' agreed Orrin.

Niclaus pushed off, leading Orrin and Aslak in a speedy descent.

'Thank God,' said Aslak, as they reached the lower, relatively safer slopes.

'What about Henik?' Aslak asked.

'We can't leave him,' said Orrin.

'Watch me,' said Niclaus. 'He left me in the water.'

'Fine, go on. Come on, Aslak.'

Without question, Aslak followed Orrin.

'This is madness,' complained Niclaus, falling into line.

*

Reaching the place where they last saw Henik, they searched anxiously. Aslak found him. Tossed to the side, he had survived.

'I saw it too late. It was too fast,' he said groggily, as he forced himself to stand.

'Come on, let's get going,' said Niclaus. 'We'll struggle to catch Ludin now.'

Henik shook down his clothes. 'I wouldn't worry.'

'Why?' asked Aslak.

'Didn't you see the ski trail?'

'No, we went over Kebnekaise,' said Niclaus, nonchalantly.

'Ah, that explains how you caught me.'

'Why aren't you worried about Ludin?' asked Aslak again.

Henik laughed. 'The stupid fool skied off a drop. He's hurt; I think it's his leg. He's been skiing on one ski.'

*

Berit paced a track in the snow. His heart sank as the first skier came into view. It was not Henik. It was Ludin. By the look of him, he was minus a ski.

'Olaf, it's your son,' he shouted.

338

Olaf ran to meet Ludin, who was clearly in distress. 'What happened?'

'I fell over a drop. I think I might have broken my ankle.'

Olaf escorted Ludin into his tent.

Soon after, Niclaus, Orrin, Aslak, and Henik arrived, bringing the camp bustling to life.

Kliim, a tall, bony faced man of pale complexion, one of the older herdsmen, brought broth and bread to Olaf and his son.

'How many of the others have arrived?' Olaf asked, on hearing the hubbub outside.

'All four.'

Although Ludin was relieved that they were all safe – Henik had not only avoided the avalanche but had somehow met up with the others – he was disappointed. 'I thought I had a bigger lead,' he said to his father.

The noise outside was increasing – by the sound of it, an ugly altercation was kicking off.

Berit broke into the tent followed by a red-faced Ealver.

Ealver was pulling at Berit, trying to restrain the taller, stronger man. Towering over Ealver, Berit made the marshal look anything but the most senior villager in the camp.

'Stop this madness,' Ealver commanded.

'I'll kill him, like he tried to kill my boy,' spat Berit.

Alive to the threat, Kliim blocked Berit's path and tried to reason with his friend. 'Calm down,' Kliim said. 'What has you so incensed?'

'He started an avalanche, tried to kill Henik.'

Berit was pointing his finger accusingly at Ludin. Olaf was on his feet, ready to meet Berit man to man. It would have been some tussle.

Olaf defended his son. 'If he started one, it must have been an accident.'

'The others saw him ski across the crest,' shouted Berit.

Three other herdsmen rushed in, getting in between the two furious men, diminishing the likelihood of a fight. An elderly man of slender build followed. Berit calmed down instantly. It was Jakob, leader of the herdsmen. He radiated calm.

'Berit, will you allow me to settle this matter?'

Berit agreed, satisfied that Jakob would resolve matters fairly.

'I would like a word with your boy. Alone.'

Reluctantly Olaf left.

Jakob moved close and examined Ludin's injured ankle without a word. It was badly swollen and extremely warm.

Ludin screamed in fear as the herdsman drew a knife from his belt.

Olaf rushed back inside but, seeing that Jakob was attending to Ludin's ankle, he promptly retreated.

Gripping Ludin's leg, Jakob pushed the point of the blade into the swelling – pus squirted out. Jakob squeezed it until he was satisfied that most of it was out. 'I need something,' he explained, leaving the tent.

He was soon back, slapping a foul-smelling mixture on to the ankle. 'Animal dung. Now, my injured friend, tell me why you would try to hurt a herdsman's son.'

Ludin did not answer. He did not dare lie to Jakob.

'At least you are man enough not to deny your actions. Is this race worth a life?'

Again, Ludin did not reply.

'I think that when the Trial is over, we should allow you and Henik to sort this matter out, man to man.'

Jakob's decision satisfied Berit and Olaf. The old herder was right; if Ludin and Henik were old enough to partake in the Trial, they were old enough to resolve their disagreement. Henik would be free to seek retribution later.

Later, Berit led a train of sleighs out into the semi-darkness. They travelled through the night, carrying many of the villagers to the finish.

*

Niclaus felt agitated and unsettled. He still could not believe that Ludin had acted in such a way. He had had another restless night's sleep, filled by a maze of contorted dreams. He tried piecing the assortment together, to see if he could make any sense of them. In one, he watched as a much younger Vidar held out a bundle, giving it to Selina. In another, Ludin was holding his head under the water. Niclaus struggled and fought, but Ludin was too strong. In another, he saw the white wolf from the attack on Ludin. He was stroking it. This dream was the calmest until he looked down at his bloodied hands.

And then there was a dream that Niclaus had had before. In it, Niclaus drove his reindeer on to the frozen surface of the lake of Torne in an act of pure madness. The next morning he tried to convince himself that they were meaningless but his doubt lingered as he took his position next to Orrin in readiness for the beginning of the final stage.

The competitors' sleighs were lined up, side by side. Jakob had insisted on bringing two extra teams because he had a concern over one of Aslak's animals. Each competitor examined his own sleigh and beasts.

Jakob tried to persuade Aslak to replace the reindeer whose soundness was in question, but Aslak declined.

Shrugging his shoulders, Jakob addressed Ealver. 'Our job's finished, we are ready to leave when you are.'

'Again, Jakob, we are in your debt,' said Ealver, sincerely.

Ealver took a step forward. 'We all know that the forest of Slarin is home to the wolf and bear. As is tradition, we offer you all a choice of weapon, a sharp knife or a strong staff. The choice is yours.' Ealver smiled. 'Don't be too frightened. No one has ever been attacked in the forest,' he reassured.

Ludin and Orrin availed of a knife, although what use it would be fending off a pack of wolves was questionable. Aslak, Henik, and Niclaus chose the staffs.

Aslak swung his over his head. 'I'll smash their heads like so if they come near me,' he said, driving it into the compacted snow.

Ludin hobbled to his sleigh. His ankle was heavily strapped. None of the others had had a chance to speak with Ludin for his father had kept him away from them.

Ealver gave Ludin the signal to go, leaving the remaining four waiting in line. Henik broke rank. 'I want to thank you for yesterday. It was a selfless act coming back for me.' He offered his hand, first to Orrin and then Aslak.

'We shouldn't have bothered,' said Orrin light-heartedly. 'You didn't need us anyway.'

Henik then offered his hand to Niclaus.

Niclaus stared at it.

'It was not me that damaged your boat.' Henik's hand remained outstretched.

Niclaus could not explain why – perhaps it was something in Henik's manner – but irrespective of the reason, he believed him. With a firm grip, he shook his hand. He, Orrin and Aslak, had had a heated discussion – mostly about Ludin and the events of the last days. Niclaus had not hidden his anger. Ludin had broken the bond of friendship. Had he not saved him from the wolf? Niclaus still could not believe he had left him in the water. To make matters worse, Niclaus now believed that he was the one responsible for sabotaging his boat. And he had deliberately started the avalance that could have killed Henik. After the Trial, Niclaus would make him pay. As for their friendship – it was lost.

'Good luck for today,' offered Henik.

'I'll need it,' replied Niclaus, looking at his reindeer. He was not looking forward to completing this stage with his unusual animals. 'You better be worth it,' he whispered into the stag's ear. 'After all, I picked you.'

CHAPTER 53

IN THE YEAR 840 AD

Morton, Vidar, Tomás, and Cado rowed back to the *Ice Maiden* as quickly as they could. Once on board, Morton issued instructions. 'Time is against us. We need to set sail to Folda immediately.'

Soon the boat had cleared the Boyne estuary and was sailing along the east coast of Erin. By late evening, following a strong north-easterly wind, Erin was fading to the south-west and Alba was gaining prominence to the east. Tomás stood at the stern, watching until his homeland was lost to the sea.

Cado stood on a small crate, next to Tomás, and leant on the bulwark. He felt old and spent. He had carried his burden for far too long and he was looking forward to 'Peace at Journey's End.' The fact that Vidar had found the Vestibule confirmed his belief that someone younger would soon take his mantle.

Cado watched Tomás for a while. He still found it hard to believe that almost forty years had passed since they had first met. Tomás looked frail – he had aged considerably.

They had been through so much together and still they had much to accomplish.

'Is this your first sailing?' he asked Tomás, aware of his friend's discomfort.

'Yes, this is the first time that I've been on a boat.'

'Well, try to keep your eyes on the horizon. There's Iona,' he said, pointing to the island, trying to distract Tomás from his seasickness.

'Have you been there?' Tomás asked.

'Yes.' Cado elaborated no further.

Tomás let out a deep sigh.

'What's on your mind?' asked Cado.

'I often wonder what would have happened if I had not lied about Damian. He would not have been exiled to Iona and Abbot Monicurr, Feargal, Conor, Darragh – all of them would still be alive.'

'Oh, Tomás, you cannot hold yourself responsible for the actions of others. None of that was your fault.'

'I wish I could believe that.'

Cado patted his shoulder. 'You have the book with you?'

'Yes, I have it here.' Tomás tapped his satchel.

Cado jumped down from his crate. 'I'll be back in a moment. I need a word with the captain.'

'Ah, Cado,' said Morton, seeing the dwarf heading his way. 'I thought that this would be a time of rejoicing, me having fulfilled our arrangement but given the circumstances … it seems we have much more pressing matters to attend to.'

'Do not be too despondent. I could not ask any more of you and your crew. When this is over, then there will be time to toast you.'

The *Ice Maiden*, aided by the strong breeze, pushed beyond the islands of Alba. The weather was favourable; the cloud above was high and unthreatening.

'We are making excellent headway,' said Morton.

Vidar gripped the gunnel and looked ahead. 'We are still too far away for my liking, but I know that there's no one who could get me there quicker,' he countered, trying to snap out of his despondency.

'Do not get downhearted. Stay positive,' advised Cado, ushering Vidar to a spot out of earshot. 'Vidar, you have suffered so much and still there comes more that will try to break you.

'With you by my side, we will accomplish everything.'

'Vidar, I am old and of little use to you now. Soon, a new younger leader will emerge. That's why I need you to see this through. It's within your power to ensure the safety of Niclaus and Orrin. Everything depends on you and I am thankful that it does, because there is no one more able.'

Vidar stood silent, deep in thought.

Cado excused himself; he had one more person to prepare. He met Jorun in the hull. 'A new captain will be hungry for new business.'

Jorun laughed. 'I was hoping that you would come and see me. Given the opportunity, I hope we can reach an accommodation.'

The negotiations proved a lot costlier for Cado than the previous arrangement agreed with Morton. Jorun, forewarned, bargained hard.

'Morton tells a tale of a dwarf paying for all his voyages in advance.'

'That I did.'

'Well, it seems only fitting that I should be paid the same way.'

'I mean you no disrespect.'

Jorun gave him a look filled with suspicion.

'The seas can be a dangerous place. I mean to settle the bill when we get back to Erin,' said Cado.

'Agreed,' they said in unison, shaking hands on the deal.

Cado climbed out of the hull and walked to the stern where Vidar had joined Tomás. From experience, Cado knew that Vidar often sought solace in Tomás' company. Their friendship, from its shaky beginning, had grown into an unbreakable alliance.

'How are you feeling?' Cado asked Tomás.

'A little better. The sickly feeling has passed but I fear it hasn't gone far away.'

'You're lucky the crossing has been calm.'

'It'll all be worth it, if we get to Niclaus and Orrin. We will, won't we?'

'Tomás, again I have placed a great burden on your shoulders.'

'It couldn't be any worse than the attack.'

'I fear it may open old scars. Put your trust in God and you shall succeed.'

'We've been through a lot. I will see this to the end,' replied Tomás.

CHAPTER 54

IN THE YEAR 840 AD

Looking over his shoulder, Ludin could see Henik almost upon him. Ludin's erratic steering coupled with the extra work that went into leading, meant that his reindeer's pace had slowed and that most of his advantage had been lost. Shaking the reins, he demanded more effort from his team. The animals quickened, furrowing the virgin snow into grooves as they went. Henik's team – using the polished tracks to minimise effort – were poised to overtake. Aslak and Orrin followed close behind. Niclaus could tell that Orrin was deliberately tucking in to Aslak's slipstream. He was conserving energy. This tactic could make a significant difference during the latter stages of the race.

Niclaus was last, by quite a considerable margin. He felt such a fool. If only he had not picked Vidar's odd-looking reindeer. Clearing the summit of a hill, with the land before him open and relatively flat, he could see where the snowy terrain met the forest of Slarin. The contrast of the pure snow against the dark wall of threatening trees instantly reignited his sense of foreboding. Slarin, so full of menace, stood expectant – he could sense its intent. It felt as though bears, wolves and other fierce animals were waiting for them.

Niclaus sped on, keeping an eye on the ground, watching for paw prints. Conscious of his anxiety rising, he tried to regain his composure. He recalled Vidar's training. Fear, he had explained, ate at a man's reasoning. If left unchecked it could drive him to act irrationally.

So Niclaus refocused on the race. If his team did not find a spurt of speed, his challenge would soon be over. If they failed to close the gap, the race would end up a contest between two of the five competitors.

To stay ahead, Ludin's reindeer were working much harder than any of the others. Niclaus suspected this would have repercussions later in the race, perhaps making the difference between winning and losing. Aslak was not going to be in contention; his reindeer were no match for Orrin's and Henik's powerful teams. In Niclaus' opinion, Orrin and Henik were the two main contenders now. Orrin had the better team but the much more experienced Henik had the technique and guile. With little between the pair, a piece of good fortune would probably decide the outcome.

Ahead, Ludin, followed by Henik, led the procession into Slarin. To either side of their path, tall snow-covered conifers stood, creating a long stretching avenue, wide enough to fit perhaps ten sleighs abreast. Ominously, heavy mauve clouds, rolling in on the strengthening easterly breeze, were replacing the white-tipped clouds overhead.

Niclaus was grateful for the shelter offered by the trees. Although they blocked most of the freshening breeze's force, the colder air was unmistakable. The temperature had dropped. Early in the season, fresh snowfalls were not unheard of. Niclaus was certain that nastier conditions would soon be upon them.

Repeatedly Ludin picked the wrong line, misread the ground, and forced his team into deep, energy-sapping snow. He battled hard, driving on at a merciless pace. Henik, on the other hand, sat tucked behind Ludin, conserving as much energy as possible.

And then, when he got within range, Henik quickened up and moved to pass.

The manoeuvre stirred Ludin and his team. They would not give up without a fight. Although Ludin's pair kept their line true, and forced their challengers on to the rougher terrain, the fresher animals gradually crept alongside.

His lead slipping, Ludin saw an opportunity and steered into Henik's sleigh. Henik was fortunate to jump clear as his reindeer crashed to the ground.

'I'll kill you,' he shouted after Ludin.

Pulling up, Aslak, Orrin and finally Niclaus stopped to help. Niclaus was again begrudging. Helping one of their main challengers seemed so ill-advised. 'He wouldn't have stopped for any of us,' he muttered under his breath.

Henik immediately checked his animals.

'How are they?' asked Aslak.

'They look fine but I'll not know until they are pulling again.'

'Come on, let's get this out,' said Orrin. The sleigh was buried in a bank of snow.

Once righted, the boys looked for any signs of damage.

'Look here,' said Niclaus, pointing to the back support of the sleigh. 'The leg's cracked.'

Henik inspected it, concluding, 'It's only splintered. It looks rigid enough. If the opportunity arises I shall repay you, I promise.'

Ahead, Ludin continued to push too hard and too fast, causing his animals to tire needlessly. Repeatedly, he steered badly, choosing the wrong lines and tracks. Reluctantly, he slowed to a pace more manageable for his animals.

Henik soon caught up with Ludin again. Aslak, closely followed by Orrin, was not much further back. Niclaus again brought up the rear. Unknown to each competitor, hungry eyes were attentively watching their progress.

*

Silently they closed. Moving in a line, each paw touched the snowy ground in perfect time with that of the dog in front. The alpha male sized up his targets. The wolf disregarded the first, fitter two teams of reindeer, and the last, which looked too powerful. Left with a choice between Aslak and Orrin's animals, it selected the former. The wolf detected the weakness in one of the reindeer's hind legs; it was landing minutely out of time.

Breaking their cover, the hunters were instantly upon the speeding train.

'Wolves,' shouted Orrin.

Aslak reacted, steering his team to the right. The sharp veering caused them to slow, allowing the lead wolf to close and lunge. Orrin sped on, miraculously guiding his terrified animals on a straight course. There was a split in the terrain in front. If he kept his line true and twisted left, there was a possibility of forcing a few of the wolves over a ledge. The drop, no more than the height of three men, offered a chance of breaking up the assault. Sailing through the middle of the pack and banking sharply, his move sent two wolves over as hoped. He felt a bump as his sleigh ran over another. The animal howled before falling silent. The runner crushed the beast high in its chest, broken shards of bone piercing its heart. Only two had made it into the killing field.

Niclaus, being too far back to help, watched horrified as the lead wolf lunged, sinking its teeth into the back of Aslak's reindeer. The animal bucked, kicked and turned tightly as it tried desperately to escape. The turn, coupled with the momentum of the sleigh, forced it to first shudder and then coup. Aslak rolled off as it overturned. He swung his staff, striking the lead wolf a powerful blow between shoulder and back.

The wolf regained its footing in readiness to attack. Aslak, who had taken a defensive position in front of his reindeer, was swinging wildly.

The second wolf closed, snarling. Aslak feigned a swipe. Distracted, defending his position, he left himself open to an attack by the lead wolf. It lunged, biting his hip, its powerful jaws ripping through clothing and flesh, gnawing to the bone. The taste of warm fresh blood sent the animal into frenzy. It tossed its head from side to side, dragging and pulling Aslak to the ground.

Orrin leapt from his sleigh. His reindeer raced off, dragging his sleigh, desperate to get away from the wolves. His knife met only air as he rolled and landed under the alpha male. It struck with ferocity, biting hard, with its ripping fangs tearing into flesh, muscle, sinew, and bone. Orrin screamed and writhed in agony. Orrin's only chance had been his dagger but he had dropped it during his fall. He gripped at the animal's throat, trying in vain to choke it.

Aslak fought to stand. He was bleeding profusely. Regaining his staff, he prodded at the second animal while trying to get to Orrin.

Much to Niclaus' surprise, his reindeer did not take fright. They obeyed his command and raced towards the wolves. Reaching the overturned sleigh, Niclaus dismounted and rushed to Orrin. His hopes sank as the two wolves Orrin had sent over the ledge came into view. It was hopeless. He had no axe, not like the other time. All he had was a staff. No plan came to mind.

Ludin and Henik would come to help.

'Help,' roared Niclaus, as he charged at the alpha male. He smashed it with his staff, catching it full on the head. He hurt it but he did not know how badly.

Seeing the extent of Orrin's injuries made Niclaus sick.

The wolves that fell over the ledge, having made up the ground, were now ready to strike. Niclaus, his staff, and wounded Aslak and Orrin would be no match against the four ravaging beasts. 'Henik, Ludin, help,' Niclaus roared again.

The wolves closed. He was despairing. Help would arrive too late.

One of Aslak's tangled reindeer broke loose and made a dart for freedom.

There was further howling. God, no, thought Niclaus, as more wolves broke from the tree line.

The original pack seemed startled. Something was not right.

Niclaus stood mesmerised – racing toward him was the

magnificent beast from the lake.

Immediately, the two lead animals met in combat. His pet was huge, dwarfing its challenger. The skirmish was brief. The smaller animals, outsized and overpowered, soon raced away.

The white wolf approached Niclaus and pawed him affectionately. Vidar's prediction had been right – this beast was bound to him.

With Niclaus safe, the white wolf led its pack away.

Niclaus rushed to assist Orrin as Henik arrived.

'That wolf … it saved you … attacked the others!' exclaimed Henik, amazed by the scene he had witnessed.

Niclaus and Henik did everything they could think of to help the injured boys. Henik, who had helped to treat many a herder who had been gashed by the antlers of rutting stags, took charge. 'Rip me some cloth.'

Niclaus, cut long strips from a blanket on his sleigh.

Crumpling up the strips, Henik packed the dressing into the neck wound. Working speedily, he applied pressure before using other strips as bandages, tying them as tightly as possible. 'That's the best I can do,' he said.

They lifted Orrin onto the back of Niclaus' sleigh. His complexion was ghostly white and his breathing shallow.

Aslak was writhing in pain and Henik tried to reassure him as he worked. 'I've seen worse,' he lied.

The position of the wounds made them much more difficult to bandage but Henik made a good stab at it. 'Don't you worry, you'll be fine.'

Aslak was crying in a mixture of pain and shock. 'I'm dying aren't I?'

Henik grabbed and shook him. 'Now you listen to me, you're in pain but you're not too bad. Stop feeling sorry for yourself. If you want to see bad take a look at Orrin.'

Henik's harshness had the desired effect. Aslak's panic eased.

As Henik said it, Niclaus caught his eye. 'Damn, I didn't mean …'

'You don't need to explain. I know what you were doing. You have done so much. Thank you.'

Henik shrugged off the compliment. 'Come on, let's get moving.'

After calming the reindeer, it took all of their might to right the sleigh and lift Aslak on to the back of it.

Niclaus thanked Henik again. 'Go on, your work is done.'

'I'm not leaving you.'

'You have to. Get to the stopping point. Get help. The quicker you go, the sooner they can bring help. And besides, I need you to win the race.'

Henik cursed the race.

'No, I need you to stop Ludin.'

Reluctantly Henik agreed to continue. 'I'll pray for them,' he said, climbing into his sleigh.

The words sounded strange coming from Henik. While the entire village had converted to Christianity years before, the herders kept their own religion, so Niclaus did not know to whom Henik would be praying. It mattered little. Niclaus felt humbled. Henik, the boy he had vilified his entire youth, had grown into a man he would be proud to call his friend.

'I'll get help as quickly as I can,' Henik called back.

Niclaus tied Aslak's sleigh to his own and encouraged his reindeer onwards. His obedient animals responded and they were immediately on their way.

CHAPTER 55

IN THE YEAR 840 AD

The dragonboat was drawing ever closer, and there was no doubt that it was flying the raven, the emblem of Hakon the Black.

'Vidar, Cado, and Tomás into the hull,' ordered Morton. 'If they find any of you, we're finished.'

'We haven't time to stop,' argued Vidar, desperate to get to Niclaus and the boys.

'We can't outrun them and besides I pay my levy to Hakon. As long as he does not find any of you, we should be fine, and should be able to continue on our journey.'

Morton followed the three into the hull. He rummaged around in a chest at the far end and produced a large flag bearing the same crest as the Norse boat.

Climbing back out, he passed the flag to Torre, who attached it to the sail.

The gaps between the boats narrowed as the Norsemen dropped oars and rowed. As soon as they were close enough, they threw and latched grappling irons onto the *Ice Maiden*, and pulled it alongside their dragonboat.

'I'm coming aboard,' shouted the Norse leader, whose angry

eyes and twisted nose added to his menace.

'It is an honour to have one of Hakon's men on my ship,' said Morton, bowing respectfully.

'What do you carry?'

'My ship is empty. I am going to pick up a cargo.'

'And you carry the flag of Hakon.'

'Yes, I agreed the handsal with Lord Hakon myself. At the end of every year, I honour him with my levy. In return, he guarantees my ship safe passage on the seas.'

Vidar was listening intently to the exchange. His face soon drained of colour.

Tomás – who was now dressed as a sailor, complete with woollen hat to cover his tonsured head – noticed Vidar's pallor. 'What is it?'

'He knows me. If he finds me, we are doomed.'

Gudny walked across deck, looking for anything of value. 'What provisions have you?'

'Nothing of worth. We mean to stock up in Folda. You are welcome to the little that we have.'

Morton gave Walrus and Torre instructions. 'Bring up whatever is below. And don't forget the casks of beer.'

Gudny's mood lightened. 'Go and help them,' he told two of the Norsemen.

Vidar whispered instructions to Cado and Tomás. 'To the forecastle.' The risk of the Norsemen turning violent meant that he wanted to stay close.

Next, he pulled his hood over his head – trying to hide his face. He dragged the casks to the steps of the hull, hoping to drown out the sound of Tomás and Cado as they scurried into the cramped forecastle. He lifted the first cask and passed it to a burly soldier who was about the same age as Niclaus. A quick glance confirmed that he did not know him.

Above, Gudny's mood soured at the sight of the meagre supplies. He punched Morton in the stomach, winding the unsuspecting captain.

'Bring that other cask here,' called the burly man.

Vidar climbed out of the hull with the cask balanced on his shoulder. He set it down and, trying not to draw attention to himself, joined the rest of the crew by the mast.

'You must have coin. All captains carry coin. How else would you pay your men?' asked Gudny.

'I have a few coins.'

'Then pay me and I'll grant you safe passage.'

Morton knew from experience that the only hope to get away was to show bravado. If he showed any weakness, chances were he and his crew would be killed. 'I have paid my levy to Hakon. I will not pay a second time.'

Gudny's men, sensing tension, drew weapons and stood by their leader. The drawn weapons alerted the men on the dragonboat. Reinforcements crossed to the *Ice Maiden*.

Morton looked irate. Vidar suspected he was not about to end his captaincy cowering on his own boat.

Vidar studied Gudny. He remembered him as a vicious man who riled easily.

The unforeseen delay was eating at Vidar. The *Ice Maiden* needed to be under way. He had to take things in hand – if he did not the boys would not survive.

'I have given you all my provisions. You have overstayed your welcome.' Morton turned his back on Gudny and walked towards his crew. 'Men, we have a ship to sail.'

Infuriated by the captain's slight, Gudny raised his sword and moved toward Morton.

Vidar rushed at Gudny without thinking and wrestled him to the deck. Before any of the Norse warriors had a chance to respond, Vidar had Gudny's own blade pointing at his neck.

'Tell your men to stay back,' Vidar warned.

'Do as he says,' Gudny spat.

Vidar dropped his hood to reveal his face.

A few of the men gasped.

A warrior in dark sheepskin stepped forward. His face was smooth and his hair braided. He knew Vidar immediately. 'We were told you were dead.'

'He's under threat of death,' spat Gudny.

'Quiet,' ordered Vidar.

'It is true,' confirmed Mord.

Vidar gripped Gudny by the shoulder of his tunic. 'I want satisfaction first.'

'What satisfaction?' Mord asked, now speaking for the Norsemen.

'Gudny has broken Hakon's pledge. Each one of you on board has refused to honour the flag of the Raven.' Vidar pointed to the fluttering banner. 'I ask for *Einvigi*.'

'I see no sense in this,' said Mord.

'Let me settle this with Gudny. If I win, the *Ice Maiden* is free to sail on her journey.'

'I cannot let you leave.'

'Let the ship sail and I will board your boat. You can bring me to Hakon. I am sure he will reward you all well. And you have my word that I will not mention this incident.'

'And if you lose?'

'Sink the boat, and leave no trace of your dishonour.' Vidar chose his words well for he believed Mord to be honourable.

'*Einvigi* must be upheld,' agreed Mord. 'What say you, Gudny?'

Gudny raised himself to a sitting position. 'Give me my sword and I'll silence his insolent tongue.'

Using the sole of his foot, Vidar pushed Gudny to the ground, throwing his sword by his side. He joined the crew of the *Ice Maiden*.

'Thanks, lad,' said Morton.

'What's *Einvigi*?' asked Anders.

'A fight. Gudny must face me or lose his honour.'

The men cleared the deck of clutter before forming a ring.

'Leif, will you second me?' Gudny asked.

'Gladly,' agreed Leif, the burly warrior.

Mord stood between Vidar and Gudny. 'You need a second.'

'Morton, will you be mine?'

'Perhaps one of the younger men would be better suited.'

'Are you too old?' asked Vidar, deliberately challenging Morton.

'What do you need me to do?'

'Pass me a shield if one breaks.'

'That's all?'

'Have you a weapon?' interrupted Mord.

'I have neither sword nor shield.'

Mord pulled out his gleaming weapon. 'Have mine.'

Behind the Norsemen jostled for position.

Mord gave out a series of orders. 'Get me six shields and two corded swords.'

Each combatant tied the smaller sword to his wrist.

'A back up in case my main sword breaks,' Vidar explained to Morton.

Similar in build and roughly the same height, Gudny was half a dozen years younger than Vidar. Vidar remembered him as a warrior of great promise.

'To first blood,' said Mord.

'No,' replied Gudny. 'To death.'

'Do you agree?' asked Mord.

Vidar consented.

Below, Tomás prayed while Cado relayed the snippets of the conversation that he picked up.

Mord checked over Gudny's weapons. 'They are fine.'

He walked to Vidar to check his. 'He's a duellist, one of the best. Beware when he pulls his sword away; he has a tendency to thrust again, catching many a man off guard.'

'Why do you help me?'

'This duel will be spoken of. Hakon will get to hear of it and I fear his vengeance if harm comes to you.'

Mord stood in the centre between both men. 'Vidar's weapons are also fine. Gudny, as challenged, you strike first. Shield against sword until no more.'

Gudny swung and Vidar parried. Then Vidar attacked. Both continued in accordance with the rules, blow after blow until Gudny's shield cracked.

'Next shield,' Gudny called to Leif.

Gudny brought his sword down through a high arc. Vidar raised his shield, his movement dispersing much of the power.

Gudny cursed Vidar.

'You strike like a woman,' Vidar whispered into Gudny's ear as their heads met.

Gudny, reacting, tried to head butt Vidar. Vidar read the move, dodged the blow and sunk his teeth into Gudny's ear, biting off a piece. Gudny screamed in pain. Mord moved quickly to separate the pair.

The duel continued. Vidar's shield split and he took his second one.

'You've got him,' encouraged Morton.

The shield felt lighter.

Gudny struck and the shield splintered badly.

'Damn it,' swore Vidar.

'What is it?' asked Morton, as Vidar got to his feet.

'We didn't check the shields. This one is made of light wood. It's more than likely a child's shield. It won't last.'

'Come on,' teased Gudny.

Vidar rubbed his ear, mocking Gudny's injury, the blood from which dripped and splattered over his tunic.

Two more blows and Vidar's shield split.

'Last shield,' warned Mord. 'When it breaks, fight to the death.'

It was made of the same soft wood.

Gudny swung again, his blade burying deeply. As Gudny retracted his sword, he lunged, just as Mord had warned, stabbing his blade.

Vidar, reacting too slowly, suffered a wound high on his shoulder.

Gudny pulled the sword free. He looked satisfied.

Vidar was in trouble. When his last flimsy shield broke, he would have to face Gudny both injured and with only a sword. Gudny would hack him to pieces.

He had to act.

Feigning a strike, Vidar stopped mid-swing and crashed his useless shield into Gudny's face, the force of the blow sending him sprawling. Vidar's shield fell to the ground. Under the rules of *Einvigi*, once either man let go of his last shield, both combatants were free to strike at will. Vidar moved in as Gudny struggled on the deck, unable to get to his feet.

Vidar swung at Gudny's head. Gudny raised his shield to parry. Vidar's lower swing sliced deeply into Gudny's exposed thigh and the wounded man dropped his guard. Seizing his opportunity, Vidar chopped into the exposed arm of his opponent.

Gudny dropped his sword. He had lost and was now reliant on the mercy of Vidar.

Behind, Leif, not prepared to watch his leader die, drew his dagger and charged at Vidar.

Morton, alive to the danger, jumped into the path of Leif's dagger. Shielding Vidar, Morton took the blade high in his chest.

CHAPTER 56

IN THE YEAR 802 AD

Cado began the long trek that he hoped would ultimately restore the monks' and Tomás' books to their rightful owners.

His ability to foretell the future was inconstant. He could not always unlock what he needed to know and all the snippets of knowledge he had unravelled so far seemed to have no bearing on this trip. Travelling south, he made for one of the many trading posts sprouting up along the coast. Dubh Linn, at the mouth of the Liffey, was perhaps the richest trading encampment along the eastern coast. It was here that a steady traffic of ships had created the perfect conditions for the beginnings of a township.

Cado loathed the place: it gave off the most pungent smell of decay, especially on warmer days. Still, the trade centre was flourishing with merchants selling every kind of ware. Traders openly bought and sold live booty: sons and daughters sold for meagre reward, as well as folk who one way or another had fallen foul of their kinsmen. It was in this backwater of a place that Cado had traded his village's resources. As well as precious metals and stones quarried in their deep mines, gold had been unearthed in the streams and mountains around the village. Newgrange and its people had amassed a fortune over the years.

Business was brisk. A stall selling fine silks caught Cado's eye.

'You'll have to pay me more than that,' said a trader to a bartering customer. 'It's from the east, from the far end of the Danube.'

Cado passed a few more stalls. A line of religious men bartering over inks and dyes caught his attention. Walking away, Cado was disgusted to find a large midden blocking his path to the dock. He believed that the pigs in Newgrange lived in better conditions. A wealthy merchant by the name of Conn greeted him as he arrived at the dock. Conn had earned the name King of the Port. Nothing moved in or out without his permission.

'I have it here,' said Conn, pointing to a small cart not far from the waterside, attended by three of his men.

Cado pointed to the nearest of two vessels. 'It's that boat over there.'

Conn's men loaded a casket on to the boat.

Like most things in his organised life, Cado had planned the sailing far in advance. The cargo ship was deep bellied, a sturdy vessel with a large rectangular sail, which made her relatively quick through the water.

'Welcome aboard,' greeted Ivar, the old captain.

It was immediately apparent to Cado that the tall and gaunt captain had few sailing days left.

Cado was soon on board and en route to Hakon's encampment for the first of what he imagined would be many distasteful meetings.

Once underway, the wind was at their backs, giving good speed and, coupled with a gentle sea, the crossing was pleasant and quicker than anticipated.

*

The planks creaked under the motion of the rocking boat as Cado walked to the stern. Glancing towards his home, he prayed for Tomás. He hoped his friend would understand that he had been powerless to intercede. He could have done nothing to stop the carnage. He was grateful that Tomás continued to wear the pendant that he had given him.

Cado asked for a private word with the captain's first mate. Tall and heavy, Morton was a match for anyone foolhardy enough to tackle him, yet his demeanour suggested that all he was interested in was earning an honest living.

'The captain is getting old. I think he could be persuaded to retire,' said Cado.

Morton said nothing.

Cado felt the man's eyes upon him. He was sizing him up, deciding whether or not he trusted him. He hoped Morton would be easily swayed.

'Don't speak in riddles,' said Morton, gruffly. Young and impetuous, he was definitely not the sort of man to get on the wrong side of.

'Perhaps if someone made him an offer for his boat, a generous offer, the old man might retire happily.'

Cado and Morton entered into a private discussion. Morton liked Cado's plan. If all worked out, Captain Morton would be in charge on the return voyage.

Having concluded his business, Cado spent the early evening amusing the crew with stories of his people. He also performed some magical tricks, one of which resulted in a young red-haired sailor by the name of Torre losing his belt and his trousers, much to the amusement of his companions.

The voyage continued to go well as Cado bonded with the crew. In Morton, Torre and the blond-haired Rune, Cado had found three new friends.

The rugged landscape of the Norse coast came slowly into view.

'It is beautiful here,' said Cado to Rune.

'No, here is a poor imitation of the northern fjords. You should see Folda, our homeland. It's a real fjord.'

A welcoming committee greeted them as they docked at Strager. Ivar and his crew were clearly popular. From what Cado could ascertain, the port was one of the ship's regular stops.

'The captain was born here. And the speedy crossing has allowed us a slightly longer break before our next sailing,' explained Morton.

'That explains his high spirits,' replied Cado.

'I have enjoyed your company, little friend,' said Morton. 'I hope we'll have the same pleasure on the way back.'

'Fear not. I'll be here.'

'Not if you continue with your planned journey.'

In seeking directions to Hakon's lair, Cado had had to give the crew some of the details of his journey.

'Don't go,' Morton pleaded. 'This venture is suicidal.'

'I have to. We have business.'

'You will suffer under his blade.'

'Morton, have faith in me,' said Cado. 'The next time we'll meet, you'll be captain.

Cado gave Morton a long list of sailings. The times and dates spanned some thirty years. The negotiations continued until they thrashed out a mutually satisfactory agreement. With coin in his hand – enough to make the captain an offer for his boat – and the contract agreed with Cado, Morton found himself in a position he could not have dreamt of. His future was secure.

Before disembarking, Cado entered into one final negotiation with Morton. 'And what would you say if I were to pay in advance for all the voyages that I wish to undertake?'

Morton laughed but Cado pressed on. 'What if I wanted all my sailings to remain a secret?'

'A secret from whom?'

'You must tell no one, not even your crew.'

'And for my silence you will pay me in full for all your journeys, now?'

'Yes. And I'll pay you ten per cent extra for your silence if you are agreeable.'

Morton spat on his palm before shaking Cado's hand. 'You have a deal.'

'Your coin is in the chest, in the hold.'

Morton laughed heartily when he opened the casket. Inside, when added to the handful of coins Cado had already given him, was the exact figure that they had settled upon.

'I started this voyage as nothing more than a ship's mate to a sickly captain. Today you have made real all my dreams and ambitions. I am indebted to you.'

Again, he tried to dissuade Cado from going to see Hakon.

'Cado, if I was a greedy man I would hope that you never make it out of Hakon's camp. I'd be rich without having to do anything. But in my heart I pray it isn't so.'

'Fret not. We have many adventures left to complete.'

Morton reluctantly repeated the directions to Hakon's encampment. 'Remember we have to sail in four days, with or without you,' warned the future captain.

Having said his goodbyes, Cado set off to meet the monster, the butcher of Ceanannus Mór.

CHAPTER 57

IN THE YEAR 840 AD

Alerted to Leif's attack, Vidar rushed to defend Morton. With one stroke, he almost beheaded the burly warrior. He was dead before he hit the ground. To his side, Morton collapsed, the dagger buried deep in his chest.

Vidar rushed to his aid. 'Quick, get Cado,' he ordered Jorun, as Mord stepped between Vidar and Gudny.

Cado and Tomás rushed from the hull.

'Help him,' pleaded Vidar.

Cado knelt beside Morton, powerless. 'If I could, I would.' He was too late.

Tomás, leaning over the body, gave Morton absolution.

Behind, Vidar dragged Leif's limp body to the bulwark where he tossed it into the sea, reciting an old Norse curse. 'May Valhalla close its gates to you.'

Then, standing tall, he breathed deeply, composing himself. He called Jorun.

Jorun, like the rest of the crew, was close to tears. 'Yes.'

'Captain, lead your men. Make Morton proud and finish his last voyage. Niclaus' and Orrin's lives depend on you.'

Torre, who stood next to Jorun, answered. 'We'll make it.'

Vidar turned to Mord. 'Let's get off this boat. This crew has a journey to complete.'

'What of Gudny?' Mord asked.

'It's your ship. He's your responsibility.'

Mord looked down at the injured warrior. 'He has disgraced Hakon. Throw him overboard.'

Cado bade farewell to Vidar. 'Be strong,' he encouraged.

'Save the boys, save my son.'

Mord called out his first orders to his crew. 'Remove the grapnels. Let's take Vidar home.'

The metal hooks were removed and the boats separated.

Tomás re-emerged from the hull dressed in his habit. 'Vidar,' he called.

Vidar stood at the side of the dragonboat. 'Yes, Tomás?'

'Take me with you.'

'I can't. This does not concern you. This is my fight.'

'I too have unfinished business.'

'It's too late. We are gone already.'

Tomás took his satchel off, held it high over his head, and jumped from the *Ice Maiden* into the water beneath.

CHAPTER 58

IN THE YEAR 840 AD

'Damn him,' shouted Jorun, at the sight of Tomás leaping from the boat. 'The old fool's endangering us all. We should be away from here at full haste.'

'Stop the boat,' roared Walrus, anxious to pick up Tomás.

'I'll get him,' called Vidar from the dragonboat, throwing a length of rope.

'Let him drown,' shouted one of the Norsemen.

Jorun leant over the gunnel. 'We haven't time for this.'

'Sail on,' said Cado. 'Vidar will need Tomás' help where he's going.'

'Are you sure?'

'Yes.'

'Good luck,' shouted Cado. 'My dearest friend,' he whispered under his breath.

The rest of the *Ice Maiden* crew offered words of encouragement as Vidar and Mord pulled Tomás from the water.

'Let's get moving,' commanded Jorun, determined to make the most of the reprieve. The men, still reeling, responded to his order and the *Ice Maiden* widened the gap between the vessels.

When they were making good progress towards Folda, Jorun called the men together. 'I think this is the place to send Morton to the waves. Perhaps Rune or Torre could say a few words.'

Rune stood next to the body of his captain. 'It's probably better that he died at sea. I couldn't really have seen him enjoying life on land.' Rune tried to force a smile as he looked at the body of his lifelong friend. 'We shall miss you …' he gulped, trying hard to suppress his emotion.

Torre took over. 'Go ahead,' he ordered. Jorun and Walrus lifted Morton's body and dropped it into the sea.

Jorun broke the hush. 'I know we are saddened by Morton's death but the best way we can honour his memory is by getting Cado to Orrin and Niclaus as quickly as possible. Cado tells me that we are in a race against time. I believe that saving the boys will ease our own grief.'

'What about Vidar and Tomás?' Rune asked.

Cado sensed he was contemplating some sort of rescue. 'Please trust me, as Morton did. There is nothing we can do for them. Their fate is in their own hands.'

Rune reacted angrily. 'We can't just leave them. Morton would go back for them.'

'No, he would not. Vidar sacrificed himself so that we could get help to Orrin and Niclaus,' said Cado.

Jorun hushed the rising voices. He was new to command but Cado sensed the authority in his voice. 'We have been paid to take this ship further north. That is where we go unless Cado deems otherwise.'

'We go to the boys,' confirmed Cado.

As the *Ice Maiden* neared Folda, Cado called the men for a final meeting. 'If Gilder learns what has happened to Vidar or Tomás, he will attempt a rescue. The result would be catastrophic and there are others to consider. There's Elwin and the girls. Please think of them. They need not know of Vidar's predicament.'

Out of earshot of Cado, Jorun spoke to his men. 'When we drop Cado off, we have no sailings. I was thinking that if I was to pay my respects to Hakon as a new captain and agree the levy, we could perhaps use the excuse of our visit to attempt a rescue.'

'If he's still alive by then,' said Rune, dejectedly.

*

'Who is it?' enquired Gilder. It was too early in the day for visitors.

His jaw dropped. 'Why are you here?' He embraced Cado. 'I haven't seen you since … Selina, come quickly, see who is here.'

Selina rushed past Gilder and lifted Cado in the tightest embrace. 'All that I have is thanks to you,' she said, kissing his cheek.

'Come, come on in,' invited Gilder.

Cado cleared his throat. 'I'm afraid I bring sad news. There is no easy way to tell you this. We lost Morton; he died on the way back. I'm so sorry.'

Gilder embraced Selina as she sobbed.

'And, although Morton's death is sad news, I have a more pressing matter I would like to speak to you about.'

Understanding Cado's tone, Selina left the men to their conversation.

'What is it?' Gilder asked.

'Niclaus and Orrin are in grave danger. We must hurry. I fear the worst if we do not get to them soon.'

'What? We need to leave …'

Cado could tell by Gilder's expression that his mind was already working on a plan of action.

'Did the *Ice Maiden* bring you here?'

'Yes.'

'And will they take us further north?'

'Wherever we want to go.'

'Selina,' Gilder called urgently.

'What is it? Is it Vidar?'

'Yes,' answered Cado, which, in his mind, was not a lie. 'Selina, I ask that you do not mention this to Elwin.'

Gilder grabbed his coat. 'I have things to organise.'

Selina kissed her husband. 'Be careful.'

Cado could see the worry etched on her face. 'Gilder, go ahead, I'll catch you up.' He need not have said anything for Gilder was almost out of the door.

Knowing Selina trusted him implicitly, Cado took a moment to reassure her. 'Do not worry. Gilder will not be in any danger, I promise.'

*

Gilder and Cado were soon sailing north aboard the *Ice Maiden* with a team of reindeer and a sleigh.

Gilder spotted the bloodstains on deck that, although scrubbed, had not faded.

'Don't ask,' warned Cado. 'We need to keep focused.'

'You said Vidar was also in trouble?'

'He is, but he and Tomás will sort that out together.'

'Don't keep things from me.'

'We must concentrate on Niclaus and Orrin. We are in a race against time and I fear we might be too late to help them,' Cado warned.

Jorun joined Gilder and Cado. 'Where am I to take you?'

'If you sail north, between Lofoten and the mainland, we can sail up Ofot fjord.'

'I know the place,' confirmed Jorun. 'We dropped Vidar there on his first trek. The north is mountainous but, to the east, you should get a clear run to Lake Torne.'

It was late in the evening as Gilder and Cado disembarked from the *Ice Maiden* with their sleigh and team of reindeer.

Gilder took the reins. 'With luck on our side, we can be at the final checkpoint before Orrin and Niclaus.'

CHAPTER 59

IN THE YEAR 840 AD

Ludin thought of Niclaus, Orrin and Aslak, he hoped that they had been able to ward off the wolves. If it had just been up to him, he would have gone back but there was his father to think of. He had promised him that he would do all in his power to avenge his defeat. He thought of Henik. It had been good fortune that he had gone to the others' aid. Yet the more he thought of Henik, the more his behaviour confused him. Why had the fool gone back? He would have lost a heavy wager betting against him doing so. Later, when quizzed, he would deny any knowledge of the attack. They would have no way of proving anything.

Out of the forest of Slarin, the snow-covered land was extremely open. Ahead lay the final checkpoint. This stop had not been part of the original race but the herders, believing the Trial pushed their animals beyond their endurance, had insisted on the stop – it allowed the competitors and their animals to eat and have a short rest.

Having the misfortune of drawing the worst duty in the Trial, Kjar and Volund stood waiting. When Ludin arrived, they immediately tended to his animals.

Ludin knew neither man.

'They're not in great shape,' complained Kjar, the more senior of the two. Volund pointed to the food. 'There is stew in the pot, help yourself.'

Ludin was keen to push on. The finish was at the other side of the lake. He studied the thickness of the ice, contemplating crossing it with his sleigh. It often froze for years at a time. The coating looked fragile. He would not risk it.

'Another sleigh is coming,' said Volund, pointing to the east. The competitors would come from the south.

Ludin had expected to be gone before any of his challengers made it to the checkpoint. He could not identify the riders in their heavy clothes. And why were there two? It was only when they dismounted that Ludin recognised Gilder. There was a second person with him – someone he did not know, someone who was half Gilder's height.

'Ludin, have you seen the others?' Gilder asked.

'They were behind. They should not be too long.'

Cado sensed that Ludin was not telling all he knew.

'Come on, let us go to them,' encouraged Gilder.

After being introduced, Cado stood beside Ludin as he ate the rest of his meal. 'Your fellow competitors: they are all your friends, aren't they?' Cado asked, instantly changing the mood.

'Yes, good friends,' he replied.

Gilder, sensing tension, moved closer to listen.

'Good enough to leave them behind when they're in trouble?'

'I don't know what you are talking about.'

'Hurry up, be on your way before I tell all,' warned Cado.

Ludin immediately did as Cado recommended. He led his reindeer to the right of the lake. Gilder watched him go, heartened to see him taking the rocky route.

Cado jumped on to Gilder's sleigh and they were instantly off. 'What's up,' asked Gilder.

'I'm afraid it is bad news. I believe the boys have been attacked by wolves. I read it from Ludin. He saw what happened and left them.'

'Are they all right?' asked a clearly worried Gilder.

'Some are injured; we need to get to them quickly.'

*

Henik's young reindeer responded to his commands, trusting him implicitly. Initially all that had mattered to Henik was summoning help but the memory of Ludin's actions made him determined to try to win at least. Further along the route, he came across Orrin's sleigh and reindeer. The animals looked unaffected by the incident with the wolves – if anything, they looked relieved to have found Henik. Tying Orrin's team to the back of his own, he spotted another reindeer, the one that had broken free from Aslak's sleigh. Apart from a few minor bite marks, it was fine. He tied the reindeer to the back of the last sleigh and set off.

Not long later, he was elated to find help coming towards him. He assumed that Ludin had not abandoned them after all – rather he had gone on to get help.

'How are they?' asked Gilder, upon reaching Henik.

Henik outlined the extent of the injuries. 'Gilder, Orrin is in bad shape.'

Gilder was shocked.

'Niclaus sent me to get help. Thank God, Ludin told you. I thought he had deserted us.'

Henik's words confirmed Cado's earlier suspicions.

Gilder could barely contain his anger. 'He told us nothing.'

'Then how did you know?'

'Ludin seemed unsettled, we were worried,' proffered Cado, not wishing to elaborate.

'I'll kill him when I find him,' promised Gilder.

'Join the queue,' muttered Henik. 'Come on, I'll lead you back.'

'No,' said Cado, forcibly. 'You've done enough, continue your race.'

Henik gave the diminutive stranger a look that said, who are you to tell me what to do?

'He's right. It's better that you continue. Someone needs to give chase to Ludin. You've done more than your share.'

Henik untied Orrin's team and sleigh and Aslak's animal.

'They belong to Orrin and Aslak.'

'I pray they're in a position to use them,' said Gilder, tying them to his own.

CHAPTER 60

IN THE YEAR 840 AD

Gilder jumped from the sleigh and rushed to his boys.

Niclaus was in tears. 'I couldn't get to him. I tried. There was nothing I could do.'

Gilder paled at the sight of Orrin. Hurrying, he wrapped more blankets around his son.

Cado raced towards the boys. 'Quick, Niclaus,' he said, throwing blankets on the ground. 'There's no time to lose. We need to keep them as warm as possible.'

Niclaus' mouth dropped open. Standing before him was the little man he had seen in his dreams.

'Now,' shouted Cado, snapping him out of his stupor.

Niclaus frantically gathered blankets and rugs from the back of his father's sleigh as Gilder carried his dying son and laid him on the woollen blankets. He then placed Aslak next to him.

Gilder examined Orrin while Niclaus checked Aslak, whose condition offered some hope: his injuries, although severe, were nowhere near as bad as Orrin's.

Niclaus bit his lip hard, topping the skin. He could feel his shoulders shaking. 'No, not my brother, please, not my brother,' he cried.

Gilder cradled Orrin. He placed loving hands over his bleeding neck, trying futilely to stem the flow, to save his boy. His hands reddened. Orrin's body was limp and his breathing shallow. 'I love you, son,' he said, leaning over and kissing his forehead.

Cado stood between Gilder and Niclaus.

Gilder tried to compose himself as he allowed Cado to inspect the wounds. He looked at him with pleading eyes. 'You've done it before. Please, do it again, I beg you.'

Cado had not set eyes on Gilder or Orrin for some eighteen years and now as then he found himself facing the same situation. Unknown to either Niclaus or Orrin, he had saved both their lives as well as Selina's.

The dwarf looked closely at Orrin's broken body. The wounds to his legs were deep. If left untreated they, alone, would be fatal. However, they paled into insignificance in comparison to his neck lacerations. The beast had savaged his throat. The only thing keeping him alive was time and that was running out.

Cado started to walk away. Niclaus thought he was giving up and moved to block him.

'You love him dearly?' Cado asked.

'I do,' said Niclaus, desperately.

'Will you do anything I ask if I can save him?'

'I will,' agreed Niclaus, eagerly.

'Then hurry, we must not delay. Do as I say if you want Orrin and Aslak to complete the race.'

'Complete the race? Can't you see they're dying?'

'Take this,' he said, passing Niclaus a battered old pouch.

'Inside you will find coloured dust. Lift a pinch of the red dust and rub it over Orrin's cuts to stem the bleeding. Then take the yellow and mix it with the red. The combination will speed up recovery and stop infection.'

Niclaus looked at him in disbelief. 'What rubbish do you ...'

'Do it, you fool, before it's too late,' shouted Gilder, unable to contain himself.

Stunned, Niclaus took the pouch and opened it. Inside were several separate compartments. Each contained a different colour of dust, as Cado had described. Touching the red dust sent a tingling sensation up his hand, warming his insides. It felt good. As instructed, he applied the dust to Orrin's wounds and watched in total amazement as the blood coagulated.

Orrin was moaning. His body twitched as spasms grew in strength and duration. Gilder held him tightly.

Working speedily, Niclaus applied the dust to Aslak's wounds, achieving the same miraculous result. Hope rose; there was a chance they would survive.

'Thank you,' Niclaus said. 'I shall repay you.'

'Hurry, Niclaus, you have not finished applying the second mixture.'

Niclaus mixed and applied the new dust.

'Is that it, have I done it correctly?'

'Yes.'

'Will they survive?'

'Yes, you have saved them.'

Niclaus handed the pouch back to Cado.

'No,' said Cado, 'That belongs to you now. However I think

it might be better if, after the race, you let me teach you how and when to use it.'

Niclaus tucked the pouch into his pocket and then hugged Cado. 'I made you a promise, what do you require me to do?'

Cado smiled. 'Now is not the time to worry about that, you can learn of the adventures that await you later. You have a race to complete.'

Niclaus looked at the dwarf. 'Are you serious?'

'Very. Now hurry up.'

Gilder followed, catching up with Niclaus as he remounted his sleigh.

'I shall go on; perhaps I can still pull it off.'

Looking into his father's face, he saw disappointment. He put it down to the possibility that his father had just realised that neither of his sons would succeed him as leader.

They hugged.

'I thought we had lost him,' confessed Niclaus.

'Me too.'

CHAPTER 61

IN THE YEAR 802 AD

Morton had described Cado's route accurately – it took half a day's trek to reach Hakon's encampment.

The camp was on a river bend, close to the sea. Surrounded by swampy ground, it would have been a difficult place to attack. The settlement was expanding. He passed a smithy under construction or extension where men were busy making weaponry. A little further along, women worked on vertical looms, twilling and wefting serge. Others warped yarn to spin. They were making a sail. Yet more were dyeing already made sails while an older woman, who looked as wide as she was tall, used experienced fingers to loosen a slub in the line.

Vigilant guards searched and interrogated Cado, before the leader of the men, thinking that the dwarf would make good entertainment, agreed to allow him an audience in the Great Hall. Cado could hear merriment from within.

A group of mischievous boys, too young to join the festivities, hung around the entrance, peeping through the main door when it opened, hoping to catch a glimpse of the banquet. Close to the water, men in chains worked on a new vessel. The three boats used in the raid on Ceanannus Mór, stripped of sail and mast, sat on wooden platforms out of the water.

The guards manhandled Cado inside.

The walls were alive with brands of soaked pitch, which, along with the cooking pits, brought light to the dark hall. Benches and tables, packed with men, covered the wood-panelled floor. A toothless cook was roasting a deer over a roaring fire, wiping his bloodied hands on the front of his apron as he did so. The fresh meat spat and hissed, sending palls of smoke into the high beams. Cado had arrived less than a day after the raiding party, finding the camp in the throes of a feast in honour of Tyr, the god of war. The banqueting hall, filled with the scent of wild garlic, was alive with revelry.

Cado was ushered in front of Hakon who sat in a high-backed chair at the centre of the main table, between Oto and Barid, and flanked by Envik and his most trusted men.

'What have we here?' Hakon asked, eyeing up the dwarf.

Although as fierce looking as Cado had imagined, Hakon was clearly drunk. A good thing, he thought – a drunken man would be easier to manipulate. Damian, who had only entered the hall, hurried to Hakon's side, eager to warn Hakon about the identity of the stranger.

'Now, little man, how can I be of service to you?'

Cado, unperturbed by his surroundings or by the arrival of Damian, took centre stage. 'Let me introduce myself. My name is Cado and I have come here to trade with you.'

'What could you possibly have that I would want?' Hakon asked.

'Let me tell you what I require and then we will see if I can interest you in an exchange.'

Hakon smiled mirthlessly. 'You certainly know how to amuse me, little man.'

'Firstly,' Cado said, 'I want you to spare the life of the monk, Damian. He has suffered enough these last few days and has a much bigger part to play in all our futures. Decree that no man harm him.'

'What makes you think any harm will come to him? We do not hurt our own.'

'If that is the case why is it that your henchman,' – Cado pointed at Oto – 'plans to kill him by morning?'

Hakon's smile changed to a frown. 'Is what he says true?'

'I don't trust him my lord. I, I, I …' stammered Oto.

'You what?'

'I thought it would be better for the camp.'

The colour drained from Damian's face. He had been oblivious to his brush with death.

'So, Oto, how does a stranger know what is in your heart when I do not?'

'I swear, I told no one of my plan. This dwarf must have used some sort of sorcery. I swear before Odin, I have never set eyes on him until today.'

Hakon lifted his latest flagon of wine and poured himself a generous cup.

Cado spoke directly to Damian.

'Is it true that you have renounced your Christian beliefs?'

'It is so,' Damian replied, bullishly.

'Then, you will have no need of the picture of the Virgin and Child you possess.' he asked, referring to the page Damian had taken with him from Iona.

'No, it's ...'

'What need of a Christian picture would you have?'

'Have it. It is of no consequence to me,' said Damian, clearly astonished that Cado knew about it.

Damian ordered a servant to collect it from his belongings.

'Do you agree to spare Damian?' Cado asked Hakon.

Intrigued now, Hakon confirmed that he would.

'Secondly, I want the Holy Book you have in your possession. I have promised to return it to its rightful place.'

'But that book belongs to me now. The jewel-encrusted cover must be worth a dwarf's fortune. The fact you dare to enter my camp proves its worth. What would you have to offer for it?'

'Keep the cover if you want. It is of little worth to me. What if I offer you something more valuable in exchange? Will you agree to my request?'

Now starting to enjoy the show, Hakon whispered to Oto, 'You can kill him after I've had my fun with him.'

'Is there anything else that you require before you leave?' Hakon asked, to the amusement of his men.

'Yes. I want the other book – the one you entrusted to Envik.'

'Ah, but Damian claims it is a powerful grimoire, a book of spells. He has been eager to get his hands on it. He says that it contains the secrets of your people. Whoever possesses it will have power beyond imagination.'

Hakon's words brought a large inhale of breath from those in the hall. He had not mentioned any of this to his men.

Cado laughed, contemptuously. 'Spells, magic, there are no such things.' Yet his eyes narrowed and his face darkened. 'But the book is priceless to me. I am prepared to barter for it. Tell me what you desire.'

'I have been told that you have the ability to foretell the future. Give me that knowledge and you can have the books.'

'I cannot give that to you.'

'Then our negotiations are over.'

'But what if I can arrange for a child of yours to learn?'

'Why not me?' asked Hakon.

'It takes years of training and dedication. Let me show you the power I possess. Imagine if I can pass this power on to your heir.' Cado walked the length of the main table, stopping in front of Baldo, the warrior who had attacked Tomás in the barn. 'This man here has broken your code.'

Cado's words instantly brought Baldo to his feet. 'I'll kill him,' he roared.

Hakon silenced his soldier with a wave of his hand. 'And the proof.'

'During your raid on the monastery, this man stole silver, silver that belongs to your family.'

Intrigued, Hakon asked Cado to explain.

'All treasure must be shared, isn't that the code?'

Murmurs of agreement echoed round the hall.

'What if someone finds treasure and keeps it for himself?'

The eyes of all the men in the hall bored into Baldo. Cado

imagined that the silver locket in his pocket must have suddenly found a new weight.

'I had a special locket made. It was to be a gift to the heir of Hakon. Baldo has it in his pocket now.'

'I forgot about it,' said Baldo ashamedly, taking the locket from his pocket and placing it on the bench in front.

The room resounded to cheers, applause and the banging of tables.

'I'll take the locket,' said Cado, slipping it into his pocket. 'I promise it shall find its way back to your family.'

'I will deal with you later, Baldo,' said Hakon before turning to Cado. 'So, Cado, what can you tell me that might persuade me to complete our negotiation?' His voice carried menace.

Cado believed it was time to ruffle Hakon. 'I can tell you that this very morning your wife has borne you a daughter.'

'You lie,' cried Hakon, a depth of despair in his voice.

'Go and find out for yourself. The women of the village are afraid to tell you. Do you also want to learn of your future son?'

The words exposed Hakon's one vulnerable spot. He hurled his goblet at the insolent dwarf. Then he leapt to his feet and sprang at Cado.

'Who have you been speaking to?' he shouted.

Hakon lifted Cado off the ground. His face turned purple and the veins in his neck bulged. 'Which one spoke to you?' he roared, spitting saliva.

Cado, unfazed, raised his head to look directly into Hakon's wild eyes. He spoke quietly. 'I offer you all you want.'

Hakon threw Cado to the ground and drew his sword. For

an inebriated man, his aim was true. His blade missed Cado by a hair's breadth as it crashed into the wooden flooring.

Cado, using his wisdom, was aware of his attacker's every move even before Hakon himself knew what he was going to do. Every lunge and stroke was just a moment late as Cado adroitly avoided the angry blade.

Envik could see Cado's smile – the little man was enjoying himself. 'I don't like this,' he hissed. 'It's as if he's playing with Hakon.' He drew his sword and stood. Oto did likewise.

Envik jumped over his table and closed on Cado from behind.

'Leave him be, he's all mine,' yelled Hakon.

Hakon thrust his sword at Cado's head. Cado danced clear but the blade cut deeply into the edge of a table next to him.

Cado spoke directly to Hakon, as he once had in the forest with Tomás. 'Why do you attack me when I offer you all that you want?'

In all his years, no one had frightened Hakon, not until now. 'Speak, little man,' he replied, understanding that he was in no position to argue.

'I believe that we should speak alone.'

Hakon turned to his men. 'Clear the hall. Every one of you out.'

'But my lord …'

Hakon cut Envik short. 'Out!'

Oto took a step towards his leader.

'You too.'

The hall quickly emptied and Cado began. 'As I said, I cannot teach you to predict the future but I shall pass the knowledge on to your son.'

Confused, Hakon looked at him, 'I have no son.'

'Within the year, your one and only son shall be born and a descendant of your line will become one of the most influential men ever to live. He shall have wisdom over many, and every man, woman and child shall know his name. This is what I offer you.'

'And for the monk's life, your book, and the manuscript, you would give this to me. Why?'

'Hakon, you have been chosen. From your line shall be born a son of promise. He shall become a great man. There is much for him to learn and at times, I will have to take him away with me. Do you agree to this?'

Hakon frowned. 'And you guarantee his safe return?'

'There are stipulations,' cautioned Cado.

'What stipulations?' Hakon asked, distrustfully.

'You must stay away from Ceanannus Mór.'

'I can live with that.'

'If this is agreed and no harm comes to Damian, your heirs will have the ability to read the future and your family will come to possess the power that Damian spoke of. Of this, you have my word.'

Hakon, having witnessed Cado's ability, agreed to the conditions.

Cado retrieved the book of Newgrange from the floor next to Envik's seat. 'The Holy Book. Where is it?'

Hakon removed a large key from around his neck. He walked to a chest which he opened in order to remove the book. Lifting a knife, he opened the cover and ran his blade along the inner joint. Repeating his action inside the back cover, he pulled the book block free and handed it to Cado. 'As agreed, the cover is mine.'

'This is a long path,' warned Cado. 'Your son's training begins on his third birthday. As to the monk, seek his counsel and his wisdom will make you wealthy.'

The meeting over, Cado set off leaving behind an astonished and shaken Hakon.

*

Yes, Hakon decided, he would keep to his side of the bargain for the year. If Cado's words were true, Hakon would have the son he yearned for.

CHAPTER 62

IN THE YEAR 840 AD

Niclaus encouraged his reindeer as best he could. He tried to stay optimistic. There was always hope, he told himself. As he rode, words buried deep in his memory rushed through his head. He smiled as he recalled a little boy walking in his father's shadow.

'… sometimes life holds different challenges … this is not the path that has been set for you … leading the village isn't what you were born to do … something greater awaits.'

Even back then, his father had known he would not be Ugter. Nevertheless, an old fortune-teller had once foretold that Niclaus would follow the same path as his father. Niclaus laughed to himself, for she had said the same thing to Orrin.

The more he thought the more muddled he became. Like Cado. How could Niclaus dream of a person he had never met? Moreover, what sort of magic had he conjured up to save Orrin and Aslak? Although Niclaus was now bound to him, he was comfortable with the debt. He supposed that this probably stemmed from his father's faith in the little man.

Fresh images came to mind, of Vidar falling through the ice and of the locket he now possessed. Moreover, what of the white wolf?

Why had it come to his aid? He needed answers. And he thought especially of Vidar. Where did he fit into all of this? Niclaus scoured his memories, searching for clues or pointers, anything that would help him understand what was happening. Had Vidar, without his knowledge, been training him for something other than the Trial? Now, the more he thought about it, the more he understood. His father and Vidar had been working to the same agenda. A conversation from an age before came to mind.

'I'm looking for a special place to hide a great treasure,' Vidar had claimed. 'When the time comes, you shall learn of my secrets. I may even entrust you with them.'

Niclaus had the gist of the unfolding story. He could not quite put it all together but he was certain that the answers he needed lay with his father and Cado.

He thought of his father, whose hopes of a son following him as Ugter must have vanished. Niclaus was determined at least to finish – at least it would give his father some small achievement to take pride in. And then it dawned on him. If his father had always known that Niclaus would not be Ugter, then all his ambitions must have been for Orrin. Vidar had trained both Orrin and himself – Orrin to win the Trial and Niclaus for … it was as if someone had taken a blindfold from his eyes.

If only Orrin and Aslak could finish the Trial. Cado's words echoed in his head: 'Do as I say if you want them to complete the race.'

A flick of the reins and the reindeer were off again. Niclaus yanked hard on his left rein. The team obeyed.

Men who completed the Trial were revered. Orrin and Aslak

deserved that honour.

Nearing the place where he had left Orrin and Aslak, Niclaus saw a solitary figure standing defiantly against the barrage of snow. As he neared, he recognised his father.

'What are you doing out here?' asked Niclaus, jumping from his sleigh.

'I was waiting for you. I knew you would return for your brother.'

'Why did you not tell me to take them?'

'I needed my son to find his own path. I had faith in you. You do know that if you take these two, they become your responsibility. The race becomes secondary in importance.'

'Yes, Father. I will not let anything happen to them, I promise.'

'Niclaus,' said Gilder. 'There is something I have wanted to tell you for a long time.'

The image of his earlier dream flashed in his mind. He saw Vidar handing over a bundle to his mother, only the image was much clearer. Gilder stood next to Selina and behind them stood Morton. The bundle was a baby. Niclaus understood. He was the baby.

'Later, Father, I shall seek my answers. Until then we have a race to complete.'

The rules of the competition were explicit: each competitor had to arrive at the finish with a sleigh and reindeer, and without outside assistance, but there was no rule to stop one competitor helping another.

First Niclaus hitched Orrin's reindeer and sleigh to the back of his own. Next, he tied Aslak's sleigh and team to the rear.

The snowfall was getting heavier and the temperature was continuing to drop. Cado spoke. 'Gilder tells me Ludin took the arduous path to the right of the river. I fear he will lose ground. What do you think?'

'I think that'll mean that Henik will win,' said Niclaus, the prospect, now, not seeming anywhere near as bad.

'I thought Vidar trained you for this race.'

'He did.'

'Surely not, for the first thing he would have taught you would have been to have heart and never to give up. You seem beaten already.'

'Do you think I still have a chance?' asked Niclaus, looking for encouragement from the little man.

'It doesn't matter what I think. It's what you think that matters.'

CHAPTER 63

IN THE YEAR 840 AD

'Are you mad?' Vidar asked Tomás, having pulled him on board.

'I think I am,' mumbled Tomás, who was already shivering with cold.

'Mord, can I have blankets for Brother Tomás?' Vidar asked, acknowledging the Norseman's leadership.

'Get this man some clothes. Vidar, let us speak.'

Mord escorted Vidar to the stern of the dragonboat.

Mord looked seaward. 'You have made my life more complicated than I would have liked it to be.'

'That was not my intention.'

'All the same, you outrank me on this vessel yet you are under death threat from Hakon. I cannot let you take command nor can I hold you as a prisoner.'

'What do you propose?'

'I shall not treat you as a prisoner or restrain you, so long as you give me your word that you will accompany me to camp without protest.'

'I'm in no position to bargain.'

Mord sighed. 'There's many on board who would follow you in

an instant … if leading our people is your intention.'

Vidar looked surprised. 'And why would they follow me?'

'Hakon is getting old, not that he's frail, mind. But younger men are looking at his position with hungry eyes.'

'Who?'

'Iarl.'

Instinctively, Vidar rubbed his old scar.

'And he has the ear of Damian. Together they … well; many in camp are looking for … many still revere you.'

'And by bringing me back, it may be seen that you are siding with me?'

'That's my worry.'

'Well, do not worry. I have no interest in the leadership. Your ways are lost to me.'

'Then why do you return?'

Vidar shook his head. 'Would you have let us sail away?'

'No.' Mord seemed to understand. 'You only came with us to spare the crew.'

'What of my father and mother?' asked Vidar.

'They are both well. There is a great sadness in them both since you left. What with Hakon putting you under sentence of death, you can imagine. Your father clings to the old ways. He takes your desertion as a personal insult. Your mother, I think, she is a mother first. The Norse way will not come between her and her son. I think by leaving, you broke both their hearts.'

'And how is it that Gudny was in command of the ship before you?'

'Iarl has much power. It was his decision. He only chooses men who are faithful to him.'

It was Mord's turn to ask a question. 'You realise you are still under threat of death?'

'Yes.'

'Your return may force Hakon's hand. Iarl will demand that the sentence is carried out immediately. If Hakon shows any hesitation Iarl could well make his move.'

'This doesn't concern me.'

Mord slapped the gunnel. 'Iarl is a monster. He will put your father and mother to death at the first opportunity.'

'Sienna won't let him.'

'Your sister is as power hungry as her husband.'

'What, she would kill her own family?'

'Iarl is her family now.'

A row erupted on the foredeck. A warrior had his sword unsheathed and was swinging wildly at Tomás. 'No White Cross Followers on my boat,' he shouted, as his blade swished past the side of Tomás' head.

Mord was quickest to react, rushing to stand between a relieved Tomás and the aggressor. 'Back down,' he warned.

The man stood his ground. 'No White Cross Followers.' Arnjlet was openly challenging Mord's leadership. 'I say we kill him,' he yelled. 'Who's with me?'

Some men fell in behind Arnjlet. Vidar estimated that the crew's allegiance was evenly split.

'This is my fight,' said Vidar.

'Stay off my deck,' warned Mord. 'You are not Norse.'

Vidar backed away.

Arnljet swung his sword from side to side as he came closer to Mord.

Mord lunged, thrusting his blade into the man's chest. His movement was graceful, his kill clean. Pulling the blade free, he continued moving forward towards the dead man's followers. He struck again, almost beheading the nearest man.

'Anyone else,' he shouted, as the dissenters cowered. 'Follow me or suffer the same. No one is to harm this White Cross Follower. Hakon will decide his fate.'

CHAPTER 64

IN THE YEAR 840 AD

Ludin's route took him into rocky hills that overlooked the frozen lake. The views were breathtaking. His reindeer stoically pulled the sleigh through the treacherous terrain. They instinctively avoided the visible rocks. A single misjudgement would prove disastrous. A reindeer could break a leg or one of the sleigh's runners could easily smash. Ludin had seen the herders' derisory looks when he chose the route to the right. He could have wiped the smugness from their faces if he had been able to share his plan with them. In the months leading up to the trial, his ambitious father had been scrupulous in his preparation. Leaving nothing to chance, Olaf and Ludin had spent many days coursing a path through the uneven land in contravention to the rules of the Trial.

The rock-strewn path was about a third shorter than the track to the left. Even allowing for a slender lead, poor steering and slower progress, Olaf estimated that it was the quickest way to go.

A flutter of snowflakes warned of the impending storm. Ludin needed the weather to hold – he was next to useless at finding his way in bad conditions. At first, the snow was fine and not troubling, but gradually the flakes thickened and the fall intensified. The wind strengthened, driving the snow with such force that Ludin found it almost impossible to breathe. Unable to see, he had no option but to stop. His reindeer huddled together as Ludin climbed over his seat and curled into a ball on the shelf behind.

*

Henik would have avoided the last checkpoint if it had not been compulsory to stop.

Between mouthfuls, Henik related the details of the wolf attack and Aslak's and Orrin's condition to Kjar and Volund.

'We'll get you on your way and then we'll go to them,' said Volund.

'This race is far from over. The fool took the path to the right. It's a near impossible path in good weather,' said Kjar, looking at the dark cloud overhead. 'That aside, his animals are in poor condition.'

The wind was icy and it was getting late in the day, although there was still enough light to see. The cold front had caused a drop in temperature. The ice would have hardened. Henik considered crossing it. It was worth a try.

Henik's reindeer tried to resist as he steered them onto the ice. Drawing on all his experience, he drove the pair onward. A few lengths out, the black-antlered reindeer's front hoof crashed through the ice, spooking both animals. Bucking in panic, its hind hoof then broke the ice. Henik steered the animals off the ice as quickly as he could – the ice held and a mightily relieved Henik, with sleigh intact, made it to shore. He cursed himself for being so reckless.

'All right, boys, take it easy,' said Henik, soothingly.

The black-antlered reindeer had hurt its hind leg. Henik could not be sure as to the extent of the damage. He feared a rupture to a tendon, a potentially fatal injury.

Henik kept a very close eye on his reindeer. From the off, he could see that the injured one was keeping weight off its hurt leg. He could see a blood trail in the snow. He soon relaxed as the bleeding stopped. Henik did not realise that, with the snowstorm reaching Ludin first, they were equidistant from the finish, and he should have had the advantage with an easier run.

Before long, though, the storm conditions made it impossible to see anything. Henik had no choice but to stop and take shelter.

*

Niclaus' initial doubts over the viability of steering all three sleighs proved unfounded as the teams ran in unison. The quick tempo was pleasantly unexpected.

What was the harm in staying positive, believing he could win? A short time ago, he was crying for his dying brother. Now, miraculously, Orrin was on the mend and so was Aslak. Moreover, the three of them would complete the Trial.

Niclaus soon met Kjar and Volund. The two herders were clearly surprised to see him leading Orrin and Aslak. After quickly telling the pair all, Niclaus convinced them that he and his party were able to continue. Kjar and Volund, much to Niclaus' consternation, examined and fed all the animals, fulfilling their obligation before they allowed him to continue.

Niclaus' challenge to the leaders was building momentum. Vidar's reindeer were slicing through the snow, each of their strides covering more ground than any stag he had ever seen. Their power surprised him. Their stocky legs and low centre of gravity meant that they could cut through the snow at a much quicker pace than the other reindeer.

The rising wind whistled and howled, drowning out the sound of the thudding hooves on the compacting snow. The land was desolate. The heavy snowfall covered all tracks leading to the finish. The light was poor. By right, he should have slowed down but his animals had other ideas. They increased their speed and ignored his steering. Somehow, they followed the invisible tracks better than he could have on the clearest day. He was now merely a passenger.

These were magnificent animals, perfectly in tune, their very breath exhaling plumes of white smoke in harmony. Niclaus was hypnotised by their grace.

He hoped that Ludin and Henik were in the middle of the worsening weather. A merciless front like the one ahead would sap the energy of even the most conditioned competitor.

With luck on his side, Niclaus could maybe skirt the edge of the front and miss the worst of it. Deep inside the clouds ahead, Henik and Ludin would struggle for direction. The thought of Ludin and, to a lesser extent, Henik being lost brought a smile to his face. He chuckled, imaging them trying to navigate. It was common knowledge that Ludin had a poor sense of direction. Niclaus would not have been surprised to see Ludin pass him, going the wrong way all together. Why should he not dare to believe?

Unlike Henik and Ludin, Niclaus had spent countless nights studying the stars under Vidar's tutelage. He was able to find his position from only a handful of stars, or from the general direction of the moonlight in relation to the seasons. Yet as he raced on, he felt as if something strange was at work: it seemed that the cloud cover broke slightly; exactly when he most needed to get a sense of his position. When he was unsure of direction, he took out the sunstone given by Vidar and watched in amazement as it caught reflected light and pointed the way.

Niclaus sailed past the last checkpoint, abandoned by Kjar and Volund. Ahead, he faced a dilemma. Which way should he take? The route to the right was stony and dangerous. Although shorter, his father had told him not to take it. 'No one has won by going that way. No matter how appealing the idea seems, dismiss it,' Gilder had said.

The only safe way was the longer route to the left, but he would never catch any one by taking the safe route. That left only one other option: to go straight ahead over the frozen lake of Torne. If he could cross it, he would have a chance. He recalled his dream, of crossing the ice. There and then, he believed that his decision had already been made for him. He would go against his instinct and follow his vision.

'Damn it,' swore Niclaus. He had not considered Orrin and Aslak's sleighs. There was no way the ice would support another two teams. Niclaus would have to untie Orrin and Aslak's sleighs and leave them, coming back to collect them when he had finished.

A wolf howled. Its call sent shivers down his spine. He imagined that it was one of the animals that had attacked Niclaus and the others in the forest. They had probably tracked him the entire time. He could not leave Orrin or Aslak.

Niclaus could not see any sign of the wolves, but he knew they were close. There was no chance of outrunning a pack. Either he could take Orrin and Aslak with him, abandoning the remaining sleighs, or he could risk pulling all three sleighs over the ice. The first choice made more sense. Although without sleighs, Orrin and Aslak would suffer disqualification. To Niclaus, it did not seem a bad swap – your life, or the pride that came with finishing the Trial. He knew which he would pick. Unfortunately, he knew what Orrin and Aslak would choose. They would both take the chance rather than live with the dishonour of failing to lift a flag.

Niclaus made up his mind – he would risk crossing the ice with the three sleighs. He did a quick check on Orrin. He was deadly still. Niclaus' heart stopped as he climbed up to have a look. He was relieved to find him breathing.

Working diligently, Niclaus slackened the reins between the sleighs as far as he could to distribute the weight as evenly as possible.

Back on his sleigh, he encouraged his reindeer on to the ice. He felt strangely relaxed and assured. I have crossed the lake already, he told himself, remembering his dream.

CHAPTER 65

IN THE YEAR 802 AD

Morton was both happy and shocked when Cado returned.

Cado was pleased to learn that Morton's negotiations had proved fruitful. He was now the proud captain and owner.

The sailing home was less comfortable than the outward journey. For days, an angry sea spat frothing waves over the brow. Cado struggled with the motion and found it difficult to keep his stomach from emptying. Somewhat battered by the ordeal, he shook hands with Torre and Rune, and waved goodbye to the rest of the crew.

Morton escorted him off the boat. 'I don't know how to thank you.'

'You are more than welcome. By the time we are finished you will have more than earned it.'

'I'm a man of my word. I will not miss an appointment.'

Disembarking, Cado walked quickly through the town and out into the countryside, on his way to the ravaged monastery. He dreaded the horrors that awaited him. The journey was a painful one. Cado normally loved the trip, having many happy memories of travelling the same road.

As the monastery came into view, all looked peaceful. The fields were absent of working monks. As Cado neared, he could make out burnt roofs and damaged buildings. Although he had envisaged the devastation that would greet him, the scene still sickened him. A bloodied handprint smudged on the whitewashed outer wall was evidence of the massacre that had taken place. The smells of charcoal and beeswax mingled. The candle store had burned, sending a torrent of flaming wax into the tannery. The stone outer walls of the tannery alone still stood, its soft centre eaten by fire.

The grounds were alive. Many of the villagers from Magority had come to help the injured. Cado walked to the refectory, which now doubled as an infirmary.

Seeing Cado enter, young Brother Sean looked up from tending one of the injured. 'Can I help you?' Sean, along with Finntoin and Brendan, had survived the attack by hiding in the tower.

'I'm here to see Brother Tomás,' replied Cado, respectfully.

Sean pointed Cado to the far end of the room. 'He's in poor shape. Second last bed from the end.'

Brother Sean went back to applying cerate to a large gash on his patient's stomach.

Behind, a monk entered, carrying a red-hot iron rod. The hall filled with horrendous screams as an infected limb was severed and then cauterised. Cado retched at the repugnant smell of burning flesh. He could stand the suffering no more. Discreetly, he removed coloured dust from his pocket and sprinkled it over the wounded. No more would die.

Making his way to Tomás' bed, Cado could not be sure if his

injured friend was asleep or unconscious.

'How has he been?' Cado asked of Tomás.

'He's been mostly unconscious. Occasionally he stirs. A good sign,' explained Maurice, who was treating another monk nearby.

Cado leant over the bed and whispered. 'Forgive me, Tomás. I was powerless to stop it, but I did everything I could to save you.'

Baldo's attack had damaged the locket that Cado had given Tomás. Cado's foresight in putting the dust into the locket had saved Tomás' life. Prior Cinaed, Monicurr's deputy, organised a single funeral for the dead. Áed mac Néill, High King of Erin, personally attended. He was so enraged by the barbarity of the attack that he gave finances to rebuild the monastery and promised to guard its walls forever. Amongst Monicurr's personal effects was a letter addressed to all the monks of Ceanannus Mór. In it, he expressed a wish that Ceanannus Mór and Iona unite under one abbot. The idea found favour and Connachtach's inauguration united both houses. In the throes of poor health, Connachtach sent Brother Cellach to oversee his work in Erin.

*

Cado enjoyed the breeze on his face as he broke from the forest. The strong sunlight forced him to squint. The sky was clear but for a single trail of high cloud that dissolved in the distance. Yet even this glorious summer day could not lift his spirits as he climbed the approach to Ceanannus Mór. His daily visits had become something of an ordeal.

He took his seat next to Tomás on the bench outside the refectory. 'Good afternoon.'

Tomás, who had been sitting quietly on his own, grunted a response, not bothering to make eye contact.

'How are you today?'

'I'm fine,' said Tomás, tersely. His eyes were fiery and his body taut. The pain was still very raw.

The two sat in silence as they had for most of Cado's recent visits. Around them, a hive of activity buzzed. Tradesmen and villagers, who should have been attending to their fields, worked alongside the monks, rebuilding and repairing the damaged monastery. Not far from where they sat, a young son was helping his father thatch one of the burnt roofs. Whilst Cado found the scene heart-warming, it did little to lighten Tomás' mood.

Tomás sighed, venting his irritation. 'You knew? You knew this was going to happen?' At last he had said what he needed to.

Cado could feel the venom in the question. 'Yes, I knew.'

'Why didn't you warn me?'

'I am not permitted to intercede. You know that if I could have, I would have.'

'I watched my brothers die. Standing in front of me, butchered and you did nothing to help.'

Cado stayed silent.

'A friend would have found a way of saving my brothers. You could have thwarted it.'

Although Tomás' words were cutting, Cado again said nothing. He suspected that what hurt Tomás the most was the belief that his friend had abandoned him and left him to die. Unaware that Cado's dust had saved his life, and with his temper soaring, Tomás hissed at Cado. 'When I thought I was dying I cursed God for failing me, I cursed the Norsemen and I cursed Damian but I should not have cursed them as much as I should you. Get out.'

Brother Cellach rushed towards the pair. 'What's going on?' he asked, standing between them, his tone soothing and conciliatory.

'He's just leaving. He has no place in the house of God.'

CHAPTER 66

IN THE YEAR 840 AD

Niclaus' dreams were coming true again. Ignoring the creaks and groans underfoot, his reindeer moved confidently over the ice.

If this action failed ... well it was not worth contemplating, thought Niclaus. He held his breath, afraid to hope.

Drawing confidence from the first team, Orrin's reindeer followed and Aslak's team did likewise. Niclaus had half expected them to panic and bolt.

Over halfway across the snow-covered lake, the ice shuddered and a peal as loud as thunder rang out.

'Help,' shouted Aslak from the back.

His sleigh had broken through the ice and its runners were slowly sinking into the freezing water. His reindeer reared up, trying to break free from the reins that secured them to the sinking sleigh.

Niclaus raced to get to Aslak, and lifted him to relative safety. He was too late to save the sleigh. Then he cut the reins that attached Aslak's reindeer to Orrin's sleigh. It seemed a cruel act. The reindeer, without the support of the other teams had no chance, and were quickly lost to the water.

Once free, the remaining two teams instinctively pulled away from the danger. For a moment, Niclaus feared they were going to run on without him. He should have known better – his surefooted stag and doe pulled to a stop.

With great effort, Niclaus hoisted Aslak into Orrin's sleigh. Orrin, still unconscious, remained ignorant to both his surroundings and the unfolding drama.

'How are you?' Niclaus asked Aslak.

'Groggy.'

'I don't think we can make the crossing tied together. We're too heavy. Do you think you could hold the reins and steer the reindeer off the ice?'

'I'll manage,' answered Aslak.

Niclaus untied the connecting reins and handed them to Aslak.

'Good luck,' he said.

'We're due some,' replied Aslak.

'Follow me,' said Niclaus, as he climbed back into his sleigh. Slowly at first, Niclaus moved across the ice. Tentative steps gave way to a light trot as the reindeer gradually increased their pace.

CHAPTER 67

IN THE YEAR 840 AD

Mord kept Vidar and Tomás apart for the remainder of the voyage. Once the boat had docked, the two guests were escorted under guard into the encampment.

'Why did you come?' Vidar asked, it being the first opportunity he had had to speak to Tomás.

Tomás did not reply.

'They will kill you.'

Tomás smiled. 'I am not under sentence of death. No, Vidar, I think they killed me back in the monastery all those years ago. I have been a shell since.'

The day was clammy, the sun surprisingly strong for autumn.

Although the camp had become much larger, its heart matched Vidar's memories. He took comfort from the familiarity. Tomás spoke aloud, encouraging himself. 'If I can teach the Devil's pup, why not the Devil?'

Vidar laughed. He had not heard the name for an age. Tomás had often referred to Vidar as the Devil's pup in his youth. He watched his friend. His stride remained assured. Vidar admired his faith and inner strength.

Word was spreading through the camp with the intensity of a gorse fire. Everywhere, men and women walked to the shore to see for themselves. He could see pleasure in the countenances of many of the men he would once have called friends. Others wore frowns – he was uncertain whether they were displeased to see him or if they were worried for his safety.

Ahead, the crowd separated. Vidar's heart leapt. His mother walked towards him. Vidar could imagine how uncomfortable she would be feeling. Despite her privileged position, his mother was a private person. She would be loath to speak to Vidar in public, yet what option had she? They would afford her no opportunity to see him on his own.

The sight of his aged mother saddened Vidar. Her raven hair had faded and her once-smooth face was lined with age.

Mord and Tomás stepped aside to allow them as private a conversation as was possible. Vidar leant forward to embrace her.

She slapped his cheek. Unashamed tears filled her eyes.

'I accepted your leaving,' she said. 'I mourned you when they said you had died. Yet in my heart, I believed you alive and free. I could have lived my days believing you were far away, that you were safe. Why have you come back?'

'I come to make my peace.'

'Peace,' she spat the word. 'Peace, no not peace.' Her words softened. 'They hunted you far and wide, they sent ships to land's end, and further. They sing ballads of the savagery they inflicted while searching for you. Some claimed that they killed you. And when they tired of their search, you come back. To what end?

Do you come to kindle the flames of their hate? Have you not tormented your father enough?'

'It is my father who I have come to see.'

*

Damian stepped from the swelling crowd. 'It is true, you did survive. I did not believe it possible. But you have done a foolish thing coming here.'

'Am I not a guest?'

Damian gave an earthy laugh, reminding Tomás of different times.

'In a strange way, it feels good to see you. Come let us walk,' said Damian, escorting Tomás away from the onlookers.

'We were friends once,' said Tomás.

'A long time ago,' agreed Damian. 'Before you deserted me.'

'No, Damian. I did not leave you to die, I did not slaughter my brothers, and I did not desert the Lord.'

'The Lord has forsaken us all. Look around you. The strength of the sword is mightier than the word of God.'

'Is your faith gone completely or is it so hidden that it is lost to you?'

'My soul,' Damian laughed, 'is damned.'

'No,' said Tomás, forcefully. 'There is always hope.'

'Do you really believe that?'

'Yes, Damian, I do. What changed you?'

'Your book. That's what changed me.'

Tomás' satchel drew Damian's attention.

'Is it the book?' he asked, covetously.

'And what good would it do you if it were? You would have to give it to your leader, unless …' Tomás began to think of a plan.

'It has haunted my dreams,' admitted Damian.

'You have the ear of Hakon do you not? If I gave you the book what would you do in return? Could you arrange mine and Vidar's escape from this camp?'

'No, Hakon would have my life.'

'Perhaps not.'

'What do you mean?'

'Perhaps it would suit all if Vidar and I slipped away.'

'And what of Iarl?' asked Damian, pondering the future leader's position on the matter.

'He could help us.'

Damian sneered. 'What makes you think that he would let you go? After all, Vidar is the only possible challenger to Iarl becoming Hakon's heir.'

'By fleeing, Vidar's reputation would be ruined. His popularity would wane.'

Damian gave a wry smile. 'Yes, I see merits in your plan.'

'And I doubt it would take you long to spread word of Vidar's cowardice. No longer would his name be revered.'

'But why would Iarl help?'

'If Vidar stays, there's always the possibility that Hakon may spare him. Do you think Iarl would want to take that chance? You have said it yourself, Vidar is held in high esteem. He could become a real threat to Iarl. This way is the safest option.'

'You have a devious mind,' agreed Damian. 'But what if Hakon gets word that Iarl helped Vidar escape?'

It was Tomás' turn to give a mischievous grin. 'Can't you see the sense in letting slip Iarl's involvement? Even the dogs know that Hakon does not want to put Vidar to death. Hakon would be eternally grateful to Iarl, not to mention the popularity his action would generate in camp. Men will respect him for saving Vidar.'

'I will speak to Iarl,' agreed Damian.

Tomás knew the proposal held appeal. He imagined Damian forming an allegiance with Iarl.

Damian's eyes narrowed. 'And why would you give the book of Newgrange to me?'

'Damian, you'll probably not believe this but I have been given a task and until now I was unsure of how to fulfil it. The task was to give the book of Newgrange to the man who craved it most. I believe I have found that man. And besides, I did promise to share this knowledge with you.'

'Are you telling me that you will hand the book over? No tricks?'

'Yes, if you arrange mine and Vidar's safe passage to Erin, the book is yours.'

CHAPTER 68

IN THE YEAR 840 AD

The blizzard dispersed rapidly. Such had been its strength that Henik had feared that he would either suffocate or freeze to death. He had spent its duration on the back of his sleigh, curled into a ball.

Henik headed off again. He had reason to be confident – he was close to clearing the lake and would soon be on the homeward stretch. He knew that the snowstorm would have finished any chance Ludin had had of making it. Henik would soon raise the red flag. Originally, he had seen the Trial as a way of getting back at Niclaus for a childhood grudge. Now, after all that had happened, the race paled into insignificance. Still, he owed it to Orrin to make sure Ludin did not win.

Not long into the trek, his team slowed. The black-antlered reindeer was panting heavily. A closer look confirmed his fear – it was bleeding from its hind leg again. Worse still, it was trying not to use it.

His team's pace gradually decreased. The freezing conditions had helped to protect the injury up to this point but now it had burst again. The injured stag would slow him down. Worse again, it would probably unsettle his healthy animal. He knew that continuing with one good deer would be better.

He decided to give the wounded animal an opportunity to keep up and tied it to the back of the sleigh. It could tag behind if it could match its partner's speed. Failing that, he would release it to its fate.

Henik had not travelled too much further when his one good reindeer became agitated, its senses alerting Henik long before he heard the first howl of a wolf. A chill ran up his spine. The wolves that had sent Niclaus scurrying on to the ice had picked up the scent of blood. Unknown to him, they had been steadily gaining and the front-runners were now passing him on the left. With the frozen lake on his right, the predators were narrowing his opportunity for escape. Henik was running out of options and was struggling to keep his sleigh moving in a straight line – the reindeer was trying to pull away from the bank to the left. He tugged hard on the reins, fighting the reindeer to a stop. Henik ran to the back of his sleigh and loosened the straps that attached the injured reindeer to the sleigh. One good yank and it would be free. Next, stepping out of the eye line of his reindeer, he lifted his staff and cruelly smashed its injured leg. The reindeer broke free, as was Henik's intention, and drew the attention of the closing pack.

Henik leapt on to his sleigh and made good his escape, although more slowly than he would have liked. He hoped that the wolves would be satisfied with the reindeer and that he had bought enough time to reach the finish. Glancing back, he saw the stricken stag fight desperately to keep the frenzied pack at bay. It lost the battle.

CHAPTER 69

IN THE YEAR 802 AD

By the autumn, Tomás' recovery was complete. The only visible sign of his ordeal was a scar that ran from above his left eyebrow along the side of his temple to the corner of his eye. He was grateful that his habit hid the rest. Although physically healed, the mental anguish was still an open sore. He sought and found the comfort of his Lord. The rediscovery of his faith brought tranquillity to his troubled heart and the anger he felt towards Cado left him. At first, he had been glad that Cado's visits had stopped but as his resentment subsided, he began to miss his little friend. He decided that he would journey to Cado's village, to make his peace and to explain about the loss of the book of Newgrange.

Tomás, his mind made-up, sought his abbot. With Connachtach having passed away peacefully, Cellach had been inaugurated abbot of Ceanannus Mór and Iona the previous month.

Tomás found Cellach in the sacristy, one of the few places undamaged in the raid. He explained his need of a leave of absence.

Abbot Cellach argued strongly but not being able to dissuade Tomás, reluctantly consented.

*

Setting off early from the monastery, Tomás followed the familiar meandering Blackwater.

The journey seemed to take twice as long as it did when he took the trip with Damian. The memories of his lost friendship did little to help his mood.

It was late in the afternoon when Tomás finally broke from the wood. The sight of the incredible monolith again captivated him – he had forgotten just how awesome it was. Strangely, he remembered little of his last visit. He recalled standing at the great mound, arguing with Damian. Damian had been adamant. He did not like the look of the village and would not set foot inside it. Strangely, Tomás could not remember why he had decided not to enter himself.

He climbed over the earth mound that encircled the great structure and continued walking towards the village, which sat in lower lying fields next to the river Boyne.

It all seemed very familiar, as if he had been to the village before. Getting closer, he recognised the unusual style of the houses. Built of brick and roofed in slate, they were of the highest standard. The streets were solid, made of crushed stone; holes and puddles were conspicuous by their absence.

The avenue, one of four running from a market square, had roughly thirty houses on either side. Like any village of its day, its square was multipurpose. A door opened in front of him and a middle-aged woman walked out.

'Afternoon, Tomás,' she said.

'Afternoon, Finola,' he replied, shocked that he knew her name.

Slowly the realisation dawned. He had been here before.

A tolling bell from somewhere ahead, signalled a near stampede of little people to the square.

A couple of kids scurried past. 'See, I told you he was back,' claimed the older boy. The chubbier of the two nodded to Tomás before both rushed off towards the square. He recalled their names, Vinc and Lamn. The crowd ahead was swelling. Tomás could make out calls and shouts but not the detail of the discussions. Somewhat nervous of interrupting the proceedings, he timidly progressed down the avenue.

'Look, there's Tomás,' a voice called out from a dais in the centre of the square. As Tomás neared, the gathering broke into muted applause. Hands patted his back, gently steering him to the stage before he had the chance to object. In front of Tomás stood his dearest friend Cado, accompanied by a dozen or so others, each of whose names he knew.

'I came to apologise,' he muttered lightly to his friend, who looked taller amidst his people.

'Tomás, you do not have to apologise. As foretold, I brought great pain to you,' Cado replied, as they embraced. 'It has been too long.'

Tomás studied the faces before him, 'It appears I have been here before,' he said, shooting an inquisitive eye at Cado.

To Cado's left stood Bram. Tomás could tell from his

demeanour that Bram was not pleased to see him.

Tomás turned to Cado. 'A friend of mine once told me of a dust that can cause memory loss. I think I may have been the victim of its powers.'

Cado gave Tomás a wry smile.

All thoughts of the actual reason behind his visit were lost, as a thousand questions raced around in Tomás' head. He forgot all about the lost book of Newgrange.

Cado addressed the gathering. 'I would like to speak to Tomás alone.'

There was a collective groan from the throng. It was evident to Tomás that many were against the idea. The mood was one of open hostility. There was bitterness in many of the villagers' words and resentment in their faces.

'It affects us all,' someone shouted.

'We want to hear what he has to say,' another shouted, to a chorus of agreement.

Stepping forward, Bram quietened his audience. 'I think I speak for us all ...'

There were shouts of agreement.

'As I said, I think I speak for us all when I say that we want to hear your conversation.'

Cado's flushed cheeks confirmed that he was unsettled. 'I have much to explain to Tomás. After we have spoken,' he had to shout to make himself heard, 'if you give me a little time with ...' His words were lost, drowned out by the clamour.

'What's said now must be said to us all,' replied Bram. 'Everyone here has a right to know how this affects our future.'

'Come, Tomás,' said Cado, leading his friend off the dais.

Rond, Bram's most loyal follower, stood to block Cado's path.

Cado gripped him by his collar and manhandled him out of his way.

A bunch of men surged forward, trying to block Cado's path, but he pushed through. Out of the throng, Cado hurried Tomás along one of the avenues and ushered his friend through the front door of one of the houses.

As Tomás waited for Cado to speak, he eyed a carved wooden sign that hung above the fireplace. He read the inscription burnt into the wood – *'Peace at Journey's End'*. He was about to ask about it when Cado spoke. 'I am so delighted to see you.'

'What is happening out there?' asked Tomás, nervously.

'Don't worry about that. Here, take your seat,' he said, pointing to the large chair.

Tomás looked at the well-worn seat, its leather cracked in places. His own chair, how could that be? He took a deep breath.

'Cado, what's going on?'

Cado shuffled on his feet. 'I do owe you an explanation, don't I?'

'Perhaps you should start with explaining how it is that I know many of the villagers, and they in turn know me? I suspect mischief afoot. I do not recall entering the village yet I remember the streets and the people. What happened?'

'Your assumption is correct; you did receive some of the dust, the one that affects your memory. You first visited us two summers ago when you came with Brother Damian. Unlike you, he did

427

not enter the village. And after that, you were back on numerous occasions.'

Cado elaborated, explaining how Darvil, a previous elder, had created a potion. When he sprayed it around the surrounding fields, it repelled all who approached the village.

'Being the first to pass this barrier, we knew you were special. In stories, handed down from our fathers, we were told that eventually a man would pass the mound. When that happened, the visitor was to undergo a series of tests. Today by re-entering our village, you have completed the last test.'

Tomás was confused, 'What test and how is it I remember names and faces?'

'We buried your memories of being here deep in your mind, a precaution, in case you failed the test. Those of the people you met, not being so deeply hidden, have merely resurfaced fastest but in time you will remember everything.'

He then told Tomás about a prophecy, foretelling the arrival of a tall walker. His coming would set about a chain of events that would ultimately see a tall walker becoming head elder. Tomás learned that he would help select the man who would take charge.

'And you say that I have to choose the man who will receive your knowledge?'

'Yes.'

'Can I select myself?'

'If you believe it to be the right decision then yes you may. Don't worry, that time is still a little while off. Come here. I have something I want to show you,' said Cado, as he lifted a book from the side of his desk.

'I am sorry – I could not retrieve the cover. It was too expensive.'

Tomás gasped. Sitting on Cado's table was the Holy Book. 'I hope that you can accept the book as a token of my remorse. I am truly sorry for your pain.'

Tomás flicked through the pages. The book was intact. Abbot Monicurr could rest in peace.

'How did you get it back?' he asked, thumbing through its pages.

'After the attack on the monastery, I travelled to the Norsemen's camp and bartered for its return. I made a deal with Hakon, lord of the Norsemen.'

'What could you have that would interest him?'

'Don't worry yourself about that; let's just say that I am happy with the outcome. I did get the book back.'

Tomás recalled the purpose of his visit. 'But the book was the reason I came. I came to tell you that the raiders also took the book of Newgrange. I was going to suggest …'

'Ah, yes, that book,' interrupted Cado. He delved into an untidy drawer in his desk, finally producing Tomás' book. 'Try not to lose it,' he teased, passing the book over. 'I have one final surprise.'

'And that is?' asked Tomás

His mouth agape, Tomás stared at the vellum page that Cado pressed into his hand. It was a replica of the one torn by Damian, only the detail was much more exquisite.

'What do you think of my handiwork?' asked Cado, handing over the page that Damian had started on Iona.

The detail was beyond compare.

'How could you produce such intricate detail?'

'Ah, my gift to you,' he said, handing Tomás a transparent crystal, 'I had it smoothed. The rock magnifies the page, allowing the most delicate touch.'

'With this I shall make the most beautiful Holy Book.'

As Tomás stared at the picture, he noticed imperfections – the copy before him was different to the original. Most notably the half disc, which should have been on the bottom of the page in the centre, had been left out and the lower angel, on the right side, was now carrying a flowering bough, where once he held an ornate fan. The two top angels were looking at the sky instead of at Jesus. Moreover, strangest of all, the illustrator had added a miniature panel containing six human busts to the outline of the vellum. Was this in reference to Newgrange and its pagan beliefs? Tomás believed that if he looked closer, he would find further faults. Even with the mistakes, the illustration was astonishingly accomplished.

Ever grateful, Tomás thought it best not to mention the mistakes.

'Now, to pressing matters,' said Cado, rising from his chair. 'We have nervous villagers waiting.'

'What has them so nervous?'

'You,'

'Me? Why?'

Cado pulled the door behind him. 'Oh, I almost forgot to tell you,' he said. 'Your arrival marks the beginning of a great upheaval. Many here are not pleased to see you.'

Before Cado got a chance to explain, they heard Bram's voice booming out, '… not stand idly by and let this happen. If Cado thinks we will let him destroy our village he has …'

Cado and Tomás' return stopped Bram's rant mid sentence.

An eerie silence descended as Cado took centre stage.

'I can confirm that the arrival of Tomás does mark the beginning of the prophecy,' he proclaimed.

There was a sharp intake of breath. The worry on numerous faces was evident even to Tomás. Cado tried to allay the rising fears but heckles drowned out his words.

The unfolding scene was becoming ugly. Tomás was shocked at the extent of the fury vented toward his friend. He had always imagined Cado a popular leader.

Bram, now conducting proceedings, stepped forward and hushed his mob. 'Please, let us hear what *our leader* has to say.'

'Rest easy. The time is still many years off. You have my word.'

Some villagers shouted questions: 'How long?', 'Do we have to leave?', 'Why can't things stay the way they are?'

Cado silenced his people. 'We have a visitor in our midst. Let us entertain him. We shall speak of this matter again.' The meeting was over.

'What of this prophecy?' Tomás asked Cado as they left the square.

'It tells of a time when we have to leave our village. Many are afraid of the transition.'

'Why would you want to leave? It is beautiful here.'

'Tomás, we will not leave through choice. When the time comes we shall leave Newgrange with heavy hearts.'

'Then why leave?'

'The murmurs of discontent that you have already heard will come to a poisonous head. The village will tear itself asunder. Many fear the future, not wanting to share our knowledge with the tall walkers. Others see themselves as prisoners trapped within the confines of the village. They long to be free of their sentence. A battle is beginning within their hearts.'

Cado tried to lighten the mood. 'All this can keep for another time. Let me reintroduce you to my people.'

Tomás spent his time reacquainting himself with many of his new, old, friends. Given the early confrontation, and much to his relief, they all treated him courteously. It was an eerie experience; memories continued to resurface.

It was late the following morning when Tomás left. He made the journey back in better time and found the walk uplifting. Not only had he made peace with Cado, he was returning to the monastery with the Holy Book and the book of Newgrange, and the secrets of Newgrange remained secure. He was in good heart when he arrived back at the monastery. He found a bemused Abbot Cellach in the scriptorium, fussing over manuscripts.

Abbot Cellach greeted Tomás with an affectionate embrace. 'Tomás, I feared you would be away much longer.'

'Father, I have accomplished what I set out to do. Better still, I have brought you a gift.'

'What sort of gift? You know we do not accept such offerings.'

'I think you'll like this one,' said Tomás, presenting Cellach with the Holy Book.

Cellach was dumbstruck for a moment. 'Praise be to God,' he

stammered, as he signed the cross. 'Cold waters to a thirsty soul. Where did you get it?'

'It was the Lord's doing. A little friend retrieved it.' Tomás said, simply. 'I'm sorry – he was unable to recover the jewelled cover.'

'Let us just be thankful.'

Word spread of Tomás' success and for much of the day the monks celebrated.

Slowly life returned to normality. Tomás set about completing the Holy Book with new vigour. Cado's visits to Ceanannus Mór resumed and they redoubled their efforts on the book of Newgrange. Cado had told him that they were running out of time.

CHAPTER 70

IN THE YEAR 840 AD

The snowstorm, when it arrived, placed Ludin at a greater disadvantage than Henik. The heavy fall, much earlier than usual in the season, blotted out many of the markers he and his father had left. To make matters worse, the thickness of the snow had covered rocks and boulders on the path, making his passage especially treacherous. Thanks to his father's trickery with the straw pulling, Ludin was using the same reindeer they had used on earlier treks. He hoped they remembered the way. He sleighed slowly, thinking it better to lose time than risk crashing.

His course swept eastward before swinging in a gentle north-easterly direction to the edge of the great lake. He hoped to see the finish as he cleared each ridge, but there was still no sign. Reaching the summit of the final ridge Ludin was horrified to see three sleighs. The furthest was closing from the far side of the lake. It had to be Henik. The sleigh, pulled by a single reindeer, had about half the distance that he himself had to cover. His only consolation was that the single sleigh had an uphill climb to complete. Given that he had two reindeer and a downhill run to the finish, he still had a chance.

He was more surprised that the other two sleighs were by the lake. Niclaus, Orrin or Aslak must have crossed the ice. Crazy fools, he thought. He had the edge on them, though: they were further away and, like Henik, had an uphill run to the finish.

*

Five flagpoles marked the finish. Beyond, fires burned between a sea of tents. Everyone eagerly waited to see who was in the lead. Sleighs were in view but still some distance away. Gunnar stood in the middle of the crowd overseeing proceedings. To his side were Olaf and Lars, waiting anxiously for their sons.

Thorsfied and Grimwald, Aslak's younger brother, acted as lookouts, hurrying back to inform the spectators what was happening. 'Henik is in the lead. Niclaus and Aslak crossed the lake but both are a good bit behind. There is no sign of Orrin or Ludin,' Grimwald told his father, disappointedly.

'Isn't that my boy coming from down the hill?' asked Olaf, hiding his disappointment. Ludin looked to be behind Henik.

*

Henik was within sight of the finish. Looking across, he could see two sleighs where they had cleared the lake. He could make out Niclaus on the leading one. Niclaus' reindeer looked fresh as they ripped through the snow. They were closing the gap but they were too far behind to catch him.

Scouring the horizon, he, at last, made out the darkened shape of Ludin's sleigh. Henik was pleased. He had a good lead. Four sleighs closed in on the red flag from differing directions. Yet his sleigh continued to slow. Henik's animal was struggling over what should have been smooth terrain. The stag, panting heavily, was thrashing with all its might. It had a lather of sweat over its body and the joints of its legs. Henik's chances of winning were evaporating with every stride. The animal was exhausted – if he did not give it a rest it was in danger of collapsing. Jumping down to check his animal for any sign of injury, he noticed that the back leg of his runner, the one damaged in the crash with Ludin, had come loose, and was dragging along the ground. The runner had broken. There was no chance of finishing the course. As he stood in the desolate wilderness, no solution came to mind. He patted his reindeer, admiring its steely determination. Resigned to defeat, he watched to see who would take the red flag. He hoped it would be Niclaus.

*

Ludin could not believe his eyes. Henik had stopped. He screamed in exhilaration as he watched him dismount. Either his sleigh was broken or the reindeer was lame. Ludin did not care. He would win.

Turning back to get a look at Niclaus' position, Ludin was shocked to find that he had lost much of his advantage and bullied his animals into one last push. It was going to be close but he believed he could make it.

For a fleeting moment, his mind wandered back to the morning before the start of the Trial. He felt no shame that he had disabled Niclaus' boat. All that mattered was winning. Niclaus, like everyone else, would just have to get used to him as Ugter.

The pain from his ankle seared, sending a burning sensation into his knee, taking his mind off his rival. He knew that tomorrow's pain would be a lot more bearable if he won.

*

Having miraculously survived the wolves and the journey over the ice, Aslak sat courageously in his seat. He had no need to steer as the reindeer followed the tracks of Niclaus' team without complaint. Behind, in the back, Orrin briefly stirred.

Aslak could see Niclaus closing on the finish. 'You can still do it,' he called.

CHAPTER 71

IN THE YEAR 806 AD

As foretold, Hakon's first and only son was born within the year. This ensured that the proud father adhered to the deal he had struck with Cado.

The vast expanse of Hakon's encampment surprised Cado – the years since his last visit had proved successful for the Norse lord. And Hakon's love of war had intensified. All along the shore men practised with swords and shields. They looked well trained. Such was their reputation that the mere mention of a dragonboat was enough to send panic through entire coastal communities. Black raven banners fluttering in the wind were feared the length of Europe.

Escorted by two guards, Cado walked towards the centre of the village, taking the same route as he had on his first visit.

Nearing the banqueting hall, Cado could hear loud laughter. The scene that greeted him caught Cado by surprise. Hakon, the mighty lord, was down on all fours, chasing a group of children. Pretending to be a bear, he caught a young boy. Pinning the child's tiny arms to the ground, he pretended to devour him by blowing on the exposed tummy, much to the amusement of the other children, who were poking and prodding at Hakon in an effort to rescue their friend.

'I'll save you,' cried the bravest girl as she jumped on the bear's back. Hakon let out a great roar of laughter as he pretended to die, dramatically tumbling over before falling on to his back. All the children piled on top in a mad frenzy. Hakon was powerless as the children tickled him mercilessly. Finally, he gave out a sigh and fell silent. The children had killed the beast.

'We killed the bear, we killed the bear, and saved the village,' cried the brave girl who had first climbed on Hakon's back. She stood astride Hakon's wide chest, soaking up the cheers of the other children.

'Children, I have a visitor, we shall play later,' Hakon said, spotting Cado. A little blond-haired girl pleaded to play longer.

'Sienna, that's enough. Now take your brother with you so that I can speak to my guest.'

The children complained and wailed as they refused to accept the end of playtime, yet Hakon displayed patience that impressed Cado. At last, he was seeing a side of the man that he liked; perhaps deep inside of him there was goodness.

Hakon walked towards Cado. 'Are you shocked to see the ogre playing?' he asked, noting his visitor's expression.

Cado grinned, showing his pleasure. 'You looked very at ease with them.'

'They are my greatest friends: they have no badness and are most loyal. If only men were of the same cloth. Come, walk with me.'

Hakon then thanked Cado for giving Damian his life. 'As

you said, he has been most useful to me, especially his gift of languages. I have lost count of the number he speaks. Even Envik has come to like him, though he denies it. Sometimes I wonder if I am really the ruler of this village, such is his wisdom.

'Under Damian's guidance, my boats have travelled across Europe, as far as Constantinople on the Black Sea, trading silk, spices, and much more. The merchants prosper under my protection.'

Hakon explained that trading was used as a means to an end – extra finance enabled him to further his warmongering, allowing him to terrorise the western islands to such an extent that his fiercest warriors had begun to colonise places as far apart as York and Dubh Linn.

As they talked, Cado mentioned that the restoration of Ceanannus Mór was complete and the monks were again working on their manuscripts. Cado caught the glint in the Norseman's eye and immediately warned him off.

'Soon I will take your son with me on his first journey,' said Cado, his words instantly changing the mood. 'At some point, I shall be bringing him to the very same monastery,' he continued, aware that the mention of doing so was an affront to Hakon and his beliefs.

'No son of mine shall follow the White Cross,' replied Hakon.

'Your son will make his own decisions. I shall teach him nothing of the White Cross ways. I am sure he will have every opportunity to follow your ways if he so desires.'

'How can I trust you?'

'Trust has to be earned,' replied Cado. 'I will not influence his religion.'

'No trickery?'

'You have my word …' Cado paused. 'That is, if I have your promise that you and your men will keep away from Ceanannus Mór.'

Hakon conceded with a grunt.

'As to the point of my visit, it is now time for your son to begin his tuition.'

'What can you teach my boy that I cannot?'

'No, you misunderstand; his first teachers will be you and Damian.'

Hakon breathed a sigh of relief.

'Your son has much to learn. Damian will teach him the various languages that he speaks and you will teach him about the stars in the sky. I shall return for his fifth birthday.'

'I suppose you'll want to meet my boy,' said Hakon, as he gave orders to a servant girl to bring the child to the hall.

Cado recognised the boy instantly; he was the very same one who Hakon had been tickling earlier. The boy looked nervous as he approached. He had thick dirty fair hair and the deepest blue eyes.

'Come here, son,' called Hakon, reassuringly.

To Cado, he looked small and fragile.

The boy ran to his father and threw confident arms around the Norse lord's neck. Hakon's love for his son was evident. The fierce warrior had a tenderness that transcended his hard exterior.

'I have someone I want you to meet,' said Hakon.

The boy turned to face Cado.

'This is Cado.'

Cado took a step forward and offered his hand.

'Don't be shy,' said Hakon, sternly.

The boy stepped nearer and shook hands.

'And this is my son, Vidar.'

CHAPTER 72

IN THE YEAR 840 AD

'Don't let me down now. Come on, you can do it,' said Niclaus, coaxing every ounce of energy out of his animals.

He was closing from the south, Ludin from the east.

Niclaus prayed that self-doubt would set in with Ludin now; after all, he had never beaten Niclaus at anything before. Why should he do so now? From the look of Ludin's team, they were close to exhaustion.

The onlookers shouted encouragement.

Both sets of reindeer gulped for air.

The finish would be too close to call. Both teams pulled as if their lives depended on the result.

Niclaus was gaining. Could he possibly be slightly ahead? It was impossible to tell.

'Go on, Niclaus,' implored Gunnar, forgetting himself.

Olaf shot him a look and Gunnar sank back into the crowd.

It was fewer than fifty strides to the finish and it was still either's race to win.

Reseth, nearest to the finish flags, could stand the tension no more. 'Go on, Niclaus,' he yelled, as he gripped his tightly curled hair.

Olaf glared at Reseth in disgust.

The last few strides were agonising. Niclaus could feel the blood pumping through his chest and neck, as if his blood vessels were about to burst. Over the final few strides, his team thundered towards the finish as Ludin's reindeer flagged. Niclaus was within reach of the flag, but his outstretched hand misjudged the distance and he sailed past. A collective groan erupted from the crowd. Niclaus would not get a second chance. It would take him too long to turn his sleigh.

Instead of slowing, Niclaus powered his team on and steered them directly into Ludin's path. Neither of his two brave reindeer flinched as they ploughed into the oncoming sleigh. Reindeer broke reindeer, sleigh broke sleigh. The force of the impact sent Ludin sprawling into a bank of snow, snapping his leg in the fall. Niclaus, prepared for the impact, had jumped just before the collision. Landing well, he was quickly on his feet, and rushing to check on his animals.

Looking down at the doe of his team, Niclaus lost all interest in the race. She was not moving. She had taken the full brunt of the crash, her neck clearly broken, and her throat deeply gashed. No amount of medicine, magical or otherwise would cure her. She was dead.

The second deer already on its feet whinnied, pleading with Niclaus to help. Niclaus turned to his stag and hugged its neck apologetically, hoping for its forgiveness. Apart from a deep gash to its snout, the stag looked fine. Removing its reins, Niclaus watched as it lay down beside its dead partner.

Niclaus may have forgotten the race but the others had not. Ludin tried to regain his feet but a broken leg and an injured shoulder meant he could not get up without assistance. His father ran to his side. 'Ludin, get up. You can still win.'

Ludin tried to stand but failed. He would not be going anywhere. Olaf went to help him.

'Leave him be,' warned Niclaus.

Olaf turned and lunged at Niclaus. Lars, Reseth, and a few others who had hurried to the crash, held him back.

Olaf was irate. 'If you had not crashed into …'

Niclaus, riled already, walked and stood boldly in front of the ranting man.

'Your son has disgraced the Trial. Help him if you must, but know that if you do, under the rules, he will be disqualified.'

Niclaus, without waiting for a response, turned and walked to his sleigh, and unhitched the dead doe.

'Come on,' he said to the stag, leading it towards the flags. 'Let's finish this.'

The red flag was his by right.

Cheers greeted Aslak as he arrived. Word quickly spread of the wolves' attack and Aslak's and Orrin's injuries. Orrin was awake and sitting backwards, resting against Aslak's seat.

Aslak and Orrin reached the flagpole slightly before Niclaus, Aslak positioning the sleigh beside the red flag. It was within reach of both Aslak and Orrin. They looked at each other knowing that if either of them lifted the flag, it would spell defeat for the other. They only had one sleigh – only one of them could finish.

Aslak nodded to Orrin, 'Without your bravery in the forest I would not be here. Please take your trophy.'

Orrin grinned and reached for the flag before stopping, 'Without your help on the sea we would have all have been doomed. If any of us are to suffer losing, we shall suffer it together. Besides I think this flag belongs to another.'

Finally, Niclaus approached; his reindeer and sleigh in tow.

'I think it belongs to you, brother,' said Orrin, pointing to the red flag.

'Yes, you deserve it,' agreed Aslak. 'You saved us both.'

'No,' said Niclaus. 'It's not mine to take. I have an obligation that stops me,' he said, handing his reins of his sleigh to Orrin.

Without waiting any longer, Aslak grabbed the pole and hoisted his flag. His father hugged him ecstatically. 'Why the blue flag?' he asked.

'Because Orrin has proved himself my leader. He saved my life.'

Niclaus beamed. 'Go on, lift it, you fool.'

Orrin looked at Niclaus, 'Without you …'

'No, listen. Without you on the ice all those years ago, many of us would not be here. Again, in the sea you showed your selflessness. You could have left me to go on and win. When the wolf attacked, you risked your life for your friend. No, Orrin, I couldn't make the harsh decisions that you will have to. You have shown that you can make difficult choices and sacrifices for the benefit of others. Without doubt, you have proved your worthiness. I would be honoured to live in a village under your leadership. You will be a great leader like your father.'

'Thank you, brother,' said Orrin, as he raised the flag.

Niclaus joined the crowd in cheering.

Turning, Niclaus walked to Ludin.

'I'll help you to the finish now,' Niclaus said.

Ludin winced in agony as Niclaus lifted him on to his sleigh. It was no small task – he had a broken leg, a broken collarbone and a broken ankle.

'It was you. You damaged my boat didn't you?'

Ludin, on his sleigh, bowed his head guiltily, 'I told you that our friendship did not count during the race. I had to win.'

'You owe me and I shall expect you to repay the debt someday,' said Niclaus. He doubted he would forgive him. He could still see the image of his friend abandoning them in the forest. 'Come, let's collect your flag. I think you need these to finish,' Niclaus said as he handed the reins to Ludin.

Cheers, whistles, and clapping greeted Ludin when he finally hoisted his flag.

The cheers continued as Olaf, Reseth, Lars and Niclaus carried Ludin to his father's tent.

Niclaus mounted Ludin's sleigh and made for where Henik sat watching.

Henik was not sure who had won. He sat patiently waiting, giving his reindeer a rest.

'Do you need a hand?' Niclaus asked as he neared.

The two old foes hugged like lifelong friends.

'Who won?'

Niclaus enlightened Henik. Together they were able to nurse the broken sleigh to the finish.

'Niclaus, I'd be honoured if you took my sleigh and raised the flag.'

'Not a chance, you deserve this.'

'No, I don't really care. I don't want to live in the village. My life's with the herders. The thought of settling there … well I just couldn't do it.'

Niclaus laughed.

'What's so funny?'

'What if neither of us raises the flag?'

'What? Fail together?'

'Yes. Why not? You aren't going to live in the fjord so it does not matter to you. And me? Well, I think I'm about to set off on another adventure that will take me far away from here.'

'Are you sure?'

'Yes, I'm sure.'

CHAPTER 73

IN THE YEAR 840 AD

'Niclaus,' said Gilder. 'This can't go on, we need to talk.'

Orrin was out, sent on an errand.

Niclaus bit hard on his lower lip. 'There's nothing to discuss,' he said, turning his back and walking away from the table.

Gilder tugged on his arm, resolutely. 'Let me explain.'

The words stabbed at Niclaus. He wanted no explanation. His rock, the man he trusted most in the world was not his father.

'Why?' he croaked, his voice full of pain

There were so many whys. Why had Gilder pretended to be his father? Did he ever truly love him? Why had he not told him the truth? Why did it have to be like this? Why couldn't things go back to the way they were?

Selina took Niclaus' hands in her own. She lifted his hands and kissed his knuckles. 'Please forgive us.'

Gilder hesitated, not exactly sure where to start. 'Niclaus, you are every bit our son. Your mother and I have raised you from the very day you were born.'

Gilder's words shocked Niclaus; his birth, he had not given

thought to his birth mother, who was she? 'My mother, you knew my mother?'

Selina blanched. 'It would be more fitting coming from Vidar. He has waited a long time for this; please wait a little longer.'

'I want to know,' Niclaus demanded.

Not prepared to tell Niclaus, Selina deftly steered the conversation. 'It was the most dangerous of times. Vidar had no choice but to give you up. Your life depended on it.'

'And why didn't you tell me? I had a right to know.'

'No, Niclaus, Vidar made us promise. It was the only way to keep you safe. And we did not know what had become of Vidar. He was under threat of death.'

'Who would threaten Vidar?'

'You know. Didn't he tell you that he was under threat from Hakon?'

'Yes.'

'Well,' Gilder paused. 'Hakon is Vidar's father.'

Niclaus felt nauseous. 'Hakon the Black is my grandfather?'

Selina patted Niclaus' hands. 'You see why we had to keep your whereabouts a secret. We had to keep you safe. Hakon would do anything to find you, you are his heir.'

Niclaus' mind was reeling.

Selina elaborated. 'Worried for your safety, Vidar turned to Gilder, his oldest friend. If anyone could keep you safe, it was Gilder. Vidar made us promise to bring you up as our son and to keep the knowledge secret. From that moment, you have been our son. You are our son.'

'We wanted to tell you,' explained Gilder, the strain of the last few days evident in his voice.

'And when Vidar arrived, you did not think to tell me?'

'We agonised over telling you. We decided that the less you knew, the safer you would be,' answered Selina.

'And Vidar?'

'Vidar, poor Vidar,' cried Selina.

Gilder stood and walked toward the dying fire. It was late and Orrin would be back shortly. 'Niclaus, Vidar is the most selfless man I have ever met. All that I have and all that I have achieved, I owe to him. It was his decision not to tell you and it nearly broke his heart.'

'Then why did he abandon me?'

Gilder defended Vidar. 'I know it's hard for you to take this all in but Vidar never abandoned you. He has dedicated his whole life to you. Can you imagine his suffering as he watched you being raised by us? It must have been unbearable. Niclaus, I made a promise to your father. I promised him that when the time came, he and I would walk with you, that you would be proud to have two fathers.'

Orrin clattered through the door, ending the discussion.

'What's going on?' he asked, catching his family hugging.

Gilder broke from the embrace. 'Aren't we allowed to miss our boy?'

'He doesn't sail until tomorrow,' answered Orrin, slapping his brother's back.

*

Niclaus was determined to soak up every minute detail of his homeland. He ran his eyes from the glistening water of the fjord, following the main stream to where it rose into a high, strong waterfall. To the west, he could make out the cloudy Lofoten Mountains. He was grateful that his task there was complete.

He wondered how long he would be gone. It was only one of the many questions swirling inside his head. He knew that Cado and Vidar would soon give him all the answers. And what of Vidar? The one subject that Niclaus wanted to talk about was the one that Gilder now refused to discuss.

Orrin, to Niclaus' side, lifted a flat stone and skimmed it across the water. One, two, three large bounces and it sank.

For Niclaus, life was changing, too quickly for his liking. He resented the responsibilities that came with maturity.

Finding an even stone, he skimmed it perfectly. It bounced more times than he could count.

'Won't you reconsider?' asked Orrin.

'I can't.'

'What about Eve? She's heartbroken.'

Niclaus swallowed hard. 'Don't make this any worse than it is.'

He had already said his tearful farewells to his parents, to Elwin and the girls, to his friends and most painfully to Eve. He had cried saying his goodbyes to her, although he had hidden his tears in their embrace. He had asked that they did not see him off, he could not bear the thought of his family and friends waving goodbye. Niclaus wanted to stay – his life in Folda was all he knew, but Orrin was alive and Niclaus had to honour the promise he had made to Cado.

They walked back to the waiting boat in silence where a small crowd waited to wave the crew off.

'And what will you do with my other reindeer while I'm gone?' Niclaus asked his brother.

'The herders have asked to look after him in your absence. Henik has sung the praises of a reindeer that is unafraid of wolves, that crosses ice that he could not and runs through deep snow as if on a stroll. Jakob has been impressed; he believes he could have a future leader of the herd.'

'What? My runt of a reindeer, the one they wouldn't let near their precious herd?'

'The very same.'

'Even with the blood bulge on his snout?' joked Niclaus.

'Yes, even with his red nose.'

They laughed.

'Yes, tell Henik. My reindeer can lead his herd but only until I come back for him.'

'Come on, hurry up lad,' shouted Jorun from the deck. Cado stood to his side.

Orrin gripped his brother in a tight embrace. 'Take care.'

'Yes, and you too, brother,' replied Niclaus, emphasising his last word.

Niclaus turned to have one last look. He was surprised to see Gilder and Selina walking to the shore. Eve followed a few paces behind.

'Did you think I would not wave my boy goodbye?' Selina cried, gripping her son, as if trying to stop him from leaving.

'I had this made for you,' said Gilder, handing Niclaus a bundle.

'What is it?' asked Niclaus, as he unravelled the gift.

It was a full-length furred coat, dyed blood-red, except for the outer trim.

'Red to signify the flag of Ugter, which was yours to take if you had wanted. I had it made from the hide of the reindeer you lost.'

It fitted perfectly.

'Thank you, it means a lot,' said Niclaus, humbly.

'Be careful, and come home to us, son,' said Gilder, his voice full of emotion.

Eve edged from behind Gilder and Selina. 'Don't be cross with …'

Niclaus kissed her. 'I'm glad you came.'

'Please don't go,' she pleaded, as they hugged. 'Don't you want to be with me?'

'Eve, I made a promise. I have to keep it.'

'Can't I come with you?'

'If only you could – but I promised to take this journey alone.'

'Come back to me.'

'I haven't got all day,' shouted Jorun.

'Look after Eve for me,' Niclaus called to Orrin.

'Keep safe,' replied Orrin.

Well-wishers offered Niclaus a few words of encouragement as he boarded.

Niclaus stood watching the solitary figure of Eve get smaller and smaller as the *Ice Maiden* sailed further out to sea. Separated by an increasing body of water, yet united in emotion, both Niclaus and Eve stood very much alone. He continued to watch her until his eyes were able to distinguish only shoreline.

'Niclaus,' someone shouted. He turned around to see who was calling him.

'Here's a present,' said Rune, tossing the bucket.

Niclaus looked at it quizzically.

'He looks just like Vidar all those years ago,' laughed Torre.

'Aye, he does too,' agreed Rune. 'I suppose you're wondering about the bucket? Don't worry – it'll become clear to you soon enough,' laughed Rune.

Cado, having finished talking to Captain Jorun, joined Niclaus.

'Where are you taking me?'

'You are going to walk in the footsteps of your father. To begin with, you will go to Ceanannus Mór and then on to Magority. You will meet your family there.'

'My family?'

Cado chuckled. 'Not only your family. I will also take you to Newgrange to meet mine. Mind you, some of them won't be best pleased to see you.'

Cado's mood turned serious. 'These are difficult times. Vidar never told Gilder the real reason he gave you up.'

Niclaus stood, stunned into silence.

'Yes, Hakon was angry with Vidar but he was family. Vidar did not fear his father. It hurt Vidar deeply to abandon his father and mother. He loved them dearly. He still does.'

'I don't understand – wasn't Vidar under threat of death?'

'Yes, when Vidar renounced the Norse way, Hakon had had no option but to pass the sentence. I do not believe that he would have carried it out.'

'Then if Hakon is not the threat, who is?'

'The person Vidar fears is Bram. He is the most popular man in my village. Everyone loves him. If only they knew him, knew how he plots and connives. He becomes more powerful by the day. And he knows the old ways – dark ways.'

'What are the dark ways?'

'Each of us has elements of the dark in us. Greed, selfishness, desire, and wickedness. Most of us choose to keep them under control but Bram embraces all their evils. He has taken a path that offers self-reward. Death and suffering of many innocents will be the result.'

'But he's only one person.'

'If it was only him … but using deceit and trickery, he has entangled a web of followers. Many have been fooled by his empty promises.'

'What has Vidar done to enrage him?'

'It's not Vidar, it's you.'

Cado was making little sense to Niclaus.

'He has sworn to kill any tall walker who tries to lead my village. He believes that you will challenge to be leader of Newgrange. Niclaus, I don't think you grasp the seriousness of the situation. You are all that stands between Bram and his victory. If you fail, all that you hold dear will be lost.'

'Me? You have the wrong person. I shall repay my debt and then return to Folda. I have a life planned here.'

'That life is over,' said Cado firmly. 'You must prepare for this future. If you do not stop Bram, Folda and its way of life will be lost forever.'

Niclaus shouted, 'What has this to do with me?'

Cado allowed himself a little grin. 'Niclaus, how many people do you know who have conversations without moving their lips?'

Niclaus' jaw dropped, he had not realised – their conversation had taken place without words.

'And you have seen things, haven't you?'

Niclaus nodded. As he did so, new visions flashed in his mind. He saw an army of Norsemen on the move – dwarfs stepping upon stones on a river of molten rock – and lastly he saw a man running, fleeing from a group of Norsemen. A tall warrior led the chase. The light was poor, making it difficult to see, but Niclaus was certain that Vidar was the man. Reaching the cliff top, he jumped. At the same time, the chaser launched his spear. The spear caught Vidar high in the back, carrying him off the ledge and into the ocean.

The vision was lost.

'What is it?' Cado asked, noticing Niclaus' alarm.

Niclaus told Cado of his vision.

Cado grimaced. 'Niclaus, forget Erin for now. I think it is time for you to meet your grandfather.'

The Beginning